TEN FROM THE TWENTIES

TEN FROM THE TWENTIES

STACY AUMONIER

J. D. BERESFORD

ELIZABETH BOWEN

A. E. COPPARD

ALDOUS HUXLEY

SHEILA KAYE-SMITH

D. H. LAWRENCE

EDEN PHILLPOTTS

G. B. STERN

HUGH WALPOLE

British Broadcasting Corporation

Published by the
British Broadcasting Corporation
35 Marylebone High Street
London W1M 4AA

ISBN 0 563 12903 4

First published in 1975

Printed in Great Britain by Love & Malcomson Ltd, Brighton Road, Redhill, Surrey

CONTENTS

The television series *Ten from the Twenties* was first shown on BBC-2 between June and August 1975.

Mr Oddy was dramatised by William Corlett, with Roland Culver, Clive Francis, Lally Bowers, John Moffatt and Angharad Rees, directed by Peter Moffatt.

An Adventure in Bed was dramatised by Michael Robson, with Rachel Gurney, Julian Holloway, Lesley-Ann Down and Michael Johnson, directed by Paul Ciappessoni.

The Indomitable Mrs Garthorne was dramatised as 'Motherlove' by Robert Muller, with Isabel Dean and Jeremy Brett, directed by Mark Cullingham.

The Eleventh Hat was dramatised as 'The Orsini Emeralds' by William Corlett, with George Chakiris, Ann Beach, Jack Watling and Ursula Howells, directed by Peter Moffatt.

Fanny and Annie was dramatised by Jack Pulman, with Gwen Watford, Tom Chadbon, Shirley Steedman and Elizabeth Bennett, directed by Valerie Hanson.

Two or Three Graces was dramatised by Peter Wildeblood, with Celia Bannermann, Tony Beckley and Eleanor Bron, directed by Peter Moffatt.

Aunt Tatty was dramatised by Fay Weldon, with Mary Morris, Fanny Rowe, Lewis Fiander and Angela Thorne, directed by Valerie Hanson.

The Anarchist was dramatised by Leslie Sands, with Cathleen Nesbitt, Patrick Barr and Nickolas Grace, directed by Valerie Hanson.

A Wedding Morn was dramatised as 'Her Wedding Morn' by Robert Muller, with Polly James, directed by Barry Letts.

Fifty Pounds was dramatised as 'The Fifty Pound Note' by Robert Muller, with Billie Whitelaw, John Hurt, Michael Gough and Vanda Godsell, directed by Mark Cullingham.

The script associate was Sue Lake, and the series producer was Pieter Rogers.

HUGH WALPOLE

MR ODDY

THIS may seem to many people an old-fashioned story; it is perhaps for that reason that I tell it. I can recover here, it may be, for myself something of the world that is already romantic, already beyond one's reach, already precious for the things that one might have got out of it, and didn't.

London of only fifteen years ago ! What a commonplace to point out its difference from the London of today and to emphasise the tiny period of time that made that difference ! We were all young and hopeful then; we could all live on a shilling a week and think ourselves well off; we could all sit in front of the lumbering horse-buses and chat confidentially with the omniscient driver; we could all see Dan Leno in pantomime and watch Farren dance at the Empire; we could all rummage among those cobwebby streets at the back of the Strand where Aldwych now flaunts her shining bosom and imagine Pendennis and Warrington, Copperfield and Traddles cheek by jowl with ourselves; we could all wait in the shilling queue for hours to see Ellen Terry in *Captain Brassbound* and Forbes Robertson in *Hamlet*; we could all cross the street without fear of imminent death, and above all we could all sink ourselves into that untidy higgledy-piggledy, smoky and beery and gas-lampy London, gone utterly and for ever. But I have no wish to be sentimental about it; there is a new London which is just as interesting to its new citizens as the old London was to myself. It is my age that is the matter; fifteen years ago, before the war, one was *so very* young.

I like, though, to try and recapture that time, and so, as a simple way to do it, I seize upon a young man : Tommy Brown we will call him. I don't know where Tommy Brown

7

may be now; that Tommy Brown of fifteen years ago, who
lived, as I did, in two very small rooms in Glebe Place,
Chelsea, who enjoyed hugely the sparse but economical
meals provided so elegantly by two charming ladies at 'The
Good Intent' down by the river, that charming hostelry
whence, looking through the bow windows, you could see
the tubby barges go floating down the river and the thin
outline of Whistler's Battersea Bridge, and in the small
room itself were surrounded by who knows what geniuses
in the lump, geniuses of art and letters, of the Stage and of
the Law. For Tommy Brown fifteen years ago this life was
Paradisical. He had come boldly from Cambridge to throw
himself upon London's friendly bosom; despite all warnings to the contrary he was certain that it would be friendly
– how could it be otherwise to so charming, so brilliant, so
unusually attractive a young man? For Tommy was conceited beyond all that his youth warranted, conceited, indeed, without any reason at all. He had, it is true, secured
the post of reviewer to one of the London daily papers; this
seemed to him, when he looked back in later years, a kind
of miracle, but at the time no miracle at all, simply a just
appreciation of his extraordinary talents. There was also re-
posing in one of the publisher's offices at that moment the
manuscript of a novel, a novel that appeared to him of
astonishing brilliance, written in the purest English, spark-
ling with wit, tense with drama. These things were fine and
reassuring enough, but there was more than that; he felt in
himself the power to rise to the greatest heights; he could
not see how anything could stop him; it was his destiny.

This pride of his might have suffered some severe shocks
were it not that he spent all of his time with other young
gentlemen quite as conceited as himself. I have heard talk
of the present young generation and its agreeable consciousness of its own merits, but I doubt if it is anything in
comparison with that little group of fifteen years ago. After

all, the war has intervened – however young we may be and however greatly we may pretend, this is an unstable world and for the moment heroics have departed from it. But for Tommy Brown and his friends the future was theirs, and nobody could prevent it. Something pathetic in that as one looks back.

Tommy was not really so unpleasant a youth as I have described him – to his elders he must have appeared a baby, and his vitality at least they could envy. After all, why check his confidence? Life would do that heavily enough in its own good time. Tommy, although he had no money and no prospects, was already engaged to a young woman, Miss Alice Smith. Alice Smith was an artist sharing with a girl friend a Chelsea studio, and she was as certain of her future as Tommy was of his.

They had met at a little Chelsea dance, and two days after the meeting they were engaged. She had no parents who mattered and no money to speak of, so that the engagement was the easiest thing in the world. Tommy, who had been in love before many times, knew, as he told his friend Jack Robinson so often as to bore that gentleman severely, that this time at last he knew what love was. Alice ordered him about – with her, at any rate, his conceit fell away – she had read his novel and pronounced it old-fashioned – the severest criticism she could possibly have made – and she thought his reviews amateur. He suffered, then, a good deal in her company. When he was away from her he told himself and everybody else that her critical judgment was marvellous, her comprehension of all the Arts quite astounding, but he left her sometimes with a miserable suspicion that perhaps, after all, he was not going to do anything very wonderful and that he would have to work very hard indeed to rise to her astonishing standards.

It was in such a mood of wholesome depression that he came one beautiful spring April day from the A.B.C. shop where he had been giving his Alice luncheon and found his way to an old bookshop on the river-side, round the corner from Oakley Street. This shop was kept by a gentleman called Mr Burdett Coutts, and the grand associations of his name gave him from the very first a sort of splendour. It was one of those old shops of which there are, thank God! still many examples surviving in London, in which the room was so small and the books so many that to move a step was to imperil your safety. Books ran in thick tight rows from floor to ceiling everywhere, were piled in stacks upon the ground and hung in perilous heaps over chairs and window-ledges.

Mr Burdett Coutts himself, a very stout and grizzled old man enveloped always in a grey shawl, crouched behind his spectacles in a far corner and took apparently no interest in anything, save that he would snap the price at you if you brought him a volume and timorously inquired. He was not one of those old booksellers dear to the heart of Anatole France and other great men, who would love to discourse to you of the beauties of *The Golden Ass*, the possibility of Homer being a lady, or the virtues of the second Hyperion over the first. Not at all; he ate biscuits which stuck in his grizzly beard and wrote perpetually in a large moth-eaten ledger, which was supposed by his customers to contain all the secrets of the universe.

It was just because he never interfered with you that Tommy Brown loved his shop so dearly. If he had a true genuine passion that went far deeper than all his little superficial vanities and egotisms, it was his passion for books, books of any kind. He had at this time no fine taste – all was fish that came to his net. The bundles of Thackeray and Dickens, parts tied up carelessly in coarse string, the old broken-backed volumes of Radcliffe and Barham and Galt, the red and gold Colburn's novelists, all these were exciting to him, just as exciting as though they had been a first

Gray's *Elegy* or an original *Robinson Crusoe*. He had, too, a touching weakness for the piles of fresh and neglected modern novels that lay in their discarded heaps on the dusty floor; young though he was, he was old enough to realise the pathos of these, so short a time ago fresh from the bursting presses, so eagerly cherished through months of anxious watching by their fond authors, so swiftly forgotten, dead almost before they were born. So he browsed, moving like a panting puppy with inquisitive nose from stack to stack with a gesture of excitement, tumbling a whole racket of books about his head, looking then anxiously to see whether the old man would be angry with him, and realising for the thousandth time that the old man never was.

It was on this day, then, rather sore from the arrogances of his Alice, that he tried to restore his confidence among these friendly volumes. With a little thrill of excited pleasure, he had just discovered a number of the volumes born of those romantic and tragedy-haunted Nineties. Here, in little thin volumes, were the stories of Crackanthorpe, the poems of Dowson, the keynotes of George Egerton, *The Bishop's Dilemma* of Ella d'Arcy, *The Happy Hypocrite* of Max Beerbohm. Had he only been wise enough to give there and then for that last whatever the old man had asked him for it, he would have been fortunate indeed, but the pennies in his pocket were few – he was not yet a book collector, but rather that less expensive but more precious thing, a book adorer. He had the tiny volume in his hand, when he was aware that someone had entered the shop and was standing looking over his shoulder.

He turned slowly and saw someone who at first sight seemed vaguely familiar, so familiar that he was plunged into confusion at once by the sense that he ought to say 'How do you do?' but could not accurately place him. The gentleman also seemed to know him very well, for he said

in a most friendly way, 'Ah, yes, the "Nineties", a very
fruitful period.' Tommy stammered something, put down
the Max Beerbohm, moved a little and pulled about him a
sudden shower of volumes. The room was filled with the
racket of their tumbling and a cloud of dust thickened
about them, creeping into eyes and mouth and nose. 'I'm
terribly sorry,' Tommy stammered, and then, looking up,
was sorry the more when he saw how extremely neat and
tidy the gentleman was and how terribly the little incident
must distress him.

Tommy's friend must have been between sixty and
seventy years of age, nearer seventy perhaps than sixty,
but his black hair was thick and strong and stood up *en
brosse* from a magnificent broad forehead. Indeed, so fine
was the forehead and the turn of the head that the face itself was a little disappointing, being so round and chubby
and amiable as to be almost babyish. It was not a weak
face, however, the eyes being large and fine and the chin
strong and determined. The figure of this gentleman was
short and thick-set and inclined to stoutness; he had the
body of a prize-fighter now resting on his laurels. He was
very beautifully clothed in a black coat and waistcoat,
pepper and salt trousers, and he stood leaning a little on
a thick ebony cane, his legs planted apart, his whole attitude that of one who was accustomed to authority. He had
the look of a magistrate, or even of a judge, and had his face
been less kindly Tommy would have said good day, nodded
to Mr Burdett Coutts and departed; but that was a smile
difficult to resist.

'Dear me,' the gentleman said, 'this is a very dusty shop.
I had never been here before, but I gather by the way that
you knock the books about that it's an old friend of yours.'

Tommy giggled in a silly fashion, shifted from foot to
foot, and then, desiring to seem very wise and learned,
proved himself only very young and foolish.

'The "Nineties" are becoming quite romantic,' he said in his most authoritative voice, 'now that we're getting a good distance from them.'

'Ah, you think so !' said the gentleman courteously; 'that's interesting. I'm getting to an age now, I'm afraid, when nothing seems romantic but one's own youth, and, ah, dear me ! that was a very long time ago.'

This was exactly the way that kindly old gentlemen were supposed to talk, and Tommy listened with becoming attention.

'In my young days,' his friend continued, 'George Eliot seemed to everybody a magnificent writer : a little heavy in hand for these days, I'm afraid. Now who is the god of your generation, if it isn't impertinent to inquire?'

Tommy shifted again from foot to foot. Who was the god of his generation? If the truth must be told, in Tommy's set there was no gods, only young men who might be gods if they lived long enough.

'Well,' said Tommy awkwardly, 'Hardy, of course – er – it's difficult to say, isn't it?'

'Very difficult,' said the gentleman. There was a pause then, which Tommy concluded by hinting that he was afraid that he must move forward to a very important engagement.

'May I walk with you a little way?' asked the gentleman very courteously; 'such a very beautiful afternoon.'

Once outside in the beautiful afternoon air everything was much easier; Tommy regained his self-confidence and soon was talking with his accustomed ease and freedom. There was nothing very alarming in his friend, after all, he seemed so very eager to hear everything that Tommy had to say. He was strangely ignorant, too; he seemed to be interested in the Arts, but to know very little about them; certain names that were to Tommy household words were to this gentleman quite unknown. Tommy began to be a little patronising. They parted at the top of Oakley Street.

'I wonder if you'd mind,' the gentleman said, 'our meeting again? The fact is that I have very little opportunity of making friends with your generation. There are so many things that you could tell me. I am afraid it may be tiresome for you to spend an hour or two with so ancient a duffer as myself, but it would be very kind of you.'

Tommy was nothing if not generous; he said that he would enjoy another meeting very much. Of course he was very busy and his spare hours were not many, but a walk another afternoon could surely be managed. They made an appointment, they exchanged names : the gentleman's name was Mr Afred Oddy.

That evening, in the middle of a hilarious Chelsea party, Tommy suddenly discovered, to his surprise, that it would please him very much to see Mr Oddy walk in through the door. Although it was a hilarious party Tommy was not very happy; for one thing, Spencer Russell, the novelist, was there, and showed quite clearly that he didn't think Tommy very interesting. Tommy had been led up and introduced to him, had said one or two things that seemed to himself very striking, but Spencer Russell had turned his back almost at once and entered into eager conversation with somebody else. This wasn't very pleasant, and then his own beloved Alice was behaving strangely; she seemed to have no eyes nor ears for anyone in the room save Spencer Russell, and this was the stranger, in that only a week or so before she had in public condemned Spencer Russell's novels, utterly and completely, stating that he was written out, had nothing to say and was as good as dead. Tonight, however, he was not dead at all, and Tommy had the agony of observing her edge her way into the group surrounding him, and then listen to him, not only as though he were the fount of all wisdom, but an Adonis as well, which last was absurd, seeing that he was fat and unwieldy and bald on the top of his head. After a while Tommy came up to her and suggested that they should go, and received then the shock of his life when she told him that he could go if he liked, but that he was not to bother her. And she told him this in a voice so loud that everybody heard, and many people tittered. He left in a fury and spent then a night that he imagined to be sleepless, although in truth he slept during most of it.

It was with an eagerness that surprised himself that he met Mr Oddy on the second occasion. He had not seen Alice for two days; he did not intend to be the one to apologise first; besides, he had nothing to apologise for; and yet during these two days there was scarcely a moment that he had not to restrain himself from running round to her studio and making it up. When he met Mr Oddy at the corner of Oakley Street he was a very miserable young man. He was so miserable that in five minutes he was pouring out all his woes. He told Mr Oddy everything; of his youth, his wonderful promise, and the extraordinary lack of appreciation shown to him by his relatives; of the historical novels that he had written at the age of anything from ten to sixteen, and found only the cook for an audience; of his going to Cambridge and his extraordinary development there, so that he became Editor of *The Lion,* that remarkable but very short-lived journal, and the President of 'The Bats', the most extraordinary Essay Club that Cambridge had ever known; of how, alas! he took only a third in history owing to the perverseness of examiners, and so on and so on, until he arrived in full flood at the whole history of his love for Alice, of her remarkable talents and beauty, but of her strange temper and arrogance and general feminine perverseness.

Mr Oddy listened to it all in the kindest way. There's no knowing where they walked that afternoon; they crossed the bridge and adventured into Battersea Park, and finally had tea in a small shop smelling of stale buns and liquorice drops. It was only as they turned homewards that it occurred to Tommy that he had been talking during the whole afternoon. He had the grace to see that an apology was necessary.

'I beg your pardon, sir,' he said, flushing a little, 'I'm afraid I have bored you dreadfully. The fact is that this last quarrel with Alice has upset me very badly. What would you do if you were in my position?'

Mr Oddy sighed. 'The trouble is,' he said, 'that I realise only too clearly that I shall never be in your position again. My time for romance is over, or at least I get my romance now in other ways. It wasn't always so; there was a lady once beneath whose windows I stood night after night merely for the pleasure of seeing her candle outlined behind the blind.'

'And did she love you,' Tommy asked eagerly, 'as much as you loved her?'

'Nobody, my dear boy,' Mr Oddy replied, 'loves you as much as you love them; either they love you more or they love you less; the first of these is often boring, the second always tragic. In the present case, I should go and make it up; after all, happiness is always worth having, even at the sacrifice of one's pride. She seems to me a very charming young lady.'

'Oh, she is,' Tommy answered eagerly. 'I'll take your advice, I'll go this very evening; in fact, if you don't mind, I think it would be rather a good time to find her in now.' Mr Oddy smiled and agreed; they parted, to meet another day. On the third occasion of their meeting, which was only two days after the second, Tommy cared for his companion enough to wish to find out something about him. His scene of reconciliation with his beautiful Alice had not been as satisfactory as he had hoped; she had forgiven him, indeed, but given him quite clearly to understand that she would stand none of his nonsense either now or hereafter. The satisfactory thing would have been for Tommy there and then to have left her, never to see her again; he would thus have preserved both his pride and his independence; but, alas! he was in love, terribly in love, and her indignation made her appear only the more magnificent. And so on this third meeting with his friend he was quite humble and longing for affection.

And then his curiosity was stirred. Who was this handsome old gentleman with his touching desire for Tommy's companionship? There was an air about him that seemed to suggest that he was someone of importance in his own world; beyond this there was an odd sense that Tommy knew him in some way, had seen him somewhere, so on this third occasion Tommy came out with his questions. Who was he? Was he married? What was his profession, or was he perhaps retired now? And another question that Tommy would have liked to have asked, and had not the impertinence, was as to why this so late interest in the Arts and, combined with this interest, this so complete ignorance? Mr Oddy seemed to know a great deal about everything else, but in this one direction his questions were childish. He seemed to never have heard of the great Spencer Russell at all (which secretly gave Tommy immense satisfaction), and as for geniuses like Mumpus and Peter Arrogance and Samuel Bird even when Tommy explained how truly great these men were, Mr Oddy appeared but little impressed.

'Well, at least,' Tommy burst out indignantly, 'I suppose you've read something by Henry Galleon? Of course he's a back number now, at least he is not modern, if you know what I mean, but then he's been writing for centuries. Why, his first book came out when Trollope and George Eliot were still alive. Of course, between ourselves, I think *The Roads,* for instance, a pretty fine book, but you should hear Spencer Russell go for it.'

No, Mr Oddy had never heard of Henry Galleon.

But there followed a most enchanting description by Mr
Oddy of his life when he was a young man, and how he
once heard Dickens give a reading of *A Christmas Carol*,
of how he saw an old lady in a sedan-chair at Brighton (she
was cracked, of course, and even then a hundred years
after her time, but still he had seen it); of how London in
his young day was as dark and dirty at night as it had been
in Pepys' time; of how crinolines when he was young were
so large that it was one of the sights to see a lady getting
into a cab; of how in the music-halls there was a chairman
who used to sit on the stage with a table in front of him,
ring a bell and drink out of a mug of beer; of how he heard
Jean de Reszke in *Siegfried* and Ternina in *Tristan*, and of
how he had been at the first night when Ellen Terry and
Irving had delighted the world with *The Vicar of
Wakefield*.

Yes, not only had Mr Oddy seen and done all these
things, but he related the events in so enchanting a way,
drew such odd little pictures of such unexpected things and
made that old London live so vividly, that at last Tommy
burst out in a volley of genuine enthusiasm : 'Why, you
ought to be a writer yourself ! Why don't you write your
reminiscences?' But Mr Oddy shook his head gently; there
were too many reminiscences, every one was always re-
miniscing; who wanted to hear these old men talk? At last,
when they parted, Mr Oddy had a request – one thing
above all things that he would like would be to attend one
of these evening gatherings with his young friend to hear
these young men and women talk. He promised to sit very
quietly in a corner – he wouldn't be in anybody's way.

Of course Tommy consented to take him; there would be
one next week, a really good one; but in his heart of hearts
he was a little shy. He was shy not only for himself but also

for his friend. During these weeks a strange and most unexpected affection had grown up in his heart for this old
man; he really did like him immensely, he was so kind and
gentle and considerate. But he would be rather out of place
with Spencer Russell and the others, he would probably say
something foolish and then the others would laugh. They
were on the whole a rather ruthless set and were no respec-
ters of persons. However, the meeting was arranged; the
evening came with Mr Oddy looking just as he always did,
quiet and gentle, but rather impressive in some way or another. Tommy introduced him to his hostess, Miss Thelma
Bennet, that well-known futuristic artist, and then carefully
settled him down in a corner with Miss Bennet's aunt, an
old lady who appeared occasionally on her niece's horizon
but gave no trouble, because she was stone deaf and cared
only for knitting.

It was a lively evening; several of the brighter spirits
were there, and there was a great deal of excellent talk
about literature. Every writer over thirty was completely
condemned, save for those few remaining who had passed
eighty years of age and ceased to produce. Spencer Russell
especially was at his best; reputations went down before his
vigorous fist like ninepins; he was so scornful that his brilliance was, as Alice Smith everywhere proclaimed, 'simply
withering'. Every one came in for his lash, and especially
Henry Galleon. There had been some article in some
ancient monthly, written by some ancient idiot, suggesting
that there was still something to be said for Galleon and
that he had rendered some service to English literature.
How Russell pulled that article to pieces! He even found a
volume of Galleon's among Miss Bennet's books, took it
down from the shelf and read extracts aloud to the laughing derision of the assembled company.

Then an odd thing occurred. Tommy, who loved to be in
the intellectual swim, nevertheless stood up and defended

Galleon. He defended him rather feebly, it is true, speaking of him as though he were an old man ready for the alms-house, who nevertheless deserved a little consideration and pity. He flushed as he spoke, and the scorn with which they greeted his defence altogether silenced him. It silenced him the more because Alice Smith was the most scornful of them all; she told him that he knew nothing and never would know anything, and she imitated his piping excited treble, and then everyone joined in.

How he hated this to happen before Mr Oddy! How humiliating after all the things that he had told his friend, the implication that he was generally considered to be one of England's most interesting young men, the implication above all that, although she might be a little rough to him at times, Alice really adored him and was his warmest admirer. She did not apparently adore him tonight, and when he went out at last with Mr Oddy into the wintry rain-driven street it was all he could do to keep back tears of rage and indignation.

Mr Oddy had, however, apparently enjoyed himself. He put his hand for a minute on the boy's shoulder. 'Good night, my dear boy,' he said. 'I thought it very gallant of you to stand up for that old writer as you did : that needed courage. I wonder,' he went on, 'whether you would allow me to come and take tea with you one day – just our two selves. It would be a great pleasure for me.' And then, having received Tommy's invitation, he vanished into the darkness.

On the day appointed Mr Oddy appeared punctually at Tommy's rooms. That was not a very grand house in Glebe Place where Tommy lived, and a very soiled and battered landlady let Mr Oddy in. He stumbled up the dark stair-case that smelt of all the cabbage and all the beef and all the mutton ever consumed by lodgers between these walls, up again two flights of stairs, until at last there was the weather-beaten door with Tommy's visiting-card nailed upon it. Inside was Tommy, a plate with little cakes, raspberry jam and some very black-looking toast. Mr Oddy, however, was appreciative of everything; especially he looked at the books. 'Why,' he said, 'you've got quite a number of the novels of that man you defended the other evening, I wonder you're not ashamed to have them if they're so out of date.'

'To tell you the truth,' said Tommy, speaking freely now that he was in his own castle, 'I like Henry Galleon awfully. I'm afraid I pose a good deal when I'm with those other men; perhaps you've noticed it yourself. Of course, Galleon is the greatest novelist we've got, with Hardy and Meredith, only he's old, and everything that's old is out of favour with our set.'

'Naturally,' said Mr Oddy, quite approving; 'of course it is.'

'I have got a photograph of Galleon,' said Tommy, 'I cut it out of a publisher's advertisement, but it was taken years ago.' He went to his table, searched for a little, and produced a small photograph of a very fierce-looking gentleman with a black beard.

'Dear me,' said Mr Oddy, 'he does look alarming!'

'Oh, that's ever so old,' said Tommy. 'I expect he's mild and soft now, but he's a great man all the same; I'd like to see Spencer Russell write anything as fine as *The Roads* or *The Pattern in the Carpet*.'

They sat down to tea, very happy and greatly pleased with one another. 'I do wish,' said Tommy, 'that you'd tell me something about yourself; we're such friends now and I don't know anything about you at all.'

'I'd rather you didn't,' said Mr Oddy. 'You'd find it so uninteresting if you did; mystery's a great thing.'

'Yes,' said Tommy. 'I don't want to seem impertinent, and of course if you don't want to tell me anything you

needn't, but – I know it sounds silly but, you see, I like you
most awfully. I haven't liked anybody so much for ever so
long, except Alice, of course; I don't feel as though you
were of another generation or anything. It's just as though
we were the same age!'

Mr Oddy was enchanted. He put his hand on the boy's
for a moment and was going to say something, when they
were interrupted by a knock on the door and the terrible-
looking landlady appeared in the room. She apologised, but
the afternoon post had come and she thought the young
gentleman would like to see his letters. He took them, was
about to put them down without opening them, when suddenly he blushed. 'Oh, from Alice,' he said, 'will you forgive me a moment?'

'Of course,' said Mr Oddy. The boy opened the letter
and read it; it fell from his hand on to the table. He got up
gropingly, as though he could not see his way, and went to
the window and stood there with his back to the room.
There was a long silence.

'Not bad news, I hope,' said Mr Oddy at last.

Tommy turned round; his face was grey and he was
biting his lips. 'Yes,' he answered, 'she's – gone off.'

'Gone off?' said Mr Oddy, rising from the table.

'Yes,' said Tommy, 'with Russell. They were married at
a registry office this morning.' He half turned round to the
window, then put his hands as though he would shield himself from some blow, then crumpled up into a chair, his
head falling between his arms on the table.

Mr Oddy waited. At last he said, 'Oh, I'm sorry, that's
dreadful for you!' The boy struggled, trying to raise his
head and speak, but the words would not come. Mr Oddy
went behind him and put his hands on his shoulders.

'You know,' he said, 'you mustn't mind me. Of course
I'll go if you like, but if you could think of me for a moment
as your oldest friend, old enough to be your father, you

know.' Tommy clutched his sleeve, then, abandoning the struggle altogether, buried his head in Mr Oddy's beautiful black waistcoat.

Later he poured his heart out. Alice was all that he had; he knew that he wasn't any good as a writer, he was a failure altogether; what he'd done he'd done for Alice, and now that she'd gone –

'Well, there's myself,' said Mr Oddy. 'What I mean is, that you're not without a friend; and as for writing, if you only write to please somebody else that's no use; you've got to write because you can't help it. There are too many writers in the world already for you to dare to add to their number, unless you're simply compelled to. But there – I'm preaching. If it's any comfort to you to know, I went through just this same experience myself once – the lady whose candle I watched behind the blind. If you cared to, would you come and have dinner with me tonight at my home? Only the two of us, you know, but don't if you'd rather be alone.'

Tommy, clutching Mr Oddy's hand, said he would come.

About half-past seven that evening he had beaten up his pride. Even in the depth of his misery he saw that they would never have got on together, he and Alice; he was quickly working himself into a fine state of hatred of the whole female race, and this helped him – he would be a bachelor all his days, a woman-hater; he would preserve a glorious independence. How much better this freedom than a houseful of children and a bagful of debts. Only, as he walked to the address that Mr Oddy had given him, he held sharply away from him the memory of those hours that he had spent with Alice, those hours in their early friendship when the world had been so wonderful a place that it had seemed to be made entirely of golden sunlight. He felt that he was an old man indeed as he mounted the steps of Mr Oddy's house.

It was a fine house in Eaton Square. Mr Oddy must be
rich. He rang the bell, and a door was opened by a footman. He asked for Mr Oddy. The footman hesitated a
little and then, smiling, said, 'Oh yes, sir, will you come
in?' He left his coat in the fine hall, mounted a broad stair-
case, and then was shown into the finest library that he had
ever seen. Books! Shelf upon shelf of books, and glorious
books, editions de luxe and, as he could see with half an
eye, rare first editions, and those lovely bindings in white
parchment and vellum that he so longed one day himself
to possess. On the broad writing-table there was a large
photograph of Meredith; it was signed in sprawling letters
'George Meredith, 1887.' What could this mean? Mr
Oddy, who knew nothing about literature, had been given
a photograph by George Meredith and had this wonderful
library! He stared bewildered about him.

A door at the far end of the library opened and an elegant young man appeared. 'Mr Galleon,' he said, 'will be
with you in a moment; won't you sit down?'

Mr Galleon! Henry Galleon! Instantly he saw it, remembered with horrid confusion his own ridiculous, conceited talk, the abusive nonsense of Russell and the rest.
'My God!' he whispered, 'what he must be thinking!'

The door opened again and Mr Oddy appeared. Tommy
Brown, his face crimson, stammered, 'It was a shame – if
I'd only known!' and then, trying to stand up for himself,
'But I had that photograph and there was the beard.'

Mr Oddy laughed. 'The beard went long ago,' he said.
'I suppose it *was* a shame, but I was hemmed in here in my
castle; I had to find out what you young people were like.
I get tired of all this sometimes; nobody tells me the truth
here. I have to go to you and your friends for that.'

So they went down to dinner together.

Yes, this is an old story. Its principal interest, perhaps,
is that it's true. I was, you see, myself Tommy Brown.

AN ADVENTURE IN BED

THERE was something essentially Chinese about the appearance of George as he lay there propped up against the pillows. His large flabby face had an expression of complete detachment. His narrowing eyes regarded me with a fatalistic repose. Observing him, I felt that nothing ever would matter. And I was angry. Pale sunlight filtered through the curtains.

'Good Lord!' I exclaimed. 'Still in bed! Do you know it's nearly twelve o'clock?'

An almost inaudible sigh greeted my explosion. George occupied the maisonette below me. Some fool of an uncle had left him a small private income, and he lived alone, attended by an old housekeeper. He did nothing, absolutely nothing at all, not even amuse himself, and whenever I went in to see him he was invariably in bed. There was nothing wrong with his health. It was sheer laziness. But not laziness of a negative kind, mark you, but the outcome of a calm and studied policy. I knew this, and it angered me the more.

'What would happen if the whole world went on like you?' I snapped.

He sighed again, and then replied in his thin, mellow voice :

'We should have a series of ideal states. There would be no wars, no crimes, no divorce, no competition, no greed, envy, hatred or malice.'

'Yes, and no food.'

He turned slightly on one side. His accents became mildly expostulating, the philosopher fretted by an ignorant child.

'How unreasonable you are, dear boy. How unthinking!

The secret of life is complete immobility. The tortoise lives four hundred years; the fox-terrier wears itself out in ten. Wild beasts, fishes, savages, and stockbrokers fight and struggle and eat each other up. The only place for a culti- vated man is – bed. In bed he is supreme – the arbiter of his soul. His limbs and the vulgar carcase of his being con- structed for purely material functioning are concealed. His head rules him. He is the autocrat of the bolster, the gallant of fine linen, the master of complete relaxation. Believe me, there are a thousand tender attitudes of repose un- known to people like you. The four corners of a feather- bed are an inexhaustible field of luxurious adventure. I have spent more than half my life in bed, and even now I have not explored all the delectable crannies and comforts that it holds for me.'

'No,' I sneered, 'and in the meantime other people have to work to keep you there.'

'That is not my fault. A well-ordered state should be a vast caravanserai of dormitories. Ninety-nine per cent of these activities you laud so extravagantly are gross and un- necessary. People should be made to stay in bed till they have found out something worth doing. Who wants tele- phones, and cinemas, and safety-razors? All that civilisa- tion has invented are vulgar luxuries and time-saving de- vices. And when they have saved the time, they don't know what to do with it. All that is required is bread, and wine, and fine linen. I – even I would not object to getting up for a few hours every week to help to produce these things.'

He stroked the three-weeks' growth on his chin, and smiled magnanimously. Then he continued :

'The world has yet to appreciate the real value of pas- sivity. In a crude form the working-classes have begun to scratch the edge of the surface. They have discovered the strike. Now, observe, that the strike is the most powerful political weapon of the present day. It can accomplish nearly everything it requires, and yet it is a condition of immobility. So you see already that immobility may be more powerful than activity. But this is only the beginning. When the nations start going to bed, and stopping there, then civilisation will take a leap forward. You can do nothing with a man in bed – not even knock him down. My ambition is to form a League of Bed-fellows. So that if one day some busy-body or group of busy-bodies says : 'we're going to war with France, or Germany, or America,' we can reply, 'Very well. Then I'm going to bed.' Then after a time, they would have to go to bed too. And they would eventually succumb to the gentle caresses of these sheets and eiderdowns. All their evil intentions would melt away. The world should be ruled not by Governments or Soviets, but by national doss-houses.'

He yawned, and I pulled up the blind.

'What about the good activities?' I replied.

For a moment I thought I had stumped him, or that he was not going to deign to reply. Then the thin rumble of his voice reached me from across the sheets.

'What you call the good activities can all be performed in bed. That is to say, they can be substituted by a good immobility. The activities of man are essentially predatory. He has learnt nothing and forgotten nothing. He is a hunter and slayer and nothing else at all. All his activities are diversions of this instinct. Commerce is war, capital is a sword, labour is a stomach. Progress means either filling the stomach or chopping someone else's head off with the sword. Science is an instrument that speeds up the execution. Politics is a game. Colonisation is straightforward daylight burglary.'

'I'm not going to waste my morning talking to a fool like you,' I said. 'But what about art, and beauty, and charity, and love?'

'In bed,' he mumbled. 'All in bed ... They are all spiritual things. Bed is the place for them. Was Keats' "Ode to a Nightingale" any finer because he got up and wrote it down and sent it off to a fool of a publisher? Charity! Give a man a bed, and charity ceases to have any significance. Love! What a fool you are! Is a bed a less suitable place for love than a County Council tramcar?'

His voice died away above the coverlet. I was about to deliver a vitriolic tirade against his ridiculous theories, but I did not know where to begin, and before I had framed a suitable opening, the sound of gentle snoring reached me.

I record this conversation as faithfully as I can recollect because it will help you to share with me the sense of extreme surprise at certain events which followed, two months later. Of course George did occasionally get up. Sometimes he went for a gentle stroll in the afternoon, and he belonged to a club down town where he would go and dine in the evening. After dinner he would watch some of the men play billiards, but he invariably returned to his bed about ten o'clock. He never played any game himself, neither did he apparently write or receive letters. Occasionally he read in bed, but he never looked at a newspaper or a magazine. He once said to me that if you read the newspapers you might as well play golf, and the tremulous shiver of disgust in his voice when he uttered the word 'golf' is a thing I shall never forget.

I ask you, then, to imagine my amazement when, two months later, George shaved himself, got up to breakfast, reached a city office at nine o'clock, worked all day, and returned at seven in the evening. You will no doubt have a shrewd idea of the reason, and you are right. She was the prettiest little thing you can imagine, with chestnut hair and a solemn, babyish pucker of the cheeks. She was as vital as he was turgid. Her name was Maisie Brand. I don't know how he met her, but Maisie, in addition to being pretty and in every way attractive, was a practical modern child. George's two hundred a year might be sufficient to keep him in bed, but it wasn't going to be enough to run a household on. Maisie had no use for this bed theory. She was a daughter of sunshine and fresh air, and frocks and theatres, and social life. If George was to win her he must get up in the morning.

On the Sunday after this dramatic change I visited him in his bedroom. He was like a broken man. He groaned when he recognised me.

'I suppose you'll stop in bed all day today?' I remarked jauntily.

'I've got to get up this afternoon,' he growled. 'I've got to take her to a concert.'

'Well, how do you like work?' I asked.

'It's torture . . . agony, hell. It's awful. Fortunately, I found a fellow-sufferer. He works next to me. We take it in turns to have twenty-minute naps, while the other keeps watch.'

I laughed, and quoted : 'Custom lies upon us with a weight, heavy as frost and deep almost as night.' Then I added venomously : 'Well, I haven't any sympathy for you. It serves you right for the way you've gone on all these years.'

I thought he was asleep again, but at last his drowsy accents proclaimed :

'What a perfect fool you are ! You always follow the line of least resistance.'

I laughed outright at that, and exclaimed : 'Well, if ever there was a case of the pot calling the kettle black !'

There was a long interval, during which I seemed to observe a slow, cumbrous movement in the bed. Doubtless he was exploring. When he spoke again, there was a faint tinge of animation in his voice.

'You are not capable I suppose, of realising the danger of it all. You fool ! Do you think I follow the line of least

resistance in bed? Do you think I haven't often wanted to
get up and do all those ridiculous things you and your kind
indulge in? Can't you see what might happen? Suppose
these dormant temptations were thoroughly aroused! Good
God! It's awful to contemplate. Habit, you say? Yes, I
know. I know quite well the risk I am running. Am I to
sacrifice all the epic romance of this life between the sheets
for the sordid round of petty actions you call life? I was a
fool to get up that day. I had a premonition of danger when
I awoke at dawn. I said to myself, "George, restrain yourself. Do not be deceived by the hollow sunlight. Above all
things, keep clear of the park." But, like a fool, I betrayed
my sacred trust. The premonitions which come to one in
bed are always right. I got up. And now . . . My God! it's
too late.'

Smothered sobs seemed to shake the bed.

'Well,' I said, 'if you feel like that about it; if you think
more of your bed than of the girl, I should break it off. She
won't be missing much.'

He suddenly sat up, and exclaimed:

'Don't you dare — '

Then he sank back on the pillow, and added dispassion-
ately:

'There you see, already the instinct of activity. A weak
attitude. I could crush you more successfully with complete immobility. But these movements are already beginning. They shake me at every turn. Nothing is secure.'

Inwardly chuckling at his discomfiture, I left him.

During the months that followed I did not have the
opportunities of studying George to the extent that I should
have liked, as my work carried me to various parts of the
country, but what opportunities I did have I found in-
triguing. He certainly improved in health. A slight colour
tinged his cheeks. He seemed less puffy and turgid. His

movements were still slow, but they were more deliberate
than of old. His clothes were neat and brushed. The girl
was delightful. She came up and chatted with me, and we
became great friends. She talked to me quite frankly about
George. She laughed about his passion for bed, but declared
she meant to knock all that sort of thing out of him. She
was going to thoroughly wake him up. She said laughingly
that she thought it was perfectly disgusting the way he had
been living. I used to try and visualise George making love
to her, but somehow the picture would never seem convincing. I do not think it could have been a very passionate
affair. Passion was the last thing you would associate with
George. I used to watch them walking down the street, the
girl slim and vivid, swinging along with broad strides,
George, rather flustered and disturbed, pottering along by
her side, like a performing bear that is being led away from
its bun. He did not appear to look at her, and when she
addressed him vivaciously, he bent forward his head and
held his large ear close to her head. It was as though he
was timid of her vitality.

At first this spectacle amused me, but after a time it produced in me another feeling altogether.

'This girl is being thrown away on him. It's horrible.
She's much too good for George.'

And when I was away I was constantly thinking of her,
and dreading the day of the wedding, praying that something would happen to prevent it. But to my deep concern
nothing did happen to prevent it, and they were duly married the following April. They went for a short honeymoon
to Brittany, and then returned and occupied George's old
maisonnette below me. The day after their return I had
to face a disturbing realisation. *I was falling hopelessly in
love with Maisie myself*. I could not think of George or
take any interest in him. I was always thinking of her. Her
face haunted me. Her charm and beauty, and the pathos

of her position, gripped me. I made up my mind that the only thing to do was to go away. I went to Scotland, and on my return took a small flat in another part of London. I wrote to George and gave him my address, and wished him all possible luck. I said I hoped 'some day' to pay them a visit, but if at any time I could be of service, would he let me know.

I cannot describe to you the anguish I experienced during the following twelve months. I saw nothing of George or Maisie at all, but the girl was ever present in my thoughts. I could not work. I lived in a state of feverish restlessness. Time and again I was on the point of breaking my resolve, but I managed to keep myself in hand.

It was in the following June that I met Maisie herself walking down Regent Street. She looked pale and worried. Dark rings encircled her eyes. She gave a little gasp when she saw me, and clutched my hand. I tried to be formal, but she was obviously labouring under some tense emotion.

'My flat is in Baker Street,' I said. 'Will you come and visit me?'

She answered huskily, 'Yes, I will come tomorrow afternoon. Thank you.'

She slipped away in the crowd. I spent a sleepless night. What had happened? Of course I could see it all. George had gone back to bed. Having once secured her, his efforts had gradually flagged. He had probably left his business – or been sacked – and spent the day sleeping. The poor girl was probably living a life of loneliness and utter poverty. What was I to do? All day long I paced up and down my flat. I dreaded that she might not come. It was just after four that the bell went. I hastened to answer it myself. It was she. I led her into the sitting-room, and tried to be formal and casual. I made some tea and chatted impersonally about the weather and the news of the day. She hardly answered me. Suddenly she buried her face in her hands, and broke into tears. I sprang to her and patted her shoulder.

'There, there,' I said. 'What is it? Tell me all about it, Maisie.'

'I can't live with him! I can't live with him any longer!' she sobbed.

I must acknowledge that my heart gave a violent bump, not entirely occasioned by contrition. I murmured as sympathetically as I could, but with prophetic assurance :

'He's gone back to bed.'

'Oh, no, no,' she managed to stammer. 'It's not that. It's just the opposite.'

'Just the opposite?'

'He's so restless, so exhausting. Oh, dear! Yes, please Mr Wargrave, give me a cup of tea, and I will tell you all about it.'

For a moment I wondered whether the poor girl's mental balance had been upset. I poured her out the tea in silence. George restless! George exhausting! Whatever did she mean? She sipped the tea meditatively; then she dabbed her beautiful eyes, and told me the following remarkable story :

'It was all right at first, Mr Wargrave. We were quite happy. He was still – you know, very lazy, very sleepy. It all came about gradually. Every week, however, he seemed to get a little more active and vital. He began to sleep shorter hours and work longer. He liked to be entertained in the evening or go to the theatre. On Sunday he would go for quite long walks. It went on like that for months. Then they raised his position in the firm. He seemed to open out. It was as though during all those years he had spent in bed he had been hoarding up remarkable stores of energy. And suddenly some demon of restlessness got possession of him. He began to work frenziedly. At first he was pleasant to me; then he became so busy he completely ignored me. At the end of six months they made him manager of a big engineering works at Walham Green. One of the directors, a Mr Sturge, said to me one day, "That husband of yours is a remarkable man. He is the most efficient and forceful person we have ever employed. What has he been doing all these years? Why haven't we heard of him before?" He would get up at six in the morning, have a cold bath, and study for two hours before he went to work. He would work all day, like a fury. They say he was a perfect slave-driver in the works. Only last week he sacked a man for taking a nap five minutes over his lunch hour. He would get home about eight o'clock, have a hurried dinner, and then insist on going to the opera or playing bridge. When we got back he would read till two or three in the morning. Oh, Mr Wargrave, he has got worse and worse. He never sleeps at all. He terrifies me. On Sunday it is just the same. He works all the morning. After lunch he motors out to Northwood, and plays eighteen holes before tea, and eighteen after.'

'What!' I exclaimed. 'Golf!'

'Golf, and science, and organisation are his manias. They say he's invented some wonderful labour-saving appli-ances on the plant, and he's planning all kinds of future activities. The business of the firm is increasing enormously. They pay him well, but he still persists in living in that maisonnette. He says he's too busy to move.'

'Is he cruel to you?'

'If complete indifference and neglect is cruelty, he is most certainly cruel. Sometimes he gives me a most curious look, as though he hated me, and yet he can't account for me. He allows me no intimacy of any sort. If I plead with him he doesn't answer. I believe he holds me responsible for all these dormant powers which have got loose and which he cannot now control. I do not think his work gives him any satisfaction. It is as though he were driven on by some blind force. Oh, Mr Wargrave, I can't go on. It is killing me. I must run away and leave him.'

'Maisie!' I murmured, and took her hand.

The immediate subsequent proceedings are not perhaps entirely necessary to record in relating this story, which is essentially George's story. The story of Maisie and myself could comfortably fill a stout volume, but as it concerns two quite unremarkable people, who were just human and workaday, I do not expect that you would be interested to read it. In any case, we have no intention of writing it, so do not be alarmed. I can only tell you that during that year of her surprising married life, Maisie had thought of me not a little, and this dénouement rapidly brought things to a head. After this confession we used to meet every day. We went for rambles and picnics, and to matinées, and of course that kind of thing cannot go on indefinitely. We both detested the idea of an intrigue. And eventually we decided that we would cut the Gordian knot and make full confession. Maisie left him and went to live with a married sister. That same morning I called on George. I arrived at the maisonnette just before six o'clock as I knew that that was the most likely time to catch him. Without any preliminary ceremony I made my way into the familiar bedroom. George was in bed. I stood by the door and called out:

'George!'

Like a flash he was out of bed, and standing in his pyjamas, facing me. He had changed considerably. His face was lined and old, but his eyes blazed with a fury of activity. He awed me. I stammered out my confession.

'George, I'm awfully sorry, old chap. I have a confession to make to you. It comes in the first place from Maisie. She has decided that she cannot live with you any longer. She thinks you have neglected her, and treated her badly. She refuses to come back to you under any circumstances. Indeed, she – she and I – er — '

I tailed off dismally, and looked at him. For a moment I thought he was going to bear down on me. I know that if he had I should have been supine. I should have stood there and let him slaughter me. I felt completely overpowered by the force of his personality. I believe I shivered. He hovered by the edge of the bed, then he turned and looked out of the window. He stood there solemnly for nearly a minute; then he emitted a profound sigh. Without more ado, he got back into bed. There was an immense upheaval of the sheets. He seemed to be burrowing down into some vast and as yet unexplored cave of comfort. He rolled and heaved, and at length became inert. I stood there, waiting for my answer. Sparrows twittered outside on the window-box. I don't know how long I waited. I felt that I could not go until he had spoken.

At length his voice came. It seemed to reach me across dim centuries of memory, an old, tired, cosy, enormously contented, sleep-encrusted voice.

' 'S'all right,' said the voice. 'Tell Mrs Chase she needn't bring up my shaving-water this morning.'

J. D. BERESFORD

THE INDOMITABLE
MRS GARTHORNE

IT was one of those still bright days in early February, on which the warmth of the Southern sun charms one with the illusion that spring is already come hot-foot across the Spanish border; and I, who prefer illusion to fact, was watching the play of the swell that rolled in now and again from the Atlantic, when I was so unexpectedly summoned to play my small part in a drama that was to affect four lives so profoundly, to say nothing of my own.

The introduction was commonplace enough. I had arrived in Biarritz the previous afternoon only; and although I knew perhaps a score of the English and American visitors who were spending the season there, I was not aware that young Hugh Garthorne and his mother were among the number until he suddenly invaded my high retreat on the island rock, near the complicated little harbour of the fishermen.

I heard the sound of someone mounting with an evident hesitation the twisting flight of steps that gives access to the little railed plateau on the summit of the rock, and turned my head to see Hugh slowly coming into view, rather as if (even then the metaphor occurred to me) he were rising to join me on the stage by means of a badly worked 'trap'.

I can't pretend that I was glad to see him. Apart from the fact that I was in a mood to dream rather than to talk, I was not greatly drawn to young Garthorne. He was spoilt by his mother, who, though she certainly spoilt no one else, permitted, even encouraged, this only child of hers to lounge through life with no occupation save that afforded by playing games and dressing himself. Judging from his appearance, he must have spent a considerable time every day in dressing himself. A great pity, I thought, for he was a handsome intelligent-looking youngster.

He gave no sign of surprise at seeing me alone there. 'Hallo, Edwardes!' he said casually. And 'Hallo, Garthorne!' I replied, adding, as he came and sat down beside me, the inevitable : 'I didn't know that you were in Biarritz.'

'Been here for five weeks,' he said.

'Oh! Have you?' I returned, mentally cursing the necessity for politeness. Why should I sit here exchanging inanities with the spoilt child of a rich widow whom I disliked, when I might be indulging my fancy with enticing dreams? It was so good, so stimulating, to be back again by the open sea; to be able to watch on this day of calm sunshine the occasional roller coming from across the world, heave magnificently against the rocks in front of us, split, break into foam, and then in sudden petulance dash at the base of the island, hissing and chattering.

'Do all the big things in life get broken up like that?' Hugh remarked unexpectedly, glancing at me with a faint blush.

I was startled. I had been anticipating some gossip of the last tennis tournament, or of where the best jazz-band was to be found for a *thé-dansant*; some fritter of that kind. But now that I looked at him more closely, I thought I could see signs of a new seriousness in his face.

'The wave at least dies in splendour,' I said.

'There's that, of course,' he replied, watching the sea and slightly shrugging his shoulders before he continued, after a moment's pause : 'I saw you come up here. I followed you on purpose. You see, you're different from the other people in our set . . . being a poet and so on . . . I got a feeling you might understand.'

That speech warmed me toward him. I was flattered by

his description of me, even with the doubtful qualification
of his 'and so on' – for, indeed, I am not known to the world
at large as a poet.

'Understand what?' I asked gently.

I have said that the introduction to my drama was commonplace enough, and I saw no probability of its ever de-
veloping on other than purely conventional lines when, with
the freedom from self-consciousness that came in his case
from being the petted and adored son of his rich mother, he
confessed to having fallen in love with a young violinist who
played at the Casino. The whole thing was, it seemed to
me, so trite, so hackneyed, so precisely what one might have
anticipated.

'What does your mother say?' I asked. 'She has always
given you everything you wanted; won't she give you
this?'

'I haven't dared to say anything to her about it,' he said.

I raised my eyebrows. 'But I thought . . .' I began.

'She wants me to marry Lady Rose Whitley,' he interrupted me. 'Some people imagine that we're engaged
already. She'll be my partner in the Mixed Doubles next
week. I like her, too. Nice kid. But it isn't only that. You
don't know my mother well, do you?'

I did not. I had never wished to. I had always heard her
spoken of as a hard, self-seeking, intolerant woman; and
that report of her had been confirmed by my own observa-
tions. She was, I believed, a woman with but one weakness:
the boy to whom I was now speaking.

'No; I don't know her at all well,' I admitted.

'Then the thing you don't know about her,' he explained,
'is that she's a bit crazy on this subject. I don't know why.
She's sensible enough about everything else. But the only
real row we've ever had was about something of this sort,
when I was at Balliol. I was a young ass, of course, and I
saw afterwards that she'd been perfectly right on that occa-

sion. But – well – she gave me a sort of scare. First time she'd ever gone on at *me* like that, you know – told me then that if ever I married without her consent she'd disown me, you understand.' He paused and grinned at me cheerfully as he concluded : 'And considering that I haven't got a bean of my own and no profession, that might be dashed awkward.'

'It certainly might,' I agreed. His frank confession, however trite, had warmed my heart towards him.

'You don't mind my telling you all this?' he half-apologised. 'Fact is, I wondered if you'd feel like helping me.'

'Helping you?' I temporised, my mind suddenly full of romantic cinematographic pictures of waiting motor-cars, frenzied escapes, and sentimental reconciliations; with myself, modestly in the background, performing some unobtrusive miracle.

'I wondered if you'd talk to my mother about it?' he said.

But no; that was more than I felt prepared to do. Mrs Garthorne was the kind of woman that I have always been afraid of; tall, handsome, commanding, with a kind of solidity, both of the flesh and the mental outlook, that greatly intimidates me. I would have been ready to commit some not too desperate offence against the law in order to help Hugh, but I could not face his mother on such an errand.

'My dear chap, what would be the use of that?' I said. 'I shouldn't have the least influence with her.'

'Tell you what,' he replied; 'come and see her this afternoon. She's playing at the Casino.'

'Your mother's playing ! . . .' I stammered.

'Good Lord !' he ejaculated with another grin. 'My hat ! no. Come and see Her.'

It was probably relief at the relative simplicity of this so suddenly substituted alternative that made me agree to his proposal without demur. But even as I did so, I had an uneasy feeling that I was letting myself in for something that I should do much better to avoid. This new Hugh Garthorne whom I saw for the first time on the little island rock at Biarritz was, I felt, going to be uncommonly difficult to influence. He had the look of a man who has definitely made up his mind; he had something of his mother's air of resolution.

'Though I don't quite understand why you should imagine that *I* can help you,' I added feebly.

'Well, you know all about psychology and that sort of thing,' was the only explanation I had from him.

When I saw the name of the girl on the programme, the feeling that this affair of Hugh's was, after all, essentially commonplace and uninteresting returned to me with new force. The name given was 'Paula Gonzalez'; an obvious and clumsy pseudonym, I decided; and was instantly prepared for a figure to match it – a young woman with a striking profile, handsome, common and loud.

Hugh, sitting beside me, nudged my elbow. 'That's her father,' he whispered. 'Just come into the orchestra. With the violin. The chap with white hair.'

The man he indicated was still standing with, as it seemed to me, an effect of hesitation. Despite the absolute whiteness of his thick hair, his eyebrows were dark and his moustache and neat pointed beard only slightly tinged with grey. I guessed him to be still on the sunny side of sixty. As I watched him, he shot one quick glance at Hugh, and then sat down, turning his back on us.

'He knows about you, then?' I murmured to Hugh.

'He has probably guessed,' he returned.

'Is he likely to be – difficult?' I asked.

'Can't say yet,' was the answer. 'You see, I've never spoken to either of 'em.'

'But how could he guess in that case?' I protested.

'Spotted me, I expect,' Hugh said. 'I'm always here

when she plays. Besides which I generally wait about to see them come out.'

With that, although there may appear to have been little cause for my change of attitude, the sense of being drawn into a hackneyed, common intrigue definitely left me. It may have been due to this evidence of restraint on Hugh's part, or it may have been the effect that that glimpse of the white-haired first violin had had upon me. I could not understand that look he had thrown at Hugh. Reflecting on the man's hesitation, the way in which he had stood with a half-abstracted, half-attentive air before he had, as it were, dared that one brief glance, it came to me that the action had been timorously planned. I wondered if the man were one of those reserved self-conscious people who never outgrow a childish dread of appearing conspicuous.

I was certainly becoming intrigued by Hugh's love-affair even before I saw the object of his adoration. She was below the average height and looked smaller perched up alone there on the platform; a rather pathetic childish figure, with a child's mouth, set, at the moment, in a mould of intent determination that did not break into a smile when she bowed to her audience. She was undoubtedly pretty; but I hardly remarked that, being drawn from the first moment by her air of intelligence, combined with that effect of girlish seriousness; as if she would attack and conquer her world by sheer endeavour. She was dark enough to carry off her Spanish name, but she was not a Spanish type; she was altogether too reserved and too tender.

I admired her at once, and when she played I fell in love with her in my paternal, middle-aged way – deep enough to feel that the Hugh Garthorne I had known was not worthy of her. She looked so sweet and yet so vital as she played to us, so eager and so intent to give us her very best. But though her best was very good for a child of nineteen, full of fire and feeling, I knew that she would never make a first-class violinist. She had worked hard, I guessed; but she was not a born musician. Of course, all her pieces were encored. There was not a man in the audience, and only a few women, who would not have rewarded her so evident wish to please them.

As she came to the end of her last encore, I became aware that Hugh was trembling as if he were shaking with cold, an impossible contingency in that overheated concert-room. I turned towards him, wondering if he had been deeply stirred by the music, and saw that his eyes were fixed upon that delightful child on the stage with a gaze that expressed at once anticipation and the keenest anxiety – the look of a man who expects some greatly longed-for sign, but is tremulously afraid that it may be denied him.

A little startled, I turned my attention back to Paula Gonzalez. She had finished playing and was bowing her acknowledgments of the enthusiastic applause, smiling gratefully as if she loved us all for our kindness to her. And then, just as the white-haired man in the orchestra had done, and with the same effect of nervous resolution, she gave one quick but unmistakable glance at Hugh before she made her exit. She did not smile as she did it. It seemed rather as if she were conscious of taking a liberty.

'You were expecting her to look at you,' I said to him as soon as we were outside.

'She did it yesterday,' he admitted.

'But you've never attempted to speak to her or her father !' I commented.

'Look here, Edwardes !' he exclaimed, taking me by the arm. 'I've told you about this because you're the only chap I know who I thought might understand. Anyway, I don't know anyone else who'd be likely to. I couldn't say much to you this morning, but now you've seen her it's different. Surely you understand now?'

I did, up to a point. I was beginning to understand, for

instance, that the Hugh Garthorne I had known hitherto was not the real man, and that I had a distinct feeling of liking for the new one who was now being revealed to me.

'I can quite understand your being in love with her,' I said. 'She's adorable.'

He gave a little sigh, perhaps at the hopelessness of expressing her quality in mere language, before he replied : 'Well, then, don't you see how impossible it would be to try and scrape up an acquaintance in the usual way, the usual caddish way? I couldn't. She's – well, you've seen her now, so you ought to know. That's why I want you to come and talk to my mother. I want her to invite them to our house. It's the only way I've been able to think of – of getting to know them decently.'

We had come down to the *Plage* and he was facing the wind that was coming up fitfully out of the great distances of the open Atlantic, and already tossing the crests of the increasing rollers into a spume of white spray. There was, I thought, something almost heroic in the calm certainty of his expression just then.

'We're going to have a storm,' I said.

'The sooner the better,' he replied unexpectedly. 'But look here, will you try first if you can do anything with my mother?'

'I'll try,' I said. I could not deny him that, though I knew it was hopeless. 'And if I don't succeed?' I added.

'She'll have to disown me,' he returned quietly. 'I expect I'll be able to earn a living somehow. And, anyway, it would prove what I was willing to do for Her.'

And that was how I came to have an interview with the terrible, intimidating woman, his mother.

I went the next afternoon while Hugh was at the Casino.

Mrs Garthorne received me politely enough. There was no reason why she should not do so; she had nothing against me; but the consciousness of my mission made me feel more uncomfortable than usual in her presence. She was so essentially a woman *rangée*. She had long since finally made up her mind on every conceivable question of society, politics and religion. She would not have taken the advice of an Archbishop if it had not suited her own views; and what chance had I when I proposed to attack what I had gathered to be the most cherished of all her fixed opinions?

The apparent effect of my foolish embassy was not, however, quite what I had anticipated. I began, tactfully, by talking of Hugh, a subject to which she was always attentive, and presently ventured the suggestion that his character had developed considerably since we had last met.

She was pouring out the tea, and paused at that with the teapot still poised in her hand.

'You find him more serious?' she asked shrewdly.

'I do, yes; and more . . .' I twiddled my fingers, searching for a word. 'More thoughtful,' I concluded weakly.

She put down the teapot and passed me my cup, holding my gaze the while with a resolute stare that made me tremble. 'You know that he's in love?' she asked.

I had forgotten about Rose Whitley, and thought that she had already got wind of the affair and that the game was up. The fact gave me courage. 'Most beautifully, even heroically in love,' I said. 'It will be the making of him.'

'Ah!' she commented quietly. I had never seen her look more solid.

'He's inspired,' I continued; 'and, I feel, worthily.'

'You've seen her?' she put in.

'Yesterday afternoon, at the Casino de la Plage,' I admitted.

'Ah!' she commented again with that effect of immense resolution. 'And her name?'

I hesitated. I was ashamed of the poor little tinsel name, so suggestive of yellow skirts, black lace and castanets, that suited so ill that earnest child with the violin. 'Paula Gonzalez,' I said.

'I'm greatly obliged to you, Mr Edwardes,' she returned, and immediately began to talk – not about Hugh or his entanglement, but about Biarritz society and its doings; a steady stream of hard, fluent conversation that gave me no chance to do more than interpolate a brief monosyllable. She talked me out of my chair and out of the house. I do not believe that anything short of physical violence would have stopped her. And though she said nothing impolite, I received very clearly the impression that I need not call on her again.

I met Hugh by appointment at the Miramont. It was a day of rain and blustering wind and the *Plage* was impossible.

'So you've done it?' he remarked as I sat down by him.

I explained that what I had done was to give him away, and nothing more.

'Good,' he replied; surprisingly, I thought.

'But, my dear chap,' I began.

'That's all right,' he interrupted me. 'It's exactly what I wanted. Cursed odd, I admit, but you know, I just hadn't got the courage to break *it* to her. That was where I stuck, somehow. I've given her a hint or two, but she pretended not to notice. Now she knows, I don't care a damn. No end obliged to you, old top.'

'But what are you going to do?' I asked.

'Split,' he said quietly. 'Make a clean break-away. What else could I do?'

I felt bound to remonstrate with him. 'That's all very well, my dear old chap,' I said; 'but you owe a lot to your mother. She may be a bit queer on this subject of your marriage, but she's utterly devoted to you; given you everything you asked for, simply lived for you. Even if she were not your mother – common gratitude, I mean – what?'

He was more impressed by that than I had expected. 'Yes, you're right,' he admitted. 'Besides . . .'

'How are you going to live?' I concluded for him.

'Oh! It isn't that,' he replied contemptuously. 'I'd make a living somehow. Scene-shifting or something. I've faced that idea. That's nothing. What I was going to say was that it was just funking to run away. Paula's so tremendously worth winning, isn't she? Worth the very greatest thing I could possibly do.'

'Which is?' I inquired, puzzled.

'Face it out,' he said. 'Make my mother give in. Go on living with her, and back my will against hers.'

'By Heaven!' I exclaimed. 'That would be magnificent.'

'I'll do it,' he announced, and for a moment he looked capable of anything. Then he frowned, sighed and slightly pushed his chair away from the table. 'Only,' he said, 'you must come back with me – just to start with. I know it looks like weakness; but, you see, I've got to snap the chain, if you know what I mean. My mother has dominated me all these years, and I've got the habit of giving in to her. But if I could once break that habit, I could go on. I'm perfectly certain I could go on. And if you're there, I should *have* to do it.'

I felt at the moment as if I would sooner parade Biarritz in pyjamas than face Mrs Garthorne again so soon; but I understood exactly how he felt about the great preliminary effort needed to 'snap the chain' of habit and agreed to lend him my support, assuming, I hope, such an appearance of careless courage as would be most likely to stiffen his own.

'Very well. Come on,' I said, getting to my feet. 'We'll go at once.'

So far as I was concerned, that, I knew, was the only chance. I should never do it if I had time to think.

Mrs Garthorne was in the same room and the same chair

in which I had left her barely an hour earlier. She turned
her head when we came in, but gave us no other greeting.
She was fully prepared for what we had to say and was perfectly confident of utterly routing us; but, like the great
general that she was, she took no risks, her first piece of
strategy being to lay all the burden of the attack upon us.
She intended to give no sign until we had revealed our
tactics and discovered our artillery, such as it was.

I looked at Hugh and realised that it was for me to open
the battle. He was gazing abstractedly out of the window,
apparently lost in some mental calculation; but whether
he was already funking the engagement or not, I couldn't
guess. In any case, I had to offer myself up as a forlorn
hope to tempt the enemy out of cover.

I did not, I confess, display either great courage or remarkable intelligence in my opening; but I have an incur-
able habit of politeness. If Hugh's life, instead of only
his happiness, had depended upon the issue, I do not think I
could have been rude to Mrs Garthorne at that moment.

'I must apologise for returning so soon,' I said. 'But I
met Hugh in the town and, realising what a very poor hand
I had made of my ambassadorship earlier, I felt that I must
ask you to let me tell you what I really had no opportunity
of telling you this afternoon. . . .'

I could have gone on from that if she had permitted me,
worked myself up, perhaps, into an appeal by the practice
of my own eloquence, but she cut me short. The sound she
made is usually written 'Faugh!' but nothing can express
the insolence and contempt she put into it. I was utterly
rejected and dismissed. Never in my life have I felt so
abominably insulted.

Nevertheless, it seemed that I had served some purpose
in thus drawing the enemy's guns, if the forlorn hope itself
had been completely annihilated by that single discharge.
Hugh had had time to find his method, time enough to

screw up his courage to the sticking-point. After all, what he had chiefly required of me was my witness.

'I came to tell you that I'm going to marry Miss Paula Gonzalez, mother, if she'll have me,' he said, still with his gaze on some ultra-terrestrial vision – possibly the imagined features of his ideal.

Mrs Garthorne remained perfectly still, perfectly contemptuous. A faint snort was her only audible reply.

'And,' Hugh continued with a faint smile – 'and with your full consent.' That seemed to be a good shot.

He had, at least, succeeded in surprising her. She looked at him sharply, as if it had crossed her mind that he might possibly have some card up his sleeve. Indeed, I thought I caught a hint of something in her expression that looked rather like alarm.

'Hugh!' she apostrophised him sharply. 'Don't be absurd.'

'I mean to get my own way this time, you see,' he said.

Her fear, if I had been correct in my diagnosis, was evidently relieved by his answer. She got to her feet, looking bigger and more impressive than ever in her cold wrath.

'You'd better go to your room, Hugh,' she pronounced majestically. 'And never let me hear another word from you on this subject.'

It was the method of the autocrat, of the governess with the small child, by which she had always ruled him. In reverting to it she played on his familiar reactions; re-stimulated the sensations of the helpless boy who had always been dependent upon her.

And I knew that if Hugh submitted now he would be beaten. It was here that he had either to snap that chain of habit which had bound him for more than twenty years or submit for ever to his mother's imperious will. I looked at him, expecting to see the signs of the coming defeat, a bent head, a nervous movement of the hands; but his head

was raised, his hands were loosely clasped behind his back
and he was smiling.

'In future you will hear from me on this subject, mother,
whenever we meet,' he said steadily. 'I shall talk of nothing
else.'

She looked straight into his eyes and he returned her
gaze with equal steadiness.

I left them there still locked in that grip. I had played
my part. Hugh had taken his line – the only right line, I believed – and no one could help him now. But what the end
of it would be I could not guess. Somehow I could not
imagine Mrs Garthorne giving in.

I did not see Hugh again for three days, and then we
met, by accident, on the *Plage* about four o'clock. He took
me by the arm. 'Good, I wanted to see you,' he said.
'There's something I want you to do for me.'

I shuddered with a horrible premonition that I was to be
called upon for yet another interview with his mother. A
dozen excuses rose to my mind, but there was a new force
and resolution about Hugh's voice and manner that
checked them from finding utterance.

'Oh! What's that?' I asked.

'I want you to make the acquaintance of Mr Gonzalez
and Paula,' he said. 'I can't yet. I've told her that I won't
see them again until I've got her consent to bring them to
the house. But I should like you to get in touch with them.
You can't give 'em any message from me, of course, but
you might sort of interest 'em in me, what?'

I agreed almost with enthusiasm, so relieved was I.

'And how goes the battle royal?' I asked.

'Pretty stiff,' he said. 'But I'm getting into training. I
started with an infernal handicap, you know, but I'm
picking up now. All this'll be splendid practice in keeping
a stiff upper lip and that sort of thing if it comes to the
scene-shifting after all.'

Who would ever have thought that the boy had such fine
stuff in him, I reflected, as I waited by the artists' entrance
to the Casino. I felt a sudden warm confidence in him; not
in his chances of winning that fearful contest of wills with
his mother – I believed her to be indomitable – but in the
certainty that he would eventually make good. I could help
him to a better start in life than a job as a scene-shifter
would give him, and I was fully prepared to do it. Not alone
for the sake of Hugh and that appealing little violinist,
although they came first. No; let me be honest and admit
that Mrs Garthorne's contemptuous 'Faugh!' still rankled
in my mind. I could never forgive her for that.

I found no difficulty in making the acquaintance of
Gonzalez and Paula; indeed, they seemed to be expecting
me. More than that, when they had accepted my invitation
to tea and we had settled ourselves into a corner of the
inner room at the Miramont, they made it very easy for me
to introduce the subject I had been charged to interest
them in.

At the first casual mention of 'a young friend of mine
who had greatly admired Miss Gonzalez' playing', they
exchanged a quick glance of understanding, and then Gonzalez, with a very obvious embarrassment of manner, said:

'Are you speaking of the young friend who was with you
in the Casino three days ago? I – I noticed him.'

'We have seen him there every day, almost,' Paula put
in; 'until last Tuesday, that is, when he was there with
you. He hasn't been since.'

'Yes, that is the one I mean,' I said. 'His name is Garthorne, Hugh Garthorne.'

Gonzalez bent over his plate to hide his face, but the clear
eyes of Paula were shining as she watched him; shining, I
thought, a little triumphantly, almost as if they were saying, 'I told you so.'

I had but one explanation of their behaviour and it repelled me. I imagined that, as so often before I had been deceived in my judgment, they were in fact no more than just two poverty-stricken musicians, eager to entrap the wealthy young man who had by his behaviour already proclaimed himself to be this outwardly charming young girl's admirer. Poor Hugh, I reflected; was it for such a tinsel prize as this that he had engaged in that tremendous conflict of wills with his indomitable mother? Yet it was not for me to oppose his desire. The one adversary he had would be quite sufficient. If she could not deter him, it was very certain that I could not.

'He would so much like to meet you,' I continued, 'a little later on. For the moment he is – er – very much occupied.'

To my surprise Gonzalez shook his head. 'Oh! no, no. That would never do,' he said.

'I don't see, dear, really, why not,' Paula remonstrated. 'Just once, you know.'

Had they guessed my suspicion of them, I wondered, and were they now trying to disguise their trap by a piece of shoddy play-acting? It looked like that. And Gonzalez' next question confirmed my original inference.

'His mother, I suppose, is very rich?' he asked shyly.

'I presume so,' I said.

'A widow?' he mumbled, still without raising his head.

'For more than twenty years,' I told him. 'Hugh was, I believe, a posthumous child.'

Gonzalez raised his eyes then, not to look at me, but to exchange another of those understanding glances with Paula, whose regard of him this time appeared to be no longer triumphant, but tender, consolatory. Then, as if to distract my attention from Gonzalez, she turned to me with one of her pathetic appealing little smiles and said : 'Me, too, you see.'

I did not understand, and in reply to my look of blank astonishment she explained :

'I'm an orphan really. My father died a few weeks before I was born and my mother a few weeks after. If daddy hadn't adopted me I should have died, too, of course.'

An obvious question suggested itself. 'You are married?' I asked Gonzalez.

He hesitated a moment and then said, 'Yes; but I have not seen my wife for more than twenty years.'

'And where were you when you adopted Miss Paula?' I inquired.

'The Argentine,' he replied, 'Buenos Aires. Paula's father was an English engineer. He died of yellow fever . . .'

A pathetic little history of struggle and self-sacrifice it appeared to me, thinking it all over after I had left them and guessing at much that they had not told me. And reflecting upon it that evening I suffered another reaction; blamed myself for having attributed such grossly mercenary motives to them. Yet I was mightily puzzled to explain otherwise their obvious interest in Hugh; puzzled and presently so piqued that I determined to talk to Gonzalez again at the earliest opportunity.

It presented itself no later than the next morning, when I found him, by chance, on that other island rock connected to the mainland by a bridge, known as the Rocher de la Vierge. He was at the farthest point where the nose of the spit dips into deep water, but the tide was half out, the sea fairly calm, and there was little danger of being drenched by the spray of a sudden swell.

He greeted me with a shy eagerness; at once glad to see me, I thought, and a little afraid; as if he braced himself to some intimidating task.

'I – I would like to ask you rather a queer question, Mr Edwardes,' he began immediately, with a nervous rush that made me think of my own futile attack upon Mrs Garthorne.

I tried to put him at his ease.

'By all means,' I said, smiling. 'If I can help you in any way, I shall be delighted. I am, I assure you, greatly interested in your charming adopted daughter.'

He leaned on the low stone parapet that guards the end of the rock, and stared out across the magnificent breadth of the great Atlantic that even in its sunniest hours hardly conceals the menace of its destructive strength.

'It's just this, sir,' he murmured; 'can I trust you with a secret? Trust you, that's to say, not to mention it to – to any of the people concerned?'

'You can,' I returned quietly.

'It concerns your young friend, Mr Hugh Garthorne,' he continued with a little catch in his breath. 'You see – you see – although he must never know it – I'm his father.'

I may be forgiven for not believing him. His announcement seemed so utterly unlikely. I did not suspect him of any criminal tendency towards blackmail, I merely supposed that his mind was a trifle weak, and that he was probably subject to harmless illusions of this kind.

'Really! That's very interesting,' I humoured him.

'And if I could just meet him once without his having any suspicion who I am,' he continued, with a deep sigh, still staring out across the sea, 'it would be something to remember. I would be very careful.' He turned to me with a sudden appeal in his face : 'Oh, I would not for anything interfere with his happiness.'

If this were acting, it was of the very finest quality; nevertheless, it was not his expression and the tones of his voice that convinced me, but the likeness to Hugh I had unexpectedly seen when the little man had gazed out at some illusory vision across the world, just as his son had gazed from his mother's window four days earlier.

'Do you know,' I said, 'I think I can help you to more than that; but couldn't you tell me something of your story first?'

A sordid little story enough, it may appear, set out in dull words, but to me it was quick with the breath of life, inspired by my sight of this sensitive little artist and my realization of what his sufferings must have been during the mercifully short year and a half of his married life. For to me there was something heroic in the fact that he had dared the law for the sake of the child that was coming; had committed a terrible indiscretion with the paper of the firm by which he had been employed and had suffered the full penalty of a term of imprisonment.

They had been poor in those days, the Garthornes, grindingly poor; but when he came out of prison, it was to find that his wife had become suddenly rich through some inheritance that might have given him, I thought, an excuse for leaving her; though it certainly gave her none for refusing to see him again. Truly she must have been an abominable woman, even when all allowance is made for my immense personal prejudice against her. It is true that she offered him money, but he refused to take it and went off to South America, taking little more than the violin, which, hitherto the solace of his worst hours, was now to become his source of livelihood.

How he lived in those years is of no importance; what is of far more interest is that the little visionary should have built up for himself an ideal of the son he had hardly seen. That had been his chief compensation, and one that Paula, as she grew up, had willingly shared. Between them, they had created the picture of the hero that should be Hugh Garthorne; a picture that had grown so vivid and convincing with the years that it had at last drawn them home by way of Spain, earning their living on the road. And at San Sebastian they had found to their infinite relief that the journey they were planning to England might not be necessary. He had seen an English paper published in Paris, giving the list of visitors at Biarritz, and his belief

that the Mrs Garthorne there mentioned was his own wife
had been confirmed three days after his arrival by a sight
of her in the street. She had even glanced at him, but without the least recognition. The years had changed him
more than her.

'So you'll understand,' he concluded, 'what it would
mean to us just to speak to him. And you can trust us never
to let him know. God forbid that I should do anything
more to spoil his life.'

He seemed to have never a doubt that Hugh was in very
truth the splendid hero of his father's dream. Hugh! The
youngster whom I had known, until less than a week ago,
as nothing more than an idle, over-dressed, game-playing
young waster!

'Listen,' I said, 'the best thing that ever happened to
Hugh was when he fell in love with your adopted daughter.'

He gasped as if I had thrown cold water over him. 'With
Paula!' he ejaculated. 'But then . . .'

I saw the threat of flight in his eyes, and knew that he
would utterly sacrifice himself and Paula, too, rather than
risk the shadow of harm to his ideal.

'No; but listen,' I interrupted him, and gave him a suc-
cinct account of all that I had seen and hoped for in Hugh
since our meeting on the rock four days earlier, together
with a hint of what he had been before that time.

Even then he was not to be convinced all at once. He
had been so poor all his life, and the possession of money
to him loomed so vastly important. Not until I insisted on
the necessity of getting Hugh away from his mother did
the little man show signs of conviction. It was an argument
that seemed to weigh with him, and I left him wondering
if it were possible that his wife had been privy to his fraud
before he had committed it, and had turned against him
afterwards. I believed her capable even of that infamy.

When I got in I sent a messenger from my hotel with a

note to Hugh saying no more than that I wished to see him; and he turned up after dinner, looking, I thought, a trifle weary.

'Well, how goes it?' I asked him.

'I'm sticking it,' he said; 'but it's going to be a long job. I wish I could see Paula again. Did you do what I asked you?'

'And more! Oh, very much more,' I said.

Watching him carefully as I told him Gonzalez' story – something too deliberately, perhaps, and withholding the essential statement until Hugh was on the verge of guessing it for himself – I could trace in him so clearly the two almost incompatible strains he had inherited. But while I admired the evidences of sympathy, understanding, idealism he had inherited from his father, I knew that they would constitute an almost insuperable handicap in the fight he had undertaken with his mother. *He* might be tempted to see her point of view. *She* would be absolute.

'But, good Lord, I say,' he murmured when the truth was out. 'What had I better do now?'

It was the paternal strain that, at first, made him unwilling to take my advice.

Perhaps I was hardly justified in my proposition. That insulting dismissal of me as a person quite unworthy of the least consideration still rankled, and I may be accused of a paltry wish for revenge – more particularly as there seemed to be no real justification for my taking part in the interview I insisted upon between Mrs Garthorne, her husband and Hugh. My excuse was that I went to support Gonzalez, as I may still call him, and he certainly needed a power of stiffening. But in the end both he and his son consented to my plan, chiefly for Paula's sake.

She, dear child that she was, remained in ignorance still of the fact that Hugh had fallen in love with her; but she was all alight with eagerness, not only herself to meet the ideal hero of their dreams, but also at the possibility that her foster-father might be forgiven and allowed free communication with his son, a pardonable deception. I do not reproach myself for that.

We had to await Mrs Garthorne in her drawing-room. Hugh had given her no warning that she was to meet the supposed father of the girl he was in love with, knowing that she would simply and blankly refuse to see him. But no doubt she suspected some ambush, for she kept us waiting long enough to aggravate almost unendurably our natural nervousness.

When she came at last, however, she made a mistake in her pretence of completely overlooking me. That put me on my mettle.

'Who is this, Hugh?' were her first words, indicating Gonzalez. She had closed the door behind her, but remained standing before it, dominating the room.

'This,' I said, 'is Mr Gonzalez – it is not his real name – the adopted father of the charming young lady your son proposes to marry.'

'And what have you to do with the affair, may I ask, Mr Edwardes?' she inquired, fixing me with her bitter stare.

'That would take too long to explain,' I said; 'more particularly as there is a far more important explanation to be made. Is it really possible, Mrs Garthorne, that you do not recognise – er – Mr *Gonzalez*?' I underlined the name with a peculiar emphasis.

Her stare travelled almost indolently from me to her husband, and rested there with a calm scrutiny.

'You see, Helen,' he began, and I fancy it was the phrase and the manner that enlightened her rather than her memory of his face.

Her self-possession was almost incredible. Her strength lay in the fact that she could be neither shocked nor wounded. She turned to her son, and said without a tremor : 'You know that your father has served a sentence of twelve months' imprisonment for forgery?'

'But, good God, mater, that was more than twenty years ago,' Hugh returned indignantly. I was glad to note his warmth.

And then, just for a moment, I caught the least flicker of her eyes in the direction of her husband, a glance that held the hint of a question, a doubt. And although I have no other evidence, for Gonzalez has preserved his faithful silence, I would swear that she had been accessory to his fraud and was debating how far she could trust him to reserve that damning fact.

Apparently she was satisfied of his trustworthiness, for she continued with the same effect of inviolable calm; 'And what do you hope to gain by this most unseemly revival of forgotten scandals, Hugh? Are you trying to blackmail me into consenting to your marriage with this trumpery little violinist, picked up Heaven knows where by an ex-convict? You have tried, quite unsuccessfully, to bully me for a week. Is it to be blackmail now? If so, I can assure you that you will find that method equally unavailing.'

She had neither humour nor imagination. If she had combined intelligence with that colossal resolution of hers she might have been great. But she was essentially a stupid woman, or she would have known that her one chance with Hugh was to make an appeal to his sympathy, his gratitude. As it was, she stung him into open revolt.

'There's no question of blackmail,' he said, and there was something very like hate in his eyes as he spoke. 'I have done my level best to persuade you, and I hoped this might help. Now, I tell you straight out that I'm going to marry Paula, if she'll have me, with your consent or without it.'

'And what do you propose to live upon?' she retorted. 'Your wife's earnings?'

'Great Scot! no,' Hugh said. 'I'll make a living some-how. And, as Edwardes says, that'll be jolly well the best thing that could happen to me.'

She was incapable of understanding that. She sneered. She believed that his education had been too carefully neglected to permit of his earning his own living. And it was on that she counted for her ultimate triumph. 'I cannot prevent you,' she said. 'But look to me for no help, Hugh; until you come back – *alone.*'

It was her last word. With that she turned and left us, to all appearances as unruffled as fate itself. No doubt she was supremely confident that time would win the battle for her; that after three – six – months, a year or two at most, Hugh would return, alone and defeated, to submit himself finally to her intolerable yoke. She could not believe that he would stand the test of poverty. Had she not suffered it herself?

And if I can judge by the sight I had of her a few days ago, she still awaits her son's return in perfect confidence. She was driving in the Park, massive and imperturbable as ever, not a thread of white in her hair nor an added line on her face.

And thinking at that moment of Hugh's joy in his wife and little son, of the success he was already making for himself; and of how he had, almost miraculously, fulfilled the dreams of those two dear people who had come across the world merely for a sight of their fairy hero; thinking also, perhaps, that I had, after all, secretly accomplished my revenge and that she must know it, I lifted my hat and bowed to her.

Her glance travelled past me. She made no movement. But on her lips and in her attitude I read again the signal of her insulting 'Faugh!'

Terrible, indomitable woman!

THE ELEVENTH HAT

I

TEDDY MOSTYN's behaviour was certainly open to suspicion. He distinctly resembled a 'gentleman cracksman', slim in evening clothes and silk hat, as he lurked and lingered and peered from the opaque green shadows of the chestnut trees which swept pompously up the drive to the doors of The Sanctuary, Hampstead Heath. Behind those doors, Sir Runnymede Clarke, professor of theological, ethical and spiritual research, was usually to be found – or rather, not to be found – blandly researching, his mind far from all thought of notoriety, his hand modestly waving away the laurel wreath – a favourite affectation of that eminent gentleman, widely applauded by the general public, but most irritating to the Press.

But on this hot, bright evening at the end of May, the doors were open wide to the visitors who were arriving in cars and on foot. Not a large crowd – but enough to justify the word 'party'. Sir Runnymede was giving a select party. Sir Runnymede was 'showing off'. He had gently enveloped the famous medium 'Jehane' in his hospitality, from the first moment of her first arrival in England, so that when she could be coaxed to function, it should be nowhere else but under his benign patronage. . . . 'She is so delicately poised, so harmoniously adjusted to her environment,' he explained. 'The least infinitesimal jar to the psyche – phut! the sitting is over !'

So that his invitations to assist at the séance were issued with the extremest care. It was unthinkable, of course, that a single member of the Press should receive permission to be present. Quite unthinkable, which was a pity, because Jehane was emphatically of news value.

And so Teddy Mostyn, journalist, hung about in the dense shade of the chestnuts, in obedience to Anthea's instructions : 'Wait in the drive till you see a group of four, walking; nearly everyone else will be in cars, of course; but the Burlington-Webbs live so near here. Then stroll in just behind them. Father will take it for granted that you're of their party, especially when he sees how prettily I receive you. . . .'

Anthea was Sir Runnymede's daughter; though she was only nineteen, she had ruled his home for him since the death of her mother, two years before. Teddy thought her (a) a goddess (b) a radiant woodland sprite (c) an angel . . . d, e, f, g, h, etc., can be imagined.

It was thoroughly impudent of her to help him to a chance of writing up tonight's séance for his sensational rag, *The Daily Snap.* But it would mean so much in Teddy's career – 'Such a stunt, Anthea, if mine should be the only description published the next morning !' Anthea was a mischievous, human child, and liked Teddy, and secretly thought her father an 'old dug-out' for his prejudice.

'She's divine,' flashed Teddy's emotional half; and '*What* a stunt if I pull it off,' his professional half, like a sky-sign that changes from green to yellow. – Were these the four Webbs? No, only another car. 'Lucky for me it's fine, waiting here. Wonder if old Sir Magna Charta'll spot me. Doesn't know me by sight, so if he thinks I'm a pal of Anthea's – she's the bravest, sweetest, noblest . . . what a rotter Philip was, not to let me come in with him !'

'My dear man,' Philip Asterley had previously replied to the request, in those low, clear, carefully restrained accents which gave an impression that, after years of tense struggle, the owner had managed at last to curb his wild and impetuous youth to a decent calm, 'my dear man, it simply can't be done. You don't quite realise what bad form it would be for me to abuse the mutual trust which is understood between host and guest, by exposing Sir Runnymede to the vulgarity of a column in *The Daily Snap*. Just because we're friends – it simply can't be done.' And Teddy had felt duly snubbed.

But Anthea, bless her, had more daring in her little finger (the bewitching little finger!) than Philip in —

Ah! four people walking together up the drive. The Burlington-Webbs at last!

A few moments later, and Teddy, in obedience to directions, had left his hat with the butler in the hall, and was following the Burlington-Webbs through the lounge and into a room on the left, where Sir Runnymede and Anthea were receiving their guests. He was swayed by an awful giddiness . . . panic . . . a wild impulse to fly . . . but checked it . . . a fleeting wish that he were more like Philip in demeanour, and less like Teddy . . . and then he moved forward to receive Anthea's courteously indifferent greeting; Anthea, a tiny, imperious naiad in her pale tints of water-blue and lily-green. Sir Runnymede, he was thankful to see, was engrossed at the buffet with some very special and exalted visitors.

Gradually Teddy recovered from a sweating preoccupation that the whole roomful was about to point at him with loud jeers of recognition : 'That's Teddy Mostyn of *The Daily Snap*.' 'Mostyn of *The Daily Snap*.' 'What's he doing here?' 'Who invited him?' 'Push him out!' – and was able to look about and recognise here and there some prominent persons in society, or from the scientific and literary worlds. There was Philip, as usual, most disconcertingly at his ease. Teddy, to relieve his feelings, fiercely cut him, and Philip slightly raised his brows . . . he did not mind Mostyn being present as long as the responsibility were not his, but if Mostyn chose to be puppyish —

And indeed, the description fitted Teddy, who was given to clumsy, lovable gambollings, to high spirits and swift remorse, and to ingenuous displays of affection.

Philip Asterley, lately his inseparable, was one year younger than Teddy's twenty-four, but frequently wondered when the latter would begin to show signs of growing up : 'D'you despise me for my illusions, Philip?' Teddy had once asked anxiously, and his blue eyes widened at the weary reply : 'Not half as much as you envy me for my disillusions, my son.' – You can see by this example of epigram, as Teddy saw at once, that Philip really was simply wonderful at times !

The Burlington-Webbs had been almost the last visitors to arrive; and not long afterwards Sir Runnymede gave the signal for adjournment into an inner room on the farther side of the sombre black and bronze curtains which were draped over an aperture opposite the door into the hall. 'Jehane' was waiting for them, seated on a raised platform. She was a peasant girl, and always wore a prim and rather shabby black stuff dress with a high collar – nothing picturesque, nothing exotic – 'We look upon this as scientific experiment, not as a fancy dress ball,' Sir Runnymede had courteously explained to a guest who expressed disappointment at the medium's commonplace appearance. Beside her sat a gentleman who apparently blended the offices of trainer, impresario, and guardian angel. An absence of crystals, bowls of ink and other old-fashioned apparatus of the mystics, denoted again, with some firmness, that a high-class séance was not to be confused with a conjuring entertainment.

The babel of tongues sank to a few expectant whispers. . . . Sir Runnymede had ensured that only two or three sceptics were present, to flavour the atmosphere of credulity. 'They say her powers are quite super-normal' . . . 'gets through to a Chinese child-martyr who died before

Confucius' . . . Queer blank eyes she has.' . . . 'Broadhurst
Challoner is here, y'know – the Wimpole Street man –
such a triumph if he gets converted. . . .' '. . . I do feel – well,
not frightened, but nervy . . . on the jump . . . as though
something – ' ' – Any test, Sir Runnymede says – afterwards. All he asks for is quiet attention and an open mind.'
'Hush . . . hush.' . . . Everybody was in their seats by now.
Teddy, obedient to a swift signal from Anthea, found himself next to his love, half way down a row near the back
of the room.

On his other side was a stately patrician woman with a
disdainful mouth, whom Teddy recognised as Philip's
mother – the Beautiful Mrs Asterley, they called her. He
could claim no personal acquaintance – she had but just
returned from winter and spring on the Riviera; and he
had only begun to play Damon to Philip's Pythias, in
January. But Philip had shown him photographs, and, on
this one topic, hardly even troubled to tone down his boyish
enthusiasm – 'She looks as though she could be uncomfortably noble,' reflected Teddy; and then, remembering
Anthea, was lost to the rest of the world.

. . . The bronze and black curtains fell back over the
doorway. The windows had all been carefully darkened.
Absolute darkness was Jehane's one requisite. The stillness
was oppressive, and the sudden chirp of a bird outside
seemed sacrilege. . . . The Chinese child-martyr of before
Confucius, took possession of Jehane's slumbering consciousness, and spoke through her lips – falteringly at first,
then more fluently. Fortunately it – he – could speak
English.

. . . Anthea's hand flew out sideways, and excitedly
grabbed Teddy's. He, like Jehane, at once became possessed – not with child-martyrs, but with passionate
clamorous ecstasy. The overwrought sensibilities of everybody present worked upon his own, infecting him reck-

lessly – Anthea ! Anthea ! how lovely she was. . . . So magic-
ally close to him, there in the warm thick gloom . . . what
else existed? What else mattered?

'I love you, Anthea, love you – Oh, do tell me – yes,
now, I can't stand it any longer you must say you love me
too or I'll – I'll – Oh, I don't know what I'll do . . . kill
somebody. . . . Anthea – ' he poured his soul out in fervent
whispers. Anthea, helpless, tried to stop him – he was not
to be stopped. She desired to give all her attention to the
séance, to that queer thin little voice trickling out its strange
wisdom from the platform . . . but the intoxicated Teddy
would not let her. The more she hushed him, the more
persistent he became. Anthea, irritated and then furious
by his untimely proposals and absolute loss of tact, at last
whispered back, softly but distinctly : 'No. I don't love you.
I hate you. I'm sick of you. I never want to see you again.'

It was the most unlucky measure that she could have
taken, if her idea was mainly to silence him. Teddy forgot
everything except that he had been refused, his adoration
mocked and baffled. His one primitive need was now to
rush away. He sprang up and plunged distractedly for the
door. His chair scraped backwards and clattered on to the
parquet. . . . He stumbled over innumerable feet. . . . Somebody cried out. . . . Somebody else sharply said 'Silence !' . . .
Teddy stumbled again, kicking another chair . . . ah, here
were the curtains of the door at last. . . .

But Sir Runnymede Clarke's séance had been reduced
by one young lover's supreme egoism, to pandemonium.
The awful, the irremediable catastrophe had happened.
Jehane, her trance rudely broken, had gone off into hysterics, and was thrilling the air with scream after scream.
. . . Everybody was on their feet now . . . every tongue talking . . . 'Who was it?' 'What was it?' 'Where is he?' 'Who?'
'Why?' – and then the masterful voice of their host, calling
for the lights to be switched on.

II

' – Mother, your emeralds!'

Philip Asterley's sudden exclamation drew the shocked attention of the little clumps of three and four guests within hearing. They crowded round : 'Oh, Mrs Asterley, have you lost them? What was it? A pendant? When did you last notice?' Mrs Asterley's hand was roaming over her bare neck in that incredulous fashion of believing the missing article must be still there because one believes it there. . . . 'Yes – a pendant – emeralds. Exquisite stones. I . . . Philip!' she was very pale.

'You had it on just before the séance,' Furness Lequesne, A.R.A., asserted positively. 'I noticed it when you were holding your liqueur – the crême-de-menthe. Two dabs of bright colour, and the dead black lace of your dress . . . it made a picture.'

'Old-fashioned art, but useful evidence,' murmured his irreverent sister.

A thorough search over that part of the floor where Mrs Asterley had been sitting, discovered nothing. By this time, all Sir Runnymede's guests knew that Mrs Asterley's emerald pendant had been . . . lost? . . . within the last twenty minutes. The second sensation of the evening eclipsed the first. It was not long before the two were linked —

'Lost? No. *Stolen*,' declared a plump gentleman with aggressively angry eyebrows. He was Professor Brax, a lecturer at the College of Ethical Research. 'Stolen!' he repeated. The hitherto unspoken word, uttered so abruptly, ripped aside the silken blandness of uncertainty, and left the company stark and uneasy. 'Not much doubt about the thief. We'll find out who it was who ran away so quickly in the middle of the sitting. Meanwhile,' fussily, 'we must insist, of course – I think I may speak in the name of every-

body present? – we must insist. . . . Oh, a mere matter of
form, Sir Runnymede – on turning out our pockets, and
the ladies their bags, before leaving this room. For our own
satisfaction, you understand? A mere matter of form.' He
echoed this phrase so often and with such sinister emphasis,
that some of the more nervous among the innocent visitors,
began to feel suspected, and wondered uncomfortably
whether the investigation might indeed reveal the missing
pendant concealed about their persons. . . .

' – And now,' continued Professor Brax, when the formal search had revealed no traces of the stolen emeralds,
'if we can't find the missing jewels, what about the missing
guest, hey? One of your visitors, Sir Runnymede, escaped
from the room, in the middle of the séance. Now – are we
all here? That's to say,' getting rather muddled, 'which of
us whom you invited, isn't?'

Sir Runnymede Clarke vainly wished it had been Professor Brax himself. Scientifically, they were rivals.
Socially, they were cronies. Intimately, they detested one
another.

'I did just notice one or two young men who were strange
to me,' he replied sulkily.

Brax pounced : 'One or two. That won't do, Sir Runnymede. Was it one or was it two. Hey? . . . Or – perhaps I'm
being officious. Yes, you think I'm being officious. You'd
rather I didn't meddle, and left it to the police.'

'No, no, Brax – ' Sir Runnymede was overcome with
horror at the notion. 'It would be all over the papers tomorrow – Do let us, that is to say, if Mrs Asterley will allow
it, try our utmost to discover the thief amongst ourselves,
as it were.' He realised that this might have been expressed
with greater advantage. 'I mean – our own common sense
– a little private detective work – and if that fails, naturally we must call in Scotland Yard. But I certainly am
anxious to avoid – ' he shuddered – 'newspaper reporters

in the house.' If he had glanced at his daughter Anthea then, he might have been struck by her piteous guilty look. But he had turned enquiringly to Mrs Asterley, who re-assured him with 'Certainly, my dear Sir Runnymede, I quite agree with you that it's pleasanter for all of us if the matter need not develop into a newspaper sensation. It's most kind of Professor Brax to bother – '

Professor Brax, being then given his head, so to speak, enjoyed himself heartily, taking down the name of each guest before permitting them to leave, and calling on Sir Runnymede to identify them, and compare the list with his list of invited guests. It tallied. Ten men and seven ladies. Thus was established the fact that the person who had so noisily rushed away in the dark, must have been the same as the 'one or two' strange young men recalled by Sir Runnymede – he was still obstinately vague about their number : 'I tell you, my dear Brax, I thought that they – he – were friends of Anthea, and concerned myself no further in the matter.'

'The confusion and upsetting of chairs was quite close to me,' Mrs Asterley's charming, well-bred voice parted the cross old men in their wrangle, like a rivulet of cool water. 'And before that I heard a lot of whispering – quite indistinguishable, though.'

'A-h-h !' the professor pounced, delighted, on this fresh evidence. 'But you saw nothing of the criminal's eyes, for instance? or his clothes?'

'My dear Professor – I could not have seen my own hand if I had held it up in front of my face. The atmosphere was like the best blue-black ink.'

' "Jehane's" psychic partner told me that it was essential,' Sir Runnymede interposed.

'Well, but who did you see in your neighbourhood when you first sat down, Mrs Asterley? Someone else must have heard the whispering.'

'You weren't far off, I think, Dr Challoner. And Miss Clarke.'

'I – did – hear – some whispering,' faltered Anthea, speaking the truth, but hardly the whole truth.

Challoner had heard it too.

'Well – but people don't whisper to themselves,' argued Professor Brax, who, like the old lady who lived in a shoe, had so many clues he didn't know what to do !

The butler, when questioned, produced a fresh clue. He had opened the french windows of the refreshment room, he said, to air it after the visitors had withdrawn into the inner room for the séance. Then he busied himself with clearing up the buffet. Suddenly someone rushed through from within, and out at the windows into the garden. He might in his frantic haste have mistaken that way out, for the ordinary door into the hall; or he might simply have preferred the garden exit – 'H'I couldn't say, sir. I was standing at the buffet at that moment with my back to the room, you understand, sir. Naturally surprised by the h'incident, I crossed to the windows, and beheld the retreating figure of a young gentleman in evening clothes, sir, but bare-'eaded, running down the flagged path. I moved a few paces after him before I realised, sir, that there was no hope of h'overtaking him.' The butler's well-turned phrases were a credit to The Sanctuary.

The company now took their leave in rather an embarrassed fashion, murmuring conventional sympathy or thanks to their host and hostess. All except the Asterleys and Professor Brax. The latter, tremendously excited, invited Sir Runnymede and Mrs Asterley to accompany him in quest of footprints down the dim garden to where the flagged path bent round to join the drive. Philip was about to accompany them, when Anthea, by a look, detained him, and drew him out into the now deserted hall.

'Philip, do help me – I must tell someone.'

'Why, certainly, Anthea. What is it?' it streaked across his mind that she might herself have taken his mother's pendant to pay a gambling debt . . . but this he dismissed as sensational folly.

'You know – it was Teddy – '

'What? who took the – ?'

'Of *course* not!' with a little stamp of indignation. 'Teddy who made all that noise while Jehane – You see, he – he was proposing to me, and I was in such a rage with him for doing it just then, that I refused him. And he just clutched at his hair and rushed away.'

Philip fought with laughter and conquered it.

'And left me in this terrible position,' continued the distressful naiad. 'And then,' unreasonably, 'your mother goes and gets her emeralds stolen !'

Philip's desire to laugh was over. He suddenly saw Teddy's reputation and liberty seriously menaced by his 'absurdly juvenile behaviour'.

'I'm afraid you'll have to tell them just why he left in such a hurry, won't you, Anthea? It's embarrassing for you, but – '

'I can't – I can't – At least, I can't while there's a hope that I needn't. Because father would never forgive me for smuggling a newspaper reporter into his séance. It's the one thing that would – '

' – Get his goat,' finished her hearer, lending a savour to inelegance by his correct and precisely articulated accents.

'But I still think, in fairness to Teddy, that you ought to clear him,' he added. 'Why, they're all down there looking for his footmarks – as though he were a criminal.'

'If I clear him, I'll have to explain him. And father will dislike him equally much as a reporter than as a criminal. So what's the good? No, what I thought was this : They,' with a nod towards the garden, 'are all on the hunt for

Teddy. But you and I, knowing that why Teddy rushed out of the room, wasn't because of the pendant, are the only ones who know that therefore somebody else must have taken it. If you could only track down the *real* thief, Philip dear . . .' she coaxed him. 'After all, you have two advantages over old Brax.'

'One of them being, as you say, that I needn't waste time tracking down Mostyn,' he mused. And paused. . . .

'Brains,' murmured Anthea, supplying the other.

It was not unnatural that, after this display of minxhood, Philip should accept the responsibility of a private detective. And, moreover, that he should feel a certain boyish thrill and gusto, carefully concealed, at the prospect. 'First of all, Anthea, we must eliminate. The theft must have occurred between the time when Lequesne noticed mother's emeralds all mixed up with the crême-de-menthe, just before she went into the inner room – and the switching on of the lights. Now, not one of your father's seventeen guests was missing when the lights were turned on. They all let themselves be searched. Nothing was found. What do we deduce from that?' Philip was unaware of his lapse into the professional vernacular. 'Why, that another uninvited guest had been present, besides Mostyn. And had escaped under cover of Mostyn's hullabaloo.'

'Oh . . .' breathed Anthea, admiringly.

'Do you remember the queer persistent way in which your father clung to it that he had noticed "One or two strange young men", and wouldn't limit it to one only; to Teddy, in fact? Did *you* notice any strangers in the male line, when receiving the guests?'

'Two or three,' promptly. Philip groaned. 'Oh, please, Phil, I don't mean to be troublesome like father. But I don't even know by sight all his cronies and students and disciples and things. Especially the spiritual research ones. By the way,' with an inspiration, 'it couldn't have been

Jehane herself, or her stage-manager person? I believe
Professor Brax quite forgot their pockets.'

Philip shook his smooth fawn-coloured head. 'They
couldn't have scrambled across the room as far as my
mother and back again without being heard, even in the
dark. No – the thief – the other strange young man who
impressed himself so indelibly on your father's attentive
subconsciousness, must have escaped, as I said before, under
cover of Mostyn's hullabaloo.'

'But Johnson was busy at the buffet and would have
seen him,' Anthea objected.

'Not while Johnson was standing outside the french
windows, with his back to the room, watching Teddy in full
flight. Here is our data then :' he had given in to the fact
that there was only one set of phrases for detectives, and
that these must be employed. 'A young man, presumably
well dressed and a gentleman, or you'd have spotted him,
passes himself off as a guest, mingles with the small crowd
you have invited, seats himself somewhere near my mother;
and takes advantage first of the darkness, then of an unexpected noise and confusion, to slip away with the emerald
pendant, through the outer room, into the deserted hall,
and out. In his hurry, however – ' and though Philip usually
kept such commonplace emotions as triumph and drama
tightly on the leash, he could not forbear giving them a run
now – 'for we can assume that the other ten men at your
party would have been fairly calm and leisurely over their
departure, with Johnson to assist them – In his hurry, our
Raffles happened to leave something behind him, *and
there it is* ! Philip flung out his arm and pointed to a peg.
. . . 'Ten guests – and the eleventh hat !'

'I noticed that topper ages ago,' remarked Anthea, not
at all impressed by the climax. 'It's Teddy's of course. He
must have been wearing one when he arrived; and, don't
you remember? Johnson described : "the retreating figure

of a young gentleman in evening-clothes but bare-'eaded".'

Philip was almost too disappointed to hide his chagrin.

'I'll toddle round to Mostyn now, I think,' he said, shortly. 'He ought to be warned that he's quite likely to find himself in a mess – and he might just be able to throw some fresh light on the affair.' He took up his own hat from where it lay on the oak chest behind him.

'If you're going to see Teddy,' Anthea betrayed suddenly a wave of shy, warm blushes, 'I mean – if you're going to see Teddy – '

'I *am* going to see Teddy.'

'You might tell him – from me – that girls, when something has upset them, very often say the exact opposite – of what they would have said – '

' – If something hadn't upset them,' finished her messenger, gravely. 'You may trust me to make that quite clear to him, my dear Anthea – and I might as well return him his lid, while I'm about it.' Philip lifted it down from the peg, glanced casually inside it – and remained staring. . . .

'Looking for goldfish, Phil?' enquired Anthea, with dainty impertinence.

'. . . It's a queer thing,' slowly, 'to find the initials O'D.J.F. on the lining of Teddy Mostyn's hat.'

*　　　*　　　*　　　*　　　*

' – And so don't let it surprise you, my son,' Philip added, when he had finished telling Teddy the exact sequence of events leading up to, and down from, the theft of his mother's emerald pendant that evening, 'if a couple of policemen should call any time within the next few days. Your improbably idiotic conduct,' severely, 'in dashing away from the séance in that guilty fashion, makes it almost too easy for Professor Brax to land you in the dock !'

'I don't care if he lands me in the hanging-shed,' replied

the dejected Teddy, racked with unrequited love.

'Oh, yes – by-the-bye – I forgot – Anthea sent you a message.'

Teddy showed faint signs of returning life.

' "Girls, when something has upset them" – I quote the little lady verbatim – "very often say the exact opposite of what they would have said – " '

Teddy bounded to his feet – his wan cheeks glowed – his countenance was radiant – he clutched distractedly at his hair. . . .

'I'll reward you some day, Philip, old man. I must rush off now – I must see her tonight – I must see her father . . ask his consent. . . . O Lord, what ought I to say, d'you think?'

'You're just like the sort of young lover Shakespeare used to write about,' commented Philip, surveying him in dispassionate criticism. 'Do sit down. You can't go to Sir Runnymede tonight. You're too damp and hot and breathless to go anywhere. Besides, he doesn't like journalists.'

'*She* loves me after all,' gasped Teddy, who was incapable of hearing any except angel voices in the heavenly choir. 'She meant to say "yes"! If I hadn't upset her – but I'll spend my life putting that right. Where's my hat? I haven't got a hat. I left it in the hall. I can't ask her father's consent without a hat. Oh, you've brought it along – good – excellent – ' he grabbed it, thrust it on his head – 'Why . . .' taking it off again, 'it's too small. It isn't mine at all, Philip, you dunder-headed . . . no, I forgot, you're a frightfully good fellow—'

Philip negotiated the turbulent youth backwards on to a chair : 'Let me remind you,' with weary patience, 'that besides the fact that you haven't a hat, you are also under grave suspicion of stealing my mother's emerald pendant, and that you can't clear yourself without betraying

Anthea's little treachery to Anthea's father-who-already-doesn't-like-journalists. The moment is, therefore, not propitious for approaching him. Stop spluttering and try to help me discover who O'D.J.F. is . . . and in fifteen years' time you may be able to get married.'

'Who's O'D.J.F.?' demanded Teddy, more bewildered than ever; his hair in rakish confusion.

'The owner of this hat. At present in possession of yours. When we find him we find the pendant.'

'How d'you know.'

Philip brought him up to date in the process of elimination, deduction and inspiration, along which he had travelled.

'You're really a damned wonder, Philip!'

'Thanks. . . .' The tribute was not unpleasant.

'Hats . . .' went on Teddy vaguely, 'I seem to be seeing hats . . . everywhere . . . hats and hats and *hats*. . . .'

'My dear man, pull yourself together. There were precisely twelve. Sir Runnymede's ten male visitors had, presumably, one head each. This is the eleventh hat which O'D.J.F. left behind; taking, by mistake yours, which *you* had left behind – being in a dazed and half-witted condition when you fled.'

Teddy grinned feebly: 'O'D. is an unusual initial,' he remarked, 'I've heard it before. Where was it? O'D. No, I've written it – in my column. . . .' He wrote personal paragraphs twice a week for *The Daily Snap.*

'You're getting warm,' the other encouraged him. 'O'D. Think of the apostrophe! O'D. Was it recently?'

Teddy began to rummage through a pile of old *Daily Snaps.*

'No – several months ago. November or December. . . . *Ah*!' about a quarter of an hour later.

Philip, wildly excited, managed to achieve a yawn. 'Got it?' he queried, lighting a cigarette.

'O'Donnell. James Ferrier, O'D.J.F. How's that?'

'Who is he?'

Teddy triumphantly read out the paragraph: Mr O'Donnell James Ferrier, known on Wall Street as "O'D.", is expected on Thursday by the *Arctic*, the Red Star Company's latest leviathan. He proposes to divide much of his time in future between London and Copenhagen. Mr Ferrier (inset) is one of the youngest powers in American finance. His dramatic negotiation of the Consolidated North American Beef Trust is too recent to have been forgotten. O'D. hopes to hunt with the Quytchley this season, and, as he first learnt to ride in Arizona, he ought to be some thruster.'

'God! how badly you write!' was Philip's comment on this.

Teddy was not unnaturally irritated that his valuable contribution of evidence should have been taken in such a scornful spirit. 'If you'd had to interview the blighter – '

'I'm going to interview him now,' said Philip, rising languidly and throwing away his cigarette with airy grace. 'It all seems to fit in all right. Rash young speculator, ruined by the sudden fall in beef, in desperate need of ready cash, and then the sudden temptation and fall. . . . What did you say was the address?'

'I didn't.'

'Find it out for me, then, there's a good fellow. And don't be long, because it's getting late.'

'I suppose I'll have to ring up "Mrs Chitter-Chat". She'll know if anyone does. She does "A Woman Lunches Out" in *The Evening Snap*, and knows everybody's affairs, everybody's income, and everybody's skeleton in the cupboard. Heaven grant she's in – ' with which Teddy betook himself to the telephone, and, after some bright badinage with his co-worker, extracted from her three pieces of information: that Lady Lavender Lestrange really *had* broken off her engagement with Gustav Beckenheimer; that O'Donnell James Ferrier lived at the Albany; and that a very luscious scandal was brewing over P. L. Raven's new revue, 'Biff'. 'The engagement and the scandal I got her to throw in as a disguise for the address!' boasted Teddy, 'and d'you know, she was in bed – at the other end!'

'When you are as old as I am, my dear Teddy, you will have learnt that beds are as boring as breakfasts. At present you really are more like a débutante than any débutante I've ever met.' Philip tilted his hat with meticulous care; and, for the second time that evening, picked up the hat of the mysterious O'D., who lived in the Albany, manipulated Beef Trusts and stole emerald pendants.

Philip was rather surprised when his steely request for an interview with Mr Ferrier on urgent private business, met with instant success. He had anticipated more difficulty.

'I called to return your hat, Mr Ferrier; and it struck me that it might be convenient for you to give me the emerald pendant in exchange. You have it in your pocket, I presume?'

'Why, sure. Here it is.' And not a whit disturbed by Philip's dramatic opening to their conversation, Ferrier, small, wiry and brown, plunged his hand into his pocket, and produced a heap of glittering green fire. 'Lovely stones!' he murmured, shaking it out and rippling it through his fingers.

Philip could not help a thrill of admiration at the man's effrontery. Had he been a thief himself, thus would he have liked to face a crisis. He leant back in his chair, and, smiling a little, said : 'Well, Mr Ferrier, and what do you propose to do about that pretty little toy?'

Ferrier grinned back, genially.. 'Give it to my fiancée, I reckon.'

But this was carrying insolence and bluff too far. Philip's

mouth hardened. 'The police of this country, Mr Ferrier, though hitherto you may not have found them your equals in mental agility, have nevertheless certain obvious uses. I'd rather hoped, as a matter of fact, to leave them out of this affair, if you could have been persuaded to return me the pendant quietly, as some slight amends for the theft – '

'Easy! you're going a bit too far, Mr —— , I don't think you told me your name. I certainly had Mrs Asterley's pendant in my pocket, but I'm not the thief who stole it.'

'Then,' with languid irony, 'would it be bad manners on my part to enquire who was?'

'Mrs Asterley.'

'It's a lie!' Philip's pose was shattered at last.

'Pardon me, I can quite understand that my statement may have sounded ridiculous, but when you have heard my explanation – '

'Your explanation – yes.' The boy had regained command of himself again. 'Your inspiration, you mean. Well? – go on.'

The American was a little annoyed. He showed his annoyance by the curt, cold manner of his narrative: 'Mrs Asterley was a great friend of my mother's. Several years ago – roughly about fifteen – she stayed with us in New York. I was a youngster at the time; I remember, though, that I thought her very beautiful, and always very beautifully dressed. But she must have been hard up, at the time, though we didn't know it, or why should she have stolen my mother's pendant? She vanished before we discovered the loss, and my mother, who was generosity itself, wouldn't follow her up. The loss of a friend meant more to her than the loss of a jewel, and I believe she was sorry about it till her death, eighteen months ago. I came to England then, and if Miss Pamela Carew hadn't done me the honour to become engaged to me, I'd never have thought again about that pendant. But it happened that emeralds are her birth-stone, and she's got a real craze for them. So when I read in *The Daily Snap* that the beautiful Mrs Asterley had just returned from the Riviera, and was to be one of the guests at Sir Runnymede Clarke's séance tonight – last night, I ought to say – it just occurred to me that I might take the chance of talking privately to the lady, and even suggest she should send me back my property. It was too late to get an invitation, so I went uninvited. I turned up as they were all squeezing into the inner room, and spotted that she was actually wearing it. Pretty cool, eh? But still, New York, and fifteen years ago. . . . I got a seat just behind her, and when that young fellow bolted out of the room like a range-steer, it seemed to me a good chance to take what belonged to me, and make off as well – without any confidential talk about it, which, anyhow, wasn't much in my line. The outer room and the hall were empty, and I went straight through and out – helped myself to my hat, which, by the way, turned out to be somebody else's, and came back here. Pam'll like these little green fellers; they're not large, but the colour's first-rate. Now, are you satisfied, Mr Sherlock Holmes?' and his dryness relaxed to a smile.

'Very ingenious, but, as I said before, purely the inspira-tion of the moment,' laughed Philip, rather hectic now.

'All right, m'lad. Step right over to the phone. I guess Mrs Asterley's number will be in the book. Ring her up, and, apologising for the lateness of the hour, tell her you've discovered who stole her pendant : That it's one O'Donnell James Ferrier from New York, and *does she wish to prosecute?*'

Philip, amused at the man's undaunted optimism, turned over the pages of the telephone book in pretended search for the name Asterley. For some reason unaccountable to himself, he did not wish Ferrier to guess his identity.

'Hello! Give me Mayfair 40039. No, nine – not five.'

Silence. Then : 'Hullo ! Is that Mayfair 40039? . . . Yes, it is. . . . The pendant is found. The – thief is one O'Donnell James Ferrier from New York. . . .'

A long pause while Philip listened to the voice which answered him. Then he replaced the receiver, and turned to O'Donnell.

'I must apologise,' he said quietly. 'My mother . . . does not wish to prosecute.'

D. H. LAWRENCE

FANNY AND ANNIE

FLAME-LURID his face as he turned among the throng of flame-lit and dark faces upon the platform. In the light of the furnace she caught sight of his drifting countenance, like a piece of floating fire. And the nostalgia, the doom of homecoming went through her veins like a drug. His eternal face, flame-lit now! The pulse and darkness of red fire from the furnace towers in the sky, lighting the desultory, industrial crowd on the wayside station, lit him and went out.

Of course he did not see her. Flame-lit and unseeing! Always the same, with his meeting eyebrows, his common cap, and his red-and-black scarf knotted round his throat. Not even a collar to meet her! The flames had sunk, there was shadow.

She opened the door of her grimy, branch-line carriage, and began to get down her bags. The porter was nowhere, of course, but there was Harry, obscure, on the outer edge of the little crowd, missing her, of course.

'Here! Harry!' she called, waving her umbrella in the twilight. He hurried forward.

'Tha's come, has ter?' he said, in a sort of cheerful welcome. She got down, rather flustered, and gave him a peck of a kiss.

'Two suitcases!' she said.

Her soul groaned within her, as he clambered into the carriage after her bags. Up shot the fire in the twilight sky, from the great furnace behind the station. She felt the red flame go across her face. She had come back, she had come back for good. And her spirit groaned dismally. She doubted if she could bear it.

82

There, on the sordid little station under the furnaces, she stood, tall and distinguished, in her well-made coat and skirt and her broad grey-velour hat. She held her umbrella, her bead chatelaine, and a little leather case in her grey-gloved hands, while Harry staggered out of the ugly little train with her bags.

'There's a trunk at the back,' she said in her bright voice. But she was not feeling bright. The twin black cones of the iron foundry blasted their sky-high fires into the night. The whole scene was lurid. The train waited cheerfully. It would wait another ten minutes. She knew it. It was all so deadly familiar.

Let us confess it at once. She was a lady's maid, thirty years old, come back to marry her first-love, a foundry worker : after having kept him dangling, off and on, for a dozen years. Why had she come back? Did she love him? No. She didn't pretend to. She had loved her brilliant and ambitious cousin, who had jilted her, and who had died. She had had other affairs which had come to nothing. So here she was, come back suddenly to marry her first-love, who had waited – or remained single – all these years.

'Won't a porter carry those?' she said, as Harry strode with his workman's stride down the platform towards the guard's van.

'I can manage,' he said.

And with her umbrella, her chatelaine, and her little leather case, she followed him.

The trunk was there.

'We'll get Heather's greengrocer's cart to fetch it up,' he said.

'Isn't there a cab?' said Fanny, knowing dismally enough that there wasn't.

'I'll just put it aside o' the penny-in-the-slot, and Heather's greengrocer's'll fetch it about half-past eight,' he said.

He seized the box by its two handles and staggered with it across the level-crossing, bumping his legs against it as he waddled. Then he dropped it by the red sweetmeats machine.

'Will it be safe there?' she said.

'Ay – safe as houses,' he answered. He returned for the two bags. Thus laden, they started to plod up the hill, under the great long black building of the foundry. She walked beside him – workman of workmen he was, trudging with that luggage. The red lights flared over the deepening darkness. From the foundry came the horrible, slow clang, clang, clang of iron, a great noise, with an interval just long enough to make it unendurable.

Compare this with the arrival at Gloucester : the carriage for her mistress, the dog-cart for herself with the luggage; the drive out past the river, the pleasant trees of the carriage-approach; and herself sitting beside Arthur, everybody so polite to her.

She had come home – for good ! Her heart nearly stopped beating as she trudged up that hideous and interminable hill, beside the laden figure. What a come-down ! What a come-down ! She could not take it with her usual bright cheerfulness. She knew it all too well. It is easy to bear up against the unusual, but the deadly familiarity of an old stale past !

He dumped the bags down under a lamp-post, for a rest. There they stood, the two of them, in the lamplight. Passersby stared at her, and gave good night to Harry. Her they hardly knew, she had become a stranger.

'They're too heavy for you, let me carry one,' she said.

'They begin to weigh a bit by the time you've gone a mile,' he answered.

'Let me carry the little one,' she insisted.

'Tha can ha'e it for a minute, if ter's a mind,' he said, handing over the valise.

And thus they arrived in the streets of shops of the little ugly town on top of the hill. How everybody stared at her; my word, how they stared ! And the cinema was just going in, and the queues were tailing down the road to the corner. And everybody took full stock of her. 'Night, Harry !' shouted the fellows, in an interested voice.

However, they arrived at her aunt's – a little sweet-shop in a side street. They 'pinged' the door-bell, and her aunt came running forward out of the kitchen.

'There you are, child ! Dying for a cup of tea, I'm sure. How are you ?'

Fanny's aunt kissed her, and it was all Fanny could do to refrain from bursting into tears, she felt so low. Perhaps it was her tea she wanted.

'You've had a drag with that luggage,' said Fanny's aunt to Harry.

'Ay – I'm not sorry to put it down,' he said, looking at his hand which was crushed and cramped by the bag handle.

Then he departed to see about Heather's greengrocery cart.

When Fanny sat at tea, her aunt, a grey-haired, fair-faced little woman, looked at her with an admiring heart, feeling bitterly sore for her. For Fanny was beautiful : tall, erect, finely coloured, with her delicately arched nose, her rich brown hair, her large lustrous grey eyes. A passionate woman – a woman to be afraid of. So proud, so inwardly violent ! She came of a violent race.

It needed a woman to sympathise with her. Men had not the courage. Poor Fanny ! She was such a lady, and so straight and magnificent. And yet everything seemed to do her down. Every time she seemed to be doomed to humiliation and disappointment, this handsome, brilliantly sensitive woman, with her nervous, overwrought laugh.

'So you've really come back, child?' said her aunt.

'I really have, Aunt,' said Fanny.

'Poor Harry! I'm not sure, you know, Fanny, that you're not taking a bit of an advantage of him.'

'Oh, Aunt, he's waited so long, he may as well have what he's waited for.' Fanny laughed grimly.

'Yes, child, he's waited so long, that I'm not sure it isn't a bit hard on him. You know, I *like* him, Fanny – though as you know quite well, I don't think he's good enough for you. And I think he thinks so himself, poor fellow.'

'Don't you be so sure of that, Aunt. Harry is common, but he's not humble. He wouldn't think the Queen was any too good for him, if he'd a mind to her.'

'Well – It's as well if he has a proper opinion of himself.'

'It depends what you call proper,' said Fanny. 'But he's got his good points –'

'Oh, he's a nice fellow, and I like him, I do like him. Only, as I tell you, he's not good enough for you.'

'I've made up my mind, Aunt,' said Fanny, grimly.

'Yes,' mused the aunt. 'They say all things come to him who waits –'

'More than he's bargained for, eh, Aunt?' laughed Fanny rather bitterly.

The poor aunt, this bitterness grieved her for her niece.

They were interrupted by the ping of the shop-bell and Harry's call of 'Right!' But as he did not come in at once, Fanny, feeling solicitous for him presumably at the moment, rose and went into the shop. She saw a cart outside, and went to the door.

And the moment she stood in the doorway, she heard a woman's common vituperative voice crying from the darkness of the opposite side of the road.

'Tha'rt theer, ar ter? I'll shame thee, Mester. I'll shame thee, see if I dunna.'

Startled, Fanny stared across the darkness, and saw a woman in a black bonnet go under one of the lamps up the side street.

Harry and Bill Heather had dragged the trunk off the little dray, and she retreated before them as they came up the shop step with it.

'Wheer shall ha'e it?' asked Harry.

'Best take it upstairs,' said Fanny.

She went first to light the gas.

When Heather had gone, and Harry was sitting down having tea and pork pie, Fanny asked:

'Who was that woman shouting?'

'Nay, I canna tell thee. To somebody, Is'd think,' replied Harry. Fanny looked at him, but asked no more.

He was a fair-haired fellow of thirty-two, with a fair moustache. He was broad in his speech, and looked like a foundry-hand, which he was. But women always liked him. There was something of a mother's lad about him – something warm and playful and really sensitive.

He had his attractions even for Fanny. What she rebelled against so bitterly was that he had no sort of ambition. He was a moulder, but of very commonplace skill. He was thirty-two years old, and hadn't saved twenty pounds. She would have to provide the money for the home. He didn't care. He just didn't care. He had no initiative at all. He had no vices – no obvious ones. But he was just indifferent, spending as he went, and not caring. Yet he did not look happy. She remembered his face in the fire-glow: something haunted, abstracted about it. As he sat there eating his pork pie, bulging his cheek out, she felt he was like a doom to her. And she raged against the doom of him. It wasn't that he was gross. His *way* was common, almost on purpose. But he himself wasn't really common. For instance, his food was not particularly important to him, he was not greedy. He had a charm, too, particularly for

women, with his blondness and his sensitiveness and his
way of making a woman feel that she was a higher being.
But Fanny knew him, knew the peculiar obstinate limited-
ness of him, that would nearly send her mad.

He stayed till about half past nine. She went to the door
with him.

'When are you coming up?' he said, jerking his head in
the direction, presumably, of his own home.

'I'll come tomorrow afternoon,' she said brightly. Between Fanny and Mrs Goodall, his mother, there was
naturally no love lost.

Again she gave him an awkward little kiss, and said
good night.

'You can't wonder, you know, child, if he doesn't seem
so very keen,' said her aunt. 'It's your own fault.'

'Oh, Aunt, I couldn't stand him when he was keen. I
can do with him a lot better as he is.'

The two women sat and talked far into the night. They
understood each other. The aunt, too, had married as
Fanny was marrying : a man who was no companion to
her, a violent man, brother of Fanny's father. He was dead.
Fanny's father was dead.

Poor Aunt Lizzie, she cried woefully over her bright
niece, when she had gone to bed.

Fanny paid the promised visit to his people the next afternoon. Mrs Goodall was a large woman with smooth-parted
hair, a common, obstinate woman, who had spoiled her
four lads and her one vixen of a married daughter. She was
one of those old-fashioned powerful natures that couldn't
do with looks or education or any form of showing off. She
fairly hated the sound of correct English. She *thee'd* and
tha'd her prospective daughter-in-law, and said :

'I'm none as ormin' as I look, seest ta.'

Fanny did not think her prospective mother-in-law
looked at all orming, so the speech was unnecessary.

'I towed him mysen,' said Mrs Goodall, ' 'Er's held back all this long, let 'er stop as 'er is. 'E'd none ha' had thee for *my* tellin' – tha hears. No, 'e's a fool, an' I know it. I says to him : "Tha looks a man, doesn't ter, at thy age, goin' an' openin' to her when ter hears her scrat' at th' gate, after she's done gallivantin' round wherever she'd a mind. That looks rare an' soft.' But it's no use o' any talking : he answered that letter o' thine and made his own bad bargain.'

But in spite of the old woman's anger, she was also flattered at Fanny's coming back to Harry. For Mrs Goodall was impressed by Fanny – a woman of her own match. And more than this, everybody knew that Fanny's Aunt Kate had left her two hundred pounds : this apart from the girl's savings.

So there was high tea in Princess Street when Harry came home black from work, and a rather acrid odour of cordiality, the vixen Jinny darting in to say vulgar things. Of course Jinny lived in a house whose garden end joined the paternal garden. They were a clan who stuck together, these Goodalls.

It was arranged that Fanny should come to tea again on the Sunday, and the wedding was discussed. It should take place in a fortnight's time at Morley Chapel. Morley was a hamlet on the edge of the real country, and in its little Congregational Chapel Fanny and Harry had first met.

What a creature of habit he was! He was still in the choir, Morley Chapel – not very regular. He belonged just because he had a tenor voice, and enjoyed singing. Indeed his solos were only spoilt to local fame because when he sang he handled his aitches so hoplessly.

> 'And I saw 'eaven hopened
> And be'old, a wite 'orse – '

This was one of Harry's classics, only surpassed by the fine outburst of his heaving :

'Hangels – hever bright an' fair –'

It was a pity, but it was inalterable. He had a good voice, and he sang with a certain lacerating fire, but his pronunciation made it all funny. And *nothing* could alter him.

So he was never heard save at cheap concerts and in the little, poorer chapels. The others scoffed.

Now the month was September, and Sunday was Harvest Festival at Morley Chapel, and Harry was singing solos. So that Fanny was to go to afternoon service, and come home to a grand spread of Sunday tea with him. Poor Fanny ! One of the most wonderful afternoons had been a Sunday afternoon service, with her cousin Luther at her side, Harvest Festival in Morley Chapel. Harry had sung solos then – ten years ago. She remembered his pale blue tie, and the purple asters and the great vegetable marrows in which he was framed, and her cousin Luther at her side, young, clever, come down from London, where he was getting on well, learning his Latin and his French and German so brilliantly.

However, once again it was Harvest Festival at Morley Chapel, and once again, as ten years before, a soft, exquisite September day, with the last roses pink in the cottage gardens, the last dahlias crimson, the last sunflowers yellow. And again the little old chapel was a bower, with its famous sheaves of corn and corn-plaited pillars, its great bunches of grapes, dangling like tassels from the pulpit corners, its marrows and potatoes and pears and apples and damsons, its purple asters and yellow Japanese sunflowers. Just as before, the red dahlias round the pillars were dropping, weak-headed among the oats. The place was crowded and hot, the plates of tomatoes seemed balanced perilously on the gallery front, the Rev Enderby was weirder than ever to look at, so long and emaciated and hairless.

The Rev Enderby, probably forewarned, came and shook hands with her and welcomed her, in his broad northern melancholy singsong, before he mounted the pulpit. Fanny was handsome in a gauzy dress and a beautiful lace hat. Being a little late, she sat in a chair in the side-aisle wedged in, right in front of the chapel. Harry was in the gallery above, and she could only see him from the eyes upwards. She noticed again how his eyebrows met, blond and not very marked, over his nose. He was attractive too : physically lovable, very. If only – if only her *pride* had not suffered ! She felt he dragged her down.

> 'Come, ye thankful people come,
> Raise the song of harvest-home.
> All is safely gathered in
> Ere the winter storms begin –'

Even the hymn was a falsehood, as the season had been wet, and half the crops were still out, and in a poor way.

Poor Fanny ! She sang little, and looked beautiful through that inappropriate hymn. Above her stood Harry – mercifully in a dark suit and dark tie, looking almost handsome. And his lacerating, pure tenor sounded well, when the words were drowned in the general commotion. Brilliant she looked, and brilliant she felt, for she was hot and angrily miserable and inflamed with a sort of fatal despair. Because there was about him a physical attraction which she really hated, but which she could not escape from. He was the first man who had ever kissed her. And his kisses, even while she rebelled from them, had lived in her blood and sent roots down into her soul. After all this time she had come back to them. And her soul groaned, for she felt dragged down, dragged down to earth, as a bird which some dog had got down in the dust. She knew her life would be unhappy. She knew that what she was doing

was fatal. Yet it was her doom. She had to come back to
him.

He had to sing two solos this afternoon : one before the
'address' from the pulpit and one after. Fanny looked at
him, and wondered he was not too shy to stand up there in
front of all the people. But no, he was not shy. He had even
a kind of assurance on his face as he looked down from the
choir gallery at her : the assurance of a common man deliberately entrenched in his commonness. Oh, such a rage
went through her veins as she saw the air of triumph,
laconic, indifferent triumph which sat so obstinately and
recklessly on his eyelids as he looked down at her. Ah, she
despised him ! But there he stood up in that choir gallery
like Balaam's ass in front of her, and she could not get beyond him. A certain winsomeness also about him. A certain
physical winsomeness, and as if his flesh were new and
lovely to touch. The thorn of desire rankled bitterly in
her heart.

He, it goes without saying, sang like a canary this particular afternoon, with a defiant passion which pleasantly
crisped the blood of the congregation. Fanny felt the crisp
flames go through her veins as she listened. Even the
curious loud-mouthed vernacular had a certain fascination.
But, oh, also, it was so repugnant. He would triumph over
her, obstinately he would drag her right back into the
common people : a doom, a vulgar doom.

The second performance was an anthem, in which Harry
sang the solo parts. It was clumsy, but beautiful, with
lovely words.

'They that sow in tears shall reap in joy,
   He that goeth forth and weepeth, bearing precious seed
   Shall doubtless come again with rejoicing, bringing his
      sheaves with him – '

'Shall doubtless come, Shall doubtless come – ' softly intoned the altos – 'Bringing his she-e-eaves with him,' the trebles flourished bright, and then again began the half-wistful solo :

'They that sow in tears shall reap in joy – '

Yet, it was effective and moving.

But at the moment when Harry's voice sank carelessly down to his close, and the choir, standing behind him, were opening their mouths for the final triumphant outburst, a shouting female voice rose up from the body of the congregation. The organ gave one startled trump, and went silent; the choir stood transfixed.

'You look well standing there, singing in God's holy house,' came the loud, angry female shout. Everybody turned electrified. A stoutish, red-faced woman in a black bonnet was standing up denouncing the soloist. Almost fainting with shock, the congregation realised it. 'You look well, don't you, standing there singing solos in God's holy house, you, Goodall. But I said I'd shame you. You look well, bringing your young woman here with you, don't you? I'll let her know who she's dealing with. A scamp as won't take the consequences of what he's done.' The hard-faced, frenzied woman turned in the direction of Fanny. '*That's* what Harry Goodall is, if you want to know.'

And she sat down again in her seat. Fanny, startled like all the rest, had turned to look. She had gone white, and then a burning red, under the attack. She knew the woman : a Mrs Nixon, a devil of a woman, who beat her pathetic, drunken, red-nosed second husband, Bob, and her two lanky daughters, grown-up as they were. A notorious character. Fanny turned round again, and sat motionless as eternity in her seat.

There was a minute of perfect silence and suspense. The audience was open-mouthed and dumb; the choir stood like Lot's wife; and Harry, with his music-sheet, stood there uplifted, looking down with a dumb sort of indifference on Mrs Nixon, his face naïve and faintly mocking. Mrs Nixon sat defiant in her seat, braving them all.

Then a rustle, like a wood when the wind suddenly catches the leaves. And then the tall, weird minister got to his feet, and in his strong, bell-like, beautiful voice – the only beautiful thing about him – he said with infinite mournful pathos :

'Let us unite in singing the last hymn on the hymn-sheet, the last hymn on the hymn-sheet, number eleven.

> 'Fair waved the golden corn,
>   In Canaan's pleasant land.'

The organ tuned up promptly. During the hymn the offertory was taken. And after the hymn the prayer.

Mr Enderby came from Northumberland. Like Harry, he had never been able to conquer his accent, which was very broad. He was a little simple, one of God's fools, perhaps, an odd bachelor soul, emotional, ugly, but very gentle.

'And if, O our dear Lord, beloved Jesus, there should fall a shadow of sin upon our harvest, we leave it to thee to judge, for thou art judge. We lift our spirits and our sorrow, Jesus, to thee, and our mouths are dumb. O, Lord, keep us from froward speech, restrain us from foolish words and thoughts, we pray thee, Lord Jesus, who knowest all and judgest all.'

Thus the minister said in his sad, resonant voice, washed his hands before the Lord. Fanny bent forward open-eyed during the prayer. She could see the roundish head of Harry, also bent forward. His face was inscrutable and expressionless. The shock left her bewildered. Anger perhaps was her dominating emotion.

The audience began to rustle to its feet, to ooze slowly and excitedly out of the chapel, looking with wildly-interested eyes at Fanny, at Mrs Nixon, and at Harry. Mrs Nixon, shortish, stood defiant in her pew, facing the aisle, as if announcing that, without rolling her sleeves up, she was ready for anybody. Fanny sat quite still. Luckily the people did not have to pass her. And Harry, with red ears, was making his way sheepishly out of the gallery. The loud noise of the organ covered all the downstairs commotion of exit.

The minister sat silent and inscrutable in his pulpit, rather like a death's-head, while the congregation filed out. When the last lingerers had unwillingly departed, craning their necks to stare at the still seated Fanny, he rose, stalked in his hooked fashion down the little country chapel and fastened the door. Then he returned and sat down by the silent young woman.

'This is most unfortunate, most unfortunate!' he moaned. 'I am so sorry, I am so sorry, indeed, indeed, ah, indeed!' he sighed himself to a close.

'It's a sudden surprise, that's one thing,' said Fanny brightly.

'Yes – yes – indeed. Yes, a surprise, yes. I don't know the woman, I don't know her.'

'I know her,' said Fanny. 'She's a bad one.'

'Well! Well!' said the minister. 'I don't know her. I don't understand. I don't understand at all. But it is to be regretted, it is very much to be regretted. I am very sorry.'

Fanny was watching the vestry door. The gallery stairs communicated with the vestry, not with the body of the chapel. She knew the choir members had been peeping for information.

At last Harry came – rather sheepishly – with his hat in his hand.

'Well!' said Fanny, rising to her feet.

'We've had a bit of an extra,' said Harry.

'I should think so,' said Fanny.

'A most unfortunate circumstance – a most *unfortunate* circumstance. Do you understand it, Harry? I don't understand it at all.'

'Ah, I understand it. The daughter's goin' to have a childt, an' 'er lays it on to me.'

'And has she no occasion to?' asked Fanny, rather censorious.

'It's no more mine than it is some other chap's,' said Harry, looking aside.

There was a moment of pause.

'Which girl is it?' asked Fanny.

'Annie – the young one – '

There followed another silence.

'I don't think I know them, do I?' asked the minister.

'I shouldn't think so. Their name's Nixon – mother married old Bob for her second husband. She's a tanger – 's driven the gel to what she is. They live in Manners Road.'

'Why, what's amiss with the girl?' asked Fanny sharply. 'She was all right when I knew her.'

'Ay – she's all right. But she's always in an' out o' th' pubs, wi' th' fellows,' said Harry.

'A nice thing!' said Fanny.

Harry glanced towards the door. He wanted to get out.

'Most distressing, indeed!' The minister slowly shook his head.

'What about tonight, Mr Enderby?' asked Harry, in rather a small voice. 'Shall you want me?'

Mr Enderby looked up painedly, and put his hand to his brow. He studied Harry for some time, vacantly. There was the faintest sort of a resemblance between the two men.

'Yes,' he said. 'Yes, I think. I think we must take no notice, and cause as little remark as possible.'

Fanny hesitated. Then she said to Harry.

'But *will* you come?'

He looked at her.

'Ay, I's'll come,' he said.

Then he turned to Mr Enderby.

'Well, good afternoon, Mr Enderby,' he said.

'Good afternoon, Harry, good afternoon,' replied the mournful minister. Fanny followed Harry to the door, and for some time they walked in silence through the late afternoon.

'And it's yours as much as anybody else's?' she said.

'Ay,' he answered shortly.

And they went without another word, for the long mile or so, till they came to the corner of the street where Harry lived. Fanny hesitated. Should she go on to her aunt's? Should she? It would mean leaving all this, for ever. Harry stood silent.

Some obstinacy made her turn with him along the road to his own home. When they entered the house-place, the whole family was there, mother, father and Jinny, with Jinny's husband and children and Harry's two brothers.

'You've been having your ears warmed, they tell me,' said Mrs Goodall grimly.

'Who told thee?' asked Harry shortly.

'Maggie and Luke's both been in.'

'You look well, don't you!' said interfering Jinny.

Harry went and hung his hat up, without replying.

'Come upstairs and take your hat off,' said Mrs Goodall to Fanny, almost kindly. It would have annoyed her very much if Fanny had dropped her son at this moment.

'What's 'er say, then?' asked the father secretly of Harry, jerking his head in the direction of the stairs whence Fanny had disappeared.

'Nowt yet,' said Harry.

'Serve you right if she chucks you now,' said Jinny. 'I'll bet it's right about Annie Nixon an' you.'

'Tha bets so much,' said Harry.

'Yi – but you can't deny it,' said Jinny.

'I can if I've a mind.'

His father looked at him inquiringly.

'It's no more mine than it is Bill Bower's, or Ted Slaney's, or six or seven on 'em,' said Harry to his father.

And the father nodded silently.

'That'll not get you out of it, in court,' said Jinny.

Upstairs Fanny evaded all the thrusts made by his mother, and did not declare her hand. She tidied her hair, washed her hands, and put the tiniest bit of powder on her face, for coolness, there in front of Mrs Goodall's indignant gaze. It was like a declaration of independence. But the old woman said nothing.

They came down to Sunday tea, with sardines and tinned salmon and tinned peaches, besides tarts and cakes. The chatter was general. It concerned the Nixon family and the scandal.

'Oh, she's a foul-mouthed woman,' said Jinny of Mrs Nixon. 'She may well talk about God's holy house, *she* had. It's first time she's set foot in it, ever since she dropped off from being converted. She's a devil and she always was one. Can't you remember how she treated Bob's children, mother, when we lived down in the Buildings? I can remember when I was a little girl she used to bathe them in the yard, in the cold, so that they shouldn't splash the house. She'd half kill them if they made a mark on the floor, and the language she'd use ! And one Saturday I can remember Garry, that was Bob's own girl, she ran off when her stepmother was going to bathe her – ran off without a rag of clothes on – can you remember, mother? And she hid in Smedley's closes – it was the time of mowing-grass – and nobody could find her. She hid out there all night, didn't she mother? Nobody could find her. My word, there was a talk. They found her on Sunday morning – '

'Fred Coutts threatened to break every bone in the woman's body, if she touched the children again,' put in the father.

'Anyhow, they frightened her,' said Jinny. 'But she was nearly as bad with her own two. And anybody can see that she's driven old Bob till he's gone soft.'

'Ah, soft as mush,' said Jack Goodall.' 'E'd never addle a week's wage, nor yet a day's if th' chaps didn't make it up to him.'

'My word, if he didn't bring her a week's wage, she'd pull his head off,' said Jinny.

'But a clean woman, and respectable, except for her foul mouth,' said Mrs Goodall. 'Keeps to herself like a bull-dog. Never lets anybody come near the house, and neighbours with nobody.'

'Wanted it thrashed out of her,' said Mr Goodall, a silent, evasive sort of man.

'Where Bob gets the money for his drink from is a mystery,' said Jinny.

'Chaps treats him,' said Harry.

'Well, he's got the pair of frightenedest rabbit-eyes you'd wish to see,' said Jinny.

'Ay, with a drunken man's murder in them, *I* think,' said Mrs Goodall.

So the talk went on after tea, till it was practically time to start off to chapel again.

"You'll have to be getting ready, Fanny,' said Mrs Goodall.

'I'm not going tonight,' said Fanny abruptly. And there was a sudden halt in the family. 'I'll stop with *you* tonight, Mother,' she added.

'Best you had, my gel,' said Mrs Goodall, flattered and assured.

TWO OR THREE GRACES

THE word 'bore' is of doubtful etymology. Some authorities derive it from the verb meaning to pierce. A bore is a person who drills a hole in your spirit, who tunnels relentlessly through your patience, through all the crusts of voluntary deafness, inattention, rudeness, which you vainly interpose – through and through till it pierces to the very quick of your being. But there are other authorities, as good or even better, who would derive the word from the French *bourrer*, to stuff, to satiate. If this etymology be correct, a bore is one who stuffs you with his thick and suffocating discourse, who rams his suety personality, like a dumpling, down your throat. He stuffs you; and you, to use an apposite modern metaphor, are 'fed up with him'. I like to think, impossibly, that both these derivations of the word are correct; for bores are both piercers and stuffers. They are like dentists' drills, and they are also like stale buns. But they are characterised by a further quality, which drills and dough-nuts do not possess; they cling. That is why, though no philologist, I venture to suggest a third derivation, from 'burr'. Burr, *bourrer*, bore – all the sticking, stuffing, piercing qualities of boredom are implicit in those three possible etymologies. Each deserves to be correct.

Herbert Comfrey was above all a sticking bore. He attached himself to any one who had the misfortune to come in contact with him; attached himself and could not be shaken off. A burr-bore, vegetable and passive; not actively penetrating. For Herbert, providentially, was not particularly talkative; he was too lazy and lymphatic for that. He was just exceedingly sociable, like a large sentimental dog that cannot bear to be left alone. Like a dog, he followed people about; he lay, metaphorically speaking, at their feet in front of the fire. And like a dog, he did not talk. It was just your company that made him happy; he was quite content if he might trot at your side or doze under your chair. He did not demand that you should pay much attention to him; all that he asked was to be permitted to enjoy the light of your countenance and bask in the warmth of your presence. If once a week he got the equivalent of a pat on the head and a 'Good dog, Herbert', he wagged his spirit's tail and was perfectly happy.

To some of my friends – the quick, the impatient, the highly strung – poor vegetable Herbert was exasperating to the point of madness. His very virtues – that good nature of his, that placidity, that unshakable fidelity – infuriated them. Even his appearance drove them wild. The sight of his broad smiling face, of his big, lazy, lubberly body and limbs was alone sufficient to set their nerves twittering and jumping like a frightened aviary. I have known people who, after living in the same house with Herbert for three days, have secretly packed their trunks, caught the first convenient train, and, leaving no address, have travelled hundreds of miles in order to escape from him.

To me, poor Herbert was boring indeed, but not exasperatingly or intolerably so. Mine is a patient temper; my nerves are not easily set twittering. I even liked him in a way; he was such a good, faithful, kind old dog. And I soon acquired, in his dumb presence, a knack of quite ignoring him, of regarding him simply as a piece of furniture – so much so, that I sometimes caught myself on the point of carelessly setting down my emptied coffee-cup on his head as he sat on the floor beside me (he always sat on the floor whenever it was possible), or of flicking my cigarette ash into the inviting cranny between his neck and his coat collar.

As boys, Herbert and I had been at the same public

school. But as we were in different houses and he was two years older than I (two years, at that age, is an enormous seniority), we had hardly ever spoken to one another. But none the less, it was on the strength of our old school that Herbert reintroduced himself into my life. His return was doubly disastrous. A bore entered my existence, and in the entering, drove out, temporarily at least, a being who, whatever his other qualities, was the very antithesis of boredom.

It was in a café of the Passage du Panorama in Paris that the thing happened. We had been sitting there for an hour, Kingham and I, talking and drinking vermouth. It was characteristic of Kingham that he did most of both – drinking as well as talking. Characteristic, too, that he should have been abusing me, among many other things, for wasting my time and spirit in precisely these two occupations.

'You sit about,' he said, 'letting every thought in your head trickle out uselessly in talk. Not that there are many thoughts, of course, because you daren't think. You create futile business, you rush about seeing people you don't like and don't take the slightest interest in, you drift from bar to bar, you swill till you're stupefied – all because you daren't think and can't bring yourself to make the effort to do something serious and decent. It's the result partly of laziness, partly of lack of faith – faith in anything. *Garçon!*' He ordered another vermouth. 'It's the great modern vice,' he went on, 'the great temptation of every young man or woman who's intelligent and acutely conscious. Everything that's easy and momentarily diverting and anaesthetic tempts – people, chatter, drink, fornication. Everything that's difficult and big, everything that needs thought and effort, repels. It's the war that did it. Not to mention the peace. But it would have come gradually in any case. Modern life was making it inevitable. Look at the young people who had nothing to do with the war – were only children when it happened – they're the worst of all. It's time to stop, it's time to do something. Can't you see that you can't go on like this? Can't you see?'

He leaned across the table at me, angrily. He hated these vices which he had attributed to me, hated them with a special fury because they happened really to be his. He was confessing the weakness he hated in himself – hated and could not eradicate.

Kingham looked handsome in anger. He had dark eyes, beautiful and very bright; his hair was dark brown, fine and plentiful : a close-cut beard, redder than his hair, disguised the lower part of his face, with whose pale, young smoothness it seemed curiously incongruous. There was a brilliancy, a vividness about him. If I were less slow to kindle, I should have burned responsively with his every ardour. Being what I am, I could always remain cool, critical, and cautious, however passionately he might burn. My uninflammableness, I believe, had somehow fascinated him. I exasperated him, but he continued to frequent my company – chiefly to abuse me, to tell me passionately how hopeless I was. I winced under these dissections; for though he often talked, as far as I was concerned, wildly at random (accusing me, as he had done on this particular occasion, of the weakness which he felt and resented in himself), his analysis was often painfully exact and penetrating. I winced, but all the same I delighted in his company. We irritated one another profoundly; but we were friends.

I suppose I must have smiled at Kingham's question. Goodness knows, I am no teetotaller, I am not averse to wasting my time over agreeable futilities. But compared with Kingham – particularly the Kingham of 1920 – I am a monument of industry, dutiful steadiness, sobriety. I take no credit to myself for it; I happen to be one of nature's burgesses, that is all. I am as little capable of leading a perfectly disorderly life as I am of, shall we say, writing a good book. Kingham was born with both talents. Hence the absurdity, so far as I was concerned, of his hortatory question. I did not mean to smile; but some trace of my amusement must have appeared on my face, for Kingham suddenly became most passionately angry.

'You think it's a joke?' he cried, and thumped the marble table. 'I tell you, it's the sin against the Holy Ghost. It's unforgivable. It's burying your talent. Damn this blasted Bible,' he added with parenthetic fury. 'Why is it that one can never talk about anything serious without getting mixed up in it?'

'It happens to be quite a serious book,' I suggested.

'A lot you understand about it,' said Kingham. 'I tell you,' he went on impressively. . . . But at this moment Herbert made his second entry into my life.

I felt a hand laid on my shoulder, looked up, and saw a stranger.

'Hullo, Wilkes,' said the stranger. 'You don't remember me.'

I looked more attentively, and had to admit that I didn't.

'I am Comfrey,' he explained, 'Herbert Comfrey. I was at Dunhill's, don't you remember? You were at Struthers', weren't you? Or was it Lane's?'

At the names of these pedagogues, who had figured so largely in my boyhood, recesses in my mind, long closed, suddenly burst open, as though before a magical word. Visions of inky schoolrooms, football fields, cricket fields, fives courts, the school chapel, rose up confusedly; and from the midst of this educational chaos there disengaged itself the loutish figure of Comfrey of Dunhill's.

'Of course,' I said, and took him by the hand. Through the corner of my eye, I saw Kingham angrily frowning. 'How did you remember me?'

'Oh, I remember every one,' he answered. It was no vain

boast, as I afterwards discovered; he *did* remember. He remembered every one he had ever met, and all the trivial
incidents of his past life. He had the enormous memory of
royal personages and family retainers – the memory of
those who never read, or reason, or reflect, and whose minds
are therefore wholly free to indulge in retrospect. 'I never
forget a face,' he added, and without being invited, sat
down at our table.

Indignantly, Kingham threw himself back in his chair.
He kicked me under the table. I looked at him and made a
little grimace, signifying my helplessness.

I mumbled a perfunctory introduction. Kingham said
nothing, only frowned more blackly, as he shook hands
with Herbert. And for his part, Herbert was hardly more
cordial. True, he smiled his amiable dim smile; but he said
nothing, he hardly even looked at Kingham. He was in too
much of a hurry to turn back to me and talk about the dear
old school. The dear old school – it was the only subject
that ever made Herbert really loquacious. It metamorph-
osed him from a merely vegetable burr-bore into an active,
piercing dentist's drill of tediousness. He had a passion for
the school, and thought that all ex-members of it ought to
be in constant and friendly communication with one another. I have noticed that, as a general rule, people of decided individuality very rarely continue their schoolboy
acquaintanceships into later life. It is only to be expected.
The chances that they will have found in the tiny micro-
cosm of school the sort of friends they will like when they
are grown up – grown out of recognition – are obviously
very small. Coteries whose bond of union consists in the
fact that their component members happened to be at the
same school at the same time are generally the dreariest of
assemblages. It could scarcely be otherwise; men who have
no better reasons for associating with one another must be
colourless indeed, and insipid. Poor Herbert, who regarded

the accident of our having worn similarly striped caps and blazers at a certain period of our boyhood as being a sufficient reason for our entering into a bosom friendship, was only an extreme specimen of the type.

I put on my chilliest and most repellent manner. But in vain. Herbert talked and talked. Did I remember the exciting match against Winchester in 1910? And how poor old Mr Cutler had been ragged? And that memorable occasion when Pye had climbed on to the roof of the school chapel, at night, and hung a chamber-pot on one of the Gothic pinnacles? Anxiously, I looked towards Kingham. He had exchanged his expression of anger for one of contempt, and was leaning back, his eyes shut, tilting his chair.

Kingham had never been to a public school. He had not had the luck (or the misfortune) to be born a hereditary, professional gentleman. He was proud of the fact, he sometimes even boasted of it. But that did not prevent him from being morbidly sensitive to anything that might be interpreted as a reference to his origin. He was always on the look-out for insults from 'gentlemen'. Veiled insults, insults offered unconsciously even, unintentionally, in perfect ignorance – any sort of insult was enough to set him quivering with pain and fury. More than once I had seen him take violent offence at words that were entirely well-intentioned. Would he regard Herbert's dreary recollections of the dear old school as an insult? He was quite capable of it. I looked forward nervously to an outburst and a violent exit. But the scene, this time, was not to be acted in public. After listening for a few minutes to Herbert's anecdotage, Kingham got up, excused himself with ironical politeness, and bade us good evening. I laid my hand on his arm.

'Do stay.'

'A thousand regrets'; he laid his hand on his heart, smiled, bowed, and was gone, leaving me (I may add parenthetically that it was his habit) to pay for his drinks.

We public school men were left to ourselves.

The next morning I lay late in bed. At about eleven o'clock Kingham burst into my room. The scene which I had been spared the night before was enacted for me now with redoubled passion. Another man would have slept on the supposed insult and, waking, have found it negligible. Not so Kingham. He had brooded over his wrongs, till what was originally small had grown enormous. The truth was that Kingham liked scenes. He loved to flounder in emotion – his own and other people's. He was exhilarated by these baths of passion; he felt that he really lived, that he was more than a man, while he splashed about in them. And the intoxication was so delicious that he indulged in it without considering the consequences – or perhaps it would be truer to say that he considered the consequences (for intellectually no man could be clearer-sighted than Kingham) but deliberately ignored them.

When I say that he had a great facility for making scenes, I do not mean to imply that he ever simulated an emotion. He felt genuinely about things – genuinely and strongly, but too easily. And he took pleasure in cultivating and working up his emotions. For instance, what in other men would have been a passing irritation, held in check by self-control, to be modified very likely by subsequent impressions, was converted by Kingham, almost deliberately, into a wild fury which no second thoughts were allowed to assuage. Often these passions were the result of mere mistakes on the part of those who had provoked them. But once emotionally committed, Kingham would never admit a mistake – unless, of course, his passion for self-humiliation happened at the moment to be stronger than his passion for self-assertion. Often, too, he would take up unchanging emotional attitudes towards people. A single powerful impression would be allowed to dominate all other impressions. His intellect was put into blinkers, the most manifest facts were ignored; and until further orders the individual in question produced in Kingham only one particular set of reactions.

As he approached my bed, I could see from the expression on his white face that I was in for a bad quarter of an hour.

'Well?' I said, with an affectation of careless cordiality.

'I always knew you were an intellectual snob,' Kingham began in a low, intense voice, drawing up a chair to my bedside as he spoke. 'But really, I thought you were above being an ordinary, suburban, lower middle-class social snob.'

I made the grimace which in French novels is represented by the sign ' — ?'

'I know that my father was a plumber,' he went on, 'and that I was educated at the expense of the State and by scholarships for the encouragement of clever paupers. I know I speak Cockney, and not Eton and Oxford. I know that my manners are bad and that I eat dirtily, and that I don't wash my teeth enough.' (None of these things were true; but it suited Kingham, at the moment, to believe that they were. He wanted to feel abased, in order that he might react with greater violence. He insulted himself in order that he might attribute the insults, under which he genuinely winced, to me, and so have an excuse for being angry with me.) 'I know I'm a cad and a little bounder.' He spoke the words with an extraordinary gusto, as though he enjoyed the pain he was inflicting on himself. 'I know I'm an outsider, only tolerated for my cleverness. A sort of buffoon or tame monkey for the amusement of cultured gentlemen. I know all this, and I know you knew it. But I really thought you didn't mind, that we met as human beings, not as specimens of upper and lower classes. I was fool enough to imagine that you liked me in spite of it all. I thought you even preferred me to the people in your own herd. It only shows what an innocent I am. No sooner does a gentleman come along, an old school chum, what?' (derisively he assumed the public school accent as rendered on the music hall stage) 'than you fling your arms round his neck and leave the dirty little outsider very definitely outside.' He laughed ferociously.

'My good Kingham,' I began, 'why will you make a bloody fool of yourself?'

But Kingham, who doubtless knew as well as I did that he was making a fool of himself, only went on with the process more vehemently. He was committed to making a fool of himself, and he liked it. Shifting his ground a little, he began telling me home truths – real home truths this time. In the end, I too began to get angry.

'I'll trouble you to get out,' I said.

'Oh, I've not finished yet.'

'And stay out till you've got over your fit of hysterics. You're behaving like a girl who needs a husband.'

'As I was saying,' Kingham went on in a voice that had become softer, more sinisterly quiet, more poisonously honied in proportion as mine had grown louder and harsher, 'your great defect is spiritual impotence. Your morality, your art – they're just impotence organised into systems. Your whole view of life – impotence again. Your very strength, such as it is – your horrible passive resistance – that's based in impotence too.'

'Which won't prevent me from throwing you downstairs if you don't clear out at once.' It is one thing to know the truth about oneself; it is quite another thing to have it told one by somebody else. I knew myself a natural bourgeois; but when Kingham told me so – and in his words – it seemed to me that I was learning a new and horribly unpleasant truth.

'Wait,' Kingham drawled out with exasperating calm,' 'wait one moment. One more word before I go.'

'Get out,' I said. 'Get out at once.'

There was a knock at the door. It opened. The large, ruddy face of Herbert Comfrey looked round it into the room.

'I hope I don't disturb,' said Herbert, grinning at us.

'Oh, not a bit, not a bit,' cried Kingham. He jumped up, and with an excessive politeness proffered his vacant chair. 'I was just going. Do sit down. Wilkes was impatiently expecting you. Sit down, do sit down.' He propelled Herbert towards the chair.

'Really,' Herbert began, politely protesting.

But Kingham cut him short. 'And now I leave you two old friends together,' he said. 'Good-bye. Good-bye. I'm only sorry I shan't have an opportunity for saying that last word I wanted to say.'

Cumbrously, Herbert made as though to get up. 'I'll go,' he said. 'I had no idea. . . . I'm so sorry.'

But Kingham put his hands on his shoulders and forced him back into the chair. 'No, no,' he insisted. 'Stay where you are. I'm off.'

And picking up his hat, he ran out of the room.

'Queer fellow,' said Herbert. 'Who is he?'

'Oh, a friend of mine,' I answered. My anger had dropped, and I wondered, sadly, whether in calling him a friend I was telling the truth. And to think that, if he were no longer my friend, it was because of this lumpish imbecile sitting by my bed! I looked at Herbert pensively. He smiled at me – a smile that was all good nature. One could not bear a grudge against such a man.

The breach was complete, at any rate for the time; it was more than two years before Kingham and I met again. But if I had lost Kingham, I had acquired Herbert Comfrey – only too completely. From that moment, my life in Paris was no longer my own; I had to share it with Herbert. Being at that moment quite unattached, a dog without a master, he fastened himself to me, taking it ingenuously for granted that I would be just as happy in his company as he was in mine. He established himself in my hotel, and for the rest of my stay in Paris I was almost never alone. I ought, I know, to have been firm with Herbert; I ought to have been rude, told him to go to the devil, kicked him downstairs. But I lacked the heart. I was too kind. (Another symptom of my spiritual impotence! My morality – impotence! My morality – impotence systematised. I know, I know.) Herbert preyed on me, and, like the Brahman who permits himself, unresistingly, to be devoured by every passing blood-sucker, from mosquitoes to tigers, I suffered him to prey on me. The most I did was occasionally to run away from him. Herbert was, fortunately, a sluggard. The Last Trump would hardly have got him out of bed before ten. When I wanted a day's freedom, I ordered an eight-o'clock breakfast and left the hotel while Herbert was still asleep. Returning at night from these holidays, I would find him waiting, dog-like, in my room. I always had the impression that he had been waiting there the whole day – from dawn (or what for him was dawn – about noon) to midnight. And he was always so genuinely pleased to see me back that I was almost made to feel ashamed, as though I had committed an act of perfidy. I would begin to apologise and explain. I had had to go out early to see a man about something; and then I had met another man, who had asked me to have lunch with him; and then I had had to go to my dear old friend, Madame Dubois, for tea; after which I had dropped in on Langlois, and we had dined and gone to a concert. In fine, as he could see, I could not have got back a minute earlier.

It was in answer to the reproaches of my own conscience that I made these apologies. Poor Herbert never complained; he was only too happy to see me back. I could not help feeling that his clinging fidelity had established some sort of claim on me, that I was somehow a little responsible for him. It was absurd, of course, unreasonable and preposterous. For why should I, the victim, feel pity for my persecutor? Preposterous; and yet the fact remained that I did feel pity for him. I have always been too tender-hearted, insufficiently ruthless.

The time came for me to return to London. Herbert, who had just enough money to make it unnecessary for him to do anything or to be anywhere at any particular time, packed his bags and got into the same train. It was a very disagreeable journey; the train was crowded, the sea just choppy enough to make me sick. Coming on deck as we drew into Dover harbour, I found Herbert looking exasperatingly well. If I had not been feeling so ill, I should have found an excuse for quarrelling with him. But I had not the requisite energy. Meanwhile, it must be admitted, Herbert made himself very useful about the luggage.

Experience was shortly to teach me that, instead of feeling exasperated with poor Herbert, I ought to have been thankful that he was not far worse. For Herbert, after all, was only a burr-bore, a passive vegetable clinger. I might have been fastened on by one who was actively and piercingly as well as just clingingly boring. Herbert might, for example, have been like his brother-in-law, John Peddley; and then there would have been only three alternatives left me : murder, suicide, exile. I was feeling annoyed with Herbert as we slid slowly across Dover harbour. A few hours later, I had realised that I ought to have been feeling thankful that he was no worse than he was. On Dover quay we met John Peddley.

Peddley was an active bore, the most active, I think, that I ever met; an indefatigable piercer, a relentless stuffer and crammer. He talked incessantly, and his knowledge of uninteresting subjects was really enormous. All that I know of the Swiss banking system, of artificial manures, of the law relating to insurance companies, of pig-breeding, of the ex-sultan of Turkey, of sugar rationing during the war, and a hundred other similar subjects, is due to Peddley. He was appalling, really appalling; there is no other word. I know no human being with whom I would less willingly pass an hour.

And yet the man was extremely amiable and full of good qualities. He had a kind heart. He was energetic and efficient. He was even intelligent. One could not listen to his account of insurance companies or artificial manures without realising that he had completely mastered his subject. Moreover, a successful solicitor, like Peddley, cannot be a fool; at least, that is what those of us who are not solicitors like to believe. What made the man so afflicting was his genius for dullness; his self-assertive pedantry; his voice; his highly developed social instinct; and finally his insensitiveness. His genius for dullness caused him unfailingly to take an interest in the things which interested nobody else; and even when, by some mistake, he embarked on some more promising theme than the Swiss banking system, he had the power of rendering the most intrinsically fascinating of subjects profoundly dull. By a process of inverse alchemy he transmuted the purest gold to lead. His self-assertiveness and a certain pedagogic instinct made him ambitious to be the instructor of his fellows; he loved the sound of his own lecturing voice. And what a voice! Not unmusical, but loud, booming, persistent. It set up strange, nay, positively dangerous vibrations in one's head. I could never listen to it for more than a few minutes without feeling confused and dizzy. If I had had to live with that voice, I believe I should have begun, one day, to turn and turn like those Japanese waltzing mice – for ever. Peddley's voice affected the semicircular canals. And then there was his sociability. It was a passion, a vice; he could not live without the company of his fellow-beings. It was an agony for him to be alone. He hunted company ferociously, as wild beasts pursue their prey. But the odd thing was that he never seemed to crave for friendship or intimacy. So far as I know, he had no friends, in the ordinarily accepted sense of the term. He desired only acquaintances and auditors; and acquaintances and reluctant auditors were all that he had. In the first period of my acquaintance with Peddley I used to wonder what he did when he felt the need of confiding his intimate and private feelings. Later on I came to doubt whether, at ordinary times, he had any private life that needed talking about. Only very rarely and when something catastrophic had explosively shattered the crust of his public existence, did he ever develop a private life. When things were running smoothly in their regular daily grooves, he lived only on the public surface, at the office, at the club, at his own dinner-table, perfectly content so long as there was somebody present to listen to his talk. It mattered not that his auditors might be listening with manifest and extreme reluctance. Like Herbert – and indeed like most bores – John Peddley was more than half unaware of the people upon whom he inflicted himself. He realised that they were there, physically there; that was all. To their feelings and thoughts he was utterly insensitive. It was this insensitiveness, coupled with his passionate sociability, that gave him his power. He could hunt down his victims and torture them without remorse. The wolf, if he were really sensitive to the feelings of the lamb, might end by turning vegetarian. But he is not sensitive. He is aware only of his own hunger and the deliciousness of mutton. It was the same with John Peddley. Ignorant of the terror which he inspired, of the mental agonies which he inflicted, he could pursue his course relentlessly and with a perfect equanimity.

My first impressions of John Peddley were not unfavourable. True, the halloo with which he greeted Herbert from the quay-side, as we were waiting our turn in the shoving crowd of human sheep to pass down the gangway on to dry land, sounded to me, in my present condition, rather distressingly hearty. And his appearance, when Herbert pointed him out to me, offended me by its robustious healthiness. Nor, when Herbert had introduced us, did I much appreciate the vehemence of his handshake and the loud volubility of his expressions of sympathy. But, on the other hand, he was very kind and efficient. He produced a silver flask from his pocket and made me take a swig of excellent old brandy. Noticing that I was chilled and green with cold, he insisted on my putting on his fur coat. He darted to the custom-house and returned, in an incredibly short space of time, with the official hieroglyph duly chalked upon our suit-case. A minute later we were sitting in his car, rolling briskly out of Dover along the Canterbury road.

I was feeling, at the time, too ill to think; and it hardly occurred to me that the situation was, after all, rather odd. Peddley had been waiting on the quay – but not for us; for we were unexpected. Waiting, then, for whom? The question did propound itself to me at the time, but uninsistently. There was no room in my mind for anything but the consciousness of sea-sickness. I forgot to wonder, and took my seat in the car, as though it were the most natural thing in the world that we should have been met at the quay by somebody who did not know that we were crossing. And the apparent naturalness of the situation was confirmed for me by the behaviour of my companions. For Peddley had taken it for granted from the first that we should come and stay with him at his country house. And Herbert, for whom one place was always just as good as another, had accepted the invitation at once. I began by protesting; but feebly, and more out of politeness than in earnest. For it was not essential for me to get back to London that evening; and the prospect of that dismal journey from Dover, of the cab drive in the chill of the night across London, of a home-coming to fireless and deserted rooms, was very dreadful to me. If I accepted Peddley's invitation, I should find myself in less than half an hour in a warm, comfortable room, at rest and without responsibilities. The temptation to a sea-sick traveller was great; I succumbed.

'Well,' said Peddley heartily, in his. loud, trombone-like voice, 'well, this *is* luck.' He brought down his hand with a tremendous clap on to my knee, as though he were patting a horse. 'The greatest luck! Think of running into you and Herbert at the gangway! And carrying you off like this! Too delightful, too delightful!'

I was warmed by his gladness; it seemed so genuine. And genuine it was – the genuine gladness of an ogre who has found a chubby infant straying alone in the woods.

'Extraordinary,' Peddley went on, 'how many acquaintances one meets at Dover quay. I come every day, you know, when I'm staying in the country; every day, to meet the afternoon boat. It's a great resource when one's feeling dull. All the advantages of a London club in the country. And there's always time for a good chat before the train starts. That's what makes me like this district of Kent so much. I'm trying to persuade my landlord to sell me the house. I've nearly coaxed him, I think.'

'And then,' said Herbert, who had a way of occasionally breaking his habitual silence with one of those simple and devastatingly judicious reflections which render children so dangerous in polite, adult society, 'and then you'll find that every one will be travelling by aeroplane. You'll have to sell the house and move to Croydon, near the aerodrome.'

But Peddley was not the man to be put out by even the most terrible of terrible infants. Wrapped in his insensitiveness, he was not so much as aware of the infant's terribleness.

'Pooh!' he retorted. 'I don't believe in aeroplanes. They'll never be safe or cheap or comfortable enough to compete with the steamers. Not in our day.' And he embarked on a long discourse about helicopters and gyroscopes, air pockets and the cost of petrol.

Meanwhile, I had begun to wonder, in some alarm, what manner of man this kind, efficient, hospitable host of mine could be. A man who, on his own confession, drove into Dover every afternoon to meet the packet; who waylaid sea-sick acquaintances and had good chats with them while they waited for the train; and who so much loved his afternoon diversions at the quay-side that he felt moved to refute in serious, technical argument the prophet of aerial travel. . . . Decidedly, a strange, a dangerous man. And his voice, meanwhile, boomed and boomed in my ears till I felt dizzy with the sound of it. Too late, it occurred to me that it might have been better if I had faced that dreary journey, that chilly drive, that icy and inhospitable homecoming to empty rooms. Too late.

I discovered afterwards that Peddley's holidays were always spent at railway junctions, frontier towns and places of international resort, where he was likely to find a good supply of victims. For week-ends, Whitsun and Easter, he had his country house near Dover. At Christmas time he always took a week or ten days on the French Riviera. And during the summer he simultaneously satisfied his social passions and his passion for mountain scenery by taking up some strategic position on the Franco-Swiss, Italo-French, or Swiss-Italian frontier, where he could go for walks in the hills and, in the intervals, meet the trans-continental trains. One year he would take his family to Pontarlier; another to Valorbes; another to Modane; another to Brigue; another to Chiasso. In the course of a few years he had visited all the principal frontier towns in the mountainous parts of central and southern Europe. He knew the best seasons for each. Valorbes, for example, had to be visited early in the season. It was in July and at the beginning of August that the greatest number of English people passed through on their way to Switzerland. When he had seen them on their homeward way at the end of August, Peddley would move on for a fortnight's stay to one of the Italian frontier towns, so as to catch the September tourists on their way to Florence or Venice. His favourite haunt at this season was Modane. There are lots of good walks round Modane; and the principal trains wait there for two and a half hours. Rosy with healthful exercise, Peddley would come striding down at the appointed hour to meet the express. The victim was marked down, caught, and led away to the station buffet. For the next two hours Peddley indulged in what he called 'a *really* good chat'.

Peddley's circle of acquaintanceship was enormous. There was his legal practice, to begin with; that brought him into professional contact with a great variety of people. Then there were his clubs; he was a member of three or four, which he frequented assiduously. And, finally, there was his own constantly hospitable dinner-table; it is astonishing what even the richest men will put up with for the sake of a good free meal. He was on talking terms with hundreds, almost thousands, of his fellows. It was not to be wondered at if he often spied familiar faces in the Modane custom-house. But there were many days, of course, when nobody of his acquaintance happened to be going South. On these occasions Peddley would seek out some particularly harassed-looking stranger and offer his assistance. The kindness, so far as Peddley was concerned, was entirely wholehearted; he was not conscious of the wolf concealed beneath his sheep's clothing. He just felt a desire to be friendly and helpful and, incidentally, chatty. And helpful he certainly was. But in the buffet, when the ordeal of the custom-house was over, the stranger would gradually come to the conclusion, as he listened to Peddley's masterly exposition of the financial policy of Sweden, that he would have preferred, on the whole, to face the rapacious porters and the insolent douaniers alone and unassisted.

John Peddley had not yet enumerated all his reasons for supposing that aeroplanes would never cut out the cross-channel steamers, when we reached our destination.

'Ah, here we are,' he said, and opened the door for me to get out. 'But as I was saying,' he added, turning back to Herbert, 'the great defect of gyroscopes is their weight and the excessive rigidity they give to the machine. Now I grant you, my dear boy . . .'

But I forget what he granted. All I remember is that he was still granting it when we entered the drawing-room, where Mrs Peddley was sitting with her children.

From the first, I found Grace Peddley charming. Positively and actively charming. And yet she was Herbert's own sister and in many respects very like him. Which only shows (what, after all, is sufficiently obvious) that we are prepared to tolerate and even admire in persons of the opposite sex qualities which infuriate us when we meet with them in persons of our own. I found Herbert a bore because he was mentally blank and vague, because he was without initiative, because he attached himself and clung. But Grace, whose character was really very similar to Herbert's, charmed me, in spite, or perhaps even because, of these qualities which made me rank her brother among the minor calamities of my existence.

But it is not only the moral and mental qualities of our fellow-beings that inspire our love or hate. I should not, I am sure, have found Herbert so deplorable if he had been smaller and less cumbrous, less clumsy of body. He was altogether too much the lubber fiend for my taste. Physically, Grace displayed little resemblance to her brother. She was tall, it is true, but slim and light of movement. Herbert was thick, shambling and leaden-footed. In a heavy, large-featured way, Herbert was not unhandsome. He had a profile; his nose and chin were Roman and positively noble. At a distance you might mistake him for some formidable Caesarean man of action. But when you came close enough to see his eyes and read the expression on that large pretentious face, you perceived that, if Roman, he was the dullest and blankest Roman of them all.

Grace was not in the least imposing or classical. You could never, at however great a distance, have mistaken her for the mother of the Gracchi. Her features were small and seemed, somehow, still indefinite, like the features of a child. A lot of dark red-brown hair which, at that epoch, when fashion still permitted women to have hair, she wore looped up in a couple of spirally coiled plaits over either ear, emphasised the pallor of that childish face. A pair of very round, wide-open grey eyes looked out from under the hair with an expression of slightly perplexed ingenuousness. Her face was the face of a rather ugly but very nice little girl. And when she smiled, she was suddenly almost beautiful. Herbert smiled in the same way – a sudden smile, full of kindness and good nature. It was that smile of his that made it impossible, for me at any rate, to treat him with proper ruthlessness. In both of them, brother and sister, it was a singularly dim and helpless goodness that expressed itself in that smile – a gentle, inefficient kindliness that was tinged, in Herbert's case, with a sort of loutish rusticity. He was a bumpkin even in his goodness. Grace's smile was dim, but expressive at the same time of a native refinement which Herbert did not possess. They were brother and sister; but hers was a soul of better, more aristocratic birth.

It was in her relations with her children that the inefficiency of Grace's benevolence revealed itself most clearly in practice. She loved them, but she didn't know what to do with them or how to treat them. It was lucky for her – and for the children too – that she could afford to keep nurses and governesses. She could never have brought her children up by herself. They would either have died in infancy, or, if they had survived the first two years of unpunctual and hopelessly unhygienic feeding, would have grown up into little savages. As it was, they had been well brought up by professional child-tamers, were healthy and, except towards their mother, beautifully behaved. Their mother, however, they regarded as a being of another species – a lovely and eminently adorable being, but not serious, like nurse or Miss Phillips, not really grown up; more than half a child, and what wasn't child, mostly fairy. Their mother was the elfin being who permitted or even herself suggested the most fantastic breaches of all the ordinary rules. It was she, for example, who had invented the sport of bathing, in summer-time, under the revolving sprinkler which watered the lawn. It was she who had first suggested that excellent game, so strenuously disapproved of by Miss Phillips, nurse and father, of biting your slice of bread, at dinner-time, into the shape of a flower or a heart, a little bridge, a letter of the alphabet, a triangle, a railway engine. They adored her, but they would not take her seriously, as a person in authority; it never even occurred to them to obey her.

'You're a little girl,' I once heard her four-year-old daughter explaining to her. 'You're a little girl, mummy. Miss Phillips is an old lady.'

Grace turned her wide, perplexed eyes in my direction. 'You see,' she said despairingly, yet with a kind of triumph, as though she were conclusively proving a disputed point, 'you see! What *can* I do with them?'

She couldn't do anything. When she was alone with them, the children became like little wild beasts.

'But, children,' she would protest, 'children! You really

mustn't.' But she knew that she might as well have expostu-
lated with a litter of grizzly bears.

Sometimes, when the protest was more than ordinarily
loud and despairing, the children would look up from their
absorbing mischief and reassuringly smile to her. 'It's all
right, mummy,' they would say. 'It's quite all right, you
know.'

And then, helplessly, their mother would give it up.

In Herbert I found this helpless inefficiency intolerable.
But the ineptitude of his sister had a certain style; even her
clumsiness was somehow graceful. For clumsy she was.
When it came to sewing, for example, her fingers were all
thumbs. She had quite given up trying to sew when I first
knew her. But she still regarded it as part of her maternal
duty to knit warm mufflers – she never attempted anything
more complicated than a muffler – for the children. She
knitted very slowly, painfully concentrating her whole
attention on the work in hand until, after a few minutes,
exhausted by the mental strain, she was forced, with a great
sigh, to give up and take a little rest. A muffler took months
to finish. And when it was finished, what an extraordinary
object it was ! A sort of woollen fishing-net.

'Not *quite* right, I'm afraid,' Grace would say, holding it
out at arm's length. 'Still,' she added, cocking her head on
one side and half closing her eyes, as though she were looking at a *pointilliste* picture, 'it isn't bad, considering.'

Secretly, she was very proud of these mufflers, proud
with the pride of a child who has written its first letter or
embroidered on canvas its first kettle-holder, with practically no help at all from the nurse. It still seemed to her
extraordinary that she could do things all by herself, unassisted.

This graceful ineptitude of hers amused and charmed
me. True, if I had had to marry it, I might not have found
it quite so enchanting, if only for the reason that I should

never have been able to afford a sufficiency of servants and child-tamers to counteract its effects on domestic, daily life. Nor, I am afraid, would the absurd charm of her intellectual vagueness have survived a long intimacy. For how vague, how bottomlessly vague she was! For example, she was quite incapable – and no experience could teach her – of realising the value of money. At one moment she was lavishly extravagant, would spend pounds as though they were pence. The next, overvaluing her money as wildly as she had undervalued it, she would grudge every penny spent on the first necessities of life. Poor Peddley would sometimes come home from his office to find that there was nothing for dinner but lentils. Another man would have been violently and explosively annoyed; but Peddley, whose pedagogic passions were more powerful than his anger, only made a reasoned expostulation in the shape of a discourse on the meaning of money and the true nature of wealth, followed by a brief lecture on dietetics and the theory of calories. Grace listened attentively and with humility. But try as she would, she could never remember a word of what he had said; or rather she remembered, partially, but remembered all wrong. The phrases which Peddley had built up into a rational discourse, Grace re-arranged in her mind so as to make complete nonsense. It was the same with what she read. The arguments got turned upside down. The non-essential facts were vividly remembered, the essential forgotten. Dates were utterly meaningless to her. Poor Grace! she was painfully conscious of her inefficiency of mind; she longed above everything to be learned, authoritative, capable. But though she read a great number of serious books – and read them with genuine pleasure, as well as on principle – she could never contrive to be well read. Inside her head everything got muddled. It was as though her mind were inhabited by some mischievous imp which delighted in taking to pieces the beautifully composed mosaics of learning and genius, and resetting the tesserae (after throwing a good many of them away) in the most fantastic and ludicrous disorder.

The consciousness of these defects made her particularly admire those who were distinguished by the opposite and positive qualities. It was this admiration, I am sure, which made her Peddley's wife. She was very young when he fell in love with her and asked her to marry him – eighteen to his thirty-four or thereabouts – very young and (being fresh from school, with its accompaniment of examination failures and pedagogic reproaches) more than ordinarily sensitive to her own shortcomings, and to the merits of those unlike herself. Peddley made his entry into her life. The well-documented accuracy of his knowledge of artificial manures and the Swiss banking system astonished her. True, she did not feel a passionate interest in these subjects; but for that she blamed herself, not him. He seemed to her the personification of learning and wisdom – omniscient, an encyclopaedia on legs.

It is not uncommon for schoolgirls to fall in love with their aged professors. It is the tribute paid by youth – by flighty, high-spirited, but passionately earnest youth – to venerable mind. Grace was not lucky. The most venerable mind with which, at eighteen, she had yet come into contact was Peddley's. Peddley's! She admired, she was awed by what seemed to her the towering, Newtonian intellect of the man. And when the Newtonian intellect laid itself at her feet, she felt at first astonished – was it possible that he, Peddley, the omniscient, should abase himself before one who had failed three times, ignominiously in the Cambridge Locals? – then flattered and profoundly grateful. Moreover, Peddley, unlike the proverbial professor, was neither grey-bearded nor decrepit. He was in the prime of life, extremely active, healthy, and energetic; good-looking, too, in the ruddy, large-chinned style of those Keen Business Men one sees portrayed in advertisements and the illustrations of magazine stories. Quite inexperienced in these matters, she easily persuaded herself that her gratitude and her schoolgirl's excitement were the genuine passion of the novels. She imagined that she was in love with him. And it would have mattered little, in all probability, if she had not. Peddley's tireless courtship would have ended infallibly by forcing her to surrender. There was no strength in Grace; she could be bullied into anything. In this case, however, only a very little bullying was necessary. At his second proposal, she accepted him. And so, in 1914, a month or two before the outbreak of war, they were married.

A marriage which began with the war might have been expected to be a strange, unusual, catastrophic marriage. But for the Peddleys, as a matter of fact, the war had next to no significance; it did not touch their life. For the first year John Peddley made Business as Usual his motto. Later, after being rejected for active service on account of his short sight, he enrolled himself as a temporary bureaucrat; was highly efficient in a number of jobs; had managed, when the medical boards became stricter, to make himself indispensable, as a sugar rationer; and ended up with an OBE. Grace, meanwhile, lived quietly at home and gave birth, in three successive years, to three children. They kept her occupied; the war, for her, was an irrelevance. She witnessed neither its tragedies, nor its feverish and sordid farces. She knew as little of apprehension, suspense, grief, as she knew of the reckless extravagances, the intoxications, the too facile pleasures, the ferocious debaucheries which ran parallel with the agonies, which mingled and alternated with them. Ineffectually, Grace nursed her babies; she might have been living in the eighteenth century.

At the time I knew her first Grace had been married

about six years. Her eldest child was five years old, her youngest about two. Peddley, I judged, was still in love with her – in his own way, that is. The wild passion which had hurried him into a not very reasonable marriage, a passion mainly physical, had subsided. He was no longer mad about Grace; but he continued to find her eminently desirable. Habit, moreover, had endeared her to him, had made her indispensable; it had become difficult for him to imagine an existence without her. But for all that, there was no intimacy between them. Possessing, as I have said, no private life of his own, Peddley did not understand the meaning of intimacy. He could give no confidences and therefore asked for none. He did not know what to do with them when they came to him unasked. I do not know if Grace ever tried to confide in him; if so, she must soon have given it up as a bad job. One might as well have tried to confide into a gramophone; one might whisper the most secret and sacred thoughts into the trumpet of the machine, but there came back only a loud booming voice that expounded the financial policy of Sweden, food controls, or the law relating to insurance companies – it depended which particular record out of the large, but still limited repertory, happened at the moment to be on the turntable. In the spiritual home of the Peddleys there was only a bedroom and a lecture-room – no sentimental boudoir for confidences, no quiet study pleasantly violated from time to time by feminine intrusion. Nothing between the physical intimacies of the bedroom and the impersonal relations of pupil and sonorously braying professor in the reverberant lecture-hall. And then, what lectures!

Grace, who still believed in the intellectual eminence of her husband, continued to blame herself for finding them tedious. But tedious they were to her; that was a fact she could not deny. Long practice had taught her to cultivate a kind of mental deafness. Peddley's discourses no longer got on her nerves, because she no longer heard them. I have often seen her sitting, her wide eyes turned on Peddley with an expression, apparently, of rapt attention, seeming to drink in every word he uttered. It was so she must have sat in those first months of her marriage, when she really did listen, when she still tried her hardest to be interested and to remember correctly. Only in those days, I fancy, there can never have been quite so perfect a serenity on her face. There must have been little frowns of concentration and agonisingly suppressed yawns. Now there was only an un-ruffled calm, the calm of complete and absolute abstraction.

I found her out on the very first evening of our acquaint-ance. John Peddley, who must have been told (I suppose by Herbert) that I was interested, more or less professionally, in music, began, in my honour, a long description of the mechanism of pianolas. I was rather touched by this mani-fest effort to make me feel spiritually at home, and, though I was dizzied by the sound of his voice, made a great show of being interested in what he was saying. In a pause, while Peddley was helping himself to the vegetables (what a bless-ing it was to have a moment's respite from that maddening voice!), I turned to Grace and asked her politely, as a new guest should, whether she were as much interested in piano-las as her husband. She started, as though I had woken her out of sleep, turned on me a pair of blank, rather fright-ened eyes, blushed scarlet.

'As much interested as John in *what*?' she asked.

'Pianolas.'

'Oh, pianolas.' And she uttered the word in a puzzled, be-wildered tone which made it quite clear that she had no idea that pianolas had been the subject of conversation for at least the last ten minutes. 'Pianolas?' she repeated almost incredulously. And she had seemed so deeply attentive.

I admired her for this power of absenting herself, for being, spiritually, not there. I admired, but I also pitied.

To have to live in surroundings from which it was necessary, in mere self-preservation, to absent oneself – that was pitiable indeed.

Next morning, assuming an invalid's privilege, I had breakfast in bed. By the time I came down from my room, Peddley and Herbert had set out for a hearty walk. I found Grace alone, arranging flowers. We exchanged good-mornings. By the expression of her face, I could see that she found my presence rather formidable. A stranger, a highbrow, a musical critic – what to say to him? Courageously doing her duty, she began to talk to me about Bach. Did I like Bach? Didn't I think he was the greatest musician? I did my best to reply; but somehow, at that hour of the morning, there seemed to be very little to say about Bach. The conversation began to droop.

'And the *Well-Tempered Clavichord*,' she went on desperately. 'What lovely things in that!'

'And so useful for torturing children who learn the piano,' I replied, as desperately. Facetiousness, the last resort.

But my words had touched a chord in Grace's mind. 'Torture,' she said. 'That's the word. I remember when I was at school . . .'

And there we were, happily launched at last upon an interesting, because a personal, subject.

Grace was as fond of her dear old school as Herbert was of his. But, with the rest of her sex, she had a better excuse for her fondness. For many women, the years spent in that uncomplicated, companionable, exciting, purely feminine world, which is the world of school, are the happiest of their lives. Grace was one of them. She adored her school; she looked back on her schooldays as on a golden age. True, there had been Cambridge Locals and censorious mistresses; but on the other hand, there had been no Peddley, no annual child-bearing, no domestic responsibilities, no social duties, no money to be too lavish or too stingy with, no servants. She talked with enthusiasm, and I listened with pleasure.

An hour and a half later, when the bores came back, red-faced and ravenous, from their walk, we were sorry to be interrupted. I had learned a great many facts about Grace's girlhood. I knew that she had had an unhappy passion for the younger of the visiting music mistresses; that one of her friends had received a love-letter from a boy of fifteen, beginning : 'I saw a photograph of you in the *Sketch*, walking in the Park with your mother. Can I ever forget it?' I knew that she had had mumps for five weeks, that she had climbed on the roof by moonlight in pyjamas, that she was no good at hockey.

From time to time most of us feel a need, often urgent and imperious, to talk about ourselves. We desire to assert our personalities, to insist on a fact which the world about us seems in danger of forgetting – the fact that we exist, that we are we. In some people the desire is so chronic and so strong, that they can never stop talking about themselves. Rather than be silent, they will pour out the most humiliating and discreditable confidences. Grace was afflicted by no such perverse and extravagant longings; there was nothing of the exhibitionist in her. But she did like, every now and then, to have a good talk about her soul, her past history, her future. She liked to talk, and she too rarely had an opportunity. In me she found a sympathetic listener and commentator. By the end of the morning she was regarding me as an old friend. And I, for my part, had found her charming. So charming, indeed, that for Grace's sake I was prepared to put up even with John Peddley's exposition of the law regarding insurance companies.

Within a few weeks of our first introduction we were finding it the most natural thing in the world that we should be constantly meeting. We talked a great deal, on these

E

occasions, about ourselves, about Life and about Love –
subjects which can be discussed with the fullest pleasure
and profit only between persons of opposite sexes. On none
of these three topics, it must be admitted, did Grace have
very much of significance to say. She had lived very little
and loved not at all; it was impossible, therefore, that she
should know herself. But it was precisely this ignorance and
her ingenuous, confident expression of it that charmed me.

'I feel I'm already old,' she complained to me. 'Old and
finished. Like those funny straw hats and leg-of-mutton
sleeves in the bound volumes of the *Illustrated London
News*,' she added, trying to make her meaning clearer for
me.

I laughed at her. 'You're absurdly young,' I said, 'and
you haven't begun.'

She shook her head and sighed.

When we talked about love, she professed a sad, middle-
aged scepticism.

'People make a most ridiculous fuss about it.'

'Rightly.'

'But it's not worth making a fuss about,' she insisted.
'Not in reality. Not outside of books.'

'Isn't it?' I said. 'You'll think differently,' I told her,
'when you've waited two or three hours for somebody who
hasn't turned up, when you can't sleep for wondering
where somebody's been and with whom, and you want to
cry – yes, you do cry – and you feel as though you were just
going to have influenza.'

'Ah, but that isn't love,' Grace retorted sententiously, in
the tone of one who has some private and certain source of
information.

'What is it, then?'

'It's . . .' Grace hesitated, and suddenly blushed, 'it's . . .
well, it's physical.'

I could not help laughing, uproariously.

Grace was vexed. 'Well, isn't it true?' she insisted obstinately.

'Perfectly,' I had to admit. 'But why isn't that love?' I added, hoping to elicit Grace's views on the subject.

She let me have them. They were positively Dantesque. I can only suppose that Peddley's ardours had left her cold, disgusted even.

But Life and Love were not our only topics. Grace's ignorance and my own native reticence made it impossible for us to discuss these themes with any profit for very long at a stretch. In the intervals, like John Peddley, I played the pedagogic part. Through casual remarks of mine, Grace suddenly became aware of things whose very existence had previously been unknown to her – things like contemporary painting and literature, young music, new theories of art. It was a revelation. All her efforts, it seemed to her, all her strivings towards culture had been wasted. She had been laboriously trying to scale the wrong mountain, to force her way into the wrong sanctuary. At the top, if she had ever reached it, within the holy of holies, she would have found – what? a grotesque and moth-eaten collection of those funny little straw hats and leg-of-mutton sleeves from the bound volumes of the *Illustrated London News*. It was dreadful, it was humiliating. But now she had caught a glimpse of another sanctuary, upholstered by Martine, enriched by the offerings of the Poirets and Lanvins of the spirit; a modish, modern sanctuary; a fashionable Olympus. She was eager to climb, to enter.

Acting the part of those decayed gentlewomen who, for a consideration, introduce *parvenus* into good society, I made Grace acquainted with all that was smartest and latest in the world of the spirit. I gave her lessons in intellectual etiquette, warned her against aesthetic *gaffes*. She listened attentively, and was soon tolerably at home in the unfamiliar world – knew what to say when confronted by a

Dada poem, a picture by Picasso, a Schoenberg quartet, an Archipenko sculpture.

I was working, at that period, as a musical critic, and two or three times a week I used to take Grace with me to my concerts. It did not take me long to discover that she had very little feeling for music and no analytical understanding of it. But she professed, hypocritically, to adore it. And as it bored me most excruciatingly to have to go by myself to listen to second-rate pianists playing the same old morsels of Liszt and Chopin, second-rate contraltos fruitily hooting Schubert and Brahms, second-rate fiddlers scraping away at Tartini and Wieniawski, I pretended to believe in Grace's enthusiasm for the musical art and took her with me to all the most painful recitals. If the hall were empty – which, to the eternal credit of the music-loving public, it generally was – one could get a seat at the back, far away from the other sparsely sprinkled auditors, and talk very pleasantly through the whole performance.

At first, Grace was terribly shocked when, after listening judicially to the first three bars of *Du bist wie eine Blume* or the *Trillo del Diavolo*, I opened a conversation. She herself had a very perfect concert-goer's technique, and listened with the same expression of melancholy devotion, as though she were in church, to every item on the programme. My whispered chatter seemed to her sacrilegious. It was only when I assured her, professionally and *ex cathedra*, that the stuff wasn't worth listening to, that she would consent, albeit with considerable misgivings in the early days of our concert-going, to take her part in the conversation. In a little while, however, she grew accustomed to the outrage; so much so, that when the music or the performance happened to be good (a little detail which Grace was not sufficiently musical to notice) it was I who had to play the verger's part and hush her sacrilegious chatter in a place suddenly made holy. She learned in the end to take her cue from me – to look devout when I looked devout, to chatter when I chattered.

Once, rather maliciously, I put on my raptest expression while some maudlin incompetent was pounding out Rachmaninoff. After a quick glance at me through the tail of her eye, Grace also passed into ecstasy, gazing at the pianist as St Theresa might have gazed at the uplifted Host. When the ordeal was over, she turned on me a pair of bright, shining eyes.

'Wasn't that splendid?' she said. And such is the power of self-suggestion, that she had genuinely enjoyed it.

'I thought it the most revolting performance I ever listened to,' was my answer.

Poor Grace turned fiery red, the tears came into her eyes; to hide them from me, she averted her face. 'I thought it very good,' she insisted, heroically. 'But of course I'm no judge.'

'Oh, of course it wasn't as bad as all that,' I made haste to assure her. 'One exaggerates, you know.' The sight of her unhappy face had made me feel profoundly penitent. I had meant only to make mild fun of her, and I had managed somehow to hurt her, cruelly. I wished to goodness that I had never played the stupid trick. It was a long time before she completely forgave me.

Later, when I knew her better, I came to understand why it was that she had taken my little clownery so hardly. Rudely and suddenly, my joke had shattered one of those delightful pictures of herself which Grace was for ever fancifully creating and trying to live up to. What had been a joke for me had been, for her, a kind of murder.

Grace was a born visualiser. I discovered, for example, that she had what Galton calls a 'number form'. When she had to do any sort of arithmetical calculation, she saw the figures arranged in space before her eyes. Each number had its own peculiar colour and its own position in the form.

After a hundred the figures became dim; that was why she always found it so difficult to work in large numbers. The difference between three thousand, thirty thousand, and three hundred thousand was never immediately apparent to her, because in the case of these large numbers she could *see* nothing; they floated indistinctly on the blurred fringes of her number form. A million, however, she saw quite clearly; its place was high up, to the left, above her head, and it consisted of a huge pile of those envelopes they have at banks for putting money in – thousands and thousands of them, each marked with the word MILLION in large black letters. All her mental processes were a succession of visual images; and these mental pictures were so vivid as to rival in brightness and definition the images she received through her eyes. What she could not visualise, she could not think about.

I am myself a very poor visualiser. I should find it very difficult, for example, to describe from memory the furniture in my room. I know that there are so many chairs, so many tables, doors, bookshelves, and so on; but I have no clear mental vision of them. When I do mental arithmetic, I see no coloured numbers. The word Africa does not call up in my mind, as Grace assured me once that it always did in hers, a vision of sand with palm trees and lions. When I make plans for the future, I do not see myself, as though on the stage, playing a part in imaginary dramas. I think without pictures, abstractly and in the void. That is why I cannot pretend to write with complete understanding of the workings of Grace's mind. The congenitally deaf are not the best judges of music. I can only guess, only imaginatively reconstruct.

From what I gathered in conversation with her, I imagine that Grace was in the habit of vividly 'seeing herself' in every kind of situation. Some of these situations had no relation to her actual life, were the purely fantastic and

hypothetical situations of day-dreams. Others were real, or
at any rate potentially real, situations. Living her life, she
saw herself living it, acting in the scenes of the flat quoti-
dian drama a very decided and definite part. Thus, when
she went for a walk in the country, she saw herself walking
– a female mountaineer of tireless strength and energy.
When she accompanied Peddley on his annual expeditions
to the Riviera, she saw herself as she climbed into the *wagon
lit*, or swam along the Promenade des Anglais, as an immensely rich and haughty milady, envied by the *canaille*,
remote and star-like above them. On certain socially important occasions at home, a similar character made its
appearance. I saw the milady once or twice during the first
months of our acquaintanceship. Later on the milady
turned into a very Parisian, very twentieth-cum-eighteenth
century *grande dame*. But of that in its place.

Grace was much assisted in these visualisations of herself
by her clothes. In the costume which she donned for a two-
mile walk in Kent she might have crossed the Andes. And
in all her garments, for every occasion, one noticed the
same dramatic appropriateness. It was a pity that she did
not know how to change her features with her clothes. Her
face, whether she lolled along the sea-fronts of the Riviera
or addressed herself, in brogues, short skirts, and sweaters
to the ascent of some Kentish hillock, was always the same –
the face of a rather ugly but very nice little girl; a face that
opened on to the world through large, perplexed eyes, and
that became, from time to time, suddenly and briefly beautiful with a dim benevolence when she smiled.

Grace's visions of herself were not merely momentary
and occasional. There was generally one predominating
character in which she saw herself over considerable periods
of time. During the first four years of her marriage, for example, she had seen herself predominantly as the housewife
and mother. But her manifest incapacity to act either of

these parts successfully had gradually chilled her enthusiasm for them. She wanted to run the house, she saw herself tinkling about with keys, giving orders to the maids; but, in practice, whenever she interfered with the rule of her masterful old cook, everything went wrong. She loved her children, she pictured them growing up, healthy and good, under her influence; but they were always sick when she fed them, they behaved like beasts when she tried to make them obey. To one who tried to see herself as the complete, the almost German matron, it was not encouraging. By the time her last child was born, she had practically abandoned the attempt. From the first, the baby had been handed over, body and soul, to the nurses. And except when she was seized with a financial panic and forbade the ordering of anything but lentils, she let the old cook have her way.

When I first met her, Grace was not seeing herself continuously in any one predominating role. Punctured by sharp experience, the matron had flattened out and collapsed; and the matron had had, so far, no successor. Left without an imaginary character to live up to, Grace had relapsed into that dim characterlessness which in her, as in Herbert, seemed to be the natural state. She still saw herself vividly enough in the separate, occasional incidents of her life – as the mountain climber, as the rich and haughty milady. But she saw no central and permanent figure in whose life these incidents of mountaineering and opulently visiting the Riviera occurred. She was a succession of points, so to speak; not a line.

Her friendship with me was responsible for the emergence into her consciousness of a new permanent image of herself. She discovered in my company a new role, not so important, indeed, not so rich in potentialities as that of the matron, but still a leading lady's part. She had been so long without a character that she eagerly embraced the opportunity of acquiring one, however incongruous. And incongruous it was, this new character; odd and eminently unsuitable. Grace had come to see herself as a musical critic.

It was our concert-going – our professional concert-going – that had done it. If I had happened not to be a journalist, if we had paid for admission instead of coming in free on my complimentary tickets, it would never have occurred to her to see herself as a critic. Simple mortals, accustomed to pay for their pleasures, are always impressed by the sight of a free ticket. The critic's *jus primae noctis* seems to them an enviable thing. Sharing the marvellous privilege, Grace came to feel that she must also share the judicial duties of a critic. She saw herself distributing praise and blame – a rapturous listener when the performance was worth listening to, a contemptuous chatterer when it wasn't. Identifying herself with me – not the real but an ideal exalted me – she pictured herself as the final arbiter of musical reputations. My malicious little practical joke had thrown down this delightful image of herself. The critic had suddenly been murdered.

At the time I did not understand why poor Grace should have been so deeply hurt. It was only in the light of my later knowledge that I realised what must have been her feelings. It was only later, too, that I came to understand the significance of that curious little pantomime which she used regularly to perform as we entered a concert hall. That languid gait with which she strolled across the vestibule, dragging her feet with a kind of reluctance, as though she were on boring business; that sigh, that drooping of the eyelids as she stood, patiently, while the attendant looked at my tickets; that air, when we were in the concert-room, of being perfectly at home, of owning the place (she used, I remember, to put her feet up on the seat in front); and that smile of overacted contempt, that wearily amused smile with which she used (once she had got over the idea that

she was committing a sacrilege) to respond, during a bad
performance, to my whispered chatter – these were the
gait, the bored patience, the possessive at-homeness, the
contempt of a hardened critic.

And what a quantity of music she bought at this time and
never played ! How many volumes of musical criticism and
biography she took out of the library ! And the grave pro-
nouncements she used to make across the dinner-table !
'Beethoven was the greatest of them all'; and so on in the
same style. I understood it all afterwards. And the better I
understood, the more I regretted my cruel little joke. As
the critic, she had been so happy. My joke destroyed that
happiness. She became diffident and self-conscious, got
actor's fright; and though I never repeated the jest, though
I always encouraged her, after that, to believe in her
musicianship, she could never whole-heartedly see herself
in the part again.

But what a poor part, at the best of times, the critic's
was ! It was too dry, too intellectual and impersonal to be
really satisfying. That it lay within my power to provide
her with a much better role – the guilty wife's – I do not
and did not at the time much doubt. True, when I knew her
first Grace was a perfectly virtuous young woman. But her
virtue was founded on no solid principle – on a profound
love for her husband, for example, or on strong religious
prejudices. It was not a virtue that in any way involved her
intimate being. If she happened to be virtuous, it was more
by accident than on principle or from psychological necessity. She had not yet had any occasion for not being virtuous, that was all. She could have been bullied and cajoled
by Peddley into marriage. Grace floated vaguely on the surface of life without compass or destination; one had only to
persuade her that adultery was Eldorado, and she would
have shaped her course forthwith towards that magical
shore. It was just a question of putting the case sufficiently

speciously. She still retained, at this time, the prejudices of her excellent upper middle-class upbringing; but they were not very deeply rooted. Nothing in Grace was so deeply rooted that it could not quite easily be eradicated.

I realised these facts at the time. But I did not try to take advantage of them. The truth is that, though I liked Grace very much, I was never urgently in love with her. True, one can very agreeably and effectively act the part of the 'lover', in the restricted and technical sense of that term, without being wildly in love. And if both parties could always guarantee to keep their emotions in a state of equilibrium, these little sentimental sensualities would doubtless be most exquisitely diverting. But the equilibrium can never be guaranteed. The balanced hearts begin sooner or later, almost inevitably, to tilt towards love or hatred. In the end, one of the sentimental sensualities turns into a passion – whether of longing or disgust it matters not – and then, farewell to all hope of tranquillity. I should be chary of saying so in Kingham's presence; but the fact remains that I like tranquillity. For me, the love-game, without love, is not worth the candle. Even as a mere hedonist I should have refrained. And I had other scruples – scruples which an overmastering passion might have overridden, but which were sufficient to keep a mere mild sensuality in check. I was never Grace's lover; neither genuinely, by right of passion, nor technically by the accident of physical possession. Never her lover. An ironic fate had reserved for me a less glorious part – the part, not of the lover, but of the introducer of lovers. All unintentionally, I was to play benevolent Uncle Pandarus to Grace's Cressida. And there were two Troiluses.

The first of them was no less – or shouldn't I rather say 'no more'? for how absurdly his reputation was exaggerated! – than Clegg, *the* Clegg, Rodney Clegg, the painter. I have known Clegg for years and liked him, in a way –

liked him rather as one likes Grock, or Little Tich, or the Fratellini : as a comic spectacle. This is not the best way of liking people, I know. But with Rodney it was the only way. You had either to like him as a purveyor of amusement, or dislike him as a human being. That, at any rate, was always my experience. I have tried hard to get to know and like him intimately – off the stage, so to speak. But it was never any good. In the end, I gave up the attempt once and for all, took to regarding him quite frankly as a music-hall comedian, and was able, in consequence, thoroughly to enjoy his company. Whenever I feel like a tired business man, I go to see Rodney Clegg.

Perhaps, as a lover, Rodney was somehow different from his ordinary self. Perhaps he dropped his vanity and his worldliness. Perhaps he became unexpectedly humble and unselfish, forgot his snobbery, craved no longer for cheap successes and, for love, thought the world well lost. Perhaps. Or more probably, I am afraid, he remained very much as he always was, and only in Grace's eyes seemed different from the Rodney whose chatter and little antics diverted the tired business man in me. Was hers the correct vision of him, or was mine? Neither, I take it.

It must have been in the spring of 1921 that I first took Grace to Rodney's studio. For her, the visit was an event; she was about to see, for the first time in her life, a famous man. Particularly famous at the moment, it happened; for Rodney was very much in the papers that season. There had been a fuss about his latest exhibition. The critics, with a fine contemptuous inaccuracy, had branded his pictures as post-impressionistic, cubistic, futuristic; they threw any brick-bat that came to hand. And the pictures had been found improper as well as disturbingly 'modern'. Professional moralists had been sent by the Sunday papers to look at them; they came back boiling with professional indignation. Rodney was delighted, of course. This was fame – and a fame, moreover, that was perfectly compatible with prosperity. The outcry of the professional moralists did not interfere with his sales. He was doing a very good business.

Rodney's conversion to 'modern art', instead of ruining him, had been the source of increased profit and an enhanced notoriety. With his unfailing, intuitive knowledge of what the public wanted, he had devised a formula which combined modernity with the more appealing graces of literature and pornography. Nothing, for example, could have been less academic than his nudes. They were monstrously elongated; the paint was laid on quite flatly; there was no modelling, no realistic light and shade; the human form was reduced to a paper silhouette. The eyes were round black boot-buttons, the nipples magenta berries, the lips vermilion hearts; the hair was represented by a collection of crinkly black lines. The exasperated critics of the older school protested that a child of ten could have painted them. But the child of ten who could have painted such pictures must have been an exceedingly perverse child. In comparison, Freud's Little Hans would have been an angel of purity. For Rodney's nudes, however unrealistic, were luscious and voluptuous, were even positively indecent. What had distressed the public in the work of the French post-impressionists was not so much the distortion and the absence of realism as the repellent austerity, the intellectual asceticism, which rejected the appeal both of sex and of the anecdote. Rodney had supplied the deficiences. For these engagingly luscious nudities of his were never represented in the void, so to speak, but in all sorts of curious and amusing situations – taking tickets at railway stations, or riding bicycles, or sitting at cafés with negro jazz-bands in the background, drinking *crème de menthe*. All the people who felt that they ought to be in the movement, that it was a disgrace not to like modern art, discovered in

Rodney Clegg, to their enormous delight, a modern artist whom they could really and honestly admire. His pictures sold like hot cakes.

The conversion to modernism marked the real beginning of Rodney's success. Not that he had been unknown or painfully poor before his conversion. A man with Rodney's social talents, with Rodney's instinct for popularity, could never have known real obscurity or poverty. But all things are relative; before his conversion, Rodney had been obscurer and poorer than he deserved to be. He knew no duchesses, no millionairesses, then; he had no deposit at the bank – only a current account that swelled and ebbed capriciously, like a mountain stream. His conversion changed all that.

When Grace and I paid our first visit, he was already on the upward path.

'I hope he isn't very formidable,' Grace said to me, as we were making our way to Hampstead to see him. She was always rather frightened by the prospect of meeting new people.

I laughed. 'It depends what you're afraid of,' I said. 'Of being treated with high-brow haughtiness, or losing your virtue. I never heard of any woman who found him formidable in the first respect.'

'Oh, that's all right, then,' said Grace, looking relieved.

Certainly, there was nothing very formidable in Rodney's appearance. At the age of thirty-five he had preserved (and he also cultivated with artful care) the appearance of a good-looking boy. He was small and neatly made, slim, and very agile in his movements. Under a mass of curly brown hair, which was always in a state of picturesque and studied untidiness, his face was like the face of a lively and impertinent cherub. Smooth, rounded, almost unlined, it still preserved its boyish contours. (There were always pots and pots of beauty cream on his dressing-table.) His eyes were blue, bright and expressive. He had good teeth, and when he smiled two dimples appeared in his cheeks.

He opened the studio door himself. Dressed in his butcher's blue overalls, he looked charming. One's instinct was to pat the curly head and say: 'Isn't he too sweet! Dressed up like that, pretending to be a workman!' Even I felt moved to make some such gesture. To a woman, a potential mother of chubby children, the temptation must have been almost irresistible.

Rodney was very cordial. 'Dear old Dick!' he said, and patted me on the shoulder. I had not seen him for some months; he had spent the winter abroad. 'What a delight to see you!' I believe he genuinely liked me.

I introduced him to Grace. He kissed her hand. 'Too charming of you to have come. And what an enchanting ring!' he added, looking down again at her hand, which he still held in his own. 'Do, please, let me look at it.'

Grace smiled and blushed with pleasure as she gave it him. 'I got it in Florence,' she said. 'I'm so glad you like it.'

It was certainly a charming piece of old Italian jewellery. Sadly I reflected that I had known Grace intimately for more than six months and never so much as noticed the ring, far less made any comment on it. No wonder that I had been generally unlucky in love.

We found the studio littered with specimens of Rodney's latest artistic invention. Naked ladies in brown boots leading borzoi dogs; tenderly embracing one another in the middle of a still-life of bottles, guitars and newspapers (the old familiar modern still-life rendered acceptable to the great public and richly saleable by the introduction of the equivocal nudes); more naked ladies riding on bicycles (Rodney's favourite subject, his patent, so to say); playing the concertina; catching yellow butterflies in large green nets. Rodney brought them out one by one. From her armchair in front of the easel, Grace looked at them; her face wore that rapt religious expression which I had so often noticed in the concert-room.

'Lovely,' she murmured, as canvas succeeded canvas, 'too lovely'.

Looking at the pictures, I reflected with some amusement that, a year before, Rodney had been painting melodramatic crucifixions in the style of Tiepolo. At that time he had been an ardent Christian.

'Art can't live without religion,' he used to say then. 'We must get back to religion.'

And with his customary facility Rodney had got back to it. Oh, those pictures! They were really shocking in their accomplished insincerity. So emotional, so dramatic, and yet so utterly false and empty. The subjects, you felt, had been apprehended as a cinema producer might apprehend them, in terms of 'effectiveness'. There were always great darknesses and tender serene lights, touches of vivid colour and portentous silhouettes. Very 'stark', was what Rodney's admirers used to call those pictures. I remember. They were too stark by half for my taste.

Rodney set up another canvas on the easel.

'I call this "The Bicycle made for Two",' he said.

It represented a negress and a blonde with a Chinese white skin, riding on a tandem bicycle against a background of gigantic pink and yellow roses. In the foreground, on the right, stood a plate of fruit, tilted forward towards the spectator, in the characteristic 'modern' style. A greyhound trotted along beside the bicycle.

'Really too . . .' began Grace ecstatically. But finding no synonym for 'lovely', the epithet which she had applied to all the other pictures, she got no further, but made one of those non-committal laudatory noises, which are so much more satisfactory than articulate speech, when you don't know what to say to an artist about his works. She looked up at me. 'Isn't it really . . . ?' she asked.

'Yes, absolutely . . .' I nodded my affirmation. Then, rather maliciously, 'Tell me, Rodney,' I said, 'do you still paint religious pictures? I remember a most grandiose Descent from the Cross you were busy on not so long ago.'

But my malice was disappointed. Rodney was not in the least embarrassed by his reminder of the skeleton in his cupboard. He laughed.

'Oh, *that*,' he said. 'I painted it over. Nobody would buy. One cannot serve God and Mammon.' And he laughed again, heartily, at his own witticism.

It went into his repertory at once, that little joke. He took to introducing the subject of his religious paintings himself, in order to have an opportunity of bringing out the phrase, with a comical parody of clerical unction, at the end of his story. In the course of the next few weeks I heard him repeat it, in different assemblages, three or four times.

'God and Mammon,' he chuckled again. 'Can't be combined.'

'Only goddesses and Mammon,' I suggested, nodding in the direction of his picture.

Later, I had the honour of hearing my words incorporated into Rodney's performance. He had a wonderfully retentive memory.

'Precisely,' he said. 'Goddesses, I'm happy to say, of a more popular religion. Are you a believer, Mrs Peddley?' He smiled at her, raising his eyebrows. 'I am – fervently. I'm *croyant* and' (he emphasised the 'and' with arch significance) '*pratiquant*.'

Grace laughed rather nervously, not knowing what to answer. 'Well, I suppose we all are,' she said. She was not accustomed to this sort of gallantry.

Rodney smiled at her more impertinently than ever. 'How happy I should be,' he said, 'if I could make a convert of you!'

Grace repeated her nervous laugh and, to change the

subject, began to talk about the pictures.

We sat there for some time, talking, drinking tea, smoking cigarettes. I looked at my watch; it was half-past six. I knew that Grace had a dinner-party that evening.

'We shall have to go,' I said to her. 'You'll be late for your dinner.'

'Good heavens!' cried Grace, when she heard what the time was. She jumped up. 'I must fly. Old Lady Wacker-bath – imagine if I kept her waiting!' She laughed, but breathlessly; and she had gone quite pale with antici-patory fright.

'Stay, do stay,' implored Rodney. 'Keep her waiting.'

'I daren't.'

'But, my dear lady, you're young,' he insisted; 'you have the right – I'd say the duty, if the word weren't so coarse and masculine – to be unpunctual. At your age you must do what you like. You see, I'm assuming that you like being here,' he added parenthetically.

She returned his smile. 'Of course.'

'Well then, stay; do what you like; follow your caprices. After all, that's what you're there for.' Rodney was very strong on the Eternal Feminine.'

Grace shook her head. 'Good-bye. I've loved it so much.'

Rodney sighed, looked sad and slowly shook his head. 'If you'd loved it as much as all that,' he said, 'as much as I've loved it, you wouldn't be saying good-bye. But if you must. . . .' He smiled seductively; the teeth flashed, the dimples punctually appeared. He took her hand, bent over it and tenderly kissed it. 'You must come again,' he added. 'Soon. And,' turning to me with a laugh, and patting my shoul-der, 'without old Dick.'

'He's frightfully amusing, isn't he?' Grace said to me a minute later when we had left the studio.

'Frightfully,' I agreed, laying a certain emphasis on the adverb.

'And really,' she continued, 'most awfully nice, I thought.'

I made no comment.

'And a wonderful painter,' she added.

All at once I felt that I detested Rodney Clegg. I thought of my own sterling qualities of mind and heart, and it seemed to me outrageous, it seemed to me scandalous and intolerable that people, that is to say women in general, and Grace in particular, should be impressed and taken in and charmed by this little middle-aged charlatan with the pretty boy's face and the horribly knowing, smart, impertinent manner. It seemed to me a disgrace. I was on the point of giving vent to my indignation; but it occurred to me, luckily, just in time that I should only be quite superfluously making a fool of myself if I did. Nothing is more ridiculous than a scene of jealousy, particularly when the scene is made by somebody who has no right to make it and on no grounds whatever. I held my tongue. My indignation against Rodney died down; I was able to laugh at myself. But driving southward through the slums of Camden Town, I looked attentively at Grace and found her more than ordinarily charming, desirable even. I would have liked to tell her so and, telling, kiss her. But I lacked the necessary impudence; I felt diffident of my capacity to carry the amorous undertaking through to a successful issue. I said nothing, risked no gesture. But I decided, when the time should come for us to part, that I would kiss her hand. It was a thing I had never done before. At the last moment, however, it occurred to me that she might imagine that, in kissing her hand, I was only stupidly imitating Rodney Clegg. I was afraid she might think that his example had emboldened me. We parted on the customary handshake.

Four or five weeks after our visit to Rodney's studio, I went abroad for a six months' stay in France and Germany. In the interval, Grace and Rodney had met twice, the first time in my flat, for tea, the second at her house, where she had asked us both to lunch. Rodney was brilliant on both occasions. A little too brilliant indeed – like a smile of false teeth, I thought. But Grace was dazzled. She had never met any one like this before. Her admiration delighted Rodney.

'Intelligent woman,' was his comment, as we left her house together after lunch.

A few days later I set out for Paris.

'You must promise to write,' said Grace in a voice full of sentiment when I came to say good-bye.

I promised, and made her promise too. I did not know exactly why we should write to one another or what we would write about; but it seemed, none the less, important that we should write. Letter-writing has acquired a curious sentimental prestige which exalts it, in the realm of friendship, above mere conversation; perhaps because we are less shy at long range than face to face, because we dare to say more in written than in spoken words.

It was Grace who first kept her promise.

'My dear Dick,' she wrote. 'Do you remember what you said about Mozart? That his music seems so gay on the surface – so gay and careless; but underneath it is sad and melancholy, almost despairing. I think life is like that, really. Everything goes with such a bustle; but what's it all for? And how sad, how sad it is! Now you mustn't flatter yourself by imagining that I feel like this just because you happen to have gone away—though as a matter of fact I *am* sorry you aren't here to talk about music and people and life and so forth. No, don't flatter yourself; because I've really felt like this for years, almost for ever. It's so to speak, the bass of my music, this feeling; it throbs along all the time, regardless of what may be happening in the treble. Jigs, minuets, mazurkas, Blue Danube waltzes; but the bass remains the same. This isn't very good counterpoint, I

· know; but you see what I mean? The children have just left me, yelling. Phyllis has just smashed that hideous Copenhagen rabbit Aunt Eleanor gave me for Christmas. I'm delighted, of course; but I mayn't say so. And in any case, why must they always act such knockabouts? Sad, sad. And Lecky's *History of European Morals*, that's sadder still. It's a book I can never find my place in. Page 100 seems exactly the same as page 200. No clue. So that – you know how conscientious I am – I always have to begin again at the beginning. It's very discouraging. I haven't the spirit to begin again, yet again, this evening. I write to you instead. But in a moment I must go and dress for dinner. John's partner is coming; surely no man has a right to be so bald. And Sir Walker Magellan, who is something at the Board of Trade and makes jokes; with Lady M —, who's *so* affectionate. She has a way of kissing me, suddenly and intently, like a snake striking. And she spits when she talks. Then there's Molly Bone, who's so nice; but why can't she get married? And the Robsons, about whom there's nothing to say. Nothing whatever. Nothing, nothing, nothing. That's how I feel about it all. I shall put on my old black frock and wear no jewels. Good-bye. GRACE.'

Reading this letter, I regretted more than ever my lack of impudence and enterprise in the taxi, that day we had driven down from Rodney's studio. It seemed to me, now, that the impudence would not have been resented.

I returned a letter of consolation; wrote again a week later; again ten days after that; and again, furiously, after another fortnight. A letter at last came back. It smelt of sandalwood and the stationery was pale yellow. In the past, Grace's correspondence had always been odourless and white. I looked and sniffed with a certain suspicion; then unfolded and read.

'I am surprised, my good Dick,' the letter began, 'that you don't know us better. Haven't you yet learned that we

women don't like the sound of the words Must and Ought?
We can't abide to have our sense of duty appealed to. That
was why I never answered any of your impertinent letters.
They were too full of "you must write", and "you promised". What do I care what I promised? That was long
ago. I am a different being now. I have been thousands of
different beings since then – reborn with each caprice.
Now, at last, I choose, out of pure grace and kindness, to
relent. Here's a letter. But beware of trying to bully me
again; don't ever attempt to blackmail my conscience. I
may be crueller next time. This is a warning.

'Were you trying, with your descriptions of diversions
and entertainments, to make me envious of your Paris? If
so, you haven't succeeded. We have our pleasures here too
– even in London. For example, the most exquisite masked
ball a few days since. Like Longhi's Venice or Watteau's
Cythera – and at moments, let me add, towards the end of
the evening, almost like Casanova's Venice, almost like the
gallant, *grivois* Arcadia of Boucher. But hush! It was in
Chelsea; I'll tell you no more. You might come bursting in
on the next dance, pulling a long face because the band
wasn't playing Bach and the dancers weren't talking about
the "Critique of Pure Reason". For the fact is, my poor
Dick, you're too solemn and serious in your pleasures. I
shall really have to take you in hand, when you come back.
You must be taught to be a little lighter and more fantastic.
For the truth about you is that you're absurdly Victorian.
You're still at the Life-is-real-life-is-earnest, Low-living-
and-high-thinking stage. You lack the courage of your in-
stincts. I want to see you more frivolous and sociable, yes,
and more gluttonous and lecherous, my good Dick. If I
were as free as you are, oh, what an Epicurean I'd be!
Repent of your ways, Dick, before it's too late and you're
irrecoverably middle-aged. No more. I am being called
away on urgent pleasure. GRACE.'

I read through this extraordinary epistle several times. If the untidy, illegible writing had not been so certainly Grace's, I should have doubted her authorship of the letter. That sham *dix-huitième* language, those neorococo sentiments – these were not hers. I had never heard her use the words 'caprice' or 'pleasure'; she had never generalised in that dreadfully facile way about 'we women'. What, then, had come over the woman since last she wrote? I put the two letters together. What could have happened? Mystery. Then, suddenly, I thought of Rodney Clegg, and where there had been darkness I saw light.

The light, I must confess, was extremely disagreeable to me, at any rate in its first dawning. I experienced a much more violent return of that jealousy which had overtaken me when I heard Grace expressing her admiration of Rodney's character and talents. And with the jealousy a proportionately violent renewal of my desires. An object hitherto indifferent may suddenly be invested in our eyes with an inestimable value by the mere fact that it has passed irrevocably out of our power into the possession of someone else. The moment that I suspected Grace of having become Rodney's mistress I began to imagine myself passionately in love with her. I tortured myself with distressing thoughts of their felicity; I cursed myself for having neglected opportunities that would never return. At one moment I even thought of rushing back to London, in the hope of snatching my now suddenly precious treasure out of Rodney's clutches. But the journey would have been expensive; I was luckily short of money. In the end I decided to stay where I was. Time passed and my good sense returned. I realised that my passion was entirely imaginary, home-made, and self-suggested. I pictured to myself what would have happened if I had returned to London under its influence. Burning with artificial flames, I should have burst dramatically into Grace's presence, only to discover, when I was actually with her, that I was not in love with her at all. Imaginary love can only flourish at a distance from its object; reality confines the fancy and puts it in its place. I had imagined myself unhappy because Grace had given herself to Rodney; but the situation, I perceived, would have been infinitely more distressing if I had returned, had succeeded in capturing her for myself, and then discovered that, much as I liked and charming as I found her, I did not love her.

It was deplorable, no doubt, that she should have been taken in by a charlatan like Rodney; it was a proof of bad taste on her part that she had not preferred to worship me, hopelessly, with an unrequited passion. Still, it was her business and in no way mine. If she felt that she could be happy with Rodney, well then, poor idiot! let her be happy. And so on. It was with reflections such as these that I solaced myself back into the indifference of a mere spectator. When Herbert turned up a few days later at my hotel, I was able to ask him, quite without agitation, for news of Grace.

'Oh, she's just the same as usual,' said Herbert.

Crass fool! I pressed him. 'Doesn't she go out more than she used to?' I asked. 'To dances and that sort of thing? I had heard rumours that she was becoming so social.'

'She may be,' said Herbert. 'I hadn't noticed anything in particular.'

It was hopeless. I saw that if I wanted to know anything, I should have to use my own eyes and my own judgment. Meanwhile, I wrote to tell her how glad I was to know that she was happy and amusing herself. She replied with a long and very affected essay about 'pleasures'. After that, the correspondence flagged.

A few months later – I had just returned to London – there was a party at Rodney's studio, at which I was present. Rodney's latest masterpiece looked down from an

easel set up at the end of the long room. It was an amus-
ingly indecent pastiche of the Douanier Rousseau. 'Wedding', the composition was called; and it represented a
nuptial party, the bride and bridegroom at the centre, the
relatives standing or sitting round them, grouped as though
before the camera of a provincial photographer. In the
background a draped column, palpably cardboard; a rustic
bridge; fir-trees with snow and, in the sky, a large pink
dirigible. The only eccentric feature of the picture was that,
while the bridegroom and the other gentlemen of the party
were duly clothed in black Sunday best, the ladies, except
for boots and hats, were naked. The best critics were of
opinion that 'Wedding' represented the highest flight, up to
date, of Rodney's genius. He was asking four hundred and
fifty pounds for it; a few days later, I was told, he actually
got them.

Under the stonily fixed regard of the nuptial group Rodney's guests were diverting themselves. The usual people
sat, or stood, or sprawled about, drinking white wine or
whisky. Two of the young ladies had come dressed identi-
cally in the shirts and black velvet trousers of Gavarni's
débardeurs. Another was smoking a small briar pipe. As I
came into the room I heard a young man saying in a loud,
truculent voice : 'We're absolutely modern, we are. Anybody can have my wife, as far as I'm concerned. I don't
care. She's free. And I'm free. That's what I call modern.'

I could not help wondering why he should call it modern.
To me it rather seemed primeval – almost pre-human.
Love, after all, is the new invention; promiscuous lust
geologically old-fashioned. The really modern people, I reflected, are the Brownings.

I shook hands with Rodney.

'Don't be too contemptuous of our simple London
pleasures,' he said.

I smiled; it amused me to hear on his lips the word with

which Grace's letters had made me so familiar.

'As good as the pleasures of Paris, any day,' I answered, looking round the room. Through the crowd, I caught sight of Grace.

With an air of being spiritually and physically at home, she was moving from group to group. In Rodney's rooms, I could see, she was regarded as the hostess. The mistress of the house, in the left-handed sense of the word. (A pity, I reflected, that I could not share that little joke with Rodney; he would have enjoyed it so much, about anyone else.) In the intervals of conversation I curiously observed her; I compared the Grace before my eyes with the remembered image of Grace as I first knew her. That trick of swaying as she walked – rather as a serpent sways to the piping of the charmer – that was new. So, too, was the carriage of the hands – the left on the hip, the right held breast-high, palm upwards, with a cigarette between the fingers. And when she put the cigarette to her lips, she had a novel way of turning up her face and blowing the smoke almost perpendicularly into the air, which was indescribably dashing and Bohemian. Haughty milady had vanished to be replaced by a new kind of aristocrat – the gay, terrible, beyond-good-and-evil variety.

From time to time snatches of her talk came to my ears. Gossip, invariably scandalous; criticisms of the latest exhibitions of pictures; recollections or anticipations of 'perfect parties' – these seemed to be the principal topics, all of them, in Grace's mouth, quite unfamiliar to me. But the face, the vague-featured face of the nice but ugly little girl, the bewildered eyes, the occasional smile, so full of sweetness and a dim benevolence – these were still the same. And when I overheard her airily saying to one of her new friends of I know not what common acquaintance, 'She's almost too hospitable – positively keeps open bed, you know,' I could have burst out laughing, so absurdly incongruous with the face, the eyes, the smile, so palpably borrowed and not her own did the smart words seem.

Meanwhile, at the table, Rodney was doing one of his famous 'non-stop' drawings – a figure, a whole scene rendered in a single line, without lifting the pencil from the paper. He was the centre of an admiring group.

'Isn't it too enchanting?'

'Exquisite!'

'Ravishing!'

The words exploded laughingly all around him.

'There,' said Rodney, straightening himself up.

The paper was handed round for general inspection. Incredibly ingenious it was, that drawing, in a single sinuous line, of a fight between a bull and three naked female toreros. Every one applauded, called for more.

'What shall I do next?' asked Rodney.

'Trick-cyclists,' somebody suggested.

'Stale, stale,' he objected.

'Self-portrait.'

Rodney shook his head. 'Too vain.'

'Adam and Eve.'

'Or why not Salmon and Gluckstein?' suggested someone else.

'Or the twelve Apostles.'

'I have it,' shouted Rodney, waving his pencil. 'King George and Queen Mary.'

He bent over his scribbling block, and in a couple of minutes had produced a one-line portrait of the Britannic Majesties. There was a roar of laughter.

It was Grace who brought me the paper. 'Isn't he wonderful?' she said, looking at me with a kind of eager anxiety, as though she were anxious to have my commendation of her choice, my sacerdotal benediction.

I had only seen her once, for a brief unintimate moment, since my return. We had not mentioned Rodney's name.

But this evening, I saw, she was taking me into her confidence; she was begging me, without words, but none the less eloquently, to tell her that she had done well. I don't exactly know why she should have desired my blessing. She seemed to regard me as a sort of old, grey-haired, avuncular Polonius. (Not a very flattering opinion, considering that I was several years younger than Rodney himself.) To her, my approval was the approval of embodied wisdom.

'Isn't he wonderful?' she repeated. 'Do you know of any other man now living, except perhaps Picasso, who could improvise a thing like that? For fun – as a game.'

I handed the paper back to her. The day before, as it happened, finding myself in the neighbourhood, I had dropped in on Rodney at his studio. He was drawing when I entered, but, seeing me, had closed his book and come to meet me. While we were talking, the plumber called and Rodney had left the studio to give some instructions on the spot, in the bathroom. I got up and strolled about the room, looking at the latest canvases. Perhaps too inquisitively, I opened the notebook in which he had been drawing when I entered. The book was blank but for the first three or four pages. These were covered with 'non-stop' drawings. I counted seven distinct versions of the bull with the female toreros, and five, a little corrected and improved each time, of King George and Queen Mary. I wondered at the time why he should be practising this peculiar kind of art; but feeling no urgent curiosity about the subject, I forgot, when he came back, to ask him. Now I understood.

'Extraordinary,' I said to Grace, as I returned her the paper. 'Really extraordinary!'

Her smile of gratitude and pleasure was so beautiful that I felt quite ashamed of myself for knowing Rodney's little secret.

Grace and I both lived in Kensington; it was I who drove her home when the party was over.

'Well, that was great fun,' I said, as we settled into the taxi.

We had driven past a dozen lamp-posts before she spoke.

'You know, Dick,' she said, 'I'm so happy.'

She laid her hand on my knee; and for lack of any possible verbal comment, I gently patted it. There was another long silence.

'But why do you despise us all?' she asked, turning on me suddenly.

'But when did I ever say I despised you?' I protested.

'Oh, one needn't say such things. They proclaim themselves.'

I laughed, but more out of embarrassment than because I was amused. 'A woman's intuition, what?' I said facetiously. 'But you've really got too much of it, my dear Grace. You intuit things that aren't there at all.'

'But you despise us all the same.'

'I don't. Why should I?'

'Exactly. Why should you?'

'Why?' I repeated.

'For the sake of what?' she went on quickly. 'And in comparison with what do you find our ways so despicable? I'll tell you. For the sake of something impossible and inhuman. And in comparison with something that doesn't exist. It's stupid, when there's real life with all its pleasures.' That word again – Rodney's word! It seemed to me that she had a special, almost unctuous tone when she pronounced it. 'So delightful. So rich and varied. But you turn up your nose and find it all vapid and empty. Isn't it true?' she insisted.

'No,' I answered. I could have told her that life doesn't necessarily mean parties with white wine and whisky, social stunts, fornication and chatter. I might have told her; but however studiously I might have generalised, it was obvious that my remarks would be interpreted (quite correctly, in-

deed) as a set of disparaging personalities. And I didn't
want to quarrel with Grace or offend her. And besides,
when all was said, I did go to Rodney's parties. I was an
accomplice. The knockabout amused me; I found it hard
to deny myself the entertainment. My objection was only
theoretical; I did what I denounced. I had no right to strike
pontifical attitudes and condemn. 'No, of course it isn't
true,' I repeated.

Grace sighed. 'Of course, I can't really expect you to
admit it,' she said. 'But bless you,' she added with a forced
and unnatural gaiety, 'I don't mind being despised. When
one is rich, one can afford the luxury of being disapproved
of. And I am rich, you know. Happiness, pleasures – I've
got everything. And after all,' she went on, with a certain
argumentative truculence in her voice, 'I'm a woman.
What do I care for your ridiculous masculine standards. I
do what I like, what amuses me.' The quotation from
Rodney rang a little false, I thought. There was a silence.

I wondered what John Peddley thought about it all, or
whether any suspicion of what was happening had yet
penetrated the horny carapace of his insensitiveness.

And as though she were answering my unspoken question, Grace began again with a new seriousness. 'And
there's my other life, parallel. It doesn't make any difference to that, you know. Doesn't touch it. I like John just as
much as I did. And the children of course.'

There was another long silence. All at once, I hardly
know why, I felt profoundly sad. Listening to this young
woman talking about her lover, I wished that I too were in
love. Even the 'pleasures' glittered before my fancy with a
new and tempting brilliance. My life seemed empty. I
found myself thinking of the melody of the Countess's
song in *Figaro: Dove sono i bei momenti di dolcezza e di
piacer?*

That Grace's adventure made little or no difference to

her other life, I had an opportunity of judging for myself in the course of a subsequent week-end with the Peddleys in Kent. John was there – 'in great form', as he put it himself; and Grace, and the children, and Grace's father and mother. Nothing could have been more domestic and less like Rodney's party, less 'modern'. Indeed, I should be justified in writing that last word without its inverted commas. For there was something extraordinarily remote and uncontemporary about the whole household. The children were geologically remote in their childishness – only a little beyond the pithecanthropus stage. And Peddley was like a star, separated from the world by the unbridgeable gulfs of his egoism and unawareness. The subjects of his discourse might be contemporary; but spiritually, none the less, he was timeless, an inhabitant of blank and distant space. As for Grace's parents, they were only a generation away; but goodness knows, that was far enough. They had opinions about socialism and sexual morality, and gentlemen, and what ought or ought not to be done by the best people – fixed, unalterable, habit-ingrained and by now almost instinctive opinions that made it impossible for them to understand or forgive the contemporary world.

This was especially true of Grace's mother. She was a big, handsome woman of about fifty-five, with the clear ringing voice of one who has been accustomed all her life to give orders. She busied herself in doing good works and generally keeping the poor in their places. Unlike her husband, who had a touch of Peddley's star-like remoteness, she was very conscious of contemporaneity and, consequently, very loud and frequent in her denunciations of it.

Grace's father, who had inherited money, filled his leisure by farming a small estate unprofitably, sitting on committees, and reading Persian, an acquirement of which, in his quiet way, he was very proud. It was a strangely disinterested hobby. He had never been to Persia and had not the slightest intention of ever going. He was quite uninterested in Persian literature or history, and was just as happy reading a Persian cookery book as the works of Hafiz or Rumi. What he liked was the language itself. He enjoyed the process of reading the unfamiliar letters, of looking up the words in the dictionary. For him, Persian was a kind of endlessly complicated jigsaw puzzle. He studied it solely for the sake of killing time and in order not to think. A dim, hopeless sort of man was Mr Comfrey. And he had an irritating way of looking at you over the top of his spectacles with a puzzled expression, as though he had not understood what you meant; which, indeed, was generally the case. For Mr Comfrey was very slow of mind and made up for his knowledge of Persian by the most extraordinary ignorance of almost all other subjects under the sun.

'Say that again,' he would say, when his incomprehension was too complete.

How strange, how utterly fantastic it seemed, that weekend. I felt as though I had been suddenly lifted out of the contemporary world and plunged into a kind of limbo.

John Peddley's latest subject was the Einstein theory.

'It's so simple,' he assured us the first evening, between the soup and the fish. 'I don't pretend to be a mathematician or anything like one; but I understand it perfectly. All that it needs is a little common sense.' And for the next half-hour the common sense came braying out, as though from the mouth of a trombone.

Grace's father looked at him dubiously over the top of his spectacles.

'Say that again, will you?' he said, after every second sentence.

And John Peddley was only too delighted to oblige.

At the other end of the table, Grace and her mother were discussing the children, their clothes, characters, education, diseases. I longed to join in their conversation. But the simple domesticities were not for me. I was a man; John Peddley and the intellect were my portion. Reluctantly, I turned back towards my host.

'What I'd like you to explain,' Grace's father was saying, 'is just exactly how time can be at right angles to length, breadth, and thickness. Where precisely does it come in?' With two forks and a knife he indicated the three spatial dimensions. 'Where do you find room for another right angle?'

And John Peddley set himself to explain. It was terrible.

Meanwhile, at my other ear, Grace's mother had begun to talk about the undesirable neighbours who had taken the house next to theirs on Campden Hill. A man and a woman, living together, unmarried. And the garden behind the houses was the common property of all the householders. What a situation! Leaving Peddley and the old gentleman to find room for the fourth right angle, I turned definitively to the ladies. For my benefit, Grace's mother began the horrid story again from the beginning. I was duly sympathetic.

Once, for a moment, I caught Grace's eye. She smiled at me, she almost imperceptibly raised her eyebrows. That little grimace was deeply significant. In the first months of our friendship, I had often seen her in the company of her father and mother, and her bearing, on these occasions, had always impressed me. I had never met a young woman of the generation which had come to maturity during the war who was so perfectly at ease with her elders, so unconstrainedly at home in their moral and mental atmosphere as was Grace. She had taken her father and mother entirely for granted, had regarded their views of life as the obvious, natural views of every sane human being. That embarrassment which – in these days, more perhaps than at any other period – afflicts young people when in the presence of their

F

elders had never, so far as I had observed, touched Grace. This smile of apologetic and slightly contemptuous indulgence, this raising of the eyebrows, were symptomatic of a change. Grace had become contemporary, even (in inverted commas) 'modern'.

Outwardly, however, there was no change. The two worlds were parallel; they did not meet. They did not meet, even when Rodney came to dine *en famille*, even when John accompanied his wife to one of Rodney's less aggressively 'artistic' (which in inverted commas means very much the same as 'modern') evening parties. Or perhaps it would be truer to say that Rodney's world met John's, but did not meet Rodney's. Only if Rodney had been a Zulu and his friends Chinese would John have noticed that they were at all different from the people he was used to meeting. The merely spiritual differences which distinguished them were too small for his notice. He moved through life surrounded by his own atmosphere; only the most glaring lights could penetrate that half opaque and intensely refractive medium. For John, Rodney and his friends were just people, like everybody else; people who could be button-holed and talked to about the Swiss banking system and Einstein's theory, and the rationing of sugar. Sometimes, it was true, they seemed to him rather frivolous; their manners, sometimes, struck him as rather unduly brusque; and John had even remarked that they were sometimes rather coarse-spoken in the presence of ladies – or, if they happened to be ladies themselves, in the presence of gentlemen.

'Curious, these young people,' he said to me, after an evening at Rodney's studio. 'Curious.' He shook his head. 'I don't know that I quite understand them.'

Through a rift in his atmosphere he had caught a glimpse of the alien world beyond; he had seen something, not refracted, but as it really was. But John was quite incurious;

careless of its significance, he shut out the unfamiliar vision. 'I don't know what your opinion about modern art may be,' he went on, disappointing me of his comments on modern people. 'But what I always say is this.'

And he said it, copiously. Modern art became another gramophone record added to his repertory. That was the net result of his meeting with Rodney and Rodney's friends.

For the next few months I saw very little either of Grace or of Rodney. I had met Catherine, and was too busy falling in love to do or think of anything else. We were married towards the close of 1921, and life became for me, gradually, once more normal.

From the first Catherine and Grace were friends. Grace admired Catherine for her coolness, her quiet efficiency, her reliableness; admired and liked her. Catherine's affection for Grace was protective and elder-sisterly; and at the same time, she found Grace slightly comic. Affections are not impaired by being tempered with a touch of benevolent laughter. Indeed, I would almost be prepared to risk a generalisation and say that all true affections are tempered with laughter. For affection implies intimacy; and one cannot be intimate with another human being without discovering something to laugh at in his or her character. Almost all the truly virtuous characters in fiction are also slightly ridiculous; perhaps that is because their creators were so fond of them. Catherine saw the joke – the rather pathetic joke – of Grace. But she liked her none the less; perhaps, even, the more. For the joke was appealing; it was a certain childishness that raised the laugh.

At the time of my marriage, Grace was acting the eternally feminine part more fervently than ever. She had begun to dress very smartly and rather eccentrically, and was generally unpunctual; not very unpunctual (she was by nature too courteous for that), but just enough to be able to say that she was horribly late, but that she couldn't help it; it was in her nature – her woman's nature. She blamed Catherine for dressing too sensibly.

'You must be gayer in your clothes,' she insisted, 'more fantastic and capricious. It'll make you *feel* more fantastic. You think too masculinely.'

And to encourage her in thinking femininely, she gave her six pairs of white kid gloves, marvellously piped with coloured leather and with fringed and intricately scalloped gauntlets. But perhaps the most feminine and fantastic thing about them was the fact that they were several sizes too small for Catherine's hand.

Grace had become a good deal more loquacious of late and her style of conversation had changed. Like her clothes, it was more fantastic than in the past. The principle on which she made conversation was simple : she said whatever came into her head. And into that vague, irresponsible head of hers the oddest things would come. A phantasmagoria of images, changing with every fresh impression or as the words of her interlocutor called up new associations, was for ever dancing across her field of mental vision. She put into words whatever she happened to see at any given moment. For instance, I might mention the musician Palestrina.

'Yes, yes,' Grace would say, 'what a marvellous composer !' Then, reacting to the Italian reference, she would add in the same breath : 'And the way they positively *drink* the macaroni. Like those labels that come out of the mouth of caricatures. You know.'

Sometimes I did know. I skipped over the enormous ellipses in this allusive thinking and caught the reference. Sometimes, when the association of her ideas was too exclusively private, I was left uncomprehending. The new technique was rather disconcerting, but it was always amusing, in a way. The unexpectedness of her remarks, the very nonsensicality of them, surprised one into finding them witty.

As a child, Grace had been snubbed when she talked in this random, fantastic fashion. 'Talk sense,' her governesses had said severely, when she told them during the geography lesson that she didn't like South America because it looked like a boiled leg of mutton. 'Don't be silly.' Grace was taught to be ashamed of her erratic fancy. She tried to talk sense – sense as governesses understand it – found it very difficult, and relapsed into silence. Peddley was even more sensible, in the same style, than the governesses themselves; devastatingly sensible. He was incapable of understanding fancy. If Grace had ever told Peddley why she didn't like South America, he would have asked her to explain herself. And learning that it was the mutton-like shape of the continent on the map that prejudiced Grace against it, he would have given her statistics of South America's real dimensions, would have pointed out that it extended from the tropics almost into the antarctic circle, that it contained the largest river and some of the highest mountains in the world, that Brazil produced coffee and the Argentine beef, and that consequently, in actual fact, it was not in the very least like a boiled leg of mutton. With Peddley, Grace's only resources were laboriously talked sense or complete silence.

In Rodney's circle, however, she found that her gift of nonsense was appreciated and applauded. An enthusiast for the 'fantastic' and the 'feminine', Rodney encouraged her to talk at random, as the spirit of associative fancy might move her. Diffidently at first, Grace let herself go; her conversation achieved an immediate success. Her unstitched, fragmentary utterances were regarded as the last word in modern wit. People repeated her *bons mots*. A little bewildered by what had happened, Grace suddenly found herself in the movement, marching at the very head of the forces of contemporaneity. In the eighteenth century, when logic and science were the fashion, women tried to talk like the men. The twentieth century has reversed the process. Rodney did Grace the honour of appropriating to himself the happiest of her extravagances.

Success made Grace self-confident; and confident, she went forward triumphantly to further successes. It was a new and intoxicating experience for her. She lived in a state of chronic spiritual tipsiness.

'How stupid people are not to be happy !' she would say, whenever we discussed these eternal themes.

To Catherine, who had taken my place as a confidant – my place and a much more intimate, more confidential place as well – she talked above love and Rodney.

'I can't think why people manage to make themselves unhappy about love,' she said. 'Why can't everybody love gaily and freely, like us? Other people's love seems to be all black and clotted, like Devonshire cream made of ink. Ours is like champagne. That's what love ought to be like : champagne. Don't you think so?'

'I think I should prefer it to be like clear water,' said Catherine. To me, later on, she expressed her doubts. 'All this champagne and gaiety,' she said; 'one can see that Rodney is a young man with a most wholesome fear of emotional entanglements.'

'We all knew that,' I said. 'You didn't imagine, I suppose, that he was in love with her?'

'I hoped,' said Catherine.

'Because you didn't know Rodney. Now you do. Champagne – you have the formula. The problem is Grace.'

Was she really in love with him? Catherine and I discussed the question. I was of opinion that she was.

'When Rodney flutters off,' I said, 'she'll be left there, broken.'

Catherine shook her head. 'She only imagines she's in love,' she insisted. 'It's the huge excitement of it all that makes her happy; that, and the novelty of it, and her sense

of importance, and her success. Not any deep passion for
Rodney. She may think it's a passion – a champagnish passion, if you like. But it isn't really. There's no passion; only
champagne. It was his prestige and her boredom that made
her fall to him originally. And now it's her success and the
fun of it that make her stick to him.'

Events were to show that Catherine was right, or at least
more nearly right than I. But before I describe these events,
I must tell how it was that Kingham re-entered my world.

It was I who took the first step to end our ridiculous quarrel. I should have made the attempt earlier, if it had not
been for Kingham's absence from Europe. A little while
after our squabble he left, with a commission to write
articles as he went, first for North Africa and thence for the
further East. I heard of him once or twice from people who
had seen him at Tunis, at Colombo, at Canton. And I read
the articles, the admirably original articles, as they appeared at intervals in the paper which had commissioned
them. But direct communication with him I had none. I
did not write; for I was uncertain, to begin with, if my
letter would ever reach him. And in any case, even if we
had made up our quarrel by letter, what good would that
have been? Reconciliations across eight thousand miles of
space are never very satisfactory. I waited till I heard of his
return and then wrote him a long letter. Three days later
he was sitting at our dinner-table.

'This is good,' he said, 'this is very good.' He looked this
way and that, quickly taking in everything – the furniture,
the books, Catherine, me – with his bright, quick eyes.
'Definitely settled.'

'Oh, not so definitely as all that, let us hope.' I laughed
in Catherine's direction.

'I envy you,' he went on. 'To have got hold of something
fixed, something solid and absolute – that's wonderful.
Domestic love, marriage – after all, it's the nearest thing to

an absolute that we can achieve, practically. And it takes on more value, when you've been rambling round the world for a bit, as I have. The world proves to you that nothing has any meaning except in relation to something else. Good, evil, justice, civilisation, cruelty, beauty. You think you know what these words mean. And perhaps you do know, in Kensington. But go to India or China. You don't know anything there. It's uncomfortable at first; but then, how exciting ! And how much more copiously and multifariously you begin to live ! But precisely for that reason you feel the need for some sort of fixity and definition, some kind of absolute, not merely of the imagination, but in actual life. That's where love comes in, and domesticity. Not to mention God and Death and the Immortality of the Soul and all the rest. When you live narrowly and snugly, those things seem absurd and superfluous. You don't even appreciate your snugness. But multiply yourself with travelling, knock the bottom out of all your old certainties and prejudices and habits of thought; then you begin to see the real significance of domestic snugness, you appreciate the reality and importance of the other fixities.'

He spoke with all his old passionate eagerness. His eyes had the same feverish, almost unearthly brightness. His face, which had been smooth and pale when I saw it last, was burnt by the sun and lined. He looked more mature, tougher and stronger than in the past.

'Yes, I envy you,' he repeated.

'Then why don't you get married yourself?' asked Catherine.

Kingham laughed. 'Why not, indeed? You'd better ask Dick. He knows me well enough to answer, I should think.'

'No, tell us yourself,' I said.

Kingham shook his head. 'It would be a case of cruelty to animals,' he said enigmatically, and began to talk about something else.

'I envy you,' he said again, later that same evening, when Catherine had gone to bed and we were alone together. 'I envy you. But you don't deserve what you've got. You haven't earned your right to a fixed domestic absolute, as I have. I've realised, intimately and personally realised, the flux and the interdependence and the relativity of things; consequently I know and appreciate the meaning and value of fixity. But you – you're domestic just as you're moral; you're moral and domestic by nature, unconsciously, instinctively, without having known the opposites which give these attitudes their significance – like a worker bee, in fact; like a damned cabbage that just grows because it can't help it.'

I laughed. 'I like the way you talk about flux and relativity,' I said, 'when you yourself are the fixed, unchanging antithesis of these things. The same old Kingham ! Why, you're a walking fixity; you're the Absolute in flesh and blood. How well I know those dear old home truths, for example !'

'But that doesn't prevent their being true,' he insisted, laughing, but at the same time rather annoyed by what I had said. 'And besides, I *have* changed. My views about everything are quite different. A sensitive man can't go round the world and come back with the same philosophy of life as the one he started with.'

'But he can come back with the same temperament, the same habits of feeling, the same instinctive reactions.'

Kingham ran his fingers through his hair and repeated his petulant laughter. 'Well, I suppose he can,' he admitted reluctantly.

I was only too well justified in what I had said. A few days of renewed intimacy were enough to convince me that Kingham preserved all his old love of a scene, that he enjoyed as much as ever the luxury of a hot emotional bath. He burst in on me one morning, distracted with fury, to tell me about a violent quarrel he had had the previous evening with some insignificant young undergraduate – rather tipsy at that – who had told him (with considerable insight, I must admit, in spite of his tipsiness) that he, Kingham, was either insincere or hysterical.

'And the awful thing is that he may be right,' he added, when he had finished his story. 'Perhaps I *am* insincere.' Restlessly, he walked about the room. From time to time he withdrew a hand from the pocket into which it was deeply plunged and made a gesture, or ran the fingers through his hair. 'Perhaps I'm just a little comedian,' he went on, 'just a mouther of words, a ranter.' The self-laceration hurt him, but he enjoyed the pain. 'Do I really feel things deeply?' he went on speculating. 'Or do I just deceive myself into believing that I care? Is it all a mere lie?' The operation continued interminably.

The tipsy undergraduate had diagnosed insincerity or hysteria. It was in my power to relieve Kingham of his haunting fear of insincerity by assuring him that the second of these alternatives was the more correct. But I doubted the efficacy of the consolation; and besides I had no desire for a quarrel. I held my tongue.

I did not make Kingham known to Grace; for knowing that he had a passionate and rooted dislike of Rodney, I was afraid that, in spite of my preliminary warnings (or even precisely because of them, for the sake of creating an intolerably unpleasant situation) he might burst out, in Grace's presence, into some violent denunciation of her lover. It was a risk that was not worth running. And besides, I did not imagine that they would get on well together. We were intimate with both; but we kept them, so to speak, in separate water-tight compartments of our intimacy.

One day, when I came home to dinner, I was greeted by Catherine with a piece of news.

'Rodney's being unfaithful,' she said. 'Poor little Grace was here for tea today. She pretends not to mind – to be very modern and hard and gay about it. But I could see that she was dreadfully upset.'

'And who's the lucky lady?' I asked.

'Mrs Melilla.'

'A step up in the world.' I thought of the emeralds and the enormous pearls, which added lustre to the already dazzling Jewish beauty of Mrs Melilla. 'He'll be in the baronetcy and peerage soon.'

'What a pig!' said Catherine indignantly. 'I'm so dreadfully sorry for poor Grace.'

'But according to your theory, she isn't really in love with him.'

'No, she isn't,' said Catherine. 'Not *really*. But she thinks she is. And she'll think so much more, of course, now that he's leaving her. And besides, she has put so many of her eggs into his basket; this smashes them all. She'd committed herself body and soul to Rodney and Rodneyism. This affair with Rodney gave sense to her whole existence. Can't you see that?'

'Perfectly.' I remembered the days when Grace had seen herself as a musical critic and how cruelly I had murdered this comforting vision of herself by my little practical joke about the player of Rachmaninoff. A much more significant, much more intimately cherished dream was being murdered now.

She did her best, as Catherine had said, to be very 'modern' about it. I saw her a few days later at one of Rodney's parties; she was smoking a great many cigarettes, drinking glass after glass of white wine and talking more wildly than ever. Her dress was a close-fitting sheath of silver tissue, designed so as to make the wearer look almost naked. Fatigued with sleeplessness, her eyes were circled with dark, bruise-coloured rings; seen in conjunction with the bright, unnatural red of her rouged cheeks and lips, these dark circles looked as though they had been painted on with a fard, to heighten the brilliance of the eyes, to hint provocatively at voluptuous fatigues and amorous vigils. She was having a great success and her admirers had never been more numerous. She flirted outrageously with all of them. Even when she was talking with me, she seemed to find it necessary to shoot languorous sidelong glances; to lean towards me, as though offering her whole person to my desires. But looking at her, I could see, under the fard, only the face of the nice but rather ugly little girl; it seemed, I thought, more than usually pathetic.

Rodney sat down at the table to do his usual non-stop drawing.

'What shall it be?' he asked.

'Draw Jupiter and *all* his mistresses,' cried Grace, who was beginning to be rather tipsy. 'Europa and Leda and Semele and Danae,' she clapped her hands at each name, 'and Io and . . . Clio and Dio and Scio and Fi-fio and O-my-Eyeo. . . .'

The jest was not a very good one. But as most of Rodney's guests had drunk a good deal of wine and all were more or less intoxicated by the convivial atmosphere of a successful party, there was a general laugh. Grace began to laugh too, almost hysterically. It was a long time before she could control herself.

Rodney, who had made no preparations for improvising a picture of Jove's mistresses, found an excuse for rejecting the suggestion. He ended by drawing Mrs Eddy pursued by a satyr.

Deserted by Rodney, Grace tried to pretend that it was she who was the deserter. The role of the capricious wanton seemed to her more in harmony with the Rodneyan conception of the eternal feminine as well as less humiliating than that of the victim. Provocatively, promiscuously, she flirted.

In those first days of her despair she would, I believe, have accepted the advances of almost any tolerably presentable man. Masterman, for example, or Gane the journalist, or Levitski – it was one of those three, I surmised, judging by what I saw at the party, who would succeed to Rodney's felicity, and that very soon.

The day after the party, Grace paid another visit to Catherine. She brought a small powder-puff as a present. In return, she asked, though not in so many words, for comfort, advice, and above all for approval. In a crisis, on the spur of the moment, Grace could be rashly and unreflectingly impulsive; but when there was time to think, when it was a question of deliberately planning she was timorous, she hated to stand alone and take responsibilities. She liked to know that the part in which she saw herself was approved of by some trustworthy judge. The powder-puff was a bribe and an argument; an argument in favour of the eternal feminine, with all that that connoted, a bribe for the judge, an appeal to her affection, that she might approve of Grace's sentiments and conduct.

Grace put her case. 'The mistake people make,' she said, 'is getting involved, like the man on the music-halls who does that turn with the fly-paper. I refuse to be involved; that's my principle. I think one ought to be heartless and just amuse oneself, that's all. Not worry about anything else.'

'But do you think one can really be amused if one doesn't worry and takes things heartlessly?' asked Catherine. '*Really* amused, I mean. Happy, if you'll permit me to use an old-fashioned word. Can one be happy?' She thought of Levitski, of Gane and Masterman.

Grace was silent; perhaps she too was thinking of them. Then, making an effort, 'Yes, yes,' she said with a kind of obstinate, determined gaiety, 'one can; of course one can.'

I was at the Queen's Hall that afternoon. Coming out,

when the concert was over, I caught sight of Kingham in the issuing crowd.

'Come home for a late cup of tea and stay to dinner.'

'All right,' he said.

We climbed on to a bus and rode eastward. The sun had just set. Low down in the sky in front of us there were streaks of black and orange cloud, and above them a pale, watery-green expanse, limpid and calm up to the zenith. We rode for some time in silence, watching the lovely death of yet another of our days.

'It's all very well,' said Kingham at last, indicating these western serenities with a gesture of his fine, expressive hand, 'it's all very well, no doubt, for tired business men. Gives them comfort, I dare say; makes them feel agreeably repentant for the swindles they've committed during the day, and all that. Oh, it's full of uplift, I've no doubt. But I don't happen to be a tired business man. It just makes me sick.'

'Come, come,' I protested.

He wouldn't listen to me. 'I won't have Gray's "Elegy" rammed down my throat,' he said. 'What I feel like is *The Marriage of Heaven and Hell,* or *Zarathustra,* or the *Chants de Maldoror.*'

'Well, all that I can suggest' (I suggested it mildly) 'is that you should travel inside the bus and not look at the sunset.'

'Ass !' he said contemptuously.

We came in, to find Grace still sitting there, over the tea-cups, with Catherine. I was annoyed; still, there was nothing to be done about it. I introduced Kingham. All unconsciously, I was playing Pandarus for the second time.

My sources for the history of Grace's second love affair are tolerably copious. To begin with, I had opportunities of personally observing it, during a considerable part of its duration. I heard much, too, from Kingham himself. For

Kingham was not at all a discreet lover. He was as little capable of being secretive about this class of experiences as about any other. He simply had to talk. Talking renewed and multiplied the emotions which he described. Talk even created new emotions – emotions which he had not felt at the time but which it occurred to him, when he was describing the scene, to think that he ought to have felt. He had no scruples about projecting these *sentiments d'escalier* backwards, anachronistically, into his past experience, falsifying history for the sake of future drama. To his memories of a scene with Grace he would add emotional complications, so that the next scene might be livelier. It was in the heat of talk that his finest emendations of history occurred to him. The genuine, or at any rate the on the whole more genuine, story came to me through Catherine from Grace. It was to Catherine that, in moments of crisis (and this particular love affair was almost uninterruptedly a crisis) Grace came for solace and counsel.

The affair began with a misunderstanding. No sooner had Kingham entered the room than Grace, who had been talking quite simply and naturally with Catherine, put on her brazen 'modern' manner of the party and began with a kind of desperate recklessness to demand the attention and provoke the desires of the newcomer. She knew Kingham's name, of course, and all about him. In Rodney's circle it was admitted, albeit with some reluctance, that the man had talent; but he was deplored as a barbarian.

'He's one of those tiresome people,' I once heard Rodney complain, 'who will talk about their soul – and your soul, which is almost worse. Terribly Salvation Army. One wouldn't be surprised to see him on Sundays in Hyde Park telling people what they ought to do to be saved.'

At the sight of him, Grace had felt, no doubt, that it would be amusing to bring this curious wild animal to heel and make it do tricks. (It did not occur to her that it might be she who would be doing the tricks.) Kingham was a quarry worthy of any huntswoman. Still, I believe that she would have flirted as outrageously with almost any stranger. This provocative attitude of hers – an attitude which might be described as one of chronic and universal unfaithfulness was her retort to unkind fate and unfaithful Rodney. She wanted to capture a new lover – several lovers, even – in order to prove to Rodney, to the world at large and above all, surely, to herself, that she was modern, knew how to take love lightly and gaily, as the most exquisite of entertainments, and that, in a word, she didn't care a pin. In another woman, this promiscuous flirtatiousness might have been distasteful, detestable even. But there was, in Grace, a certain fundamental innocence that rendered what ought, by all the rules, to have been the most reprehensible of actions entirely harmless. Text-book moralists would have called her bad, when in fact she was merely pathetic and a trifle comic. The text-books assign to every action its place in the moral hierarchy; the text-book moralists judge men exclusively by their actions. The method is crude and unscientific. For in reality certain characters have power to sterilise a dirty action; certain others infect and gangrene actions which, according to the book, should be regarded as clean. The harshest judges are those who have been so deeply hypnotised by the spell of the text-book words, that they have become quite insensitive to reality. They can think only of words – 'purity', 'vice', 'depravity', 'duty'; the existence of men and women escapes their notice.

Grace, as I have said, possessed an innocence which made nonsense of all the words which might have been used to describe her actions. To any one but a text-book theorist it was obvious that the actions hardly mattered; her innocence remained intact. It was this same innocence which enabled her to give utterance – with perfect unconcern and a complete absence of daring affectation – to those scabrous sentiments, those more than scientific expressions which were almost *de rigueur* in the conversation of Rodney's circle. In a foreign language one can talk of subjects, one can unconcernedly use words, the uttering, the mention of which in one's native idiom would horribly embarrass. For Grace, all these words, the most genuinely Old English, all these themes, however intimately connected by gossip with the names of known men and women, were foreign and remote. Even the universal language of coquettish gestures was foreign to her; she acted its provocations and innuendoes with a frankness which would have been shameless, if she had really known what they meant. Kingham entered the room; she turned on him at once all her batteries of looks and smiles – a bombardment of provocations. I knew Grace so well that, in my eyes, the performance seemed merely absurd. These smiles, these sidelong glances and flutteringly dropped eyelids, this teasing mockery by which she irritated Kingham into paying attention to her, struck me as wholly uncharacteristic of Grace and therefore ridiculous – above all, unconvincing. Yes, unconvincing. I could not believe that any one could fail to see what Grace was really like. Was it possible that Kingham didn't realise just as well as I did that she was, in spirit, as in features, just a nice little girl, pretending without much success – particularly in this role – to be grown up?

It seemed to me incredible. But Kingham was certainly taken in. He accepted her at her face value for this particular moment – as an aristocratically reckless hedonist in wanton search of amusement, pleasure, excitement, and power. To the dangerous siren he took her to be, Kingham reacted with a mixed emotion that was half angry contempt, half amorous curiosity. On principle, Kingham violently disapproved of professional *femmes fatales*, sirens, vampires – all women, in fact, who make love and the subjugation of lovers the principal occupation of their lives. He thought it outrageous that self-respecting and useful men should suddenly find themselves at the mercy of these dangerous and irresponsible beings. What perhaps increased his moral indignation was the fact that he himself was constantly falling a victim to them. Youth, vitality, strong personality, frank and unbridled vice had irresistible attractions for him. He was drawn sometimes to the vulgarest possessors of these characteristics. He felt it an indignity, a humiliation (and yet, who knows? perhaps with Kingham this sense of humiliation was only another attraction); but he was none the less unfailingly drawn. He resisted, but never quite firmly enough (that, after all, would have spoiled all the fun). He resisted, succumbed and was subjected. But it must be admitted that his love, however abject it might be in the first moment of his surrender, was generally a vengeance in itself. Kingham might suffer; but he contrived in most cases to inflict as much suffering as he received. And while he, with a part of his spirit at any rate, actually enjoyed pain, however acutely and genuinely felt, the tormentors whom he in his turn tormented were mostly quite normal young women with no taste for the pleasures of suffering. He got the best of it; but he regarded himself, none the less, as the victim, and was consequently in a chronic state of moral indignation.

This first meeting convinced Kingham that Grace was the sort of woman she wanted to persuade him (not to mention herself) that she was – a vampire. Like many persons of weak character and lacking in self-reliance, Grace was often extraordinarily reckless. Passive generally and acquiescent, she sometimes committed herself wildly to the most extravagant courses of action – not from any principle of decision, but because, precisely, she did not know what decision was, because she lacked the sense of responsibility, and was incapable of realising the irrevocable nature

of an act. She imagined that she could do things irresponsibly and without committing herself; and feeling no inward sense of commitment, she would embark on courses
of action which – externalised and become a part of the
great machine of the world – dragged her, sometimes
reluctant, sometimes willing, but always ingenuously surprised, into situations the most bewilderingly unexpected.
It was this irresponsible impulsiveness of a character lacking the power of making deliberate decisions (this coupled
with her fatal capacity for seeing herself in any role that
seemed, at the moment, attractive) that had made her at
one moment a socialist canvasser at the municipal elections;
at another, an occasional opium smoker in that sordid and
dangerous den near the Commercial Docks which Tim
Masterman used to frequent; at another, though she was
terrified of horses, a rider to hounds; and at yet another –
to her infinite distress; but having light-heartedly insisted
that she didn't know what modesty was, she couldn't draw
back – the model for one of Levitski's nudes. And if she
now threw herself at Kingham's head (just as, a few nights
before, she had thrown herself at Masterman's, at Gane's,
at Levitski's), it was irresponsibly, without considering what
might be the results of her action, without even fully realising that there would be any results at all. True, she saw
herself as a 'modern' young woman; and her abandonment
by Rodney had made her anxious, for the mere saving of
her face, to capture a new lover, quickly. And yet it would
be wrong to say that she had decided to employ coquettish
provocations in order to get what she wanted. She had not
decided anything; for decision is deliberate and the fruit of
calculation. She was just wildly indulging in action, in
precisely the same way as she indulged in random speech,
without thinking of what the deeds or the words committed
her to. But whereas logical inconsistencies matter extremely
little and false intellectual positions can easily be aban-

doned, the effects of action or of words leading to action are not so negligible. For action commits what is much more important than the intellect – the body. To get the bodily self out of a false position is a difficult and often painful business. Grace, the indecisive, the all too easily and lightly moved to action, had often found it so to her cost. But that did not prevent her from repeating her mistake. Experience never does.

Kingham, as I have said, took her for what she irresponsibly wanted him to believe she was. He was duly provoked by what had been meant to be provocative. To this sort of amorous teasing he was extraordinarily susceptible. So much so, indeed, that his interest in Grace was no great tribute to her style. It was enough that a woman should exhibit a certain lively, vampirish interest in him; Kingham was almost certain to succumb to the attack. I remember one occasion in Paris when he was positively swept off his feet by the shrill, metallic sallies of an American chorus-girl from the Folies Bergère.

This first impression of Grace – as a 'modern', dangerously provocative, actively wanton vampire – persisted in Kingham's mind and no evidence to the contrary could obliterate it. In the course of their first meeting, he had taken up his emotional attitude towards her; and the attitude once taken, he would not shift his ground, however palpable the proofs that he was wrong. Whether he ceased to be able to use his intelligence and became incapable of recognising the facts that would have upset his prejudices, or whether he deliberately shut his eyes to what he did not wish to see, I do not exactly know. A powerful emotion had the double effect, I surmise, of rendering him at one and the same time stupid and most ingeniously perverse.

'I think there's something really devilish about the women of this generation,' he said to me, in his intense, emphatic way, some two or three days later. 'Something devilish,' he repeated, 'really devilish.' It was a trick of his, in writing as well as in speech, to get hold of a word and, if he liked the sound of it, work it to death.

I laughed. 'Oh, come,' I protested. 'Do you find Catherine, for example, so specially diabolic?'

'She isn't of this generation,' Kingham answered. 'Spiritually, she doesn't belong to it.'

I laughed again; it was always difficult arguing with Kingham. You might think you had him cornered; you raised your logical cudgel to smash him. But while you were bringing it down, he darted out from beneath the stroke through some little trap door of his own discovery, clean out of the argument. It was impossible to prove him in the wrong, for the simple reason that he never remained long enough in any one intellectual position to be proved anything.

'No, not Catherine,' he went on, after a little pause. 'I was thinking of that Peddley woman.'

'Grace?' I asked in some astonishment. 'Grace devilish?'

He nodded. 'Devilish,' he repeated with conviction. The word, I could see, had acquired an enormous significance for him. It was the core round which, at the moment, all his thoughts and feelings were crystallising. All his universe was arranging itself in patterns round the word 'devilish', round the idea of devilishness in general, and Grace's devilishness in particular.

I protested. 'Of all the un-devilish people I've ever known,' I said, 'Grace seems to me the most superlatively so'.

'You don't know her,' he retorted.

'But I've known her for years.'

'Not really known,' insisted Kingham, diving through another of his little trap doors out of the argument. 'You've never inspired her with one of her devilish concupiscences.' (I thought of Grace and could not help smiling; the smile exasperated Kingham.) 'Grin away,' he said. 'Imagine you're omniscient, if it gives you any pleasure. All I say is this : she's never tried to hunt you down.'

'I suppose you mean that she was rather stupidly flirtatious the other evening,' I said.

Kingham nodded. 'It was devilish,' he said softly, more for himself than for me. 'Devilish concupiscence.'

'But I assure you,' I went on, 'that business the other night was all mere silliness. She's childish, not devilish. She still sees herself in terms of Rodney Clegg, that's all. And she wants to pretend, now that he's deserted her, that she doesn't care. I'm not sure, indeed, that she doesn't want to make us believe that it was she who deserted him. That's why she wants to get hold of another lover quickly – for the sake of her prestige. But as for devilishness – why, the idea's simply absurd. She isn't definite enough to be a devil. She's just what circumstances and her imagination and other people happen to make her. A child, that's all.'

'You may think you know her,' Kingham persisted obstinately, 'but you don't. How can you, if you've never been hunted by her?'

'Bosh !' I said impatiently.

'I tell you she's devilish,' he insisted.

'Then why on earth did you accept her invitation to lunch with such alacrity?'

'There are things that are unescapable,' he answered oracularly.

'I give you up,' I said, shrugging my shoulders. The man exasperated me. 'The best thing you can do,' I added, 'is to go to your devil and be damned as quickly as possible.'

'That's exactly where I am going,' he said. And as though I had reminded him of an appointment, Kingham looked at his watch. 'And by God,' he added, in a different voice, 'I shall have to take a taxi, if I'm to get there in time.'

Kingham looked deeply put out; for he hated parting with money unnecessarily. He was tolerably well off now;

but he still preserved the habits of prudence, almost of avarice, which he had acquired, painfully, in the days of his lower-middle-class boyhood and his poverty-stricken literary novitiate. He had asked Grace to dine with him in Soho; that had already cost him an effort. And now he was going to be compelled to take a taxi, so as to be in time to pay for the dinner. The thought of it made him suffer. And suffering for her sake, suffering a mean, unavowable pain for which he could not hope to get any sympathy, even his own, he found the ultimate cause of it, Grace, all the more devilish.

'Unescapable,' he repeated, still frowning, as he put on his hat to go. There was an expression positively of ferocity on his face. 'Unescapable.' He turned and left me.

'Poor Grace!' I was thinking, as I closed the front door and walked back to my study. It was just as unescapable for her as for Kingham. And I knew Kingham; my sympathies were all with Grace.

I was quite right, as it turned out, in according my sympathies as I did. For if any one ever needed, ever deserved sympathy, it was poor Grace, during those deplorable months of 1922. She fell in love with Kingham – fell in love, though it was the third time she had given herself, for the first, the very first time in her life, painfully, desperately, insanely. She had proposed to herself a repetition of her affair with Rodney. It was to be all charmingly perverse dalliances, with champagne and sandwiches and lightly tender conversation in the intervals; and exquisite little letters in the *dix-huitième* manner; and evening parties; and amusing escapades. That was what it had been with Rodney. He made this kind of love, it must be admitted, with real style; it was charming. Grace imagined that she would make it in just the same way with Rodney's successor. And so she might have, more or less, if the successor had been Levitski, or Masterman, or Gane. But the successor was Kingham. The choice was fatal; but the worst results of it might have been avoided if she had not loved him. Unloving, she might simply have left him when he made things too insupportable. But she did love him and, in love, she was utterly at his mercy.

Kingham had said that the thing was unescapable; and if for him it was so, that was due to the need he perversely felt of giving himself over periodically to strong emotions, the need of being humiliated and humiliating, of suffering and making other people suffer. What he had always loved was the passion itself, not the women who were the cause or excuse of it. These occasional orgies of passion were necessary to him, just as the periodical drinking bout is necessary to the dipsomaniac. After a certain amount of indulgence, the need was satisfied and he felt quite free to detach himself from the lover who had been dear to him only as the stimulator of his emotions, not for her own sake. Kingham could satisfy his craving; it was an appetite that could be quenched by indulgence. But Grace's desire was one of those desperate, hopeless desires that can only be assuaged by a kind of miracle. What she desired was nothing less than to unite herself wholly with another being, to know him through and through and to be made free of all his secrets. Only the all but miraculous meeting of two equal loves, two equally confiding temperaments can bring fulfilment to that longing. There was no such meeting here.

Kingham made a habit of telling all his acquaintances, sooner or later, what he thought of them – which was invariably disagreeable. He called this process a 'clearing of the atmosphere'. But in point of fact, it never cleared anything; it obscured and made turbid, it created thunder in clear skies. Kingham might not admit the fact; but this was, none the less, precisely what he intended should happen. Clear skies bored him; he enjoyed storms. But always, when he had succeeded in provoking a storm, he expressed a genuine astonishment at the inability of the world at large to tolerate frankness, however sincere, however manifestly for its own good. Hurt by his brutally plain speaking, his old friends were reproached for being hurt. Few of Kingham's loves or friendships had long survived the effects of his frankness. The affair with Grace was one of the exceptions.

From the very beginning, Kingham had found it necessary to 'clear the atmosphere'. Even at their first meeting, in our house, he was rather rude. Later on, he developed into a kind of Timon of Athens. Her frivolity, her voluptuary's philosophy of life, her heartlessness, her 'devilish concupiscence' – these were the characteristics about which he told her, with all the concentrated passion of which he was capable, what he indignantly thought.

I met him again, at the Queen's Hall, on the day after his dinner in Soho.

'I told her what I thought of her,' he let me know.

'And what did she think about what you thought?' I asked.

Kingham frowned. 'She seemed to be rather pleased than otherwise,' he answered. 'That's the devilish strength of these women. They simply glory in the things they ought to be ashamed of. It makes them impervious to anything decent. Impervious, and therefore utterly ruthless and unscrupulous.'

'How incorrigibly romantic you are !' I mocked at him.

Told–and very mildly, after all–what I thought of him, Kingham winced like a stung horse. Other people's frankness hurt him just as much as his hurt other people; perhaps more. The only difference was that he enjoyed being hurt.

'What nonsense !' he began indignantly.

His retort lasted as long as the interval and was only

drowned by the first blaring chords of the *Meistersinger* overture. Bottled up within compulsory silence, what were his emotions? It amused me to speculate. Various, emphatic, tirelessly unflagging and working themselves up into ever more and more clotted complications – were they not the spiritual counterpart of this music to which we were now listening? When the Wagnerian tumult was over, Kingham continued his interrupted protest.

'She seemed to be rather pleased.' That, according to Kingham, had been Grace's reaction to his home truths. I felt sure, on reflection, that he had observed her rightly. For Grace still saw herself in terms of Rodneyism – as 'modern' and 'eighteenth-century' (curious how these terms have come to be largely interchangeable) and what Rodney imagined to be 'eternally feminine'. Of course she would be pleased at finding that Kingham had accepted her at her own valuation – and not only accepted her valuation but even voluntarily outbidden it by adding devilishness to the modernity, eighteenth-centuriness, and eternal femininity which she had mostly – too modestly, as she now perceived – attributed to herself. She took Kingham's denunciations as compliments and smiled with unaffected pleasure when he talked to her of her vampire's ruthlessness, when he reproached her with her devilish concupiscence for the shuddering souls as well as the less reluctant flesh of her victims. In Rodney's circle a temperament was as much *de rigueur* as a train and ostrich feathers at Court. Grace saw herself as a prodigy of temperament; but she liked to have this vision of herself confirmed by outside testimony. Kingham's home truths convinced her that she had seen herself correctly. The more abusive Kingham became, the better pleased she was and the more she liked him. She felt that he was really taking her seriously as a frivolous woman, that he was appreciating her as she deserved. His appreciation heightened her confidence and, under the rain of his anathemas, she played her part with an easier grace, a more stylish perfection. The spectacle of Grace impertinently blossoming under what had been meant to blast exasperated Kingham. He abused her more violently; and the greater his violence, the more serenely airy her eternal, modern, eighteenth-century femininity.

Underneath, meanwhile, and almost unconsciously, Grace was falling in love with him.

I have seen Kingham in his relations with many men and women. To none of them was he merely indifferent. Either they detested him – and I have never known a man who had more and bitterer enemies – or else they loved him. (Many of the lovers, I may add, turned subsequently into haters.) When I analyse my own feelings towards him, I am forced to the conclusion that I myself was in some manner in love with him. For why should I, who knew him so well and how insufferable he could be and, indeed, generally was, why should I have put up with him, in spite of everything? And why should I always have made such efforts to patch up all our incessant quarrels? Why shouldn't I have allowed him to go to the devil, so far as I was concerned, a dozen times? or at least thankfully accepted the estrangement which followed our most violent squabble – the squabble over poor loutish Herbert – and allowed the separation to lengthen into permanency? The only explanation is that, like all those who did not loathe him, I was somehow in love with Kingham. He was in some way important for me, deeply significant and necessary. In his presence I felt that my being expanded. There was suddenly, so to speak, a high tide within me; along dry, sand-silted, desolate channels of my being life strongly, sparklingly flowed. And Kingham was the moon that drew it up across the desert.

All those whom we find sympathetic exercise, in a greater or less degree, this moon-like influence upon us, drawing up the tides of life till they cover what had been, in an antipathetic environment, parched and dead. But there are certain individuals who, by their proximity, raise a higher tide, and in a vastly greater number of souls, than the ordinary man or woman. Kingham was one of these exceptional beings. To those who found him sympathetic he was more sympathetic than other and much more obviously amiable acquaintances. There was a glow, a vividness, a brilliance about the man. He could charm you even when he was saying things with which you disagreed, or doing things which you disapproved. Even his enemies admitted the existence and the power of this brilliant charm. Catherine, who was not exactly an enemy, but who profoundly disliked his way of life and habits of mind, had to confess that, whenever he wanted and took the trouble to do so, he could silence, for the moment at any rate, all her prejudices and compel her, so long as he was actually there, in the room with her, to like him. Grace started with no prejudices against him – no prejudices, beyond the opinion, inherited from Rodney, that the man was a savage; and savages, after all, are more attractive than repellent. She was suggestible and easily swayed by stronger and more definite personalities than her own. It was not surprising that she should succumb to his charm to the extent of first liking the man and soon wildly loving him.

It was some little time, however, before Grace discovered that she loved him. In the first days of their intimacy, she was too busy playing the modern part to realise that she felt so un-Rodneyan an emotion. Love, the real insane thing, was out of harmony with the character she had assumed. It needed a sudden, startling shock to make her understand what she felt for him, to make her, in the same moment, forget to be 'modern' and 'feminine' in Rodney's sense of the terms, and become – what? I had meant to say 'herself'. But after all, can one be said to be 'oneself' when one is being transfigured or dolorously distorted by love? In love, nobody is himself; or if you prefer, romantically, to put it the other way round, nobody is really himself when he is not in love. It comes to very much the same thing. The difference between Grace in love and Grace out of it seemed all the wider, because it was the difference between a Rodneyan eternal female and a woman, and a Kingham-ised woman at that. For even in love, Grace saw herself in the part and saw herself, inevitably, in terms of her lover. Her Rodneyisms disappeared and were replaced by King-hamisms. She saw herself no longer as a modern young aristocrat, but as the primevally 'passional' incarnation ('passional' was one of Kingham's too favourite words) of her new lover's feminine ideal.

Their intimacy had lasted more than a month before Grace discovered the true nature of her feelings. King-ham's courtship had been unremitting. Denunciations of her devilishness had alternated with appeals to her to be-come his mistress. Grace took the denunciations as compli-ments and laughingly replied to them at random with any nonsense that came into her head. These airy irrelevant retorts of hers, which Rodney would have applauded as the height of modern wit, seemed to Kingham the very height of diabolism.

'She's like Nero,' he said to me one day, 'fiddling over Rome'.

He was Rome – the centre of the universe – in flames. Grace, having kindled, watched him burn and, in the face of his destruction, talked nonsense.

What was more, she would not quench his conflagration. In spite of the 'devilish concupiscence', which Kingham had attributed to her, she refused, during the first five or six weeks of their acquaintance, to become his mistress. She had captivated Kingham; that was sufficient to restore her self-confidence and that fantastic image of herself, as a success-ful modern siren, which Rodney's desertion had temporarily shattered. To have tumbled into his arms at once might, perhaps, have been in the *dix-huitième* part; but a certain native modesty prevented Grace from being perfectly consistent.

Kingham regarded her refusal to capitulate immediately as yet another piece of devilishness; according to his theory, she was exercising an unnatural self-control merely in order to torment him. A perverse taste for cruelty was added to his list of accusations. Grace was charmed by this soft impeachment.

Kingham's attacks had seemed to her, so far, more amusing than painful, more complimentary than insulting. She was still protected by the armour of her indifference. The realisation that she loved him was soon to strip her of that armour, and with every increase of that love, her naked spirit was to grow more tremulously sensitive to Kingham's assaults upon it.

The critical, the apocalyptic event took place in Kingham's rooms. It was a damp, hot afternoon of early summer. The sky was overcast when Grace arrived, and there was thunder in the air. She was wearing – the fact came out in her account to Catherine of the afternoon's events – she was wearing, for the first time, a brand-new frock from Paris; mouse-coloured, with two subtly harmonious, almost discordant, tones of red about the collar, and a repetition of the same colours at the cuffs and in a panel let into the skirt. Poiret, I think, was the inventor; and it was very modern and rather eccentrically elegant. In a word, it was a dress created for Rodney's mistress.

Grace, who was very much aware of herself in her clothes, had felt the incongruity most painfully, afterwards. The more so, since, when she came in, she was feeling so happy about her dress. She was thinking what a success it was and how elegant, how original the people who saw her in the street must find her. And she was wondering what effect the dress would have on Kingham. She hoped, she thought that he would like it.

In his way, Kingham was nearly as observant in the matter of clothes as Rodney. True, he had not Rodney's almost professional eye for style and cut and smartness. Rodney was a great couturier *manqué*. The fashionable dressmaker was visible in every picture he painted; he had mistaken his profession. Kingham's way of looking at clothes was different. His was the moralist's eye, not the couturier's. For him, clothes were symbols, the visible expressions of states of soul. Thus, Grace's slightly eccentric, very dashing elegance seemed to him the expressive symbol of her devilishness. He regarded her clothes as an efflorescence of her spirit. They were part of her, and she was directly and wholly responsible for them. It never seemed to strike him that tailors, dressmakers and advisory friends might share the responsibility. He took in Grace's frock at a glance.

'You've got a new dress on,' he said accusingly.

'Do you like it?' she asked.

'No,' said Kingham.

'Why not?'

'Why not?' he repeated. 'Well, I suppose it's because the thing's so expressive of you, because it suits you so devilishly well.'

'I should have thought that would be a reason for liking it.'

'Oh, it would be, no doubt,' said Kingham, 'it would be, if I could just regard you as a spectacle, as something indifferent, to be looked at – that's all – like a picture. But you're not indifferent to me, and you know it and you deliberately torture me. How can I be expected to like what makes you seem more devilishly desirable and so increases my torture?'

He glared at her ferociously. It was with an effort that Grace kept her own gaze steady before those bright, dark, expressive eyes. He advanced towards her and laid his two hands on her shoulders.

'Today,' he said, 'you're going to be my lover.'

Grace shook her head, smiling a capricious, eternally feminine smile.

'Yes, you are.' His grip on her shoulders tightened.

'No, I'm not,' Grace answered. She drew in her breath rather sharply; he was hurting her.

'I tell you, you are.'

They looked at one another, face close to face, enemies. Grace's heart violently beat.

'At one moment, I thought he was going to throttle me,' she told Catherine.

But she braved it out, and conquered.

Kingham withdrew his hands from her shoulders and turned away. He walked across to the other side of the room and, leaning against the wall in the embrasure of the window, looked out in silence at the grey sky.

Greatly relieved, Grace sat down on the divan. With a saucy and defiant movement that was, unfortunately, quite lost on Kingham's stubbornly presented back, she tucked up her feet under her. Opening her handbag, she took out her cigarette case, opened that in its turn, extracted a cigarette and lighted it – all very nonchalantly and deliberately. She was steadying her nerves to resist another attack – steadying her nerves and perhaps, at the same time, preparing to annoy him, when he should turn round, by the spectacle of her unconcernedness.

She had expected a repetition of the violences of a moment since, of the familiar denunciations of all the other days. She was not prepared to resist the new kind of attack which he now launched against her emotions. When at last – and she had more than half finished her cigarette before the long silence was broken – Kingham turned round and came towards her, she saw that he was weeping.

Kingham, as I have said, was no comedian. All that he professed to feel he felt, I am sure, genuinely. But he felt too easily and he was too fond of feeling. In situations where others would have exercised a restraint upon themselves, Kingham gave free rein to his emotions, or even actually roused and goaded them into a more violent and more prolonged activity. He needed no dervish tricks to work himself up, no dancing, no howling and drumming, no self-laceration. He could do the thing inwardly, by intense concentration on the object of his desire or hatred, or the cause of his pain or pleasure. He brooded over his loves or his grievances, making them seem more significant than they really were; he brooded, conjuring up in his imagination appropriate visions – of unpermitted raptures, when he was suffering from the pangs of desire; of scenes of insult, humiliation, rage, when he was angry with any one; of his own miserable self, when he desired to feel self-pity – himself, pictured as unloved, in solitude, utterly deserted, even dying. . . .

Long practice had made him an adept in the art of working up his emotions, of keeping himself uninterruptedly on the boil, so to speak, over a long period of time. In the course of these few brief weeks of his courtship, he had managed to convince himself that the interest he took in Grace was the most violent of passions and that he was suffering excruciatingly from her refusal – her devilish, her sadistic refusal – to be his mistress. Painfully and profoundly, he was enjoying it. The zest was still in the orgy; he felt no sense of satiety.

These tears were the result of a sudden and overwhelming feeling of self-pity, which had succeeded his mood of violence. He had perceived, all at once, that his violence was futile; it was absurd to suppose that he could shake or beat or throttle her into accepting him. He turned away in despair. He was alone, an outcast; nobody cared for him;

he was expending his spirit in a waste of shame – his precious, beautiful spirit – and there was no saving himself, the madness was too strong. He was done for, absolutely done for.

Standing there, in the embrasure of the window, he had brooded over his miseries, until his sense of them became all of a sudden intolerable. The tears came into his eyes. He felt like a child, like a tired child who abandons himself, hopelessly, to misery.

All the animation went out of his face; it became like the face of a dead man, frozen into a mask of quiet misery. Pale, ruddy-bearded, delicately featured, it was like the face of a dead or dying Christ in some agonising Flemish picture.

It was this dead Christ's face that now turned back towards Grace Peddley. This dead Christ's face – and it had been the face of Lucifer, burning with life and passion, menacingly, dangerously beautiful, that had turned away from her. The eyes, which had shone so brightly then, were almost shut, giving the face an appearance of blindness; and between the half-closed lids there was a slow welling out of tears.

The first sight of this suffering face startled her into a kind of terror. But the terror was succeeded almost at once by a great pity. That face, at once lifeless and suffering! And those tears! She had never seen a man shed tears before. She was overwhelmed by pity – by pity and, at the thought that it was all her fault, by a passion of repentance and self-abasement, by a desire to make amends. And at the same time she felt another and greater emotion, an emotion in which the pity and the repentance were included and from which they derived their strange intensity. It was the feeling that, for her, Kingham was the only person in the world who in any way mattered. It was love.

In silence he crossed the room, dropped down on his knees before the divan where Grace, her cigarette still smoking between her fingers, half sat, half reclined, frozen by astonishment into a statue of lolling modernity, and laying his head in her lap, silently sobbed.

The spell of Grace's immobility was broken. She bent forward over him, she caressed his hair. The gesture recalled to her attention the half-smoked cigarette; she threw it into the fire-place. Her fingers touched his scalp, the nape of his neck, his ears, his averted cheek.

'My darling,' she whispered, 'my darling. You mustn't cry. It's terrible when you cry.'

And she herself began to cry. For a long time they remained in the same position, Kingham kneeling, his face pressed against her knees, Grace bending over him, stroking his hair, both weeping.

Our thoughts and feelings are interdependent. It is only in language, not in fact, that they are separate and sharply differentiated. Some men are better mathematicians when they are in love than when they are out of it; some are worse. But in either case the emotion of love conditions the working of the intellect. Still more powerfully does it affect the other emotions, such as pity, courage, shame, fear of ridicule, which it enhances or diminishes as the case may be. It may be laid down as a general rule that the feeling of one strong emotion predisposes us automatically to the feeling of other emotions, however apparently incongruous with the first. Thus joy may predispose to pity and shame to anger. Anger and grief may both dispose to sensual desire. Violent disputes often end in love-making; and there are sometimes strange orgies over new-made graves, orgies, to the eye of the indifferent spectator, most unseemly, but which, as often as not, should be attributed less to a cynical lack of feeling than to its abundant presence. Grief creates a sense of loneliness, a desire in those who feel it to be comforted. At the same time, by throwing the whole personality into commotion, it renders the soul of the sufferer peculiarly susceptible to voluptuous influences and peculiarly unapt, in its state of disorganisation, to exercise the customary self-restraints; so that when the desired comforter appears, it sometimes happens (conditions of sex and age being propitious) that sympathy is transformed, not merely into love, but into desires demanding immediate satisfaction. Some such transformation took place now. Tears gave place to kisses less and less tearful, to caresses and embracements. There were languors and ecstatic silences.

'I love you, I love you,' Grace repeated, and was almost frightened by the vehemence of the new emotions, the intensity of the new and piercing sensations which she expressed in these old, blunted words. 'I love you.'

And Kingham kissed her and permitted himself, for the moment, to be happy without reserve or inward comment, without a touch of that anticipated afterthought which turns the present into history, even as it unrolls itself, and – criticising, appraising, judging and condemning – takes all the zest out of immediacy. He was simply happy.

The time came for them to part.

'I must go,' said Grace, sighing.

But the Grace who went was a different woman from the Grace who had come, two hours before. It was a worshipping, adoring Grace, a Grace made humble by love, a Grace for whom being modern and a *grande dame* and eighteenth-century and intellectually fashionable had suddenly ceased to have the slightest importance. Adjusting her hair before the glass, she was struck by the incongruity, the garish out-of-placeness of her new frock. Her love for Kingham, she felt, was something vast and significant, something positively holy; in the presence of that love, the new dress seemed a clown's livery worn in a church. Next day she wore an old, pre-Rodney dress – white muslin with black dots; not at all showy, fashionable, or eccentric. Her soul had dressed itself, so to speak, to match.

But Kingham, who had had time in the intervening hours to poison the memory of yesterday's joy with every kind of venomous afterthought, to discover subtle and horrible explanations for actions that were obviously innocent and simple, received her as though she had changed neither her dress nor her spirit and were indeed the woman whose part she had been playing all these weeks.

'Well,' he said, as he opened the door to her, 'I see you've come for more.'

Grace, who had expected to be received with the gentle and beautiful tenderness which he had displayed on the previous day, was cruelly surprised by the brutality of his tone, the coldness and bitterness of his expression.

'More what?' she asked; and from brightly exultant her eyes became apprehensive in their expression, the smile with which she had so eagerly entered the room faded, as she halted in front of him. Anxiously she looked into his face. 'More what?'

Kingham laughed a loud, unpleasant, mirthless laugh, and pointed to the divan. Grace's devilish concupiscence – that was what he had been chiefly dwelling on since last he saw her.

For the first second Grace did not understand what he meant. This particular aspect of their love was so far from her mind, that it did not occur to her to imagine that it could be in Kingham's. Then all at once his meaning dawned upon her. The blood ran up into her cheeks.

'Kingham!' she protested. (Kingham was one of those men whom everybody, even his closest intimates, called by his surname. For the rest, he had only a pair of initials – J. G. I never knew what they stood for. John George, I should think. But it was quite irrelevant; he was always 'Kingham', pure and simple.) 'Kingham! How can you say such things?'

'How can I?' he repeated mockingly. 'Why, by not keeping a fig-leaf over my mouth, which is where the truly respectable, who never talk about their vices, always keep it. Do what you like, but don't talk about it; that's respectability. But dear me,' he bantered on, 'I thought you were as much beyond respectability as you are beyond good and evil – or below, whichever the case may be.'

Grace, who had come in expecting a kiss and gentle words, walked slowly away from him across the room, sat down on the divan and began to cry.

A moment later Kingham was holding her in his arms and kissing away her tears. He spoke no word; the kisses became more passionate. At first, she averted her face from them. But in the end she abandoned herself. For a time she was happy. She forgot Kingham's cruel words, or if she remembered them, she remembered them as words spoken in a nightmare – by mistake, so to say, not on purpose, not seriously.

She had begun to feel almost perfectly reassured, when Kingham disengaged himself suddenly and roughly from her embrace, jumped up and began restlessly walking up and down the room, ruffling his hair as he went.

'What a horrible thing it is to have a vice!' he began. 'Something you carry about with you, but that isn't yourself. Something that's stronger than you are, that you want to resist and conquer, but can't. A vice, a vice.' He was enchanted by the word; it became, for the moment, the core of his universe. 'It's horrible. We're possessed by devils, that's what's wrong with us. We carry our private devils about with us, our vices, and they're too strong for us. They throw us down and horribly triumph.' He shuddered disgustedly. 'It's horrible to feel yourself being murdered by your vice. The devil spiritually murdering you, suffocating your soul with warm soft flesh. My devil uses you as his instrument of murder; your devil uses me. Our vices conspire; it's a conspiracy, a murder plot.'

By this time Grace was unhappier than she had ever been in her life before. (And yet, if Rodney had said the same thing, expressed a little differently – in terms of compliments on her 'temperament' – she would have been delighted, two months ago.)

'But you know I love you, you *know*,' was all that she could say. 'What makes you say these things, when you know?'

Kingham laughed. 'Oh, I know,' he answered, 'I know, only too well. I know what women like you mean by "love".'

'But I'm not a woman like . . .' Grace hesitated; 'like me' didn't sound quite sensible, somehow. '. . . like that.'

'Not like yourself?' Kingham asked derisively.

'Not like what you think,' Grace insisted through the tangled confusion of words.' Not silly, I mean; not frivolous and all that. Not really.' All those months with Rodney seemed a dream; and yet she had really lived through them. And there had really been champagne and sandwiches, and more than scientific conversations. . . . 'Not now, at any rate,' she added. 'Now I know you. It's different; can't you understand. Utterly different. Because I love you, love you, love you, love you.'

Any one else would have allowed himself to be convinced, at any rate for the moment; would have begged pardon, kissed and made friends. But, for Kingham, that would have been too easy, too emotionally flat. He stuck to his position.

'I know you do,' he answered, averting his gaze, as he spoke, from that pathetic, suffering face, from those wideopen grey eyes, perplexed and agonised, that looked up at

him so appealingly, so abjectly even. 'So do I. Your devil
loves me. My devil loves you.'

'But no,' Grace brokenly protested. 'But why? . . .'

'Loves violently,' he went on in a loud voice, almost
shouting, 'irresistibly.' And as he spoke the words he swung
round and precipitated himself upon her with a kind of
fury. 'Do you know what it is,' he went on, as he held her,
struggling a little and reluctant in his arms, 'do you know
what it is to love, not a person, not even their whole body,
but just some part of it – insanely? Do you know what it is
when the vice-devil concentrates its whole desire on one
point, focuses it inexorably until nothing else exists but the
nape of a neck, or a pectoral muscle, a foot, a knee, a hand?
This hand, for example.' He took her hand and lifted it towards his face. 'And not even a whole hand,' he continued.
'Just the ball of a thumb, just that little cushion of flesh
that's marked off from the rest of the palm by the line of
life; just that soft, resilient, strong little cushion of flesh.'

He began to kiss the spot on Grace's hand.

'Don't, don't. You mustn't.' She tried to pull her hand
away.

But Kingham held it fast. He went on kissing that soft,
rounded swell of muscle at the base of her palm, insistently,
again and again; kissing and kissing. And sometimes he
would take the flesh between his teeth and would bite,
gently at first, then with a gradually increasing force, until
the pain became almost unbearable and Grace cried out,
when he would fall to kissing again, softly and tenderly, as
though he were asking forgiveness, were trying to kiss the
pain away. Grace ceased to struggle and abandoned her
hand to him, to do with what he liked. And little by little
this insanely limited devil's love-making seemed to evoke a
special voluptuous sensibility in that particular square inch
of skin upon which it was concentrated. Her whole capacity for feeling pleasure seemed to focus itself at the base of

her left hand. Even the gradually increasing pain, as his teeth closed more and more tightly on her flesh, was pleasurable. She abandoned herself; but, at the same time, she felt that there was something shameful and even horrible about this pleasure. What might have been simple and beautiful and joyous had been turned into something painful, complicated, ugly and obscure. Kingham might congratulate himself on having produced a situation full of the most promising emotional possibilities.

I have reconstructed these scenes at some length because they were characteristic and typical of the whole affair. In his search for intense and painful emotions, Kingham displayed a perverse ingenuity; he was never at a loss for a pretext to complicate the simple and distort the natural. His great resource was always Grace's devilishness. Blind, as only Kingham could be blind, to call evidence to the contrary, he persisted in regarding Grace as a frivolous vampire, a monster of heartless vice. Her vampirishness and her vice were the qualities which attracted him to her; if he could have been convinced that she was really simple, innocent and childish, that her 'devilish concupiscence' was in actual fact an abject, unhappy adoration, he would have ceased to take any interest in her. Pleading meant as little to him as evidence. If Grace protested too vigorously, Kingham would bring up the affair with Rodney. What was that but vice, plain and unvarnished? Had not she herself admitted that she didn't love the man? Miserably, despairingly, Grace would confess in answer that she had certainly been silly and frivolous and feather-headed, but that now all that was done with. Everything was different, she was different, now. Because she loved him. To which Kingham would retort by expatiating with fiery eloquence about the horrors of vice, until at last Grace began to cry.

Grace's devilishness formed the staple and chronic pretext for scenes. But Kingham was inventive and there were plenty of other excuses. Observant – for he was acutely observant, wherever he chose not to be blind – Kingham had early recognised the entirely vague and accidental nature of all Grace's ideas, convictions, principles, and opinions. He perceived that what she thought about music, for example, was only a distorted and fragmentary version of what I thought; that her opinions on art were Rodney's muddled; that her philosophic and literary convictions were like a parboiled lobster – 'the fading sable and the coming gules' – half Rodney's and half, already, his own. And perceiving these things, he mocked her for her intellectual hypocrisy and snobbery. He found plenty of opportunities for hurting and humiliating her.

On other occasions, he would reproach her with untruthfulness and mean dissimulation, because she did not frankly tell John Peddley of her infidelity to him.

'I don't want to make him unnecessarily miserable,' Grace protested.

Kingham laughed derisively. 'A lot you care about anybody's happiness,' he said, 'particularly his! The truth is that you want to make the best of both worlds – be respectable and vicious at the same time. At all costs, no frankness! It's a case of the misplaced fig-leaf, as usual.'

And then there was a terrible scene, a whole series of terrible scenes, because Grace did not want to have a child by him.

'Our only excuse,' he raged at her, 'the only thing that might justify us – and you won't hear of it. It's to be vice for vice's sake, is it? The uncontaminated aesthetic doctrine.'

At other times, becoming strangely solicitous for the welfare of Grace's children, he reproached her with being a bad, neglectful mother.

'And you know, it's true,' she said to Catherine, with remorseful conviction. 'It's quite true. I *do* neglect them.'

She invited Catherine to accompany her and the two youngest to the Zoo, the very next afternoon. Over the heads of little Pat and Mittie, among the elephants and apes, the bears and the screaming parrots, she talked to Grace about her love and her unhappiness. And every now and then Pat or Mittie would interrupt with a question.

'Mummy, why do fish swim?'

Or: 'How do you make tortoises?'

'You know, you're a great comfort,' said Grace to Catherine, as they parted. 'I don't know what I should do without you.'

The next time she came, she brought Catherine a present; not a powder-puff this time, not gloves or ribbons, but a copy of Dostoievsky's *Letters from the Underworld*.

'You must read it,' she insisted. 'You absolutely must. It's so damnably *true*.'

Grace's life during this period was one of almost uninterrupted misery. I say 'almost uninterrupted'; for there were occasions when Kingham seemed to grow tired of violent emotions, of suffering, and the infliction of suffering; moments when he was all tenderness and an irresistible charm. For these brief spells of happiness, Grace was only too pathetically grateful. Her love, which an absolutely consistent ill-treatment might finally perhaps have crushed and eradicated, was revived by these occasional kindnesses into fresh outflowerings of a passionate adoration. Each time she hoped, she almost believed, that the happiness was going to be permanent. Bringing with her a few select aphorisms of Nietzsche, a pocket Leopardi, or the reproduction of one of Goya's *Desastres de la Guerra*, she would come and tell Catherine how happy she was, how radiantly, miraculously happy. Almost she believed that, this time, her happiness was going to last for ever. Almost; but never quite. There was always a doubt, an unexpressed, secret, and agonising fear. And always the doubt was duly justified, the fear was proved to be but too well founded. After two or three days' holiday from his emotional orgy – two or three days of calm and kindness – Kingham would appear before her, scowling, his face dark, his eyes angry and accusing. Grace looked at him and her heart would begin to beat with a painful irregularity and violence; she felt suddenly almost sick with anxious anticipation. Sometimes he burst out at once. Sometimes – and that was much worse – he kept her in a state of miserable suspense, that might be prolonged for hours, even for days, sulking in a gloomy silence and refusing, when Grace asked him, to tell her what was the matter. If she ventured to approach him in one of these moods with a kiss or a soothing caress, he pushed her angrily away.

The excuses which he found for these renewals of tempest after calm were of the most varied nature. One of the periods of happiness ended by his reproaching her with having been too tenderly amorous (too devilishly concupiscent) when he made love to her. On another occasion it was her crime to have remarked, two days before he chose actually to reproach her for it, that she liked the critical essays of Dryden. ('Such an intolerable piece of humbug and affectation,' he complained. 'Just because it's the fashion to admire these stupid, boring classical writers. Mere hypocrisy, that's what it is.' And so on.) Another time he was furious because she had insisted on taking a taxi all the way to Hampton Court. True, she had proposed from the first to pay for it. None the less, when the time came for paying, he had felt constrained in mere masculine decency to pull out his pocket-book. For one painful moment he had actually thought that she was going to accept his offer. He avenged himself for that moment of discomfort by accusing her of stupid and heartless extravagance.

'There's something extraordinarily coarse,' he told her, 'something horribly thick-skinned and unfeeling about people who have been born and brought up with money. The idea of spending a couple of pounds on a mere senseless caprice, when there are hundreds of thousands of people with no work, living precariously, or just not dying, on state charity ! The idea !'

Grace, who had proposed the excursion because she thought that Hampton Court was the most romantic place in the world, and because it would be so wonderful to be two and lovers by the side of the Long Water, in the deep embrasures of the windows, before the old grey mirrors, before the triumphing Mantegnas – Grace was appalled that reality should have turned out so cruelly different from her anticipatory dreams. And meanwhile yet another moment of happiness had irrevocably passed.

It was not surprising that Grace should have come to look tired and rather ill. She was paler than in the past and perceptibly thinner. Rimmed with dark circles of fatigue, her eyes seemed to have grown larger and of a paler grey. Her face was still the face of a nice but rather ugly little girl – but of a little girl most horribly ill-treated, hopelessly and resignedly miserable.

Confronted by this perfect resignation to unhappiness, Catherine became impatient.

'Nobody's got any business to be so resigned,' she said. 'Not nowadays, at any rate. We've got beyond the Patient Griselda stage.'

But the trouble was that Grace hadn't got beyond it. She loved abjectly. When Catherine urged and implored her to break with Kingham, she only shook her head.

'But you're unhappy,' Catherine insisted.

'There's no need for you to tell me that,' said Grace, and the tears came into her eyes. 'Do you suppose I don't know it?'

'Then why don't you leave him?' asked Catherine. 'Why on earth don't you?'

'Because I can't.' And after she had cried a little, she went on in a voice that was still unsteady and broken by an occasional sob : 'It's as though there were a kind of devil in me, driving me on against my will. A kind of dark devil.' She had begun to think in terms of Kingham even about herself. The case seemed hopeless.

We went abroad that summer, to the seaside, in Italy. In the lee of that great limestone mountain which rises suddenly, like the mountain of Paradise, out of the Pomptine marshes and the blue plains of the Mediterranean, we bathed and basked and were filled with the virtue of the life-giving sun. It was here, on the flanks of this mountain, that the enchantress Circe had her palace. Circeus Mons, Monte Circeo – the magic of her name has lingered, through Roman days, to the present. In coves at the mountain's foot stand the ruins of imperial villas, and walking under its western precipices you come upon the ghost of a Roman seaport, with the fishponds of Lucullus close at hand, like bright eyes looking upwards out of the plain. At dawn, before the sun has filled all space with the quivering gauzes of heat and the colourless brightness of excessive light, at dawn and again at evening, when the air once more grows limpid and colour and distant form are reborn, a mountain shape appears, far off, across the blue gulf of Terracina, a mountain shape and a plume of white unwavering smoke : Vesuvius. And once, climbing before sunrise to the crest of our Circean hill, we saw them both – Vesuvius to the southward, across the pale sea and northwards, beyond the green marshes, beyond the brown and ilex-dark Alban hills, the great symbolical dome of the world, St Peter's glittering above the mists of the horizon.

We stayed at Monte Circeo for upwards of two months, time enough to become brown as Indians and to have forgotten, or at least to have become utterly careless of, the world outside. We saw no newspapers; discouraged all correspondents by never answering their letters, which we hardly even took the trouble to read; lived, in a word, the life of savages in the sun, at the edge of a tepid sea. All our friends and relations might have died, England been overwhelmed by war, pestilence and famine, all books, pictures, music destroyed irretrievably out of the world – at Monte Circeo we should not have cared a pin.

But the time came at last when it was necessary to return to London and make a little money. We loaded our bodies with unaccustomed garments, crammed our feet – our feet that had for so long enjoyed the liberty of sandals – into their imprisoning shoes, took the omnibus to Terracina and climbed into the train.

'Well,' I said, when we had managed at last to squeeze ourselves into the two vacant places which the extraordinary exuberance of a party of Neapolitans had painfully restricted, 'we're going back to civilisation.'

Catherine sighed and looked out of the window at the enchantress's mountain beckoning across the plain. 'One might be excused,' she said, 'for making a little mistake and thinking it was hell we were going back to.'

It was a dreadful journey. The compartment was crowded and the Neapolitans fabulously large, the weather hot, the tunnels frequent, and the smoke peculiarly black and poisonous. And with the physical there came a host of mental discomforts. How much money would there be in the bank when we got home? What bills would be awaiting us? Should I be able to get my book on Mozart finished by Christmas, as I had promised? In what state should I find my invalid sister? Would it be necessary to pay a visit to the dentist? What should we do to placate all the people to whom we had never written? Wedged between the Neapolitans, I wondered. And looking at Catherine, I could see by the expression on her face that she was similarly preoccupied. We were like Adam and Eve when the gates of the garden closed behind them.

At Genoa the Neapolitans got out and were replaced by passengers of more ordinary volume. The pressure in the compartment was somewhat relaxed. We were able to secure a couple of contiguous places. Conversation became possible.

'I've been so much wondering,' said Catherine, when at last we were able to talk, 'what's been happening all this time to poor little Grace. You know, I really *ought* to have written to her.' And she looked at me with an expression in which consciousness of guilt was mingled with reproach.

'After all,' I said, responding to her expression rather than to her words, 'it wasn't my fault if you were too lazy to write. Was it?'

'Yes, it was,' Catherine answered. 'Just as much yours as mine. You ought to have reminded me to write, you ought to have insisted. Instead of which you set the example and encouraged my laziness.'

I shrugged my shoulders. 'One can't argue with women.'

'Because they're almost always in the right,' said Catherine. 'But that isn't the point. Poor Grace is the point. What's happened to her, do you suppose? And that dreadful Kingham – what has he been up to? I wish I'd written.'

At Monte Circeo, it is true, we had often spoken of Grace and Kingham. But there, in the annihilating sunshine, among the enormous and, for northern eyes, the almost unreal beauties of that mythological landscape, they had seemed as remote and as unimportant as everything and everybody else in our other life. Grace suffered. We knew it, no doubt, theoretically; but not, so to speak, practically – not personally, not with sympathetic realisation. In the sun it had been hardly possible to realise anything beyond our own well-being. Expose a northern body to the sun and the soul within it seems to evaporate. The inrush from the source of physical life drives out the life of the spirit. The body must become inured to light and life before the soul can condense again into active existence. When we had talked of Grace at Monte Circeo, we had been a pair of almost soulless bodies in the sun. Our clothes, our shoes, the hideous discomfort of the train gave us back our souls. We talked of Grace now with rediscovered sympathy, speculating rather anxiously on her fate.

'I feel that in some way we're almost responsible for her,' said Catherine. 'Oh, I wish I'd written to her! And why didn't she write to me?'

I propounded a comforting theory. 'She probably hasn't been with Kingham at all,' I suggested. 'She's gone abroad as usual with Peddley and the children. We shall probably find that the whole thing has died down by the time we get home.'

'I wonder,' said Catherine.

We were destined to discover the truth, or at least some portion of it, sooner than we had expected. The first person I saw as I stepped out of the train at Modane was John Peddley.

He was standing on the platform some ten or fifteen yards away, scanning, with eyes that sharply turned this way and that, the faces of the passengers descending from the express. His glances were searching, quick, decisive. He might have been a detective posted there on the frontier to intercept the escape of a criminal. No crook, you felt, no gentleman cracksman, however astute, could hope to sneak or swagger past those all-seeing hunter's eyes. It was that thought, the realisation that the thing was hopeless, that made me check my first impulse, which was to flee – out of the station, anywhere – to hide – in the luggage-van, the lavatory, under a seat. No, the game was obviously up. There was no possible escape. Sooner or later, whatever I might do now, I should have to present myself at the custom-house; he would catch me there, infallibly. And the train was scheduled to wait for two and a half hours.

'We're in for it,' I whispered at Catherine, as I helped her down on to the platform. She followed the direction of my glance and saw our waiting danger.

'Heaven help us,' she ejaculated with an unaccustomed piety; then added in another tone : 'But perhaps that means that Grace is here. I shall go and ask him.'

'Better not,' I implored, still cherishing a foolish hope that we might somehow slip past him unobserved. 'Better not.'

But in that instant, Peddley turned round and saw us. His large, brown, handsome face beamed with sudden pleasure; he positively ran to meet us.

Those two and a half hours in John Peddley's company at Modane confirmed for me a rather curious fact, of which, hitherto, I had been only vaguely and inarticulately aware: the fact that one may be deeply and sympathetically interested in the feelings of individuals whose thoughts and opinions – all the products, in a word, of their intellects – are utterly indifferent, even wearisome and repulsive. We read the Autobiography of Alfieri, the Journals of Benjamin Robert Haydon, and read them with a passionate interest. But Alfieri's tragedies, but Haydon's historical pictures, all the things which, for the men themselves, constituted their claim on the world's attention, have simply ceased to exist, so far as we are concerned. Intellectually and artistically, these men were more than half dead. But emotionally they lived.

Mutatis mutandis, it was the same with John Peddley. I had known him, till now, only as a relater of facts, an expounder of theories – as an intellect, in short; one of the most appallingly uninteresting intellects ever created. I had known him only in his public capacity, so to speak, as the tireless lecturer of club smoking-rooms and dinner-tables. I had never had a glimpse of him in private life. It was not to be wondered at; for, as I have said before, at ordinary times and when things were running smoothly, Peddley had no private life more complicated than the private life of his body. His feelings towards the majority of his fellow-beings were the simple emotions of the huntsman : pleasure when he had caught his victim and could talk him to death; pain and a certain slight resentment when the prey escaped him. Towards his wife he felt the desires of a healthy man in early middle life, coupled with a real but rather unimaginative, habit-born affection. It was an affection which took itself and its object, Grace, altogether too much for granted. In his own way, Peddley loved his wife, and it never occurred to him to doubt that she felt in the same way towards him; it seemed to him the natural inevitable thing, like having children and being fond of them, having a house and servants and coming home in the evening from the office to find dinner awaiting one. So inevitable, that it was quite unnecessary to talk or even to think about it; natural to the point of being taken publicly for granted, like the possession of a bank balance.

I had thought it impossible that Peddley should ever develop a private life; but I had been wrong. I had not foreseen the possibility of his receiving a shock violent enough to shake him out of complacency into self-questioning, a shock of sufficient strength to shiver the comfortable edifice of his daily, taken-for-granted life. That shock he had now received. It was a new and unfamiliar Peddley who now came running towards us.

'I'm so glad, I'm so particularly glad to see you,' he said, as he approached us. 'Quite extraordinarily glad, you know.'

I have never had my hand so warmly shaken as it was then. Nor had Catherine, as I could see by the way she winced, as she abandoned her fingers to his crushing cordiality.

'You're the very man I particularly wanted to see,' he went on, turning back to me. He stooped and picked up a couple of our suitcases. 'Let's make a dash for the douane,' he said. 'And then, when we've got those wretched formalities well over, we can have a bit of a talk.'

We followed him. Looking at Catherine, I made a grimace. The prospect of that bit of a talk appalled me. Catherine gave me an answering look, then quickened her pace so as to come up with the energetically hurrying Peddley.

'Is Grace with you here?' she asked.

Peddley halted, a suit-case in each hand. 'Well,' he said, slowly and hesitatingly, as though it were possible to have metaphysical doubts about the correct answer to this question, 'well, as a matter of fact, she isn't. Not really.' He might have been discussing the problem of the Real Presence.

As if reluctant to speak about the matter any further, he turned away and hurried on towards the custom-house, leaving Catherine's next question – 'Shall we find her in London when we get back?' – without an answer.

The bit of a talk, when it came, was very different from what I had gloomily anticipated.

'Do you think your wife would mind,' Peddley whispered to me, when the douanier had done with us and we were making our way towards the station restaurant, 'if I had a few words with you alone?'

I answered that I was sure she wouldn't, and said a word to Catherine, who replied, to me by a quick significant look, and to both of us together by a laughing dismissal.

'Go away and talk your stupid business if you want to,' she said. 'I shall begin my lunch.'

We walked out on to the platform. It had begun to rain,

violently, as it only rains among the mountains. The water beat on the vaulted glass roof of the station, filling all the space beneath with a dull, continuous roar; we walked as though within an enormous drum, touched by the innumerable fingers of the rain. Through the open arches at either end of the station the shapes of mountains were dimly visible through veils of white, wind-driven water.

We walked up and down for a minute or two without saying a word. Never, in my presence at any rate, had Peddley preserved so long a silence. Divining what embarrassments kept him in this unnatural state of speechlessness, I felt sorry for the man. In the end, after a couple of turns up and down the platform, he made an effort, cleared his throat and diffidently began in a small voice that was quite unlike that loud, self-assured, trombone-like voice in which he told one about the Swiss banking system.

'What I wanted to talk to you about,' he said, 'was Grace.'

The face he turned towards me as he spoke was full of a puzzled misery. That commonplacely handsome mask was strangely puckered and lined. Under lifted eyebrows, his eyes regarded me, questioningly, helplessly, unhappily.

I nodded and said nothing; it seemed the best way of encouraging him to proceed.

'The fact is,' he went on, turning away from me and looking at the ground, 'the fact is . . .' But it was a long time before he could make up his mind to tell me what the fact was.

Knowing so very well what the fact was, I could have laughed aloud, if pity had not been stronger in me than mockery, when he wound up with the pathetically euphemistic understatement : 'The fact is that Grace . . . well, I believe she doesn't love me. Not in the way she did. In fact I know it.'

'How do you know it?' I asked, after a little pause, hoping that he might have heard of the affair only through idle gossip, which I could proceed to deny.

'She told me,' he answered, and my hope disappeared.

'Ah.'

So Kingham had had his way, I reflected. He had bullied her into telling Peddley the quite unnecessary truth, just for the sake of making the situation a little more difficult and painful than it need have been.

'I'd noticed for some time,' Peddley went on, after a silence, 'that she'd been different.'

Even Peddley could be perspicacious after the event. And besides, the signs of her waning love had been sufficiently obvious and decisive. Peddley might have no sympathetic imagination; but at any rate he had desires and knew when they were satisfied and when they weren't. He hinted at explanatory details.

'But I never imagined,' he concluded – 'how could I imagine? – that it was because there was somebody else. How could I?' he repeated in a tone of ingenuous despair. You saw very clearly that it was, indeed, quite impossible for him to have imagined such a thing.

'Quite,' I said, affirming comfortingly I do not know exactly what proposition. 'Quite.'

'Well then, one day,' he pursued, 'one day just before we had arranged to come out here into the mountains, as usual, she suddenly came and blurted it all out – quite suddenly, you know, without warning. It was dreadful. Dreadful.'

There was another pause.

'That fellow called Kingham,' he went on, breaking the silence, 'you know him? he's a friend of yours, isn't he?'

I nodded.

'Very able man, of course,' said Peddley, trying to be impartial and give the devil his due. 'But, I must say, the only times I met him I found him rather unsympathetic.' (I pictured the scene : Peddley embarking on the law relating to insurance companies or, thoughtfully remembering that the chap was literary, on pianolas or modern art or the Einstein theory. And for his part, Kingham firmly and in all likelihood very rudely refusing to be made a victim of.) 'A bit too eccentric for my taste.'

'Queer,' I confirmed, 'certainly. Perhaps a little mad sometimes.'

Peddley nodded. 'Well,' he said slowly, 'it was Kingham.'

I said nothing. Perhaps I ought to have 'registered amazement,' as they say in the world of the cinema; amazement, horror, indignation – above all amazement. But I am a poor comedian. I made no grimaces, uttered no cries. In silence we walked slowly along the platform. The rain drummed on the roof overhead; through the archway at the end of the station the all but invisible ghosts of mountains loomed up behind white veils. We walked from Italy towards France and back again from France towards Italy.

'Who could have imagined it?' said Peddley at last.

'Anybody,' I might, of course, have answered. 'Anybody who had a little imagination and who knew Grace; above all, who knew you.' But I held my tongue. For though there is something peculiarly ludicrous about the spectacle of a self-satisfaction suddenly punctured, it is shallow and unimaginative only to laugh at it. For the puncturing of self-satisfaction gives rise to a pain that can be quite as acute as that which is due to the nobler tragedies. Hurt vanity and exploded complacency may be comic as a spectacle, from the outside; but to those who feel the pain of them, who regard them from within, they are very far from ludicrous. The feelings and opinions of the actor, even in the morally lowest dramas, deserve as much consideration as the spectator's. Peddley's astonishment that his wife could have preferred another man to himself was doubtless, from my point of view, a laughable exhibition. But the humiliating realisation had genuinely hurt him; the astonishment had been mixed with a real pain. Merely to have mocked would have been a denial, in favour of the spectator, of the actor's rights. Moreover, the pain which Peddley felt was not exclusively the product of an injured complacency. With the low and ludicrous were mingled other, more reputable emotions. His next words deprived me of whatever desire I might have had to laugh.

'What am I to do?' Peddley went on, after another long pause, and looked at me again more miserably and bewilderedly than ever. 'What *am* I to do?'

'Well,' I said cautiously, not knowing what to advise him, 'it surely depends how you feel about it all – about Grace in particular.'

'How I feel about her?' he repeated. 'Well,' he hesitated, embarrassed, 'I'm fond of her, of course. Very fond of her.' He paused; then, with a great effort, throwing down barriers which years of complacent silence, years of insensitive taking for granted had built up round the subject, he went on : 'I love her.'

The utterance of that decisive word seemed to make things easier for Peddley. It was as though an obstruction had been removed; the stream of confidences began to flow more easily and copiously.

'You know,' he went on, 'I don't think I had quite realised how much I did love her till now. That's what makes it all so specially dreadful – the thought that I ought to have loved her more, or at least more consciously when I had the opportunity, when she loved me; the thought that if I had, I shouldn't, probably, be here now all alone, without her.' He averted his face and was silent, while we walked half the length of the platform. 'I think of her all the time, you know,' he continued. 'I think how happy we used to be together and I wonder if we shall ever be happy again, as we were, or if it's all over, all finished.' There was another pause. 'And then,' he said, 'I think of her there in

England, with that man, being happy with him, happier perhaps than she ever was with me; for perhaps she never really did love me, not like that.' He shook his head. 'Oh, it's dreadful, you know, it's dreadful. I try to get these thoughts out of my head, but I can't. I walk in the hills till I'm dead-beat; I try to distract myself by talking to people who come through on the trains. But it's no good. I can't keep these thoughts away.'

I might have assured him, of course, that Grace was without doubt infinitely less happy with Kingham than she had ever been with him. But I doubted whether the consolation would really be very efficacious.

'Perhaps it isn't really serious,' I suggested, feebly. 'Perhaps it won't last. She'll come to her senses one of these days.'

Peddley sighed. 'That's what I always hope, of course. I was angry at first, when she told me that she wasn't coming abroad and that she meant to stay with that man in England. I told her that she could go to the devil, so far as I was concerned. I told her that she'd only hear from me through my solicitor. But what was the good of that? I don't want her to go to the devil; I want her to be with me. I'm not angry any more, only miserable. I've even swallowed my pride. What's the good of being proud and not going back on your decisions, if it makes you unhappy? I've written and told her that I want her to come back, that I'll be happy and grateful if she does.'

'And what has she answered?' I asked.

'Nothing,' said Peddley.

I imagined Peddley's poor conventional letter, full of those worn phrases that make their appearance with such a mournful regularity in all the letters that are read in the divorce courts, or before coroners' juries, when people have thrown themselves under trains for unrequited love. Miserable, cold, inadequate words! A solicitor, he had often dictated them, no doubt, to clients who desired to have their plea for the restitution of conjugal rights succinctly and decorously set down in black and white, for the benefit of the judge who was, in due course, to give it legal force. Old, blunted phrases, into which only the sympathy of the reader has power to instil a certain temporary life – he had had to write them unprofessionally this time, for himself.

Grace, I guessed, would have shown the letter to Kingham. I imagined the derisive ferocity of his comments. A judicious analysis of its style can reduce almost any love-letter to emptiness and absurdity. Kingham would have made that analysis with gusto and with a devilish skill. By his mockery he had doubtless shamed Grace out of her first spontaneous feelings; she had left the letter unanswered. But the feelings, I did not doubt, still lingered beneath the surface of her mind; pity for John Peddley and remorse for what she had done. And Kingham, I felt sure, would find some ingenious method for first encouraging, then deriding these emotions. That would agreeably complicate their relations, would render her love for him a source of even greater pain to her than ever.

Peddley broke the rain-loud silence and the train of my speculations by saying : 'And if it is serious, if she goes on refusing to answer when I write – what then?'

'Ah, but that won't happen,' I said, speaking with a conviction born of my knowledge of Kingham's character. Sooner or later he would do something that would make it impossible for even that most abject of lovers to put up with him. 'You can be sure it won't.'

'I only wish I could,' said Peddley dubiously : he did not know Kingham, only Grace – and very imperfectly at that. 'I can't guess what she means to do. It was all so unexpected – from Grace. I never imagined . . .' For the first time he had begun to realise his ignorance of the woman to whom he was married. The consciousness of this ignorance was one of the elements of his distress. 'But if it is serious,' he went on, after a pause, obstinately insisting on contemplating the worst of possibilities, 'what am I to do? Let her go, like that, without a struggle? Set her free to go and be permanently and respectably happy with that man?' (At the vision he thus conjured up of a domesticated Kingham, I inwardly smiled.) 'That would be fairest to her, I suppose. But why should I be unfair to myself?'

Under the fingers of the drumming rain, in the presence of the ghostly, rain-blurred mountains, we prolonged the vain discussion. In the end I persuaded him to do nothing for the time being. To wait and see what the next days or weeks or months would bring. It was the only possible policy.

When we returned to the station restaurant, Peddley was considerably more cheerful than when we had left it. I had offered no very effectual consolation, invented no magical solution of his problems; but the mere fact that he had been able to talk and that I had been ordinarily sympathetic had been a relief and a comfort to him. He was positively rubbing his hands as he sat down beside Catherine.

'Well, Mrs Wilkes,' he said in that professionally hearty tone which clergymen, doctors, lawyers, and all those whose business it is to talk frequently and copiously with people they do not know, so easily acquire, 'well, Mrs Wilkes, I'm afraid we've shamefully neglected you. I'm afraid you'll never forgive me for having carried off your husband in this disgraceful way.' And so on.

After a little, he abandoned this vein of graceful courtesy for more serious conversation.

'I met a most interesting man at this station a few days ago,' he began. 'A Greek. Theotocopulos was his name. A very remarkable man. He told me a number of most illuminating things about King Constantine and the present economic situation in Greece. He assured me, for one thing, that . . .' And the information about King Constantine and the economic situation in Hellas came pouring out. In Mr Theotocopulos, it was evident, John Peddley had found a kindred soul. When Greek meets Greek then comes, in this case, an exchange of anecdotes about the deposed sovereigns of eastern Europe – in a word, the tug of bores. From private, Peddley had returned to public life. We were thankful when it was time to continue our journey.

Kingham lived on the second floor of a once handsome and genteel eighteenth-century house, which presented its façade of blackened brick to a decayed residential street, leading northward from Theobald's Road towards the easternmost of the Bloomsbury Squares. It was a slummy street in which since the war, a colony of poor but 'artistic' people from another class had settled. In the windows, curtains of dirty muslin alternated with orange curtains, scarlet curtains, curtains in large bright-coloured checks. It was not hard to know where respectable slumminess ended and gay Bohemianism began.

The front door of number twenty-three was permanently open. I entered and addressed myself to the stairs. Reaching the second landing, I was surprised to find the door of Kingham's rooms ajar. I pushed it open and walked in.

'Kingham,' I called, 'Kingham !'

There was no answer. I stepped across the dark little vestibule and tapped at the door of the main sitting-room.

'Kingham !' I called again more loudly.

I did not want to intrude indiscreetly upon some scene of domestic happiness or, more probably, considering the relations existing between Grace and Kingham, of domestic strife.

'Kingham !'

The silence remained unbroken. I walked in. The room

was empty. Still calling discreetly as I went, I looked into the second sitting-room, the kitchen, the bedroom. A pair of suit-cases were standing, ready packed, just inside the bedroom door. Where could they be going? I wondered, hoped I should see them before they went. Meanwhile, I visited even the bathroom and the larder; the little flat was quite empty of life. They must have gone out, leaving the front door open behind them as they went. If preoccupation and absence of mind be signs of love, why then, I reflected, things must be going fairly well.

It was twenty to six on my watch. I decided to wait for their return. If they were not back within the hour, I would leave a note, asking them to come to see us, and go.

The two small monstrously lofty sitting-rooms in Kingham's flat had once been a single room of nobly classical proportions. A lath-and-plaster partition separated one room from the other, dividing into two unsymmetrical parts the gracefully moulded design which had adorned the ceiling of the original room. A single tall sash window, having no proportionable relation to the wall in which it found itself accidentally placed, illuminated either room – the larger inadequately, the smaller almost to excess. It was in the smaller and lighter of the two sitting-rooms that Kingham kept his books and his writing-table. I entered it, looked round the shelves, and having selected two or three miscellaneous volumes, drew a chair up to the window and settled down to read.

'I have no patience,' I read (and it was a volume of Kingham's own writings that I had opened), 'I have no patience with those silly prophets and Utopia-mongers who offer us prospects of uninterrupted happiness. I have no patience with them. Are they too stupid even to realise their own stupidity? Can't they see that if happiness were uninterrupted and well-being universal, these things would cease to be happiness and well-being and become merely boredom and daily bread, daily business, *Daily Mail*? Can't they understand that, if everything in the world were pea-green, we shouldn't know what pea-green was? "Asses, apes and dogs!" (Milton too, thank God for Milton! didn't suffer fools gladly. Satan – portrait of the artist.) Asses, apes and dogs. Are they too stupid to see that, in order to know happiness and virtue, men must also know misery and sin? The Utopia I offer is a world where happiness and unhappiness are more intense, where they more rapidly and violently alternate than here, with us. A world where men and women endowed with more than our modern sensitiveness, more than our acute and multifarious modern consciousness, shall know the unbridled pleasures, the cruelties and dangers of the ancient world, with all the scruples and remorses of Christianity, all its ecstasies, all its appalling fears. That is the Utopia I offer you – not a sterilised nursing home, with Swedish drill before breakfast, vegetarian cookery, classical music on the radio, chaste mixed sun-baths, and rational free love between aseptic sheets. Asses, apes and dogs!'

One thing at least, I reflected, as I turned the pages of the book in search of other attractive paragraphs, one thing at least could be said in Kingham's favour; he was no mere academic theorist. Kingham practised what he preached. He had defined Utopia, he was doing his best to realise it – in Grace's company.

'Vows of chastity,' the words caught my eye and I read on, 'vows of chastity are ordinarily taken in that cold season, full of disgusts and remorses, which follows after excess. The taker of the oath believes the vow to be an unbreakable chain about his flesh. But he is wrong; the vow is no chain, only a hempen strand. When the blood is cold, it holds fast. But when, with the natural rebirth of appetite, the blood turns to flame, that fire burns through the hemp – the tindery hemp which the binder had thought to be a

rope of steel – burns it, and the flesh breaks loose. With renewed satiety come coldness, disgust, remorse, more acute
this time than before, and with them a repetition of the
Stygian vows. And so on, round and round, like the days of
the week, like summer and winter. Futile, you say, no
doubt; weak-minded. But I don't agree with you. Nothing
that intensifies and quickens life is futile. These vows, these
remorses and the deep-rooted feeling from which they
spring – the feeling that the pleasure of the senses is somehow evil – sharpen this pleasure to the finest of points,
multiply the emotions to which it gives rise by creating,
parallel with the body's delight, an anguish and tragedy
of the mind.'

I had read them before, these abbreviated essays or expanded maxims (I do not know how to name them; Kingham himself had labelled them merely as 'Notions'); had
read them more than once and always enjoyed their
violence, their queerness, their rather terrifying sincerity.
But this time, it seemed to me, I read them with greater
understanding than in the past. My knowledge of Kingham's relations with Grace illuminated them for me; and
they, in their turn, threw light on Kingham and his relations with Grace. For instance, there was that sentence
about love : 'All love is in the nature of a vengeance; the
man revenges himself on the woman who has caught and
humiliated him; the woman revenges herself on the man
who has broken down her reserves and reluctances, who
has dared to convert her from an individual into a mere
member and mother of the species.' It seemed particularly
significant to me, now. I remember noticing, too, certain
words about the sin against the Holy Ghost. 'Only those
who know the Holy Ghost are tempted to sin against him –
indeed, can sin against him. One cannot waste a talent
unless one first possesses it. One cannot do what is wrong,
or stupid, or futile, unless one first knows what is right, what

is reasonable, what is worth doing. Temptation begins with knowledge and grows as knowledge grows. A man knows that he has a soul to save and that it is a precious soul; it is for that very reason that he passes his time in such a way that it must infallibly be damned. You, reader,' the paragraph characteristically concluded, 'you who have no soul to save, will probably fail to understand what I am talking about.'

I was considering these words in the light of the recent increases of my knowledge of Kingham, when I was suddenly interrupted in the midst of my meditations by the voice of Kingham himself.

'It's no good,' it was saying. 'Can't you understand?' The voice sounded all at once much louder, as the door of the larger sitting-room opened to admit the speaker and his companion. Their footsteps resounded on the uncarpeted boards. 'Why will you go on like this?' He spoke wearily, like one who is tired of being importuned and desires only to be left in peace. 'Why will you?'

'Because I love you.' Grace's voice was low and dulled. It seemed to express a kind of obstinate misery.

'Oh, I know, I know,' said Kingham with an impatience that was muted by fatigue. He sighed noisily. 'If you only knew how sick I was of all this unnecessary higgling and arguing!' The tone was almost pathetic; it seemed to demand that one should condole with the speaker, that one should do one's best to spare him pain. One might have imagined, from the tone of his voice, that Kingham was the persecuted victim of a relentless Grace. And it was thus indeed that he now saw himself, if, as I guessed, he had reached that inevitable closing phase of all his passions – the phase of emotional satiety. He had drunk his fill of strong feeling; the bout was over, for this time, the zest had gone out of the orgy. He wanted only to live quietly, soberly. And here was Grace, importuning him to continue the orgy. An orgy in cold blood – ugh! For a man sobered by complete satiety, the idea was disgustful, a thought to shudder at. No wonder he spoke thus plaintively. 'I tell you,' he went on, 'it's settled. Definitely. Once and for all.'

'You mean it? You mean definitely that you're going?'

'Definitely,' said Kingham.

'Then I mean what I've said,' the miserable, dully obstinate voice replied. 'Definitely. I shall kill myself if you go.'

My first impulse, when I heard Kingham's voice, had been – goodness knows why – to hide myself. A sudden sense of guilt, a schoolboy's terror of being caught, entirely possessed me. My heart beating, I jumped up and looked about me for some place of concealment. Then, after a second or two, my reason reasserted itself. I remembered that I was not a schoolboy in danger of being caught and caned; that, after all, I had been waiting here in order to ask Kingham and Grace to dinner; and that, so far from hiding myself, I ought immediately to make my presence known to them. Meanwhile, sentence had succeeded sentence in their muffled altercation. I realised that they were involved in some terrible, mortal quarrel; and realising, I hesitated to interrupt them. One feels shy of breaking in on an exhibition of strong and intimate emotion. To intrude oneself, clothed and armoured in one's daily indifference, upon naked and quivering souls is an insult, almost, one feels, an indecency. This was evidently no vulgar squabble, which could be allayed by a little tact, a beaming face and a tepid douche of platitude. Perhaps it was even so serious, so agonising that it ought to be put an end to at all costs. I wondered. Ought I to intervene? Knowing Kingham, I was afraid that my intervention might only make things worse. So far from shaming him into peace, it would in all probability have the effect of rousing all his latent violences. To continue an intimately emotional scene in the presence

H

of a third party is a kind of indecency. Kingham, I reflected, would probably be only too glad to enhance and complicate the painfulness of the scene by introducing into it this element of spiritual outrage. I stood hesitating, wondering what I ought to do. Go in to them and run the risk of making things worse? Or stay where I was, at the alternative risk of being discovered, half an hour hence, and having to explain my most inexplicable presence? I was still hesitating when, from the other room, the muffled, obstinate voice of Grace pronounced those words :

'I shall kill myself if you go.'

'No, you won't,' said Kingham. 'I assure you, you won't.' The weariness of his tone was tinged with a certain ironic mockery.

I imagined the excruciations which might result if I gave Kingham an audience to such a drama, and decided not to intervene – not yet, at any rate. I tiptoed across the room and sat down where it would be impossible for me to be seen through the open door.

'I've played that little farce myself,' Kingham went on. 'Oh, dozens of times. Yes, and really persuaded myself at the moment that it was the genuinely tragic article.' Even without my intervention, his mockery was becoming brutal enough.

'I shall kill myself,' Grace repeated, softly and stubbornly.

'But as you see,' Kingham pursued, 'I'm still alive.' A new vivacity had come into his weary voice. 'Still alive and perfectly intact. The cyanide of potassium always turned out to be almond icing : and however carefully I aimed at my cerebellum, I never managed to score anything but a miss.' He laughed at his own jest.

'Why will you talk in that way?' Grace asked, with a weary patience. 'That stupid, cruel way?'

'I may talk,' said Kingham, 'but it's you who act. You've

destroyed me, you've poisoned me : you're a poison in my blood. And you complain because I talk !'

He paused, as if expecting an answer : but Grace said nothing. She had said all that there was for her to say so often, she had said 'I love you', and had had the words so constantly and malevolently misunderstood, that it seemed to her, no doubt, a waste of breath to answer him.

'I suppose it's distressing to lose a victim,' Kingham went on in the same ironic tone. 'But you can't really expect me to believe that it's so distressing that you've got to kill yourself. Come, come, my dear Grace. That's a bit thick.'

'I don't expect you to believe anything,' Grace replied. 'I just say what I mean and leave it at that. I'm tired.' I could hear by the creaking of the springs that she had thrown herself down on the divan. There was a silence.

'So am I,' said Kingham, breaking it at last. 'Mortally tired.' All the energy had gone out of his voice; it was once more blank and lifeless. There was another creaking of springs; he had evidently sat down beside her on the divan. 'Look here,' he said, 'for God's sake let's be reasonable.' From Kingham, the appeal was particularly cogent; I could not help smiling. 'I'm sorry I spoke like that just now. It was silly; it was bad-tempered. And you know the way one word begets another; one's carried away. I didn't mean to hurt you. Let's talk calmly. What's the point of making an unnecessary fuss? The thing's inevitable, fatal. A bad business, perhaps; but let's try to make the best of it, not the worst.'

I listened in astonishment, while Kingham wearily unwound a string of such platitudes. Wearily, wearily; he seemed to be boring himself to death with his own words. Oh, to have done with it, to get away, to be free, never again to set eyes on her ! I imagined his thoughts, his desires.

There are moments in every amorous intimacy, when such thoughts occur to one or other of the lovers, when love has turned to weariness and disgust, and the only desire is a desire for solitude. Most lovers overcome this temporary weariness by simply not permitting their minds to dwell on it. Feelings and desires to which no attention is paid soon die of inanition; for the attention of the conscious mind is their food and fuel. In due course love reasserts itself and the moment of weariness is forgotten. To Kingham, however, Kingham who gave his whole attention to every emotion or wish that brushed against his consciousness, the slightest velleity of weariness became profoundly significant. Nor was there, in this case, any real enduring love for the object of his thoughtfully fostered disgust, any strong and steady affection capable of overcoming what should have been only a temporary weariness. He loved because he felt the need of violent emotion. Grace was a means to an end, not an end in herself. The end – satisfaction of his craving for emotional excitement – had been attained; the means had therefore ceased to possess the slightest value for him. Grace would have been merely indifferent to him, if she had shown herself in this crisis as emotionally cold as he felt himself. But their feelings did not synchronise. Grace was not weary; she loved him, on the contrary, more passionately than ever. Her importunate warmth had conspired with his own habit of introspection to turn weariness and emotional neutrality into positive disgust and even hatred. He was making an effort, however, not to show these violent feelings; moreover he was tired – too tired to want to give them their adequate expression. He would have liked to slip away quietly, without any fuss. Wearily, wearily, he uttered his sedative phrases. He might have been a curate giving Grace a heart-to-heart chat about Life.

'We must be sensible,' he said. And : 'There are other

things besides love.' He even talked about self-control and
the consolation of work. It lasted a long time.

Suddenly Grace interrupted him. 'Stop!' she cried in a
startlingly loud voice. 'For heaven's sake stop! How can
you be so dishonest and stupid?'

'I'm not,' Kingham answered, sullenly. 'I was simply
saying . . .'

'You were simply saying that you're sick of me,' said
Grace, taking up his words. 'Simply saying it in a slimy,
stupid, dishonest way. That you're sick to death of me and
that you wish to goodness I'd go away and leave you in
peace. Oh, I will, I will. You needn't worry.' She uttered
a kind of laugh. There was a long silence.

'Why don't you go?' said Grace at last. Her voice was
muffled, as though she were lying with her face buried in a
cushion.

'Well,' said Kingham awkwardly. 'Perhaps it might be
best.' He must have been feeling the beginnings of a sense
of enormous relief, a joy which it would have been indecent to display, but which was bubbling only just beneath the surface. 'Good-bye, then, Grace,' he said, in a
tone that was almost cheerful. 'Let's part friends.'

Grace's laughter was muffled by the cushion. Then she
must have sat up; for her voice, when she spoke a second
later, was clear and unmuted.

'Kiss me,' she said peremptorily. 'I want you to kiss me,
just once more.'

There was a silence.

'Not like that,' Grace's voice came almost angrily. 'Kiss
me really, really, as though you still loved me.'

Kingham must have tried to obey her; anything for a
quiet life and a prompt release. There was another silence.

'No, no.' The anger in Grace's voice had turned to
despair. 'Go away, go, go. Do I disgust you so that you
can't even kiss me?'

'But, my dear Grace . . ,' he protested.

'Go, go, go.'

'Very well, then,' said Kingham in a dignified and slightly offended tone. But inwardly, what joy! Liberty, liberty! The key had turned in the lock, the prison door was opening. 'If you want me to, I will.' I heard him getting up from the divan. 'I'll write to you when I get to Munich,' he said.

I heard him walking to the door, along the passage to the bedroom, where, I suppose, he picked up his suit-cases, back along the passage to the outer door of the apartment. The latch clicked, the door squeaked on its hinges as it swung open, squeaked as it closed; there was an echoing bang.

I got up from my chair and cautiously peeped round the edge of the doorway into the other room. Grace was lying on the divan in precisely the position I had imagined, quite still, her face buried in a cushion. I stood there watching her for perhaps half a minute, wondering what I should say to her. Everything would sound inadequate, I reflected. Therefore, perhaps, the most inadequate of all possible words, the most perfectly banal, trivial and commonplace, would be the best in the circumstances.

I was pondering thus when suddenly that death-still body stirred into action. Grace lifted her face from the pillow, listened for a second, intently, then with a series of swift motions, she turned on her side, raised herself to a sitting position, dropped her feet to the ground and, springing up, hastened across the room towards the door. Instinctively, I withdrew into concealment. I heard her cross the passage, heard the click and squeak of the front door as it opened. Then her voice, a strange, inhuman, strangled voice, called 'Kingham!' and again, after a listening silence that seemed portentously long, 'Kingham!' There was no answer.

After another silence, the door closed. Grace's footsteps

approached once more, crossed the room, came to a halt. I peeped out from my ambush. She was standing by the window, her forehead pressed against the glass, looking out – no, looking down, rather. Two storeys, three, if you counted the area that opened like a deep grave at the foot of the wall beneath the window – was she calculating the height? What were her thoughts?

All at once, she straightened herself up, stretched out her hands and began to raise the sash. I walked into the room towards her.

At the sound of my footsteps, she turned and looked at me – but looked with the disquietingly blank, unrecognising eyes and expressionless face of one who is blind. It seemed as though her mind were too completely preoccupied with its huge and dreadful idea to be able to focus itself at once on the trivialities of life.

'Dear Grace,' I said, 'I've been looking for you. Catherine sent me to ask you to come and have dinner with us.'

She continued to look at me blankly. After a second or two, the significance of my words seemed to reach her; it was as though she were far away, listening to sounds that laboured slowly across the intervening gulfs of space. When at last she had heard my words – heard them with her distant mind – she shook her head and her lips made the movement of saying 'No.'

I took her arm and led her away from the window. 'But you must,' I said.

My voice seemed to come to her more quickly this time. It was only a moment after I had finished speaking that she again shook her head.

'You must,' I repeated. 'I heard everything, you know. I shall make you come with me.'

'You heard?' she repeated, staring at me.

I nodded, but did not speak. Picking up her small, close-fitting, casque-shaped hat from where it was lying on the floor, near the divan, I handed it to her. She turned with an automatic movement towards the dim, grey-glassed Venetian mirror that hung above the fireplace and adjusted it to her head : a wisp of hair straggled over her temple; tidily, she tucked it away.

'Now, let's go,' I said, and led her away, out of the flat, down the dark stairs, into the street.

Walking towards Holborn in search of a taxi, I made futile conversation. I talked, I remember, about the merits of omnibuses as opposed to undergrounds, about second-hand bookshops, and about cats. Grace said nothing. She walked at my side, as though she were walking in her sleep.

Looking at that frozen, unhappy face—the face of a child who has suffered more than can be borne – I was filled with a pity that was almost remorse. I felt that it was somehow my fault; that it was heartless and insensitive of me not to be as unhappy as she was. I felt, as I have often felt in the presence of the sick, the miserably and hopelessly poor, that I owed her an apology. I felt that I ought to beg her pardon for being happily married, healthy, tolerably prosperous, content with my life. Has one a right to be happy in the presence of the unfortunate, to exult in life before those who desire to die? Has one a right?

'The population of cats in London,' I said, 'must be very nearly as large as the population of human beings.'

'I should think so,' Grace whispered, after a sufficient time had elapsed for her to hear, across the gulfs that separated her mind from mine, what I had said. She spoke with a great effort; her voice was scarcely audible.

'Literally millions,' I pursued.

And then, fortunately, I caught sight of a taxi. Driving home to Kensington, I talked to her of our Italian holiday. I did not think it necessary, however, to tell her of our meeting with Peddley at Modane.

Arrived, I told Catherine in two words what had happened and, handing Grace over to her care, took refuge in my work-room. I felt, I must confess, profoundly and self-ishly thankful to be back there, alone, with my books and my piano. It was the kind of thankfulness one feels, motor-ing out of town for the weekend, to escape from dark and sordid slums to a comfortable, cool-gardened country house, where one can forget that there exist other human beings beside oneself and one's amusing, cultivated friends, and that ninety-nine out of every hundred of them are doomed to misery. I sat down at the piano and began to play the Arietta of Beethoven's Op. III.

I played it very badly, for more than half my mind was preoccupied with something other than the music. I was wondering what would become of Grace now. Without Rodney, without Kingham, what would she do? What would she be? The question propounded itself insistently.

And then, all at once, the page of printed music before my eyes gave me the oracular reply. *Da capo*. The hiero-glyph sent me back to the beginning of my passage. *Da capo*. After all, it was obvious. *Da capo*. John Peddley, the children, the house, the blank existence of one who does not know how to live unassisted. Then another musical critic, a second me – introduction to the second theme. Then the second theme, *scherzando*; another Rodney. Or *molto agitato*, the equivalent of Kingham. And then, in-evitably, when the agitation had agitated itself to the climax of silence, *da capo* again to Peddley, the house, the children, the blankness of her unassisted life.

The miracle of the Arietta floated out from under my fingers. Ah, if only the music of our destinies could be like this!

ELIZABETH BOWEN

AUNT TATTY

THE train stopped every ten minutes after it left the junction : each time Pellew jumped up to clutch his hat and stick in a spasm of nervousness. The screech of brakes, the jolt that passed down the coaches repeated themselves in his vitals. Each time the white station palings, the lamp and the porter slid into view again he would gulp, put a hand to his tie and experience once more that sense of fatality. At the back of the station for Eleanor's home there was a group of beeches; their beautiful bare green trunks like limbs stood boldly out in the February sunshine. He stepped from the train and stood staring : they were so beautiful they were a kind of escape, yet they brought round again his yearly chagrin, his suspicion of being cheated. Then he remembered Eleanor – if he could be said to have forgotten her – and turning saw her a few feet away, blinking, a thin colour creeping up her face.

'Hullo – Paul.'

'Eleanor . . . splendid !'

'Splendid !' They shook hands. He couldn't remember when they had last shaken hands; he supposed when they had been introduced. He looked down, sideways, at the little fiery crocuses spurting against the fence.

'I've never seen crocuses in a station before,' he said hurriedly. 'Wallflowers, of course, and stocks. I . . . some railways offer prizes. . . .'

'I saw you looking at the beech trees, too,' said Eleanor, with a triumphant, informed little air, as though she had stolen a march on him. They walked down the platform together towards the barrier. They each told themselves that they must avoid any show of emotion with people, Eleanor's

234

neighbours, about – but *wasn't* Spring. . . . As Paul tasted
the air and coming out on to the road saw the pale fields
washed over with sunshine, with knolls of trees rising here
and there like islands, he tingled. He hated constraint – this
business, this effort ahead. He wished he could have come
down and spent the day here alone. Eleanor wore – as a
kind of symbol – a straw hat, new-looking, pulled down
over her eyes, but her shoes were wintry, heavily covered in
mud; she had splashed mud over her ankles up to the edge
of her skirt. In spite of being so thin she looked womanly
and capable, a regular country girl, and he couldn't believe
he had held her crushed in his arms, helpless. London
altered her, he could only suppose.

She walked fast, swinging along with a stick. She was
embarrassed and silent. More tentatively than by an inspiration he wheeled her into a copse by the side of the
road, put his stick down and threw his arms round her. A
blackbird fluted, all round little crumpled primrose-leaves
were pushing up through the beech mould. She strained
her face away, showing the fine line of her jaw; he felt her
go rigid against him under the bulky tweed coat. 'Not here,'
she cried, 'not here, don't; it's like the village people. Don't
Paul!'

It was in the country, Paul knew, that his shortcomings
began to appear. He wasn't a gentleman. He wore a grey
suit, but it did not look right somehow. His technique was
all wrong; he should not go further than Chiswick or Rich-
mond – unless to the Continent. He reached for his stick
philosophically. 'As a matter of fact, my dear,' he said,
startled to frankness, 'there seemed nothing to say.'

She emerged from the copse ahead of him, cautiously,
and went on rapidly down the road.

Down the avenue Eleanor's mother came strolling to
meet them. Paul braced himself. His position was perfectly
simple, he was Mr Pellew, a friend of the Jennings'

(Eleanor's friends in town). He had met Eleanor with them. He just happened to be in this part of the world, seeing churches. He had suggested himself to luncheon and they had sent him a friendly reply.

'Seeing churches' – Eleanor's mother beamed on his cultivation. Diffuse yet stately, she had Eleanor's fine hardness with an alloy, melted over the edge of the mould, running into a form of its own, a privileged kind of formlessness. Little girls – they resolved themselves into three – came running out of the bushes and slung themselves on to Eleanor's arms. Young sisters.

They brought with them out of the bushes some kind of a gummy smell; twigs and little pieces of young leaf clung to their reefer coats and their pigtails. 'Scaramouches!' said their mother, contented. They stared at Paul politely but indifferently, as though he did not come into their world at all. Paul thought : he would show them. He wondered whether it would be big-boyish and popular – brotherly – if he were to tweak their pig-tails but he dared not; these were not town little girls; one never quite knew.

Eleanor seemed pervaded all at once with an anxious vexation. She kept glancing sideways – across him – at her mother's profile. She pulled little bunches of grey buds off the flowering currant trees and crumbled them between her fingers.

'You live in London,' said Eleanor's mother positively.

'I suppose in a kind of way I do.'

'So much going on there,' sighed Eleanor's mother with a polite affectation of chagrin. 'One's terribly out of it . . . Patsey, run on and look for Aunt Tatty. I can't think where she's gone to' – A child sped away – 'Mr Pellew will be hungry. Do you write about churches?'

'Mr Pellew doesn't write at all,' said Eleanor sharply.

'So many people nowadays do.' The mother wrinkled her brows up; she had got him all wrong, he wasn't an author at all; now there would be all this fearful business of readjustment. She turned to Paul with a gesture and laughed despairingly, confidentially, lovably. He laughed back, the remaining little girls tittered. Still laughing, they passed round the bend of the avenue into sight of the house.

The sun struck full on the square façade and in at the windows, which with their blinds half down had an appearance of blinking. Tufts of winter jasmine grew at the foot of the steps that went steeply and massively up to the open hall-door. Two puppies asleep at the top twitched, yawned, stretched and came bounding down curved like bows. They made straight for Paul and jumped up; they remained on their hind legs, propping their rigid fore-paws against his knees, grinning ineffably. 'Nice fellows then, nice boys,' said Paul, brushing them off politely.

'Don't they give you a welcome – dogs do *know*,' said Eleanor's mother.

'I should be sorry to think they did,' said Paul genially. He looked sideways at Eleanor, who stiffened. She said with just old stimulating perversity, that inflection . . . 'As a matter of fact, Mr Pellew doesn't care for animals.'

'Fancy!' said Eleanor's mother.

She wandered about the drawing-room, from table to table, showing him bowl after bowl of spiky leaves. He wandered after her. 'Hyacinths?'

'Oh no; I hate the waxy smell. They're unhealthy, I always think. These are tulips – muscari – daffs. They'll be out in a week. I had early tulips by Christmas.'

'Had you really? Eleanor, you are terribly un-exotic.'

Eleanor had taken her hat off; she showed her crisp, light-brown hair brushed sideways across her forehead, her thin face with the jaw a shade prominent, the nose so adorably crooked, her dark, rather deep-set eyes; her whole expression eager, serious, immature. Her smile, which came doubtfully, was also a little crooked; this crookedness lent it the air of a greater complexity than her nature possessed, of ruefulness, of subtle uncertainty, of the constant reweighing of values. She was slender and strong-looking; she stopped.

She smiled when he said she was un-exotic. 'Nobody said I was.'

'That's what so — '

' – Oh, please hush! I don't think the door's shut.' He shut it; the feeling of being shut in together evidently frightened her. 'Do remember,' she said, 'you're just someone who's come to lunch. Do be natural – like anyone of that sort would be. And don't – don't *look* at me, Paul. You make me so ashamed and uncomfortable.'

'Ashamed?'

'Oh, it's not that mother would notice, but it seems all wrong here. You see this is my home, Paul, and it's me too, what I've always been . . . Do open the door again. It's so . . . well, you know. Shutting ourselves in. I'm only supposed to be showing you the bulbs and the Bartolozzi.'

'Ah yes,' he said, 'and I haven't seen the Bartolozzi, have I?' He made no attempt to open the door again, so she opened it herself, doggedly.

'Then I can't really see,' he said in a low voice, 'why I've come down at all. You won't hear of my having it out with them all; you won't let me touch you — '

She winced. 'You don't understand,' she said. 'It was different in London. But here – I do hate feeling . . . common.'

'I'm sorry,' he said, 'I'm a man, you're a woman. Love is rather common, I dare say.'

'Don't be so intellectual!' she said bitterly. 'Do be more human – and give us all time. Can't you do what you promised? Make friends with them all. Be something more than just a man. Make mother feel you're real. Be jolly with the children, like the other men who come here.' ('Evidently,' thought Paul, 'I *ought* to have tweaked their pig-tails.') 'Then tell mother yourself about us – when she's had time to see for herself.'

'Everything?'

'Of course not – it would sound terrible put into words. I think mother would die. Just say you began to like me when I was in London.' She stood with her face turned away from him, listening distractedly all the time for a possible step in the hall, speaking confusedly.

'So you're ashamed, on the whole, of what happened in London?'

'It seems so unreal. It's got no background. It isn't what one could possibly build up one's life on.'

They heard steps at last, coming downstairs and beginning to cross the flagstones. Eleanor brought out a bundle of knitting from behind a cushion and sat down, swinging her legs, on the end of the sofa, with her shoulders clad in a fluffy blue jumper hunched forward a little. She frowned at her work like a schoolgirl, chaste and negative. Paul wheeled round to study the Bartolozzi engravings which, more than a dozen, hung in a pattern all over one wall. Chintz-covered chairs were drawn up to the fireplace in a semicircle; the women of the family would sit thus, looking up at the mantelpiece where the men, the brothers killed in the war, the dead father, the brother in India, stood lined up in their silver frames, staring out at nothing frankly and fearlessly. The family jaw repeated itself. The pendulum of the Dresden clock swung lazily, the fire rustled, Eleanor's needles clicked.

' "One's life",' he impatiently thought. 'This is living, O Daughter of the House, this is how time passes, this is how you approach death!'

A lady with white hair piled up on her forehead came in, preceded by one dog and followed by another. She glanced at Pellew a moment, penetratingly over her rimless glasses. 'Eleanor,' she said in a deep voice, 'you haven't introduced this Mr Pellew to your Aunt Tatty.'

Eleanor hated, evidently, this failure in social alertness. Aggrieved, she performed the introduction. 'Mr Pellew,' she added, 'is a friend of the Jennings'.'

'I know, I know,' said Aunt Tatty; 'you told me that twice. I'm not such an old lady.' She ran her eyes over him candidly, so intelligently that he shifted his attitude. He felt for the first time that morning in touch with a fellow-being, at once on guard and at ease. 'I hear,' said she, 'that all you friends of the Jennings', their what they call "set", are remarkably clever and modern. Splendid for Eleanor – I should be quite out of touch. Do you care for the country?'

Paul looked out of the window for reference. 'Depends,' he said guardedly.

'I daresay,' said Aunt Tatty, and glanced at his knees. 'Too bad, the dogs have been jumping up. You should control your dogs, Eleanor, they are impossible. We shall never have modern visitors . . . Dogs,' she added, in explanatory aside, 'are a habit, I think.'

Lunch went through with strands of talk spun out fine till they dwindled to thin little patches of silence. Pellew, his back to the fire, sat between two young sisters and Eleanor watched him. 'Have you got a pony?' 'Oh no, we ride horses . . .' 'Isn't that pretty!' (pointing to a coloured prism falling from the water-jug). 'What, that? Haven't you seen one before?' 'The colours . . .' 'I don't care for violet,' said the younger sister, wrinkling up her nose. 'Do you keep rabbits?' 'We did, but they died. Do you?' 'I used, but they died too.' 'Oh! I didn't know men kept rabbits.' 'That was when I was a little boy.' 'Oh.' They were here to eat not to talk and they turned from him politely and finally. 'All their lives,' thought Paul, 'they'll go on eating slabs and slabs and slabs of roast mutton. . . .'

Eleanor's mother came in to lunch with a pile of literature which she placed on the table beside her. She kept fingering leaflets. She was longing to talk to Aunt Tatty about the Women's Institute. Every now and then she would draw a long breath and lean over vaguely towards her sister-in-law. He could see thought struggling up from the depths of her mild eyes. Then she would recollect him. She kept 'bringing him in'. 'It is a great movement,' she told him, 'a great movement. Here, we have taken up basket-work. We are so keen. But I don't suppose,' she faltered, her eyebrows knitted again in despair at herself, 'that you'd know very much about basket-work! One gets so absorbed – terrible. It isn't like architecture. Do talk to me about churches. It would be lovely to know. . . .'

Aunt Tatty listened impartially. She sat with her shoulders a little shrugged, the weight of her body tilted; when she was not eating it seemed that, below the edge of the table, her hands were clasped on her knees and she were leaning upon them. She looked round at her relations as though she had not yet wholly identified herself with them, still had the faculty of seeing them. Yet she had an air of being permanently among them; she didn't exert herself. Whenever Paul looked at her she always seemed to be looking at Eleanor. She was a stoutish, aristocratic old lady in a 'good' black. During a longer pause than usual, while the mother fingered her leaflets and Eleanor stared at her plate, she said to Pellew :

'Do tell us about the Jennings.'

Ursula Jennings (Maltby before her marriage) had been a school friend of Eleanor's. He thought of her as a dark young woman, at her ease everywhere, emphasising without declaring herself, reserved, daring, patronising, subtle, discreet. Indescribable. He didn't, as a matter of fact, care for Ursula Jennings. He had 'owed her one' for her manner ever since that first evening, with Eleanor. He didn't believe she cared for Eleanor really. He had always known William and couldn't at the moment, from sheer nervousness, visualise him. Fattish . . . sceptical? Good on Venetians – seventeenth century? That wouldn't say anything *here*. He put himself into the Jennings' drawing-room, determined to build them both up from the outside, detail by detail, but all he saw was Eleanor getting up from a gold chair under the red lacquer lamp, uncertainly, with her curiously square, pale face; thin, awkward, serious, eager, to hold out her hand to him. He felt startled, a little angry as though someone had touched him, and said in an abrupt voice :

'I haven't seen anything of them lately.'

Eleanor's mother put down a brochure on rabbit-keeping. 'But surely . . .' she objected, 'Eleanor said you'd been there so much.'

'I mean, not since then.'

'That was only three weeks ago,' said Eleanor's mother, gently informative, smiling.

'In London, I expect,' said Aunt Tatty, 'people who are all friends, who are "a set", see each other almost every day.' She twinkled her spectacles at Pellew and smiled knowingly.

Pellew, standing in the open door at the top of the steps, waved an arm at some trees and exclaimed, 'Those are – splendid !' They did not, it is true, burn in like the station trees – he was tired now and could not receive impressions so sharply. These were not bare beech, stretching up full in sunshine, but elms with the sun behind them. A slight wind, imperceptible in the shelter of the house, tossed their branches so that the sky behind them twinkled. It was towards the end of the afternoon; the wheels went round more easily but he drooped, he could feel them all drooping, with social fatigue. They had paraded the garden and the paddocks; feeling high-pitched, he kept pulling them up to indicate and exclaim at what nobody else saw.

'Yes, that's our barn roof – that's moss makes it so green. Yes, isn't it green. What were you going to say?'

'Nothing. Only it's *so* green. With that light on it.'

'Yes, it is green . . .' After a little glance across at each other, a slight pause, they would pass on.

Embarrassment kept prevailing. Pellew felt an awful bounder. He wasn't used to being entertained, he kept initiating, he couldn't go properly passive. He tried to make his mind slack as an empty sack to be trailed along, but he couldn't; there was something in it that kept catching on things, bumping. He walked between Eleanor and her mother (Aunt Tatty had stayed in the house to write letters). They hesitated along the garden borders, stopping, lifting here and there a leaf with the point of a walking stick and bending down to peer under it. Meanwhile he stood behind them and yawned, stretching his whole being. He looked along the espaliers, up at the brick walls, down at the turned soil and blunt-tipped enamelled noses of young plants poking up through it, and yawned again. 'Life,' he thought, 'life!' Gravely Eleanor picked him a crocus which he gravely put in his button-hole. She walked bare-headed with her bare hands deep in her coat-pockets; keeping close beside her he slipped his fingers into a pocket and touched her wrist. Feeling the muscles contract in a shiver he thought with surprise : 'So she loves me!'

Now they were back on the steps again; her mother had gone in murmuring something, sighing. 'Those trees . . .' he repeated, pensively, with a kind of inspiration to the inept.

Eleanor said at last, 'I suppose we *feel* the country; we don't — '

'Aestheticise about it?'

'You do rather, don't you.' Absently and kindly, like a sister, she put a hand on his shoulder and leant a little upon it. 'I do care for you,' she said, frowning at the elm trees. 'It's so difficult, isn't it? Don't be discouraged.'

'I thought *you* were. I should have liked so much to have kissed you – just once.'

'Do I seem awfully different?' she asked wistfully.

He looked back over his shoulder into the hall. All round the doors stood ajar letting in panels of afternoon light; in the drawing-room window, Aunt Tatty was at a writing-table, silhouetted against a strip of sunny lawn. Loyal to Eleanor's privacy, it was for him to say rapidly, 'Hush!' She drew into herself, the hand slipped from his shoulder, there flitted across her face an expression of disappointment. He had rebuffed her.

'If you'd care,' she said with an effort, 'I'll show you the church. You may as well see *one* church, I suppose,' she added, smiling unhappily. 'Do you know, Paul, till your letter came I hadn't had to tell a lie for three years. I remember the last quite distinctly; it was something to do with Aunt Tatty's coffee, when we were abroad. I hate lying – I wish I were not such a coward . . . Would you dare, do you think, after all, speak to mother tonight?'

She was taking him to the church by a way of her own; down an overgrown track through a thicket. He went ahead, parting the interlaced branches of hazel and willow and holding them back for her. They walked unsteadily over tussocks of pale, wintry grass and desiccated bracken. 'I'm afraid,' he objected, 'we've made that rather difficult, now. Are you so certain, then, that they like me?'

She didn't answer, only stared at him.

'You see,' he said gently, 'I'm not at all their sort. I'm not your sort, really. I'm afraid you'll have to get used to the idea of their not liking it.'

'It's hard at present, naturally. We're not in the way of new people.'

'I'm too new. There's nothing to go on. I'm all in a void. I'm a phenomenon for them.'

'Paul — '

He strode on a few feet ahead of her, speaking over his shoulder, pressing his way through the branches. She cried his name again, and as he gave no sign of hearing came hurrying after him. 'I do care, I do !' she exclaimed with a catch in a her voice; 'I feel in a thicket everyway. Yet I have been happy; I came back from town feeling dazed. I prayed you might write, though I'd made you swear you wouldn't. Paul, I'm yours, honestly – look at me.'

He stepped back and put his arms round her, not ardently as he had done in the morning but with a queer mixture of diffidence and desperation. He caught one passionate and frightened look from her eyes before she closed them. 'Now we're alone,' he said, 'listen to me, Eleanor. How do you feel . . . Wouldn't you come back to town with me now, come abroad, and we'd write to them from there? Married – I meant married. It's nothing desperate we both want to do, after all; I wouldn't be spoiling your life – a life's what I want to give you. I've made myself some sort of a place in the world, I've a good deal of money. They'd get used to me afterwards. Wouldn't you come?'

'Why like that, why — '

'It's the only chance. Oh, I'm not so uncivilised really. I'd wait any time, please anyone, if I were sure of you at the end. But I couldn't be, all this is sapping us. At the end of some more of these days there wouldn't be anything of us left. We have been real people – we *are* real people, at the back of us – somewhere. And you're great; it's that that I've felt in you. Don't make life an affair of behaviour – you try but it isn't.'

'What is it then ?'

'I don't know – why make it anything ? – let it make you something. Will you come back with me?'

'Why must I come?' she cried miserably. 'It's not fair to make me decide. I don't know what's real; all today I've been absolutely bewildered. It's so difficult. I can't even imagine mother – afterwards. It might kill her, or she might hardly be worried a bit — '

' – All tomorrow,' he said, 'they'll be pulling me to pieces gently. They won't even know they're doing it, but there will be nothing left of me – and nothing in you could survive it. They couldn't tell you a thing about me I haven't told you myself, but to hear them say it would absolutely finish me for you. We wouldn't see each other again. You must decide. I felt today : this is going to be the crisis, I felt it as soon as I saw you there on the platform, more when we met your mother, most of all when we came into the house. "Think what your brothers would have thought" – that would be your mother's last shot. I shouldn't have got on well with your brothers, Eleanor.'

'I do like you for saying that – but I think you're wrong.' She added in a matter-of-fact voice, as though the ideas had followed each other in natural sequence : 'I'm coming with you – only look, Paul, what shall I do? – I haven't a hat.'

He was so much startled, he laughed aloud. She smiled, and they stood staring at one another, transformed by this one wild moment. The afternoon light came slanting on to them through the branches, they were trellised over with thin definite shadows which moved to and fro, to and fro as the branches tossed. The thicket closing round them with its damp, mossy smell, its tunnels of blue shadow, might have been a forest through which they were roving unhampered. He cried 'Beautiful!' and they kissed spontaneously and eagerly, as though meeting again. With her hands on his shoulders she looked about her triumphantly, at her lover, at the trees, as though she were having her own way at last, as though this idea had been hers and only the opposition had come from him. 'I can't go back to the house,' she said; 'I must buy a hat on the way. I'll wait here and you walk down to the village, to the Green Man, and hire a car. There are new people there who won't know me. Then we can drive to the junction. We can't go up by the slow train, feeling like this, and it wouldn't do to wait about at our station. Don't let's lose time, Paul. Come quickly.'

'Where does this path lead? Where are we going?'

It was a short cut that bisected the avenue some yards ahead. She slipped an arm through his own and was hurrying him along; she no longer smiled; she looked very serious and exalted. Her profile, the hair blown back from her forehead, made him feel he was running away with a Joan of Arc. They stumbled over the tussocks; in his hurry he stepped on the first primrose he'd seen that year, deep down in its leaves in the middle of the path. He did not realise how close they were to the avenue till Eleanor, without caution, had hurried him half way across it. Then he glanced to his left, stopped dead and said softly, 'Done in.'

Aunt Tatty, strolling from the direction of the house, had hailed them and was cheerfully waving.

'Having a look round the place?' called Aunt Tatty.

Eleanor, also turning, took her hand from Paul's arm and vaguely stared at her approaching aunt. She seemed less confused than utterly taken aback. Aunt Tatty advanced without embarrassment; possibly she had seen nothing. She wore an astrakhan coat and a decided-looking felt hat; grey Shetland muffled the amplitude of her chin.

'Don't you feel cold, Eleanor, wandering about without a hat? Seems to me it's turned chilly. I'm just taking your mother's letters and mine to post, for the sake of the walk – Will you come with me?' she turned to Pellew. 'I could show you the post-office. Pretty, but not much in the way of architecture – Eleanor, your mother's been looking for you.'

While Paul watched, something in Eleanor faded. As though at the suggestion from Aunt Tatty she shivered faintly and turned up her coat-collar. 'Don't go !' he said sharply and clumsily. 'You promised,' he insisted, holding her eyes, 'to show me the church.'

She looked blank. 'I think, Mr Pellew,' interposed Aunt Tatty, 'that while Eleanor's mother is looking for her we mustn't detain Eleanor.'

'In half an hour I'll be at the church,' said Eleanor, and, without looking again at her aunt or her lover, walked away in the direction from which Aunt Tatty had come.

Pellew wondered if just such blind black moments as this preceded murder. He found himself moving forward numbly, sucked in the wake of the stout lady. She was in full sail again, with the invulnerable complacency of a man-of-war. Yet at the very crisis of his sickness and anger there was something grateful in this contact after the aloofness and erratic fires of Eleanor.

'Fancy not having looked at the church yet,' Aunt Tatty was observing; 'wasn't that what you came for? But of course,' she went on, 'one could see that it wasn't that. You two are in love with each other, aren't you?'

Pellew began laughing awkwardy, with self-derision. 'Were we so unnatural?'

'I could guess beforehand – Eleanor is quite transparent. It occurred at once to her mother, even, although she, as I dare say you noticed, is a good deal vaguer than I am. Churches,' sniffed Aunt Tatty – 'of all the childish inventions – *Churches!*'

'I'm an architect by profession, you know,' said Pellew stiffly.

'Oh, I dare say you may be,' said Aunt Tatty, and looked at him keenly. 'But that doesn't explain, you know, why you couldn't be more direct with us. Why you couldn't have declared yourself frankly, or have let Eleanor confide in her mother – You *do*, I suppose, mean to marry her?' she sharply added.

'Of course,' said Pellew, surprised by her manner, by her queer alternations of irony and bustle. 'But I do, of course, anticipate trouble. Well, as you noticed at once, I'm not Eleanor's sort. Not any of your sort. I feel up against so much in her here that I never suspected. If I'd guessed what it was going to be like here, I wouldn't only have *funked* coming down, I wouldn't have come at all — '

'Wisest not, perhaps — ' said Aunt Tatty.

'All my feeling is for her as a woman. Socially, I find her difficult. Socially, she seems to find me impossible.'

'Really – is that really so, now?' Aunt Tatty said eagerly. Suddenly flushed, she seemed annoyed all at once by the warmth of her muffler, which she loosened with quick little tugs, poking out her pink chin impatiently over the folds.

'Not an easy basis for marriage,' she said dogmatically, with a queer note of triumph. '*I* didn't marry on that,' she informed him, '*I* wouldn't. And I might have at one time, there were a good many reasons . . besides some affection on both sides. But I didn't. Later on, I married much better. Of course I had plenty of opportunities. Which is more,' said the Aunt complacently, 'than Eleanor may have.'

'That does make a difference.'

His irony was lost upon her preoccupation. 'I have sometimes wondered — ' she began, then suddenly broke off.

'Really?'

'I was rather wild at one time,' admitted Aunt Tatty. 'Intellectually, I mean,' she qualified hastily, touching the brim of her hard hat. 'I hesitated; I suppose I was quite unhappy. He was nothing socially; quite young, but there was promise – brilliancy. But the promise,' cried Aunt

Tatty triumphantly, 'didn't fulfil itself. I'd been right all along. He went downhill in every way – rapidly.'

'Disappointed, perhaps?'

'Faugh!' said Aunt Tatty. 'One disappointment! . . . So you see I've had nothing to regret. There's no protection in life like a lack of courage. I've been a happy woman, Mr Pellew.'

Something unreal in her tone, some lack of simplicity, made him say with a touch of impertinence, 'You are to be congratulated.' They were approaching the lodge gates. 'Come out into the open,' she said, sardonic and genial, 'take your chances.'

'Which, quite frankly,' he said, 'you think are the worst in the world?'

'In so far as Eleanor is my niece, they'll be as bad as I know how to make them. In so far as you're a clever modern young man whom I quite like – well, I couldn't wish you anything better than to be clear of the lot of us. In so far,' she concluded, wistfully genuine, 'as my own curiosity is concerned (for I tell you, I *have* sometimes wondered –) I shall be sorry to see the end of this so soon. I should like to see what became of you both – though I'm perfectly certain, of course, how it must end, your marriage.'

'So you'll fight me over it?'

'Certainly.'

'By conviction?'

'By conviction,' she assented, loudly and definitely; a sharp sigh heaved up the lapels of astrakhan coat.

'Fairly?'

Silently, she handed him her letters. He took them and pushing through the lodge gates crossed the road and slipped them into the postbox. He stood a moment more with his back to her, mustering his forces, before he dared to turn round. She had remained leaning back on her walking-stick, watching his every movement, taking him in, measuring him with intensity. 'Fairly?' he asked again, coming back, raising his voice to be heard above a sudden clamour of rooks. He stared straight with some kind of a pang, a sharp conflict of confidence and antagonism, into her hard vivid face. She had touched the man in him.

'Yes,' said Aunt Tatty with a little laugh and braced herself, 'Fairly.'

'Then come back to the house,' he said. 'There is something I must say, at once, to Eleanor's mother.'

EDEN PHILLPOTTS

THE ANARCHIST

N O B O D Y knew where he got his red opinions; but there they were – a proper, right down anarchist, and full of hard words against every man who wore a black coat even o' Sundays.

Joe Manders was his name, and he was an orphan and lived at the fishing village of Wallcross and worked for old Matthew Ford, in his second boat. He had a room with a fisherman's widow, and, whatever else he might be, he stood to work.

Start Bay, you must know, is a great ground for the crab industry, and Joe was a proper masterpiece in his understanding of the creatures. He knew where all the heaviest crabs walked under the sea, and he put down the pots by a sort of instinct just in the properest places. A rare chap to labour – not an idle bone in his body, you might say – and Mr Ford thought the world of him, though, of course, he didn't hold with his rash ideas.

'So long as he works for me and earns his money and shows his great understanding of the crabs, I don't care,' said old Ford. 'I judge young men by what they do, not what they says, and if Joe talks like a fool and believes that a man with a few pence saved is a foe to the people, and so on, then let him. But this I believe; his heart is in the right place.'

He said that to Miss Nosworthy, Joe's aunt. She was a very steadfast Conservative, however, and had almost two hundred pounds a year, and her own cottage, all left to her by her father, who had worked for it. So she hadn't no opinion of Joe's anarchy and felt it might land him in trouble some day.

'But be it as it will,' said old Ford to Mary Nosworthy, 'all fruits have got to be sour afore they're sweet, so you may live in hope that your nephew will throw over this nonsense and see the dignity and might of capital, as ordained by God Almighty in the nature of things. Capital and labour be cogs of one wheel,' said Matthew, 'and us have got to see that each does its proper work and learns to trust the other. But the oil of the machine be goodwill, and where shall we find it?'

'I hope he'll get sense presently,' answered Miss Nosworthy – a little, pinicking woman, up home seventy-five years, so brittle as a shrimp owing to her rheumatics, but full of wisdom and with a seeing eye.

'I'd sooner have him than his cousin, Lance, anyways,' said old Ford. 'Joe haven't got the gentle tongue of Harry Lance, I grant; but then Harry had a secondary education; and he'll follow his father at Three Ways Farm; and his nature is to trust his betters and go to church and so on.'

'Harry will come in and pass the time of day,' answered old Mary, 'and he'll bring me a chicken now and then and a nice parcel of green stuff.'

'All to the good,' admitted Matthew Ford. 'I'm not saying nothing against Harry. I'm only saying I'd sooner have Joe with all his nonsense.'

And, being a man so wise as he was kind, the old crabber, next time he had speech with Joe, gave him a hint.

'You see a bit more of your Aunt Mary in your spare time, Joe Manders,' he said. 'She can't be above ground very much longer in my opinion, for you can look through the old lady's hands very near, and there ain't no more substance to her than a butterfly; so you be attentive and kind to her off and on; and next time you drop in, you can take her a nice, middle-sized crab.'

Joe was a dark chap, aged twenty-one, with a handsome

but scowling countenance, and a wonderful pair of eyes, so black as coal, yet full of fire. Tall and slim, and nicely put together, but discontented-looking, owing to his fixed opinions that the world was going to smash along of labour not getting its share of the spoil.

Now he shook his black hair off his forehead and gave his master a nod.

'If you command,' he said.

'I don't command. I only command in working hours, Joe, and well you know it,' answered old Ford, 'but I tell you, that you owe your aunt respect – a sort of respect that your cousin Harry don't forget to pay.'

Joe Manders sneered.

'And why? Why do he creep up her sleeve and take her things to eat and agree with every word she says and pretend he's a saint and all that? Because, well, he knows there's capital hid there what she can't take with her when she drops out. And if you think a socialist born, such as me, would sink to such hookem-snivery ways, I'm sorry, Mister Ford, because I'd sooner starve than dirt my hands of unearned money.'

'And quite right, Joe – quite right,' answered Matthew mildly. 'I know your fine feelings about cash, and what the mischief you'll do some day, when you find yourself making plenty, as you surely will with all your cleverness, be bothered if I can tell. But, meanwhile, your aunt's an old woman, and she was mighty fond of your mother, and there's no law in socialism for a young man not to brighten up his relations now and again.'

'I won't brighten up no capitalists,' said Joe.

'They might brighten you up, however. I'm not saying you did ought to keep a half-crown in your pocket, or a decent coat on your back, Joe – not if such things run contrary to your high opinions – but I'll ask you to take a real good crab to Miss Nosworthy one day next week, and if

she asks you to bide a bit and drink a cup of capitalist tea,
I'll thank you to do so.'

'Then I will do so,' answered Joe, and he obeyed.

He was received affectionately, and his aunt let him run
on, because, though a spinster, she'd had a lot to do with
men and understood 'em pretty well. And she knew Joe
was a very honest boy under his skin.

He ate hearty and fretted and fumed and showed a
wondrous warm heart and a great command of memory.
For he let out what he'd read in the Labour papers and
what he'd heard an open-air orator tell on the subject;
and it was quite clear that he believed every word of it.
And Miss Nosworthy listened and pointed out how time
was a sure healer.

'Everything that did ought to happen does happen, Joe,
according to the will of God,' she said, 'so you may be
certain that when the Almighty thinks the world be ripe for
anarchy – if ever He does – then it will happen, and capital
will be abolished. But since the world haven't yet got beyond the stage of capital, us must take things as they are.
And, if you want to be a useful man, you must help the
world as only it can be helped, by being a wise and powerful man also. And money is power, and you can't tell me
there ain't plenty of good, rich men spending their money
to help their neighbours.'

'I don't know none,' said Joe. 'Your view be a very
cowardly one in my opinion, Aunt Mary. Doles and chari-
ties ain't what we want. We want equal rights and chances.
Capital handicaps labour to hell; and so it will go on doing
for evermore, unless we on my side combine against it and
crush the dirty thing, and let the world start fair and clean
again.'

So he talked, and behind his ideas his aunt saw a big-
hearted, earnest chap, so green as a gooseberry, where truth
was concerned.

Then who should drop in but Harry Lance. He kissed Miss Nosworthy – a thing what Joe had never done – and he shook hands with his cousin and said he was glad to see him there – which was a lie.

A nice-looking, fair, frank young chap; but he'd got they white eyelashes, which to the seeing eye always mean something up a man's sleeve; and he'd got one of they easy mouths, which mean women – just like some women have got a mouth that means men.

He prattled on, but Joe dried up when he came in, and pretty soon the young fisherman cleared out, for he cherished a natural dislike of Harry. His aunt made Joe promise to come again, however, and his promise he kept; but as time went on and he saw more of her, Joe didn't appear to please her very much. She'd listen, though she'd never argue; and then she found a new sort of restlessness rising up in the young fellow, and he got that bitter and cross-grained there was no biding him.

They quarrelled once over Harry Lance, because Joe said he was after her money; and then he didn't see his aunt no more for two months, till he got a message from another party to say as she wanted to see him and commanded him to come. And that other party happened to be one Joe could always obey.

Susie Cliff it was; and if the truth had been shown up, I doubt not the people would have found that Susie was responsible for Joe's present temper and doglike way of snarling and cussing everybody in the village. Because much to his surprise and indignation, he'd fallen in love with Susie, and he felt it a shameful thing that a man with his opinions and such big ideas in general, should find himself thinking twice about a chit of a girl.

She was a lovely little piece without a doubt – graceful and pretty, with bright, grey eyes and a good large, red mouth and a mane of pale-brown hair. A very proper hard-working girl was Susie and always busy as a bee. She did chores for Miss Nosworthy of a morning, and the old lady liked her very much and thought well of her sense; but for the most part Susie was too young to be critical, and she thought more hopefully of her fellow creatures as a rule than her mistress did. On the subject of Joe, the maiden would say nothing at all, and when his aunt shook her head about the young man and feared his opinions might make a mess of his life, Susie only hoped not.

'He does a plenty good things on the quiet, Miss Nosworthy,' she said, 'and he's kind really, though such a fierce fellow by all accounts.'

She might have said more, but she did not. She knew Joe was terribly interested in her, and on the day she sought him and told him his aunt was wishful for his company, the affair went farther.

She met the young man coming up from his boat on a summer evening, and he looked at her with a stern face and told her to bide till he'd cleaned himself and then they'd have a tell. Which she did so, and a bit later they walked beside the inland lake at Wallcross.

'I want to let you know a darned queer thing and get it off my chest,' began Joe. 'Perhaps if I was to tell you, it might be better for me.'

'Yes, Joe,' she answered, reckoning she knew what was coming, but little guessing how.

'You know my opinions,' he said sternly. 'Cast iron they are; and among 'em is a feeling that folk are mad to marry young, or marry at all for that matter. I'm against it for all socialists till they get their own back, and knock out the upper classes, and put 'em where they belong. But, despite all that, there's powers in a man beyond his own control seemingly, and I may tell you strict in confidence, Susie, that I'm very much addicted to you. A silly thing without a doubt, but there it is. I love you, in fact, because it can't

I

be for no other reason that you stick in my mind and interfere with my reading and even keep me awake at nights. You don't interfere with my work, nor yet my opinions, because no woman born could do that; but there's no manner of doubt I love you.'

'I'm sorry, Joe – if you are,' said Susie in a very small voice.

'I wouldn't say I was sorry, but it's terrible ill-convenient,' explained Joe. 'What I feel is this. I'm dead sure young men didn't ought to wed, with life what it is nowadays, and far bigger things calling them, and dangers ahead. But when I say to myself, "How would you feel, Manders, if you heard that woman was going to marry somebody else?" when I ax myself that question, I get a powerful sort of feeling for some funny reason I wouldn't like it. And that's love, Susie.'

'I suppose it is, Joe.'

'Yes, and so I'm rather hoping you can see your way to let me out, so as I can bide true to my own fixed opinions. Of course, I couldn't marry anybody, even if so inclined at present, being poor as a mouse; but if you can honestly tell me that you don't feel nothing like this and ain't addicted to me, or better still, that you love somebody yourself, then my feeling would soon fade away, I expect, and I would do everything to help you. You needn't tell me his name or anything about the chap; but if you was in love by good chance, though I shall be sorry, too, in a way, it'll make it much easier for me to put this nonsense out of my head.'

Well, perhaps no girl ever heard anything quite like that before, and most of 'em would have given him a short answer; but she was honest as the morning light, and he'd put her in a parlous fix, along of the fact that she did love the ground he walked on.

She hedged a bit, seeing she had to speak.

'Most of the labour leaders be married men with families, I believe, Joe,' she said.

That ought to have told him he was on dangerous ground, but the young fool only aired his views.

'Most of our leaders be getting big money for leading,' he answered. 'All very well for them to have wives and families. We pay 'em huge salaries for what they do – too huge in my opinion. They pull in thousands of pounds; and I don't reckon many of 'em be worth so much myself. They talk and run about and lecture us working men; but they're capitalists themselves, to be honest. We can leave them to their own consciences; but if they think they be doing right in having long families and servants to wait on 'em and motor-cars and so on, I do not.

'You stick to facts, Susie. I can't marry, and don't want to, even if I could, along of my duty to the Cause. But if you can say you love somebody yourself, then my conscience is clear and I shall feel a bit freer and no strain on my mind. I ain't good enough for a beautiful, bowerly creature like you, as ought to have the fat of the land yourself, if there was any justice; but I'm just telling you that you've upset my scheme, and so I shall be mortal glad if you can assure me there's no need for me to worry no more.'

That done it, and showed Susie how she might tell the truth quick and then leave him to his wonderful opinions.

'I do love a man,' she said, and Joe breathed again.

'Thank God!' he replied. 'That cuts the knot very clever indeed, Susie. Now I'm free to go my way; and so be you. And if I knew who the man was – but I don't and I don't want to. Good night and good luck.'

With that, in his abrupt way, he left her standing by the lake, staring at the water lilies that grew in it; and when the sound of his feet was still and she stood alone, she sat down in the sand and wept buckets.

For he'd been her dream, you see, best part of a year, and

she knew he liked her and felt cruel proud of it. But now the poor maid was down and out, in a manner of speaking, and nought left to hope and live for.

A few nights later Joe came to tea with his aunt and he was so glum as a bear and scarce civil to the old lady. He fetched her a lobster, however, but forgot all about it, and Susie found it next morning, outside the door on the mud-scraper, when she was cleaning the step.

'How's the proletariat going on, Joe?' asked Miss Nosworthy, to make conversation, finding her nephew so quiet.

'There's a million and a quarter out of work – that's how they're going on,' said Joe. 'And to see you eating buttered scones and plum cake is a disgrace, Aunt Mary.'

But he didn't quarrel long. He wanted to know something. That fine relief that he'd got when he heard he was free of Susie had worn off, much to his surprise; and it had left a queer feeling that wasn't fine at all. He'd fairly cussed the woman when he found she still stuck in his mind; and he'd lost hope about himself also, because he began to fear that he was weak in his head and wouldn't be much good to the Cause after all.

He came to the subject gradually.

'They tell me,' he said, 'that the girl as works for you of a morning be tokened. Susie Cliff, I mean.'

'First I've heard of it, Joe,' answered Miss Nosworthy.

'I thought she might have told you who he was?'

'No. Yet I think she'd have named it. Be you sure?'

'Yes – I had it from her herself.'

'Fancy! I'd never have thought that; and I ask if you're sure, Joe, because the child has been a good bit under the weather lately and not herself by no means.'

'Perhaps he's chucked her, whoever it was,' suggested Joe.

'He may have done that. You young men never know your own minds nowadays.'

But her nephew didn't take no note of that challenge.

'If I thought there was a man playing about with her feelings, I'd talk to him,' said Joe.

'I hope you would then,' answered Miss Nosworthy. 'She's a girl in a thousand, in my opinion – too good for most of the Wallcross chaps.'

Joe nodded.

'Yes, she is. Do she know Harry Lance?' he asked.

'She knows him; but Harry wouldn't play with a girl's feelings, Joe – a steady, church-going chap like him.'

'It wouldn't be the first, however. He jilted Sarah Quickly.'

'There was two sides to that. He couldn't be blamed there.'

The fisherman scowled as he thought of his cousin.

'He's a tricky toad – Master Harry is – like all them capitalists and fellows that know they're snug.'

'He does his work at Three Ways Farm – so his father tells me.'

'Yes, his father would. I'll make sure, however.'

'Don't you quarrel with Harry, Joe.'

But the young man didn't pursue the subject. He was moody and troubled, yet the facts he had revealed rather pleased his aunt. She'd felt for a good bit that a wife like Susie Cliff might very like put sense into Joe; and that her nephew was evidently considering Susie in a jealous spirit cheered her a bit. But her hope died pretty quick when he went off, for she asked herself, very naturally, what a cheerful and hopeful creature like Susie would see in such a scowling, sour-tongued lad.

'Unless,' thought the old woman, 'she had the cleverness to know all his wild opinions come of good sense turned upside down – same as I do; but how can you expect an ignorant girl to see that?'

She remembered, however, that Susie always stood up

for Joe and knew about kind things he'd done, so she didn't fling over hope, for she knew exceeding well that the rash youth was sound at heart.

The next thing that her nephew meant to happen was a row between himself and his cousin, Harry, because the love-sick young idiot had got it into his head that his cousin must be the man who was vexing Susie. But a streak of sense come to him the last moment, and he bethought him that he'd go so far as to ask Susie first if Harry Lance was the man. Because he granted to his stupid self that it would be a pity to fall out with Harry unless the reason was big enough. So he tackled Susie in his savage way; and he ordered her to walk with him after dark one evening out towards the Start Lighthouse.

Of course she obeyed, and when they met and got going, Joe said :

'I hear from a private source, Susie Cliff, that you be a good bit under the weather.'

She didn't say 'yes' nor 'no' to that, but kept silent.

'If it's true, there's no reason for it,' declared the young fellow, 'and the reason I'm wishful to know. Because, though you're lost to me in a manner of speaking, me being marked for a bachelor and you wanting some other and likelier chap, yet I'm still interested in your career, I may tell you; and it's whispered to me that this here unknown you care about ain't treating you none too well. And if the love's all on your side, or if he's changed his mind, then, feeling what I do, I'm wishful to talk to the man and bring him to reason mighty quick.

'My sweeping ideas don't give me time for silly little fusses between man and man, nor nothing like that; but where you're concerned,' says Joe, 'I'll take it on and put sense into him. And if it's my cousin, Harry Lance, I'll thank you to let me know, because a chap like him would be dust in my hands.'

'Harry's got nothing to do with me,' said she. 'We're very good friends; but whenever he's serious about a girl, then you may be sure that girl will have got money. He'll be friendly with any girl; but he won't marry nought but a rich one.'

'Money's his god, as we all know. Well, that lets him out, then; and I'm rather sorry, I may tell you, for I'd so soon have a row with him as anybody, him being against all progress except his own – a selfish dog. But if it isn't him, no doubt it's somebody else and all's one to me where you're concerned.

Again Susie went dumb.

'By your silence,' he said, 'you grant I'm right. Very well then. There's a man treating you unkind and I won't have it – I won't have it, Susie. If he's offered to marry you, and you be such a fool as to think you'll be happier along with him than on your own, then married you shall be; or else you shall have him up for breach. Tell me the man's name and leave the rest to me.'

'Don't you worry about me, Joe; I'm all right,' answered Susie. 'There's other things to think of besides men. I'm troubled about a woman for the minute; far more than any man; and that's your Aunt Mary. She's failing and ought to see the doctor, I'm sure.'

'That may or may not be,' answered Joe; 'but one thing at a time, please. You can't choke me off like a child. There's a man fretting you and you don't deny it, and I'll have his name afore we part company tonight.'

'You won't have it, Joe,' said the girl, firm and sharp, 'for the good reason I ain't going to tell you.'

'Think twice,' he answered her. 'I'm pretty clever and far-seeing, and I haven't got into politics and all that for nothing. An anarchist I may be, as they say, but I know when to take direct action, as we call it, and when to keep inside the British Constitution. You tell me the man and I'll go for him well inside the constitution and the law, as it stands at present. I won't knock his silly head off nor nothing like that. I'll just argue patient and sensible, and tell him not to make a hateful fool of himself and hurt your feelings; and I'll drop a skilful hint in his stupid ear that you're one in a thousand and the best and finest creature ever come out of Wallcross and so on. Then the blighter will soon creep back and feed out of your hand, no doubt, and give you no more trouble. And if he's saucy and minded to throw you over, or any such wickedness as that, then I'll put it across him and blamed soon bring him to heel.'

'Very kind and thoughtful of you, Joe, I'm sure,' said Susie, not knowing very well whether to laugh or cry; 'but 'twill be cleverer all round, I think, if I don't mention the chap to you.'

'And why not? Shouldn't a far-seeing man like me understand how to handle the fool?'

'Not very well, I'm afraid,' said Susie; and then, of course, Joe began to get hot.

'Cuss all women!' he said. 'Be blessed if any sane man did ought to have any truck with 'em. They stand in our light and they stand in their own. Here am I – a chap a bit out of the common by all acounts – and I offer to take trouble for you, and, like a little zany, you – however, it ain't too late for you to change your mind, I suppose. So best to do so.'

'I never shall change my mind about him,' vowed Susie, though she trembled while she spoke; 'and as for you, Joe, you are out of the common, as you truly say. But – but I can't very well tell you who he is; and be it as it will, I shall never marry him – I'm sure I shan't, so there's no call to worry you.'

'He's thrown you over then?'

'Yes. He's like you – won't marry, I expect.'

'Then he's a dog and never ought to have told you he

cared for you; and whether you give me his name or not, I'll find it out and run him down and let him know how he looks in the eyes of every decent man.'

'I'd a lot rather you didn't trouble, dear Joe.'

'It won't be no trouble,' he answered her. 'It'll be a pleasure to strip that wretch naked and point the finger of scorn at him. The men here be a lot too fond of philandering and then changing their minds. That's the sort Harry Lance is, and I won't stand for 'em.'

'Please, please leave it, Joe! I – I love him still, you see, and I wouldn't like for any harm to over-get him.'

'More fool you, then. You ought to have a properer pride, I reckon. 'Tis weak-minded girls like you give love-hunting creatures like him their chance. I thought better of you, as you well knew; but I shan't no more. You're a poor thing, Susie Cliff.'

'Poor every way, Joe,' said Susie, and then she did begin to cry; but it was dark and he didn't know it. He stormed a bit, and she answered not a syllable; and then he lost his temper and used a lot of crooked words and said he'd find the chap and scrag the life out of him, whether Susie loved him or not. And then he turned on his heel and left her all alone.

He cussed himself to bed and to sleep, full of resolves to make an example of the faithless scamp, and wishing all the time it was his cousin Harry; but the very next morning that happened to make him forget everything but his own affairs; for he was eating his breakfast when Susie Cliff herself, with fatal news, rushed into the cottage where he dwelt. She'd gone as usual to Miss Nosworthy's at six of the clock, to light the fire and tidy up and carry the old woman a cup of tea and a rusk, what she always took before rising up; but when Susie did so, and went into the bedroom, there was old Mary kneeling by her bed in prayer!

A very righteous creature always; but Susie never remembered to see her praying like that before her morning cup of tea. So she called out and Miss Nosworthy didn't move, and Susie went over to her and found her stone-cold and dead as a fish. She died saying her evening prayers, you see, and she'd been kneeling there quite dead since nine o'clock the night afore and she was stiff as a board, poor dear. A beautiful end, but very difficult for the undertakers.

So Susie fled and gave the alarm, and women went into the house, and a policeman also. All sorts of things got about – that Miss Nosworthy had been murdered for her Sheffield candlesticks, and so on; but it was proved a natural death, and the doctor knew all about her state and weren't surprised. So, when the folk heard there wouldn't be no inquest, they calmed down, and after the funeral, to which Miss Nosworthy's relations come in a black swarm, knowing her so well-to-do, the will was read out. Harry Lance and his mother were there, and Miss Worthington, and two nieces of Mary's from Plymouth. In fact the only relation of the lot that didn't turn up was Joe Manders. For, after the funeral, well knowing there'd be nought for him, he doffed his black and went to the crab pots.

But wonders never cease, as they say. His aunt had left one hundred pounds to Harry Lance, and all her silver to her nieces, and a mourning ring to Mrs Lance, and fifty pounds to Mr Matthew Ford for old friendship's sake, and a hundred to Susie Cliff; but all the rest – the bulk of her money, and her house, and every darned thing, to Joe!

It shocked the other relations a good deal, for they hardly knew him more than by name, as the dark spot in the family; but law's law and nobody could say Mary Nosworthy had been out of her mind, or anything like that.

The thing sped on its own wings, as such wonders will, and though none of his relations was upon Wallcross beach to tell Joe the news when he came ashore that evening, his master, Matthew Ford done so; and there he was when Joe landed, and he said :

'Joseph Manders, your aunt's will have been read, and I may tell you that I knew the contents of it six months ago, when she made it, me being her oldest friend, and you'll be glad to know she's left me fifty of the best – free of legacy duty also.'

Joe nodded.

'I am glad,' he said. 'I thought Harry Lance would have the lot.'

'He's got a hundred, and another here and there be down for a trifle; but you are her sole residuary legatee.'

'And what might that mean?' asked Joe. 'She knew my views on capital, poor old dear.'

'It means,' explained Mr Ford, 'that you scoop the lot, my bold hero. You're a capitalist, Joe – a bloated profiteer, Joe – rich with money you never earned, Joe – one of the sort as should be put up against a wall and shot out of hand, my lad !'

'Hell !' said Joe.

Of course he had to go through with it, and likewise, of course, being only a human young fellow, he couldn't help liking the taste. But he thought very steadfast against the temptation it offered, and was full of generous, but foggy, ideas as to his duty. Two things troubled him in secret from the very first; and one concerned himself and the other somebody else. But time had to pass, and it was a fortnight or more before he brought his difficulties to his master; for though Matthew Ford was a capitalist himself and, as such, not to be trusted too far, still Joe knew him to be honest as the day, and couldn't deny that the old man had done many acts worthy of a socialist and been tolerable decent to his poorer neighbours according to his limited lights.

First, however, Joe went orderly to work and gave Susie a month's notice, because there weren't no Mary Nosworthy to wait on no more. And if ever his hard heart was touched, it was when he thought upon his Aunt Mary and her trust in him.

'She believed in me,' he told Matt Ford – 'the first as ever did.'

He had a mourning card printed about her – with a border of black and silver and a tea-urn on a pedestal under a weeping willow tree – all very nice indeed – and he sent it out to everybody, his relations included; and he also let them know that, when the time come, he should put up a fine, sizeable cross of moor stone, or perhaps white marble, over her grave. But the family weren't overmuch interested.

And then he paid an evening visit to Matt Ford, which was, in a manner of speaking, the turning-point in his life.

They drank tea, and Matt lighted his pipe and Joe explained his fine resolves.

'There's two things you can help me with, master,' began the young man. He hated the word 'master', but he still worked for the boat owner and meant so to continue.

'There's two things,' said Joe, 'and I'll take the big one first. It stands like this. My aunt's property, cash and house and sticks, mounts up to a bit over four thousand pounds; and all that hugeous dollop of money's mine; and how she came to leave it to me, the Lord knows!'

'So do I, Joe,' said Mr Ford. 'She left it to you because she was a very far-sighted old bird. She felt what you wanted to steady you down and make you a useful chap was responsibility; and now you've got it. She reckoned that, under your sour rind, you had an honest heart, that only wanted time to ripen and make you a sane and valuable sort of man. And I hope she was right.'

'I hope she was,' answered Joe. 'Anyway, this is my resolve. There's more than a million out-of-works in England at this minute, and though I don't know much about capi-

tal, and don't want to do so, I reckon that four thousand
pounds is going a tidy way to take off the strain for a bit.
That money put in the right channels is going to give all
those poor fellows a breathing space and a little passing
comfort. If 'twas only for a month, it would take the load
off their minds and provide a bit of meat for their wives and
families. And I'm going to sell up and send 'em the lot. And
I'll take it kindly of you to tell me how it's to be done.'

Mr Ford nodded.

'A very big and handsome idea, Joe, and meantime you'll
go on working for me?'

'Yes, I will, then – till things be altered in the world, and
you capitalists be all put out and equality comes in.'

'Fine, Joe – quite what I should have expected from your
high opinions. And I'll be glad to help, I'm sure.'

The old man rose up, went to his desk and fetched out a
bit of paper and pencil.

'We'll just go into figures, Joe, and put it down in black
and white. Four thousand pounds is a dollop of money, as
you say, and a million out-of-works is a dollop of men. But
there's nothing like figures for throwing light on these
problems, and as figures haven't come your way yet, along
of no education, I can help you there.'

Joe didn't answer and Matt made some calculations. He
worked slow and sure for a quarter of an hour; then he sat
up, lighted his pipe again and spoke.

'A pound is two hundred and forty pennies, Joe, and ten
pounds be two thousand, four hundred pennies. Multiply
that by ten again and you find a hundred pounds be twenty-
four thousand pennies.'

'Why for d'you fetch it down to pennies?' asked Joe
impatiently.

'I'm telling you,' replied the old man. 'Let me flow on,
Joe.'

Then he continued.

'Now a thousand pounds comes out at not less than two hundred and forty thousand pennies; and since you've got four thousand pounds to burn, you command no less than nine hundred and sixty thousand pennies. So there you are, Joe. Hand over your pennies to the out-of-works and there'll be just about enough to give the poor heroes one box of matches all round. That you can do; but no more.'

'Not a penny for each of 'em?' gasped Joe.

'If you was to dole out pennies to 'em, my dear, there would still be forty thousand penniless.'

'Damn capital!' said Joe.

'Far from it. I'm only showing you that to help a million men wants a braver bit of cash than the likes of you and me will ever see. But now I'll tell you what I'd do – not speaking as a capitalist, Joe, but as a friend to you and all poor folk. You can't do much for a million; but you can do a proper useful stroke for thirty; and since charity begins at home, I'd advise like this. You be listening?'

'Yes, I be listening,' the boy answered.

'Very well, then; since things are as they are and socialism is not yet in view, because, while this country thinks it hates "protection", it knows it hates your opinions a jolly sight worse, I should do this. You well know the fishermen here badly want a rest house and shelter – a nice place handy to the beach, where they could get a fire and a cup of cocoa in winter and meet and talk with their eyes on the Bay. Such a shelter would be bringing a powerful lot of comfort and cheer to your own neighbours, Joe; and for the price of three hundred pounds, or maybe less, a very commodious and fine affair could be set up. The food and drink would pay for themselves, and I can see a great addition to Wallcross in that way – a good, worthy piece of work.

'Then, for the rest, you buy your own boat, and take up your proper, licensed job as a crabber; and presently you find yourself lucky enough to give useful, well-paid work to

other men. And every man in steady work is one less un-
employed and one more to the good. You go and live in
your own house, and earn your own money, and enlarge
your ideas, and cut your coat according to your cloth, and
help your poorer neighbours when you can, and just wait,
patient and dignified, for anarchy to come along in God's
own time. What about that, Joe?'

'Do you mean I could lift up a proper brick and slate
shelter for the fishermen?'

'Certainly I do. A practical thing showing your opinions
— a proper sign and covenant that you're a red-hot anarchist, Joe — a building as lasting and useful in its way as
Start Lighthouse itself.'

'I'll do it!' cried Joe. 'I'll go to Dartmouth tomorrow,
if you'll let me off for the day, and tell a builder to start on
it this minute.'

'So you shall, then. And don't forget your own boat and
a bit of work for one of our chaps out of a job. And when
you leave me, then I can give another man a job; so that
will be two in work. The place shall be called the "Manders
Shelter", so as you won't be forgot in time to come.'

'No, by God!' swore Joe. 'It shall be called the "Mary
Nosworthy Shelter"! 'Tis her money, not mine.'

He was full of excitement and Matt Ford smiled at him.

Joe rattled on for half an hour; and then he remembered
the other affair.

'You've done me a power of good, master, and I thank
you, I'm sure. If anybody had told me I couldn't help the
whole lot of labour with my money, I never would have
trusted 'em; but no doubt figures can't lie. And the other
affair is that girl, Susie Cliff.'

'I know her very well,' said Matt.

'She tended my aunt, and I find she's in love with some
fool, and he's treating her bad. I may tell you in strict confidence, I think a lot of the woman; and if my opinions

were different, would have offered for her myself; but I found she cared for another man and I felt very pleased to know it – at the time. But he's no mortal good, it seems, and she won't tell me his name, so I can tackle him and knock decency into him.'

'I know his name, Joe,' said Mr Ford, thoughtful-like.

'Would you feel any objection to letting me have it, master?'

'It's like this, Joe. The man can well afford to marry her. He's in an excellent position, honest, clean-living and healthy – just the sort of man that even you would say might be trusted with a hand in the next generation. And on his own showing he's fond of Susie.'

'Then why the mischief do the lunatic hang fire?'

'That I couldn't tell you. I haven't axed him. But perhaps you might find out if you went to headquarters in your fearless way. A lunatic no doubt, as you say. His name's Joe Manders.'

SHEILA KAYE-SMITH

A WEDDING MORN

AN Easter Day was slowly breaking over one of those
Squares in North Kensington which an ebbing prosperity
has left derelict for many years. Strips of golden cloud lay
across the sky behind the houses, and a quickening light
made the rare street-lamps hang like dim fruit against the
trees of the garden. From innumerable back-yards came
the cluck and croon of waking fowls and every now and
then the shrill note of a cock, sending a dream of farms to
the sleeping country-born. The whole place was held in the
dawn like a pearl, full of mysterious glows and a brooding
dimness. It was the Square's moment – a moment in which
it was almost a landscape of high cliffs and deep pools instead of a mere agglomeration of houses, pavements and
lamp-posts, zoning a few exiled trees. The moment passed
as the light grew and revealed the faces of crumbling
stucco, the waste-paper that filled the gutters and drifted
up the doorsteps, the sooty tanglewood of the garden where
the grass grew rank and tall over the neglected paths and
forgotten beds.

The dawn came in at the uncurtained window of a room
set high in Number Seven, Lunar Square. It stroked the
sleeping face of Ivy Skedmore, and she woke, for she was
sleeping lightly. She started up, her mind full of whirling
wheels, of a dream that was scarcely done. Her big round
eyes went wildly round the room, and drew reassurance
from the hanging strips of wallpaper, the walls that were so
high that they soared into shadows under the ceiling, the
cornices of plaster fruits and the matchboard partition
which shut her off from the room where her parents and
the children slept.

Ivy slept with the lodger, who went by the name of Miss
Peach Grey, forgetting some baptismal Maud or Mabel,
and worked as mannequin at a small but aspiring dressmaker's. She was still asleep, and Ivy felt glad, for she did
not want talk or company just yet. She wanted to feel herself alone, to gather some sort of strength with which to
face the day. How many hours? Of course, she had no
watch or clock. On working days there was always the big
buzzer at the paper works. But today was not a working
day, and she suddenly huddled herself over her knees as
she realised that there never would be another working
day – no more rising in clammy dusks, no more dressing in
the darkness, no more hastily swallowed tea – she could feel
the hot catch of it now in her throat – gulped before she
ran down the huge, rickety flight of stairs, across the Square
into Lunar Street past the waking shops to the Oxford
Street restaurant where she washed up dishes all day, all
day . . . smells of grease and cabbage water, the miserable
roughness of her skin in the constant water, the unutter-
able weariness of her legs at her unresting stand before the
sink . . . all day, all day . . . No, never, never, never again.

She sprang out of bed, forgetting the slumbers of Peach,
which luckily were too deep to be disturbed. Her heart beat
quickly and her pulses tingled with the realisation of the
new world she was making for herself by this marriage. She
had escaped the tyranny of every-day and all-day, that
deadly grind of going out to work; and she had not done as
so many girls did in marriage, and merely exchanged paid
labour for unpaid, the back-breaking toil of the workshop
for the heartbreaking struggle of the home. From this day
forward she would be easy and comfortable; she would sit
in a parlour and sleep in a brass bed, she would have electric
light and eat bacon for breakfast . . . and a girl to help her
sometimes in the house. She, Ivy Skedmore, nearly twenty-
seven now, who had slaved at one ill-paid job after another

ever since she had left school, and no prospect before her but toil till her life's end, she had captured the heart of a childless widower, earning eight pounds a week as an electrician, and offering her a snug little flat over at Hammersmith, full of undreamed-of luxuries in the way of parlours and electric light.

How it had all happened she scarcely remembered now. The first casual meeting at a friend's house, the next unsought encounter, the appointed tryst, later walks and excursions, the growth of expectation and the final settlement, all were merged together in an uncertain fog, in which stood many dark shapes she was wary of as she glanced back, so she glanced but seldom. The fog stretched all the way to the year she had left school. Before that it lightened, and she had neat, clear memories of family progressions from house to house, of brothers' and sisters' births and deaths, of her work and play at school and in the streets. The Skedmores were regarded as quite one of the old families of the district as, though they had been driven, chiefly by internal expansion, to many changes of residence, they had never moved out of the withered Squares and Crescents of Royal Kensington, as she lies north and is forgotten by her own kingdom in the south.

Ivy knew nothing of East End slum tradition – of drab rows of houses and dreary pillars of tenements, which have never been anything but the homes of the poor. The houses she had always lived in – the house she lived in now – had been built with a very different intention. A tablet in the wall of Number One, Lunar Square, recorded how the first stone of it had been laid by the Honourable Mrs Addleham, in 1839. Enterprising Victorian speculators had planned a new district of wealth and fashion on the slopes behind the Notting Hill racecourse. They had designed squares and crescents and terraces, and planted trees and gardens. For a few sweet years, gay crinolines had swum over the pavements, and elegant carriages had stood at front doors pillared with gleaming stucco, the music of the waltz and the polka had sounded of a winter's night, and in the galleried churches Victorian ladies had prayed into their muffs and Victorian gentlemen into their top-hats.

It was all gone now. For some reason or other the district had never really thriven. Those who wanted suburban air went to Putney and Tooting, those who wanted the town remained clustered round Mayfair and Belgravia. No one wanted to be either so far or so near as Paddington. So rents and glory fell. The houses which had once been so respectable and inviolate became disreputable and common. They sheltered two, three, four, five families. Even their floors and finally their rooms were divided. Their basements seethed. Strings of washing were run out, fowls clucked in their areas. Their back gardens became backyards, and their Square gardens became jungles, the haunt of the sleeper-out and the unchartered lover.

II

When Ivy looked out of the window she might, had she been so made, have seen the ghosts of the happy and respectable people who once had lived in Lunar Square and must have been vexed to haunt it by its present ways. But instead of ghosts, she saw only one or two cats prowling among the rubbish in the gutter. The place was void and silent, alight, but without the sun. The dawn wind rustled to her through the trees, and she shivered.

Then she noticed a movement in the tanglewood of the Square garden. At first she thought it was the wind, then that it was a pair of those unchartered lovers. But the next moment a man pushed his way up to the railings, and beckoned to her to come down.

She stood motionless. Her round eyes staring from under

the shock of her hair. So it was Bill – so he had come over,
though she'd never thought he'd do it. Bill . . . there was no
matching him for cheek. There was nothing he'd stop at.
She caught her breath. Bill . . . he might have left her alone.
He was one of those dark shapes in the fog, and now he had
come out to stand in the dawn of her wedding day. How
dared he! How dared he, the swine! She clenched her
hands fiercely and helplessly. What was she to do? She
couldn't make him go. She couldn't shout to him across the
silence of the Square. He was making signs to her. He was
beckoning her down. His lips were forming her name. The
window was shut and she could not hear distinctly, but she
knew that he was calling her. He mustn't call her. He
musn't wake the place.

She opened the window very softly and put her head
out. She made signs to him to go away, but he only grinned
and shook his head.

'Come down,' he called to her.

'Shut up!'

'Come down.'

'I can't. Do go away. They'll hear you.'

'I don't care. If you don't come down, I'll come up.'

'You can't.'

But she knew he could. The catch of the front door at
Number Seven was a weak makeshift, and once he was in
the house there were no keys between him and her. She
would have to go down. If she wanted peace and quiet and
decorum on her wedding day she would have to go down.
She could easily talk him into sense – she had done so
many times. Then he would go, and she could get on with
her business.

Ivy did not wear a nightgown. She had always done so
until recently, but her couple were both worn out, and
though she had bought three for her wedding, a pink and a
blue and a mauve, every one knows that it is unlucky to

wear your wedding clothes before the wedding day. So for
the last month she had slept in her vest and petticoat, and
dressing this morning was merely a matter of pulling on her
old blue coat frock, thrusting a comb through the tousle of
her bobbed hair, and slipping her feet into her old black
shoes with their worn soles and trodden-over heels. What
a blessing it would be never to wear them again! Of late
they had hurt her badly, and they let in the wet besides.
She thought of the comfortable new pair waiting for her
feet.

New clothes, new shoes, new furniture, a comfortable
home, a comfortable bed, light work, warm fires, good
food. She thought of all these things as she ran down the
staircase of Number Seven. The banisters had most of them
gone for firewood, but the great and splendid width of the
stairs allowed her to run without fear of falling. She
dragged open the front door, and she was out in a sudden
snatch of cold.

The gate of the Square garden had long been pulled off
its hinges, so she was soon treading through the high grass
to where Bill waited for her, mercifully discreet, in a thicket
of lilac.

'Don't let anybody see us,' she said wildly, as he grasped
her.

'They can't see us here.'

'But they might have . . . Oh, Bill, how could you! You
nearly got me into ever such a fix.'

'Nonsense. Nobody will wake up here for hours yet.'

'Why did you come?'

'That's a pretty question. I came to see you.'

'But why should you? I mean how dare you? You've no
right to see me. I've done with you, Bill.'

'Yes, so you told me once. But that's no reason why I
shouldn't come to wish you luck on your wedding day.'

'You know that's not why you've come.'

'Of course it is; what else should it be?'

'Then why didn't you come at the proper time?'

'Because I'm going out for a day in Epping Forest. That's one reason, and another is you never asked me. If I come to your wedding I come by invite from the bride, like a proper little gentleman. But I've a feeling the card went astray in the post.'

'I didn't know you were back,' she said sulkily. 'I thought your ship didn't get in till the end of the month.'

'So that's why you fixed to get married today?'

'No, Mr Smart; I'm getting married today because it's Easter Sunday.'

'Is it really, Miss Clever? Well, we live and learn. And may I ask why you're in such a temper on your wedding morning? Haven't things been going as smooth as they ought?'

'Not since you came.'

'But I haven't been here half an hour, and that temper of yours has been brewing for days. I know my little Ivy.'

'Don't.'

She did not forbid his words so much as his hands, which had come suddenly about her waist.

'Don't, Bill.'

'Why not?'

'Because if you've only come to wish me luck, you've no right to – to mess me about.'

'Oh, so that's it. You think it should be "hands off" because I've only come to pay you the compliments of the season. But suppose I told you that I'd come to give you one last chance of changing your mind before it's too late.'

'Don't, Bill.'

'It seems you can say nothing but "don't".'

'I – I can't bear it.'

'Then *I*'ll say "don't". Don't bear it, little girl.'

Her hands flew up between them against his breast, but

it was too late. His arms were round her and his mouth on hers, forcing back her head. The tears ran out of the corners of her eyes, but she made no resistance and no sound; she merely seemed to melt and fade and grow weak, and then suddenly to break, as love and sorrow smote her at once.

III

After that they talked more quietly together. She had tried at first to be angry, but she knew all the time her anger was unjust. She was vexed with herself rather than with him – not for any moral failure, but for allowing the past to come and upset the present, now at the very last moment, when everything had seemed settled and she herself was ready for everything. The fire in her had suddenly died, and she was cold and abstracted as he talked on.

'You don't love this chap Hurley.'

'Don't I?'

'Of course you don't. You love me – you've just shown me that.'

'I dunno.'

'What d'you mean by you "dunno"? I bet you do. I bet you wouldn't have kissed me like that if you hadn't loved me.'

She shivered.

'Ivy, little Ivy, give yourself a chance. Give me a chance. You didn't, you know, last summer. There was I, all burning for love of you, and you sent me away.'

'I didn't – your ship sailed.'

'But you could have given me your promise to take with me.'

'What 'ud have been the good of it? You said yourself you couldn't marry for years?'

'If you'd loved me you could have waited.'

'That's just it – that's what I'm telling you the whole time. I don't love you.'

'Yes, you do – you've shown me that. You do love me – but it's the waiting you can't manage. You're afraid of waiting. Well, I'll tell you something. You shan't wait. I'll chuck the sea and get a job ashore. I'm handy at most things and we could manage if you didn't mind having a job of your own at the start. It was only as I didn't want you to have to work, and if I'd gone on I could have done better for myself and you, too, some day. But if waiting's all that's the matter, I tell you what I'll do. I can't do nothing now, for I've only three days' leave – on Wednesday we go to Middlesbrough to refit. But I'll make it my last voyage. We'll be back in September, and I'll marry you then. I'll get a job in a garage – or maybe we could both go as caretakers somewhere . . . I knew a chap in the Navy who got a thundering good job as porter in a block of flats . . . anyhow, we'll manage fine. So you go home, Ivy, and tell 'em the wedding's off.'

Ivy did not speak. She was still thinking – thinking, as she always thought, in a series of pictures. She saw herself as she had been, going out with Bill last summer, pleased with the places where he took her on Saturdays and Sundays, and sometimes of an evening in the week when she was not too late or too tired. He had spent money freely, and done her proud, and other girls had envied her. He had kissed her freely, too, and asked her to marry him when he was better off. At present he was just an ordinary seaman on the *Clio*, one of a small steamship line plying between London and Halifax. Like her, he knew what it was to be out of a job, though, as he said, he was handy at most things – at too many, perhaps, she had criticised in her heart, and the reviving criticism gave her a new set of pictures, this time of the future. She saw herself standing in front of the sink – standing till September – another six months of early and weary days, of roughened hands and greasy water, of aching legs . . . she'd already started what the Square called 'various' veins, and the dreaded threat of 'bad legs' was upon her . . . she had thought it all over and done with, in time, before the evil happened – another six months might bring it about, and she would have legs like those of so many women she knew, like her own mother's, aching and ulcerated, perpetually swathed in greasy bandages as one patent ointment was tried after another. . . . At the thought her mouth and nose wrinkled up adorably and her pictures were destroyed by Bill's provoked kiss.

'Sweetheart, I've got a better idea. Come away with me now, so as you won't have to face them at home. I'll take you straight to mother's, and you can stop along of her till I come back. You'll like it, you know. You and mother always did get on together. You can go to work just as easy from there as from here, and give her something for your keep and save the rest.'

Ivy laughed shortly. That showed the way he thought of things – 'save the rest' – as if there'd be any 'rest'. Bill was too cocksure by half. He saw things much too bright. He saw them married in September, when most likely they wouldn't have a penny piece to do it on. He'd have spent all his money – he always did – and she wouldn't have managed to save any of hers. He'd have to get another job, and try to save on that . . . not likely . . . more years of waiting, more years of working. Then there'd be more working after she was married – standing before the washtub just as now she stood before the sink, standing over the kitchen fire, always cleaning, always trying to manage on just too little. Bill's would be the sort of home in which there was never quite enough, because Bill's would be the sort of home in which there would always be periods of unemployment, lean weeks of struggle on the dole . . . she shivered again. She knew the dole, and so did he – it was failure to get work

on land that had sent him to sea in the first place. Poor
Bill . . . poor, darling, adored Bill! For, of course, she
adored him, loved him . . . ever so much. . . . Oh, God!
That made another picture come. She had a picture of
babies – babies coming year after year, wearing her out as
she had seen so many women worn out, binding her yoke
upon her without pity or rest. Ivy had no illusions about
marriage in general, and, more remarkably, she had no
illusions about marriage with Bill.

'Well, precious, what's it going to be?'

'Nothing,' she jerked at him shortly.

'Ain't you coming with me?'

'No. And I'm not going to stop the marriage neither.'

'Oh, yes, you are.'

He tried to pull her close for another kiss, but she pushed
him from her almost violently.

'No, I say. Stop pawing me about. I won't have it. Gawd!
You ought to know better than to speak as you do, to me as
good as married. I tell you I've made up my mind and I
know what I'm doing. You leave me alone.'

'Very well, Miss Spitfire. If you want to be miserable all
your life, you're free and welcome, and maybe I've had a
lucky escape.'

'I shan't be miserable. I'd be miserable if I married you,
but I'll be ever so happy if I marry Sid Hurley.'

'Bah! He's old enough to be your father.'

'He ain't. He's only forty-six; and, anyway, better be an
old man's darling than a young man's slave.'

'So that's it, is it?' His young face darkened, and at the
same time his lip quivered childishly. She could not bear it.
She turned from him with a little moan and fought her
way out of the bushes. He did not attempt to follow her as
she rustled through the wilderness towards the gate. One
or two sick flowers went down under her feet. Her frock
caught on a twig, tearing a shoddy seam. She cursed, and

ran on. She wanted to forget. She wanted to blot out that picture of his standing there with his angry eyes and childish trembling mouth.

I V

It was eight o'clock in the Square – very different from the eight o'clock of most days. Usually at eight o'clock the pavements echoed with the patter of girls' feet. From under the solemn porticoes, which long ago had sheltered the slow, swaying exits of crinolined ladies, tripped groups and strings of prettily dressed girls. No Victorian belle had looked smarter or sweeter than these in their stockings of sunburn silk, in their patent-leather shoes, in their big wrap coats and little cloche hats. It was incredible that they should emerge from these ruins of homes, that the muddle of the common living and sleeping room should produce anything so fresh and delicate and gay. Yet out they came, on their way to the dressmaker, the hairdresser, the café, the drapery store, to spend the day waiting on elegance and learning from it their natural lesson of charm, to return at night with step less springy and eye less bright, and maybe mud on the patent shoes (which often let in water) and spots and stains on the sunburn stockings (which often defeated the efforts of the wrap coat to protect its wearer from chills).

Ivy had never counted herself as a member of this society. She belonged to a smaller, inferior troupe that set out at an earlier, more unfashionable hour, and went to wait on necessity rather than on elegance. Yet it was she and not one of them who had been chosen to live in a four-roomed flat, to preside over the glories of a bathroom, a gas-cooker and electric light, to run an eight-pound-a-week home in unimagined honour. *They* would marry men like Bill, and in five years become middle-aged slatterns, slaving in three-pound-a-week homes, that periodically would become fourteen-and-sixpenny homes as prosperity ebbed and flowed over the district and the dole took the place of wages. Ivy Skedmore could pity them as she fled from passion to security, running across the empty Square, and up the many steps of Number Seven to where the giant door stood unlatched.

It was lucky that the Sabbath was in the Square, or she and Bill would have been discovered and the story down all the streets by this time. But on Sunday no one ever thought of getting up before nine o'clock. At nine-thirty the shops opened, and the market, and the streets were full of those who bought and sold fish and meat and vegetables that the main-road shops had not been able to get rid of on Saturday night.

The Skedmores had not on this occasion left their shopping till Sunday morning, but had done it in superior fashion on Saturday afternoon. The wedding feast had shared their sleeping chamber, the more perishable parts bestowed for safety on the window-sill. As she passed her parents' door, Ivy was surprised to hear the sound of voices. She felt uneasy. Had they somehow discovered her absence? Had Peach woken up and gone in search of her to the main room? She decided to go in and find out the worst.

But she need not have alarmed herself. Her parents' early rising was due entirely to social reasons. Today was their eldest daughter's wedding day, and they had already received one, or rather several, wedding guests. A large woman, with a baby in her arms, was seated on one of the two double beds that the room contained. Round her knees squirmed a mass of children, four of whom were her own, the other three being little Skedmores, arrayed only in their underclothing, as their wedding garments were for obvious reasons not to be taken out of the drawer till the last moment. On the other bed lay Mr Skedmore, smoking a pipe while his wife struggled with the fire.

The room was big, and even now almost handsome, with its soaring walls and richly decorated cornice. Peach's and Ivy's room was a mere slice cut off it, and much remained in the chief apartment to suggest the splendour of the rock out of which it had been hewn. It was crammed with furniture – two big beds, a big table and one or two smaller ones, a chiffonier, a chest of drawers, innumerable chairs, most of them decrepit, and a broken-backed sofa. The walls were gay with pictures, and ornaments and the family china and glass, for which there was no cupboard, adorned all available space. Clothes were everywhere – they hung from hooks on the wall, they were rolled up in piles in corners, and eked out the blankets on the beds. The place in its litter and hugeness suggested a parish hall rather inefficiently stocked for a jumble sale. The Skedmores had many possessions, none of which was intact, unblemished or really serviceable, but all of which were loved, prized and hoarded till the day of final disintegration.

'Well, dearie,' cried Mrs Skedmore cheerily, lifting a blackened face out of the smoke – 'and how are you this morning? I thought I'd leave you to have your sleep out.'

'Thanks, Mum, but I couldn't sleep late this morning.'

'Of course she couldn't,' the lady on the bed declared with cheeriness – 'when it's her wedding day and all.'

'A pity to waste a Sunday, though,' said Mrs Skedmore.

'What's that matter to her, marrying Sid Hurley? She may lay in bed all day if she likes.'

'Of course she can – and will sometimes, I dessay. It'll all be ever so nice, I tell her.'

'I bet she don't want to be told. Ivy, you're looking fine this morning.'

Ivy's cheeks were blazing and her eyes were bright.

'It's ever so kind of Mrs Housego to come in and help

us,' said her mother. 'I thought I'd got everything straight yesterday, but it's all gone and got messed up again. Drat this fire – it won't catch and I've gone and used up all the newspaper.'

'Let me help you, dear,' said Mrs Housego, heaving from the bed. There was a flaw in the Skedmores' grate which involved desperate measures every morning, with a threat of suffocation throughout the day.

'Try a drop of paraffin, dearie.'

'There isn't any in the place.'

'I'll try and find you some downstairs. Mrs Spiller has some, I know, for I saw her bring it in yesterday.'

'Don't you go chucking paraffin on the fire !' shouted Mr Skedmore from his bed. 'You got me fined a bob last year for setting fire to the chimney – it'll be half-a-crown next time.'

The matrons heaved and struggled amidst clouds of smoke. Finally, one of Mrs Housego's children found a piece of newspaper under the bed, and, by holding this in front of the grate, a flame was persuaded to kindle and grow. By the time the paper had caught fire and whirled blazing up the chimney there was some chance of the kettle being boiled for a cup of tea.

'And we'll all be glad of that,' said Mrs Skedmore. 'What you standing there for, Ivy, like a stuck pig ? You'll be tired before you've gone through half today.'

Ivy sat down upon the bed.

v

'Let's talk about the wedding,' said Mrs Housego. 'How many are you expecting, dearie ?'

'I've got food for ten besides ourselves. Mr Hurley's mother 'ull be coming and his sister Grace. And then there's yourself, Mrs Housego, and the Lockits and the

Gaits and old Mr Willard. We'll be a crowd, I tell you. But don't you worry – nobody shall go without. I've got salmon and crab and tongue and prawns, a lovely cake and some fancies and a vealanam pie, and two dozen of ale and a dozen of Guinness for a start.'

'Coo! Listen to that! Ivy, your mother couldn't have done you prouder if it had been your funeral.'

'Well, I didn't want Sid Hurley's people to think he was marrying dirt,' said Mrs Skedmore modestly.

'They won't think it after this. What a breakfast! What a treat! When I married, my mother didn't give us nothing but fish and chips and tea – not but what she didn't have to pawn her crocks to get that much. Pore mother! Which reminds me, I've got my five shilling parcel back, and it's got my best hat in it as well as the sheets, so I shan't look such a guy at your wedding, Ivy, after all.'

'Are you coming to the church?'

'You betcher life! – now I've got my hat. I'm all for the Church, as I told the clergyman the other day. Why, I was as weak as a rat after Monty was born till I had my churching. I said to the nurse, "For mercy's sake, let me out. I know what's good for me." And I did. She found me cleaning the windows the next time she came. Now that Mrs Winter, at Number Three, has never had herself churched nor her baby christened. I tell her the child won't ever be strong and healthy till it's done. And it don't cost nothing like being vaccinated, and you don't have to fuss about keeping the place clean afterwards. I tell you, I'm all for the Church.'

'Well, I wish the Church 'ud let us get married a bit earlier. They won't have us till a quarter past twelve, which means nearly half the day gone.'

'That doesn't matter to Ivy. She'll have more than the day for her holiday. Is he taking you away, Ivy?'

'We're going down to Eastbourne till Tuesday.'

'Did you ever, now! Eastbourne! I've heard that's a fashionable place. Ivy Skedmore, you're a lucky girl, as I've always said. Now, I believe I hear that kettle boiling. Let's have a nice cup of tea all round.'

She went to the tea-making, while Mrs Skedmore spread a piece of newspaper on the table and set out the heel of a loaf and some dissolving margarine.

'We don't want more than just a bite just now. There's plenty coming later.'

'Only a cup of tea to freshen us all a bit. Ivy 'ull have to think about getting dressed soon.'

'Oh, there's time enough. She might spoil her gown if she sat about in it.'

'Is she having any bridesmaids?'

'Just our Nellie. We've got her a wreath of flowers. That's why I've done up her hair like that in rags. I thought maybe it 'ud curl.'

'She'll look ever so sweet. Oh, it'll be a pretty wedding, Mrs Skedmore – quite like the ones you read about. Who else is getting married with Ivy?'

'I don't know for certain, except that there'll be young Spiller and Rose Chown – at last and not before it was time, to my way of thinking; and there'll be the gipsies.'

'Who?'

'Those Lees – Tom and Dinah. I'm sorry about it, but it can't be helped.'

'We've too many gipsies in these parts. My Jim was saying to me only yesterday as they've quite spoilt the barrer trade. They always seem to think of better things to take round on barrers than ordinary Christians.'

'Talking of barrers, Mr Skedmore's thinking of a new job. There's a chap asked him to go shares in an ice-cream stall.'

'Ice-cream's no good. People are mostly too cold these days to want it.'

K

'Well, you can do chestnuts and baked potatoes in the winter.'

'Yes, and tortusses in the spring. Don't I know it? Haven't I been through it all with my poor Jim? I tell him that's the way to keep our homes about us – ha! ha!' and she pulled out a handful of pawn-tickets. 'It ain't every woman who carries her home in her pocket.'

'I hope you haven't too many things away, dear – nothing that's really wanted, I mean.'

'Not now I've got my five-shilling parcel back. But I've not had a hat to me head nor a sheet to me bed these six months, and all because my man wants to be his own master.'

'Quite right, too,' growled Mr Skedmore into his teacup. 'It's a dog's life working for a boss. I'm all for being me own capitalist.'

'He's getting quite red – Mr Skedmore,' said his wife proudly – 'sings the "Red Rag" and all. But I'd rather he stayed at the works; then I know where I am. Even as it is, I'd have had a lot of things away if it hadn't been for Ivy's Mr Hurley's kindness, getting everything back for us in time for the wedding.'

'Did he reelly? Well, that's what I call generous and handsome. My Gawd! Ivy's in luck.'

'Ivy!' cried her mother – 'what are you staring at? Come away from that winder and take some notice of us all.'

VI

Ivy was looking down at the Square garden. She could see tracks in the grass, the spoor, as it were, of some wild animal escaped. Down in that garden a wild beast, sleek and lovely, had threatened her, had opened its jaws to devour Sid Hurley's meek head and prosperous home. But it was gone now. The garden lay empty, tossed by wind, while the

Easter sun at last shone down on it over the house-tops, spattering its undergrowth with dusty light – queer, shifting spots and speckles, as if a beast really moved there . . . Ivy turned away.

'Hallo, everybody! I'm all right!'

'Betcher life you are!'

The door had opened as she turned and Peach Grey had come in – a very different Peach from the tall girl who trod indifferently the show-rooms of Madame Bertha. Her hair lay close under the shingle-cap in which she slept, for a wave cost one and sixpence to put in and must be preserved as long as possible. She wore a shabby but still colourful wrapper, and an edge beneath it proclaimed the aristocracy of a lace-trimmed night-gown. Nevertheless Peach was not exactly your idea of a successful mannequin – even of a mannequin who is the only one employed by a small Queen's Road establishment, and has to take on occasionally the role of saleswoman, as pressure demands. Her voice was certainly different from what you would expect from those disdainful lips, and different from the voice in which she made occasional rare utterances while on duty. 'This little dress would be very becoming to Moddom.' 'A model straight from our French house, Moddom.' 'The price is really quate ridiculous, Moddom, when you look at the material.'

'A cup o' tea, Miss Grey?'

'I don't mind if I do.'

Peach sat down, and produced a packet of cigarettes from somewhere about her person.

'Have a fag, anybody?'

However, nobody smoked but Mr Skedmore, who preferred his pipe. There was a subtle social distinction of which all were conscious between Peach and the others in the room. Her wages were in point of fact no more than Ivy's, but she worked in elegance for elegance instead of in squalor for appetite, and the difference was appreciated. She sat with her kimono pulled modestly over crossed knees, while Mrs Skedmore poured her out a cup of tea, which Ivy brought to her.

'Well, Ivy, you were up fine and early this morning.'

'How d'you mean?' blurted Ivy, taken unawares.

'Well, I heard you go out, and it wasn't more'n half-past seven, for the church bells hadn't finished.'

'How do *you* know? You were asleep.'

'I heard you go out, I say, and I heard the bells, too.'

'I tell you I didn't go out – not till after eight. I didn't come in here till after eight, did I, Ma?'

'No, you didn't. Mrs Housego had been sitting with us a quarter of an hour before you came.'

'There's bells at eight, too,' continued Ivy desperately; 'what should I get up earlier for on a Sunday?'

'Oh, well, you didn't then,' said Peach airily. She felt quite sure that Ivy had got up and gone out before half-past seven, but if she didn't want it mentioned, she certainly was not going to give her away.

'Did you go to the pictures, Peach, last night?'

'I did. We went to see Norma Talmadge at the Pavilion.'

'What was she like?' asked Ivy wistfully.

'Ever so nice.'

'Ivy will be able to go to the pictures any day she chooses now,' said Mrs Skedmore – 'the price of a seat won't be no object, and she loves the pictures.'

'Well, if ever you get the chance, Ivy,' said Peach, 'go and see Norma Talmadge in "Love Makes News". It's ever such a beautiful picture.'

'What's it about?'

'Oh, about a girl in temptation. On one side there's a nice poor boy and on the other side a rich old chap, and she has to choose between them.'

Ivy wished she hadn't asked.

'Who does she choose?' asked Mrs Housego.

'Why, the boy, of course. But not till the end of the picture. The old chap brings her lovely pearls. I didn't half think I'd have married him in her place.'

'And jilted your Algy?' rallied Mrs Skedmore.

'Oh, the boy in the picture wasn't near so nice as Algy.'

Here again Peach outraged your convention of a mannequin, who is always supposed to be superior and expensive in her love affairs, having been engaged for the last four years to a young salesman at a Brixton drapers, who might be able to afford to marry her in another four years' time.

'Well, I'm all for Romance,' said Mrs Housego. 'Love in a cottage – that's what I like on the pictures. I pity the girl who sells herself for money.'

'Lots of them do,' said Mrs Skedmore, shaking her head.

'But they always regrets it,' said Mrs Housego.

'And ends up old and grey, sitting in the empty nursery,' said Mrs Skedmore with a catch in her voice.

Ivy hung down her head, and her hands quivered and locked together, though she knew that her mother and Mrs Housego were talking of another life than this, the Life of the Pictures in which things happen differently from this life, and therefore a life into which it is sometimes good to escape.

VII

'Albie,' said Mrs Skedmore, 'run down to Mrs Spiller and ask her kindly what time it is.'

The youngest Skedmore emerged from beneath a bed, and trotted off. He came back with the alarming intelligence that it was a quarter past ten.

'A quarter past ten! Did you ever! And we haven't even

begun to get things straight. Come, girls, make a start, or Sid will be here and none of us ready.'

'What time is he coming?'

'He said he'd be round with a keb at a quarter to twelve. Come, hustle, girls! Bless me! You'd never think I'd spring-cleaned this room all over yesterday.'

'We can't do nothing, Ma, with the children here. Can't they go out for a bit?'

'Of course they can – no, they can't, for they ain't dressed, and they mustn't play in the street with their new clothes on.'

'They can wear their old knickers and jerseys, just to run out. Mrs Housego's Gertie will look after them and see as they come back in time.'

'I wan'er go to church,' said Gertie.

'Did you ever!' cried her mother. 'You'll have plenty of church later, when you go to see Ivy married.'

'But I won't get a pitcher. I get a pitcher if I go to church now.'

'I wan'er pitcher – I wan'er pitcher,' chimed in the other little Housegos.

'I wan'er pitcher,' echoed the little Skedmores.

'Oh, let them go, Ma,' cried Ivy impatiently; 'they'll be out of the way, anyhow.'

'The children's service begins at a quarter to ten,' said Peach – 'not much good their going at a quarter past.'

But such a distinction was merely trivial to the Sked-more conception of time. It being decided that the children were best out of the way, that church was safer than the street, and that they were more likely to return from it than more thrilling and scattered pursuits, they were accordingly dispatched there, to add their arrival to the confusion at the end of the Children's Mass.

As soon as they were gone Mrs Housego and Mrs Skedmore settled down to what they called euphemistically a 'good clean'. The crockery of the wedding feast was washed anew and would have to be washed again more than once in the course of the meal if the glasses and plates were to go round. A bunch of flowers, bought last night in Lunar Street market, was dispersed among Mrs Skedmore's vases. Pictures and ornaments were finally dusted, the hearth cleaned, and the food spread out on the newly-washed tablecloth. In the midst of it all Mr Skedmore shaved, with blasphemous interludes, and Ivy, in the next room, helped by Peach, put on her rosewood cloth dress with the detachable cape, the nigger-brown straw-hat, the silk stockings and suède shoes that formed the chief splendours of her wedding.

'Coo, Ivy, but you look ever so nice! You pay for dressing up, you do. I wish I had a chance with you at Madame's. I could make you look sweet. But maybe you'll come some day. You'll be able to afford it, you know, once and again. I bet lots of the women who come to us don't have as much as eight pounds a week. But you're a lucky girl. I wish I had half your luck,' and she sighed.

Evidently she was not looking at Ivy from the moral viewpoint of the pictures. She did not see her friend as 'selling herself for money.' And yet she knew all about Bill. She also knew all about life, and that a girl can't always afford to live up to the exalted moral standard set by the cinema – that she must occasionally move on a lower level, simply in order to avoid bad legs. . . . Ivy's chosen course suddenly appeared to her as absolutely sordid and humdrum. Not thus would Norma Talmadge or Mary Pickford or Mae Murray have chosen. The tears began to roll down her cheeks.

'Wotever's the matter, Ive?'

'I feel so bad about it all, Peach.'

'Bad about wot?'

'Marrying Sid when I ought to be marrying Bill.'

'Now don't start all that nonsense over again. Why ever should you be marrying Bill? He's not got a penny and never will have.'

'I could go on with my job.'

'Yes, you could – till the kids came. And what then? No, you forget it, Ive. It's no good. I wouldn't say that if he was like Algy, but he isn't. My own opinion is that he's not straight. Anyhow, *I* wouldn't trust him. Now there's nothing really exciting about Sid, but he's as straight as they're made. He won't let you down. He's good stuff.'

'Do you really think so?'

'Of course I think so, and so do you. You've only got the jim-jams at the last minute, the way most girls do.'

Ivy wondered. Had she really only got the jim-jams? Or was this Conscience Roused At Last? The words seemed to flicker before her eyes, as if thrown on a screen. She went to the window and looked out – down at the garden where the sun-dappled shadows moved like some spotted beast. Suddenly she saw two figures come arm in arm round the corner of the Square. It was Bill and an unknown female, whom he led past the house. She was smartly dressed in green, with a hat to match, and her skirts displayed much silken leg. Bill's hand lay tenderly over the one he had pulled through his arm. He was bending towards her and talking eagerly.

'Cad!' shouted Ivy, and brought Peach, who was kneeling to button a shoe, startled to her feet.

'What is it? Who? – Oh!'

She looked out and saw Bill turning at the Square corner, to lead his lady back past the window that he wished to mock.

'Why, it's Bill! Who in the Lord's name has he got hold of now?'

'He's brought her to jeer at me. He's a cad. He's a – '

'Shut up, Ivy! You don't want everyone to hear. Don't be a fool and give him his chance like that. Get away from the window'; and she pulled her back into the room with such violence that she fell across the bed that filled up most of it.

'There, what did I say?' continued Peach. 'I told you he wasn't straight. He's a rotten sort of chap. You're well rid of him.'

Ivy sobbed, stifling, into her pillow.

'Now don't do that, or you'll spoil your face. Come and let me brush your dress.'

'Has he gone?'

'Yes – now you're not looking out any more. He's cleared off'; and Peach made an unladylike gesture of farewell. 'Come, Ivy, and don't be a damn fool. You'll get yourself all crumpled. Sit up. That's right. Now, let me give you just a dust over with my powder. Yes, you *must*. You can't let every one see you with a red nose and red eyes like that. They'll think you've been crying. And you've nothing to cry for. You're a lucky girl.'

'If you say that again,' said Ivy sullenly, 'I shall scream.'

'Well, then, I won't say it, but I'll think it all the same.'

A sudden clamour broke out in the next room.

'Girls! Girls!' shrieked Mrs Skedmore – 'Sid's come!'

Doors flew open, footsteps thudded, voices questioned and screamed.

'Sid's come . . . the keb's here . . . the children ain't back. Wherever can they be? They've got to be dressed, and Nellie to put on her bridesmaid's clothes and all.'

In the midst of the uproar, Sid Hurley's step came quietly up the stairs.

'Hallo, what's the matter? Where's Ivy?'

'Here I am, Sid.'

'Don't sound so sad, little girl. What's she been doing Mrs Skedmore? Is she tired?'

'No, but what am *I* to do, Sid? There's all the children out Heaven knows where.'

'Well, if they can't be found, the wedding must go on without them. It's a quarter to twelve.'

'But Nellie's to be bridesmaid. Oh, what shall we do? Ivy, you're dressed. Run down to the corner and – '

'No, no, Mrs Skedmore; Ivy mustn't do any more running about this morning. Why, she's tired already, poor little girl'; and he gently tucked back a piece of hair that had flown loose under her hat.

'Well, I'll go to the corner, dear, if you like,' said Mrs Housego. 'I can call them, but Heaven knows I can't chase after them, being the size I am.'

'Stay where you are, ma'am,' said Sid. 'I'll see if I can find 'em; and, if I find 'em, I bet I bring 'em, too.'

'There!' cried Mrs Skedmore. 'That's a man, dearie.'

Peach, too, thought that it was. She nudged Ivy in the ribs.

'Wot price Doug Fairbanks?' she whispered.

Meanwhile, the finishing touches were put to Mr Skedmore's tie and Mrs Skedmore's toque. Mrs Housego went downstairs to her own room, to put on the redeemed hat and await such of her family as the bridegroom should recover in the short time allowed him. His chief efforts were to be centred on Nellie Skedmore, but it was more than likely that the children had kept together

So it proved! just as the more trustworthy clocks in the Square pointed to twelve, Sid Hurley reappeared with a little string of grubs. It appeared that, finding themselves too late at church to receive the coveted pictures, they had gone on in hope to the Salvation Army Sunday School, where they had each been rewarded with a coloured text about the size of a postage stamp. Thus refreshed, they had endured a certain amount of instruction, agreed that they had found the Lord, and started off home, stopping on the way to join in a game of 'house' on the steps of the Parish Hall. This was not 'house' as played in the nursery, but as played in the British Army; and, though none of the players had any money, stakes were put up in the way of buttons, marbles, matchboxes and similar treasures. The little Skedmores staked their texts and lost them, and it was in the midst of the ensuing battle that Sid Hurley arrived and dragged them away.

It was decided once again to concentrate on Nellie; the others, having no prominent part in the coming ceremony, might scramble as they chose into the new jerseys and knickers laid out for them. But Nellie must be washed, combed, brushed, and clothed in white raiment, white stockings and shoes, with a wreath of daisies round her rag-curled hair. Nellie, though next in age to Ivy, was not yet twelve. She represented the other side of a gap which had been filled with a variety of births and deaths, as little Skedmores came into the world and left it in rapid succession. Three had not survived their birth more than a few weeks, one had died sensationally in a smallpox epidemic much written of in the newspapers, while another, as if to show the utter contempt of Providence for the efforts of the Skedmores, had died of a 'bad arm' caused by septic conditions after vaccination.

While Nellie was being dressed, Ivy and her bridegroom sat together by the window, their conversation screened by the general uproar.

'Sure you're not tired, darling?'

She shook her head.

'I believe you are a bit.'

'Why should I be? I've done nothing today.'

'But it's all been exciting and trying for you. I'll be ever so glad when I've got you away all quiet by the seaside.'

Ivy shivered.

'What is it, dear?'

'Nothing.'

'Ivy, you're not unhappy, are you? You're not feeling –
oh, my dear, tell me that you're glad.'

'I am glad,' said Ivy.

She suddenly knew that she was glad.

'I've only got the jim-jams at the last moment, the way
most girls have,' she repeated firmly.

She suddenly knew that she had only got the jim-jams.
That was what it was – what every girl had on her wedding
day. There was nothing else – no regrets, no flight, no
sorrow, no wild beast in the garden. . . .

VIII

'There now!' said her mother. 'She looks a pitcher!'

'Boo-hoo!' sobbed Nellie. 'There's a pin sticking into
me!'

'There ain't. I tell you there's no pin. Now you behave!
If it wasn't Ivy's wedding day you'd have been well tanned
by your dad for the dance you've led us.'

'We only went to the Salvations.'

'Well, it wasn't the Salvations who rolled you in the dirt
and spoiled your only decent pair of drawers. Now, don't
you move till we all go out together. Albie! Georgie! . . .
Oh, thank you, Peach. Now, is everybody ready? Ivy! We
can't get far without you, nor Sid either. You'll have plenty
of time for spooning later. Now everybody go out. Dad! Got
the key? That's right. Lock the door after us. Now, Albie, if
you start running . . .'

Somehow or other they all got downstairs and were not
too hopelessly involved with the emerging Housegos. There
stood the cab, and somehow or other they all got into it. As
they drove across the Square, before the windows became
too fogged to see out, Ivy looked her last into the garden.
Nobody was there, neither a spotted beast, nor a madden-

ing, jeering boy, parading his new love to mock the old. She felt quite quiet now – quiet and not unhappy. The past was over and done with, and the future looked brighter than it had looked before the sun was up. It looked bright as well as comfortable. . . . She glanced across at Sid, and remembered with a little creep of pride that Peach had compared him to Douglas Fairbanks. Not that he was really very like him, but he was certainly strong and kind . . . and Peach had also said he was 'good stuff'. . . .

The cab stopped outside the church. They were not so very late after all, for though it was twenty past twelve, the Easter morning service was not yet over. The verger came out and told them to stay in the porch till it was finished. Looking in, Ivy could see dim figures and dim lights, and sniff the soft blue haze that reminded her of her childhood's Sundays. Churchgoing was either for the very old or for the very young – the middle years were too crowded and too hard, and Saturday night ate up too much of Sunday morning. But perhaps she would go again now, for there would be leisure in her home, such as there had never been in her mother's and as there would not be in Peach's when she married.

How smart Peach looked! Smarter than any of the brides – for Ivy's was not the only glory of that wedding day. No less than eight other brides were crowding with their retinues into that narrow porch, while their friends and neighbours covered the pavement outside.

'Bang! Crash! Bang! Terrumphy!'

The service was over and the organ had began to play the congregation out. The various wedding parties made a rush for the entrance, but the verger and churchwardens held them back.

'Let the people out first.'

Out the congregation came, dribbling a thin line through the brides and bridegrooms. In the vestry a tired clergyman was taking off his vestments and scrambling into a surplice for the approaching orgy.

'I wish you'd let me take them,' said the new curate, who had not begun his day's work at five.

'My dear chap, you couldn't start with nine couples at a time. You'd get 'em mixed. I'll polish them off in twenty minutes and then thank the Lord for food, hot coffee, rest.'

He disappeared into the church, where the verger had by this time marshalled the different couples and arranged them in a long row in front of the chancel. Those who had no bridesmaids stood in front of the pews, those who had the longest trail stood in the aisle. Ivy stood a little way to the right, with Sid on one side and her father on the other, and Nell behind her, wedged against a Litany desk and still complaining of a pin. She had time to look round her while they waited for the priest. There stood the gipsies, right at the end – her hat was full of feathers like a donah. Rose Chown actually had a white veil. There was swank for you! Especially after what people said – and Hilda James . . . she didn't know Hilda was getting married. The other couples were strangers – two of them were quite middle-aged . . . getting married again . . . then it couldn't be so bad the first time. . . . She looked round shyly at Sid. Her jim-jams were all gone now – she supposed it had been just that, just like what every girl has before her wedding . . . no mistaking Peach for a bride now – she was right behind in one of the pews.

A great shuffle went through the lines. The clergyman had come in. He stood before them, turning over the pages of his book, eyeing meanwhile one of the bridegrooms who was a little drunk. Then he began to read :

'Dearly beloved, we are gathered together in the sight of God . . .'

A. E. COPPARD

FIFTY POUNDS

AFTER tea Philip Repton and Eulalia Burnes discussed their gloomy circumstances. Repton was the precarious sort of London journalist, a dark, deliberating man, lean and drooping, full of genteel unprosperity, who wrote articles about 'Single Tax', 'Diet and Reason', 'The Futility of this, that, and the other', or 'The Significance of the other, that and this' – all done with a bleak care, and signed 'P. Stick Repton'. Eulalia was brown-haired and hardy, undeliberating and intuitive; she had been milliner, clerk, domestic help, and something in a canteen; and P. Stick Repton had, as one commonly says, picked her up at a time when she was drifting about London without a penny in her purse, without even a purse, and he had not yet put her down.

'I can't understand! It's sickening, monstrous!' Lally was fumbling with a match before the penny gas-fire – for when it was evening, in September, it always got chilly on a floor so high up. Their flat was a fourth-floor one, and there were – oh, fifteen thousand stairs! Out of the window and beyond the chimneys you could see the long glare from lights in High Holborn, and hear the hum of buses. And that was a comfort.

'Lower! Turn it lower!' yelled Philip. The gas had ignited with an astounding thump; the kneeling Lally had thrown up her hands and dropped the matchbox, saying 'Damn' in the same tone as one might say 'Good morning' to a milkman.

'You shouldn't do it, you know,' grumbled Repton. 'You'll blow us to the deuce.' And that was just like Lally, that was Lally all over, always; the gas, the knobs of sugar

in his tea, the way she . . . and the, the . . . oh, dear, dear !
In their early life together, begun so abruptly and illicitly
six months before, her simple hidden beauties had delighted him by their surprises; they had peered and shone
brighter, had waned and recurred; she was less the one
star in his universe than a faint galaxy.

This room of theirs was a dingy room, very small but
very high. A lanky gas tube swooped from the middle of the
ceiling towards the middle of the table-cloth as if burning
to discover whether that was pink or saffron or fawn –
and it *was* hard to tell – but on perceiving that the cloth,
whatever its tint, was disturbingly spangled with dozens of
cup stains and several large envelopes, the gas tube, in the
violence of its disappointment, contorted itself abruptly,
assumed a lateral bend, and put out its tongue of flame at
an oleograph of Mona Lisa above the fireplace.

Those envelopes were the torment to Lally; they were
the sickening, monstrous manifestations which she could
not understand. There were always some of them lying
there, or about the room, bulging with manuscripts that no
editors – they *couldn't* have perused them – wanted; and
so it had come to the desperate point when, as Lally was
saying, something had to be done about things. Repton had
done all *he* could; he wrote unceasingly, all day, all night,
but all his projects insolvently withered, and morning,
noon and evening brought his manuscripts back as un-
wanted as snow in summer. He was depressed and baffled
and weary. And there was simply nothing else he could do,
nothing in the world. Apart from his own wonderful gift he
was useless, Lally knew, and he was being steadily and
stupidly murdered by those editors. It was weeks since they
had eaten a proper meal. Whenever they obtained any
really nice food now, they sat down to it silently, intently
and destructively. As far as Lally could tell, there seemed
to be no prospect of any such meals again in life or time,

and the worst of it all was Philip's pride – he was actually too proud to ask anyone for assistance! Not that he would be too proud to accept help if it were offered to him : oh no, if it came he would rejoice at it! But still, he had that nervous, shrinking pride that coiled upon itself, and he would not ask; he was like a wounded animal that hid its woe far away from the rest of the world. Only Lally knew his need, but why could not other people see it – those villainous editors! His own wants were so modest, and he had a generous mind.

'Phil,' Lally said, seating herself at the table. Repton was lolling in a wicker arm-chair before the gas fire. 'I'm not going on waiting and waiting any longer, I must go and get a job. Yes, I must. We get poorer and poorer. We can't go on like it any longer, there's no use, and I can't bear it.'

'No, no, I can't have that, my dear ...'

'But I will!' she cried. 'Oh, why are you so proud?'

'Proud! Proud!' He stared into the gas fire, his tired arms hanging limp over the arms of the chair. 'You don't understand. There are things the flesh has to endure, and things the spirit too must endure. ...' Lally loved to hear him talk like that; and it was just as well, for Repton was much given to such discoursing. Deep in her mind was the conviction that he had simple access to profound, almost unimaginable, wisdom. 'It isn't pride, it is just that there is a certain order in life, in my life, that it would not do for. I could not bear it, I could never rest : I can't explain that, but just believe it, Lally.' His head was empty but unbowed; he spoke quickly and finished almost angrily, 'If only I had money! It's not for myself. I can stand all this, any amount of it. I've done so before, and I shall do again and again, I've no doubt. But I have to think of you.'

That was fiercely annoying. Lally got up and went and stood over him.

'Why are you so stupid? I can think for myself and fend

for myself. I'm not married to you. You have your pride, but I can't starve for it. And I've a pride, too. I'm a burden to you. If you won't let me work now while we're together, then I must leave you and work for myself.'

'Leave! Leave me now? When things are so bad?' His white face gleamed his perturbation up at her. 'Oh, well, go, go.' But then, mournfully moved, he took her hands and fondled them. 'Don't be a fool, Lally; it's only a passing depression, this; I've known worse before, and it never lasts long; something turns up, always does. There's good and bad in it all, but there's more goodness than anything else. You see.'

'I don't want to wait for ever, even for goodness. I don't believe in it, I never see it, never feel it, it is no use to me. I could go and steal, or walk the streets, or do any dirty thing – easily. What's the good of goodness if it isn't any use?'

'But, but,' Repton stammered, 'what's the use of bad if it isn't any better?'

'I mean . . .' began Lally.

'You don't mean anything, my dear girl.'

'I mean, when you haven't any choice it's no use talking moral, or having pride, it's stupid. Oh, my darling' – she slid down to him and lay against his breast – 'it's not you, you are everything to me; that's why it angers me so, this treatment of you, all hard blows and no comfort. It will never be any different, I feel it will never be different now, and it terrifies me.'

'Pooh!' Repton kissed her and comforted her : she was his beloved. 'When things are wrong with us our fancies take their tone from our misfortunes, badness, evil. I some-times have a queer stray feeling that one day I shall be hanged. Yes, I don't know what for, what *could* I be hanged for? At other times I have felt sure that one day I shall come to be – what do you think? – Prime Minister of this country. You can't reason against such things. I even made a list of the men I would choose for my Cabinet. Yes, oh yes.'

But Lally had made up her mind to leave him; she would leave him for awhile and earn her own living. When things took a turn for the better she would join him again. She told him this. She had friends who were going to get her some work.

'But what are you going to do, Lally, I . . .'

'I'm going away to Glasgow,' said she.

Glasgow! He had heard things about Glasgow! Good heavens!

'I've some friends there,' the girl went on steadily. She had got up and was sitting on the arm of his chair. 'I wrote to them last week. They can get me a job almost anywhen, and I can stay with them. They want me to go – they've sent the money for my fare. I think I shall have to go.'

'You don't love me then!' said the man.

Lally kissed him.

'But *do* you? Tell me!'

'Yes, my dear,' said Lally, 'of course.'

An uneasiness possessed him; he released her moodily. Where was their wild passion flown to? She was staring at him intently, then she tenderly said : 'My love, don't you be melancholy, don't take it to heart so. I'd cross the world to find you a pin.'

'No, no, you mustn't do that,' he exclaimed idiotically. At her indulgent smile he grimly laughed too, and then sank back in his chair. The girl stood up and went about the room doing vague nothings, until he spoke again.

'So you are tired of me?'

Lally went to him steadily, and knelt down by his chair.

'If I was tired of you, Phil, I'd kill myself.'

Moodily he ignored that. 'I suppose it had to end like this. But I've loved you desperately,' Lally was now weeping on his shoulder, and he began to twirl a lock of her rich brown hair absently with his fingers as if it were a seal on a watch-chain. 'I'd been thinking we might as well get married as soon as things had turned round.'

'I'll come back, Phil,' she clasped him so tenderly, 'as soon as you want me.'

'But you are not really going?'

'Yes,' said Lally.

'You're not to go!'

'I wouldn't go if . . . if anything . . . if you had any luck. But as we are now I must go away, to give you a chance. You see that, darling Phil?'

'You're not to go, I object. I just love you, Lally, that's all, and of course I went to keep you here.'

'Then what are we to do?'

'I . . . don't . . . know. Things drop out of the sky. But we must be together. You're not to go.'

Lally sighed : he was stupid. And Repton began to turn over in his mind the dismal knowledge that she had taken this step in secret, she had not told him while she was trying to get to Glasgow. Now here she was with the fare, and as good as gone ! Yes, it was all over.

'When do you propose to go?'

'Not for a few days, nearly a fortnight.'

'Good God !' he moaned. Yes, it was all over then. He had never dreamed that this would be the end, that she would be the first to break away. He had always envisaged a tender scene in which he could tell her, with dignity and gentle humour, that . . . well, he never had quite hit upon the words he would use, but that was the kind of setting. And now, here she was with her fare to Glasgow, her heart turned towards Glasgow, and she as good as gone to Glasgow ! No dignity, no gentle humour – in fact he was enraged, sullen but enraged; he boiled furtively. But he said with mournful calm :

'I've so many misfortunes, I suppose I can bear this too.' Gloomy and tragic he was.

'Dear, darling Phil, it's for your own sake I'm going.'

Repton sniffed derisively. 'We are always mistaken in the reasons for our commonest actions; Nature derides us all. You are sick of me, I can't blame you.'

Eulalia was so moved that she could only weep again. Nevertheless she wrote to her friends in Glasgow promising to be with them by a stated date.

Towards the evening of the following day, at a time when she was alone, a letter arrived addressed to herself. It was from a firm of solicitors in Cornhill inviting her to call upon them. A flame leaped up in Lally's heart : it might mean the offer of some work which would keep her in London after all ! If only it were so she would accept it on the spot, and Philip would have to be made to see the reasonableness of it. But at the office in Cornhill a more astonishing outcome awaited her. There she showed her letter to a little office boy with scarcely any finger-nails and very little nose, and he took it to an elderly man who had a superabundance of both. Smiling affably the long-nosed man led her upstairs into the sombre den of a gentleman who had some white hair and a lumpy yellow complexion. Having put to her a number of questions relating to her family history, and appearing to be satisfied and not at all surprised by her answers, this gentleman revealed to Lally the overpowering tidings that she was entitled to a legacy of eighty pounds by the will of a forgotten and recently deceased aunt. Subject to certain formalities, proofs of identity, and so forth, he promised Lally the possession of the money within about a week.

Lally's descent to the street, her emergence into the clamouring atmosphere, her walk along to Holborn, were accomplished in a state of blessedness and trance, a trance in which life became a thousand times airily enlarged, movement was a delight, and thought a rapture. She would give all the money to Philip, and if he very much wanted it she would even marry him now. Perhaps, though, she would save ten pounds of it for herself. The other seventy would keep them for . . . it was impossible to say how long it would keep them. They could have a little holiday somewhere in the country together, he was so worn and weary. Perhaps she had better not tell Philip anything at all about it until her lovely money was really in her hand. Nothing in life, at least nothing about money, was ever certain; something horrible might happen at the crucial moment and the money be snatched from her very fingers. Oh, she would go mad then! So for some days she kept her wonderful secret.

Their imminent separation had given Repton a tender sadness that was very moving. 'Eulalia,' he would say – for he had suddenly adopted the formal version of her name : 'Eulalia, we've had a great time together, a wonderful time, there will never be anything like it again.' She often shed tears, but she kept the grand secret still locked in her heart. Indeed, it occurred to her very forcibly that even now his stupid pride might cause him to reject her money altogether. Silly, silly Philip! Of course, it would have been different if they had married; he would naturally have taken it then, and really, it would have _been_ his. She would have to think out some dodge to overcome his scruples. Scruples were _such_ a nuisance, but then it was very noble of him : there were not many men who wouldn't take money from a girl they were living with.

Well, a week later she was summoned again to the office in Cornhill and received from the white-haired gentleman a cheque for eighty pounds drawn on the Bank of England to the order of Eulalia Burnes. Miss Burnes desired to cash the cheque straightway, so the large-nosed elderly clerk was deputed to accompany her to the Bank of England close by and assist in procuring the money.

'A very nice errand!' exclaimed that gentleman as they crossed to Threadneedle Street past the Royal Exchange. Miss Burnes smiled her acknowledgment, and he began to tell her of other windfalls that had been disbursed in his time – but vast sums, very great persons – until she began to infer that Blackbean, Carp & Ransome were universal dispensers of heavenly largess.

'Yes, but,' said the clerk, hawking a good deal from an affliction of catarrh, 'I never got any myself, and never will. If I did, do you know what I would do with it?' But at that moment they entered the portals of the bank, and in the excitement of the business Miss Burnes forgot to ask the clerk how he would use a legacy, and thus she possibly lost a most valuable slice of knowledge. With one fifty-pound note and six five-pound notes clasped in her handbag she bade good-bye to the long-nosed clerk, who shook her fervently by the hand and assured her that Blackbean, Carp & Ransome would be delighted at all times to undertake any commissions on her behalf. Then she fled along the pavement, blithe as a bird, until she was breathless with her flight. Presently she came opposite the window of a typewriting agency. Tripping airily into its office she laid a scrap of paper before a lovely Hebe who was typing there.

'I want this typed, if you please,' said Lally.

The beautiful typist read the words on the scrap of paper and stared at the heiress.

'I don't want any address to appear,' said Lally, 'just a plain sheet, please.'

A few moments later she received a neatly typed page folded in an envelope, and after paying the charge she hurried off to a District Messenger office. Here she addressed the envelope in a disguised hand to *P. Stick Repton, Esq.*, at their address in Holborn. She read the typed letter through again :

DEAR SIR,

In common with many others I entertain the greatest
admiration for your literary abilities, and I therefore beg
you to accept this tangible expression of that admiration
from a constant reader of your articles, who, for purely
private reasons, desires to remain anonymous.

> Your very sincere
> WELLWISHER.

Placing the fifty-pound note upon the letter Lally carefully
folded them together and put them both into the envelope.
The attendant then gave it to a uniformed lad, who sauntered off whistling very casually, somewhat to Lally's alarm
– he looked so small and careless to be entrusted with fifty
pounds. Then Lally went out, changed one of her five-
pound notes and had a lunch – half-a-crown, but it was
worth it. Oh, how enchanting and exciting London was!
In two days more she would have been gone; now she
would have to write off at once to her Glasgow friends and
tell them she had changed her mind, that she was now
settled in London. Oh, how enchanting and delightful!
And tonight he would take her out to dine in some fine
restaurant, and they would do a theatre. She did not really
want to marry Phil, they had got on so well without it, but
if he wanted that too she did not mind – much. They would
go away into the country for a whole week. What money
would do! Marvellous! And looking round the restaurant
she felt sure that no other woman there, no matter how
well dressed, had as much as thirty pounds in her handbag.

Returning home in the afternoon she became conscious
of her own betraying radiance; very demure and subdued
and usual she would have to be, or he might guess the
cause of it. Though she danced up the long flights of stairs
she entered their room quietly, but the sight of Repton

staring out of the window, forlorn as a drowsy horse, over-
came her and she rushed to embrace him crying 'Darling !'

'Hullo, hullo,' he smiled.

'I'm so fond of you, Phil dear.'

'But . . . but you're deserting me !'

'Oh no,' she cried archly, 'I'm not – not deserting you.'

'All right.' Repton shrugged his shoulders, but he seemed
happier. He did not mention the fifty pounds then : perhaps it had not come yet – or perhaps he was thinking to
surprise her.

'Let's go for a walk, it's a screaming lovely day,' said
Lally.

'Oh, I dunno.' He yawned and stretched. 'Nearly tea
time, isn't it ?'

'Well, we . . .' Lally was about to suggest having tea out
somewhere, but she bethought herself in time. 'I suppose it
is. Yes, it is.'

So they stayed in for tea. No sooner was tea over than
Repton remarked that he had an engagement somewhere.
Off he went, leaving Lally disturbed and anxious. Why had
he not mentioned the fifty pounds? Surely it had not gone
to the wrong address? This suspicion once formed, Lally
soon became certain, tragically sure, that she had misad-
dressed the envelope herself. A conviction that she had put
No. 17 instead of No. 71 was almost overpowering, and she
fancied that she hadn't even put London on the envelope –
but Glasgow. That was impossible, though, but – oh, the
horror ! – somebody else was enjoying their fifty pounds.
The girl's fears were not allayed by the running visit she
paid to the messenger office that evening, for the rash imp
who had been entrusted with her letter had gone home and
therefore could not be interrogated until the morrow. By
now she was sure that he had blundered; he had been so
casual with an important letter like that ! Lally never did,
and never would again, trust any little boys who wore their

hats so much on one side, were so glossy with hair-oil, and went about whistling just to madden you. She burned to ask where the boy lived, but in spite of her desperate desire she could not do so. She dared not, it would expose her to . . . to something or other she could only feel, not name; you had to keep cool, to let nothing, not even curiosity, master you.

Hurrying home again, though hurrying was not her custom, and there was no occasion for it, she wrote the letter to her Glasgow friends. Then it crossed her mind that it would be wiser not to post the letter that night; better wait until the morning, after she had discovered what the horrible little messenger had done with her letter. Bed was a poor refuge from her thoughts, but she accepted it, and when Phil came home she was not sleeping. While he undressed he told her of the lecture he had been to, something about Agrarian Depopulation it was, but even after he had stretched himself beside her he did not speak about the fifty pounds. Nothing, not even curiosity, should master her, and so she calmed herself, and in time fitfully slept.

At breakfast next morning he asked her what she was going to do that day.

'Oh,' replied Lally off-handedly, 'I've got a lot of things to see to, you know; I must go out. I'm sorry the porridge is so awful this morning, Phil, but . . .'

'Awful?' he broke in. 'But it's nicer than usual! Where are you going? I thought – our last day, you know – we might go out somewhere together.'

'Dear Phil!' Lovingly she stretched out a hand to be caressed across the table. 'But I've several things to do. I'll come back early, eh?' She got up and hurried round to embrace him.

'All right,' he said. 'Don't be long.'

Off went Lally to the messenger office, at first as happy as a bird, but on approaching the building the old tremors

assailed her. Inside the room was the cocky little boy, who
bade her 'Good morning' with laconic assurance. Lally at
once questioned him, and when he triumphantly produced
a delivery book she grew limp with her suppressed fear, one
fear above all others. For a moment she did not want to
look at it : Truth hung by a hair, and as long as it so hung
she might swear it was a lie. But there it was, written right
across the page, an entry of a letter delivered, signed for
in the well-known hand, *P. Stick Repton*. There was no
more doubt, only a sharp indignant agony, as if she had
been stabbed with a dagger of ice.

'Oh yes, thank you,' said Lally calmly. 'Did you hand it
to him yourself?'

'Yes'm,' replied the boy, and he described Philip.

'Did he open the letter?'

'Yes'm.'

'There was no answer?'

'No'm.'

'All right.' Fumbling in her bag, she added : 'I think I've
got a sixpence for you.'

Out in the street again she tremblingly chuckled to herself. 'So that is what he is like, after all. Cruel and mean!'
He was going to let her go and keep the money in secret to
himself! How despicable! Cruel and mean, cruel and
mean. She hummed it to herself : 'Cruel and mean, cruel
and mean!' It eased her tortured bosom. 'Cruel and mean!'
And he was waiting at home for her, waiting with a smile
for their last day together. It would *have* to be their last
day. She tore up the letter to her Glasgow friends, for now
she *must* go to them. So cruel and mean! Let him wait! A
bus stopped beside her and she stepped on to it, climbing to
the top and sitting there while the air chilled her burning
features. The bus made a long journey to Plaistow. She
knew nothing of Plaistow, she wanted to know nothing of
Plaistow, but she did not care where the bus took her; she

only wanted to keep moving, and moving away, as far away as possible from Holborn and from him, and not once let those hovering tears down fall.

From Plaistow she turned and walked back as far as the Mile End Road. Thereabouts, wherever she went she met clergymen, dozens of them. There must be a conference, about charity or something, Lally thought. With a vague desire to confide her trouble to some one, she observed them; it would relieve the strain. But there was none she could tell her sorrow to, and failing that, when she came to a neat restaurant she entered it and consumed a fish. Just beyond her three sleek parsons were lunching, sleek and pink, bald, affable, consoling men, all very much alike.

'I saw Carter yesterday,' she heard one say. Lally liked listening to the conversation of strangers, and she had often wondered what clergymen talked about among themselves.

'What, Carter! Indeed. Nice fellow, Carter. How was he?'

'Carter loves preaching, you know!' cried the third.

'Oh yes, he loves preaching!'

'Ha ha ha, yes.'

'Ha ha ha, oom.'

'Awf'lly good preacher, though.'

'Yes, awf'lly good.'

'And he's awf'lly good at comic songs, to.'

'Yes?'

'Yes!'

Three glasses of water, a crumbling of bread, a silence suggestive of prayer.

'How long has he been married?'

'Twelve years,' returned the cleric who had met Carter.

'Oh, twelve years!'

'I've only been married twelve years myself,' said the oldest of them.

'Indeed!'

'Yes, I tarried very long.'

'Ha ha ha, yes.'

'Ha ha ha, oom.'

'Er . . . have you any family?'

'No.'

Very delicate and dainty in handling their food they were, very delicate and dainty.

'My rectory is a magnificent old house,' continued the recently married one. 'Built originally 1700. Burnt down. Rebuilt 1784.'

'Indeed !'

'Humph !'

'Seventeen bedrooms and two delightful tennis courts.'

'Oh, well done !' the others cried, and then they all fell with genteel gusto upon a pale blanc-mange.

From the restaurant the girl sauntered about for a while, and then there was a cinema wherein, seated warm and comfortable in the twitching darkness, she partially stilled her misery. Some nervous fancy kept her roaming in that district for most of the evening. She knew that if she left it she would go home, and she did not want to go home. The naphtha lamps of the booths at Mile End were bright and distracting, and the hum of the evening business was good despite the smell. A man was weaving sweetstuffs from a pliant roll of warm toffee that he wrestled with as the athlete wrestles with the python. There were stalls with things of iron, with fruit or fish, pots and pans, leather, string, nails. Watches for use – or for ornament – what d'ye lack? A sailor told naughty stories while selling bunches of green grapes out of barrels of cork dust which he swore he had stolen from the Queen of Honolulu. People clamoured for them both. You could buy back numbers of the comic papers at four a penny, rolls of linoleum for very little more – and use either for the other's purpose.

'At thrippence per foot, mesdames,' cried the sweating

cheapjack, lashing himself into ecstatic furies, 'that's a piece of fabric weft and woven with triple-strength Anda-lusian jute, double-hot-pressed with rubber from the island of Pagama, and stencilled by an artist as poisoned his grandfather's cook. That's a piece of fabric, mesdames, as the king of heaven himself wouldn't mind to put down in his parlour – if he had the chance. Do I ask thrippence a foot for that piece of fabric? Mesdames, I was never a daring chap.'

Lally watched it all; she looked and listened; then looked and did not see, listened and did not hear. Her misery was not the mere disappointment of love, not that kind of misery alone; it was the crushing of an ideal in which love had had its home, a treachery cruel and mean. The sky of night, so smooth, so bestarred, looked wrinkled through her screen of unshed tears; her sorrow was a wild cloud that troubled the moon with darkness.

In miserable desultory wandering she had spent her day, their last day, and now, returning to Holborn in the late evening, she suddenly began to hurry, for a new possibility had come to lighten her dejection. Perhaps, after all, so whimsical he was, he was keeping his 'revelation' until the last day, or even the last hour, when (nothing being known to her, as he imagined) all hopes being gone, and they had come to the last kiss, he would take her in his arms and laughingly kill all grief, waving the succour of a flimsy banknote like a flag of triumph. Perhaps even, in fact surely, that was why he wanted to take her out today! Oh, what a blind, wicked, stupid girl she was, and in a perfect frenzy of bubbling faith she panted homewards for his revealing sign.

From the pavement below she could see that their room was lit. Weakly she climbed the stairs and opened the door. Phil was standing up, staring so strangely at her. Helplessly and half-guiltily she began to smile. Without a word said he came quickly to her and crushed her in his arms, her burning silent man, loving and exciting her. Lying against his breast in that constraining embrace, their passionate disaster was gone, her doubts were flown; all perception of the feud was torn from her and deeply drowned in a gulf of bliss. She was aware only of the consoling delight of their reunion, of his amorous kisses, of his tongue tingling the soft down on her upper lip that she disliked and he admired. All the soft wanton endearments that she so loved to hear him speak were singing in her ears, and then he suddenly swung and lifted her up, snapped out the gaslight, and carried her off to bed.

Life that is born of love feeds on love; if the wherewithal be hidden how shall we stay our hunger? The galaxy may grow dim, or the stars drop in a wandering void; you can neither keep them in your hands nor crumble them in your mind.

What was it Phil had once called her? Numbskull! After all it was his own fifty pounds; she had given it to him freely; it was his to do as he liked with. A gift was a gift, it was poor spirit to send money to anyone with the covetous expectation that it would return to you. She would surely go tomorrow.

The next morning he awoke her early, and kissed her.

'What time does your train go?' said he.

'Train!' Lally scrambled from his arms and out of bed. A fine day, a glowing day. A bright sharp air! Quickly she dressed, and went into the other room to prepare their breakfast. Soon he followed, and they ate silently together, although whenever they were near each other he caressed her tenderly. Afterwards she went into the bedroom and packed her bag; there was nothing more to be done, he was beyond hope. No woman waits to be sacrificed, least of all those who sacrifice themselves with courage and a quiet mind. When she was ready to go she took her portmanteau into the sitting-room; he, too, made to put on his hat and coat.

'No,' murmured Lally, 'you're not to come with me.'

'Pooh, my dear!' he protested, 'nonsense.'

'I won't have you come,' cried Lally with an asperity that impressed him.

'But you can't carry that bag to the station by yourself!'

'I shall take a taxi.' She buttoned her gloves.

'My dear!' His humorous deprecation annoyed her.

'Oh, bosh!' Putting her gloved hands around his neck she kissed him coolly. 'Good-bye. Write to me often. Let me know how you thrive, won't you, Phil? And' – a little waveringly – 'love me always.' She stared queerly at the two dimples in his cheeks; each dimple was a nest of hair that could never be shaved.

'Lally darling, beloved girl! I never loved you more than now, this moment. You are more precious than ever to me.'

At that, she knew her moment of sardonic revelation had come – but she dared not use it, she let it go. She could not so deeply humilate him by revealing her knowledge of his perfidy. A compassionate divinity smiles at our puny sins. She knew his perfidy, but to triumph in it would defeat her own pride. Let him keep his gracious mournful airs to the last, false though they were. It was better to part so, better from such a figure than from an abject scarecrow, even though both were the same inside. And something capriciously reminded her, for a flying moment, of elephants she had seen swaying with the grand movement of tidal water – and groping for monkey-nuts.

Lally tripped down the stairs alone. At the end of the street she turned for a last glance. There he was, high up in the window, waving good-byes. And she waved back at him.